the
awful
secret

Bernard Knight, CBE, became a Home Office Patholo-
gist in 1965 and was appointed Professor of Forensic
Pathology, University of Wales College of Medicine in
1980. He is the author of ten novels, a biography and
numerous popular and academic non-fiction books.
The Awful Secret is the fourth book in the Crowner
John series, following *The Sanctuary Seeker*, *The Poisoned
Chalice* and *Crowner's Quest*.

THE AWFUL SECRET

A Crowner John Mystery

Bernard Knight

POCKET
BOOKS

LONDON · SYDNEY · NEW YORK · TOKYO · SINGAPORE · TORONTO

First published in Great Britain by
Simon & Schuster UK Ltd, 2000
This edition first published by Pocket Books, 2000
An imprint of Simon & Schuster UK Ltd
A Viacom Company

1 3 5 7 9 10 8 6 4 2

Simon & Schuster UK Ltd
Africa House
64–78 Kingsway
London WC2B 6AH

Simon & Schuster Australia
Sydney

A CIP catalogue record for this book is available
from the British Library

ISBN 0-671-02965-7

Typeset by Palimpsest Book Production Limited,
Polmont, Stirlingshire
Printed and bound in Great Britain by
Omnia Books Limited, Glasgow

Author's Note

Any attempt in historical novels to give modern English dialogue an 'olde worlde' flavour, is as inaccurate as it is futile. In the time and place of this story, late twelfth-century Devon, most people would have spoken early Middle English, which would be quite unintelligible to us today. Many others spoke western Welsh, later called Cornish, and the ruling classes would have spoken Norman-French. The language of the Church and virtually all official writing was Latin.

Many of the characters actually existed and the contemporary political and religious events alluded to are authentic – piracy was rife around the coasts of England, Prince John was constantly plotting against his brother Richard the Lion-Heart and the Inquisition was getting under way in France.

The author leaves it to readers to put whatever credence they wish on the substance of the Awful Secret, but for those who may have a further interest in the subject, some sources are suggested at the end of the book.

Acknowledgements

The author would like to thank the following for historical advice, though reserving the blame for any misapprehensions about the complexities of life and law in twelfth century Devon; Mrs Angela Doughty, Exeter Cathedral Archivist; the staff of Devon Record Office and of Exeter Central Library; Mr Stuart Blaylock, Exeter Archaeology; Rev Canon Mawson, Exeter Cathedral; Mr Thomas Watkin, Cardiff Law School, University of Wales; Professor Nicholas Orme, University of Exeter; to copy-editor Hazel Orme and to Gillian Holmes and Clare Ledingham of Simon & Schuster for their continued encouragement and support.

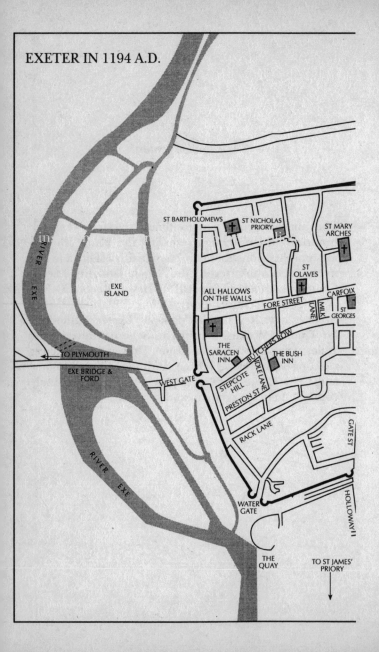

EXETER IN 1194 A.D.

RIVER EXE

EXE ISLAND

TO PLYMOUTH

EXE BRIDGE & FORD

RIVER EXE

WEST GATE

ST BARTHOLOMEWS

ST NICHOLAS PRIORY

ST MARY ARCHES

ST OLAVES

ALL HALLOWS ON THE WALLS

FORE STREET

CARFOIX

MILK LANE

ST GEORGES

BUTCHERS ROW

THE SARACEN INN

THE BUSH INN

MIDDLE LANE

STEPCOTE HILL

PRESTON ST

RACK LANE

GATE ST

WATER GATE

HOLLOWAY II

THE QUAY

TO ST JAMES' PRIORY

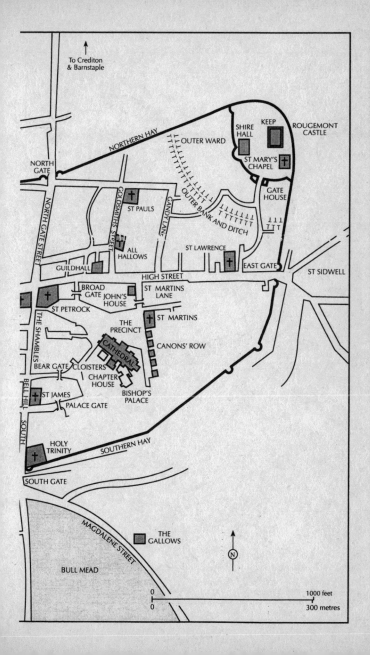

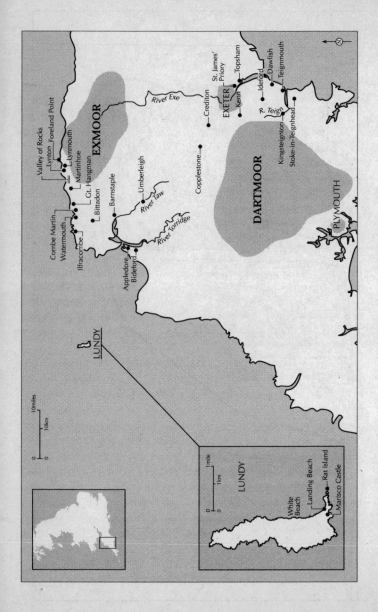

GLOSSARY

ABJURER
A criminal or accused person who sought sanctuary in a church and then elected to 'abjure the realm of England for ever' to avoid being hanged, by confessing to the coroner. He had up to forty days sanctuary, then had to proceed on foot, dressed in sackcloth and carrying a wooden cross, to a port nominated by the coroner and take the first ship available. If there was a delay, he had to wade out up to his knees at every tide, to show his willingness to leave.

ALBIGENSIAN HERESY
See Cathars.

AMERCEMENT
An arbitrary fine imposed on a person or community by a law officer, for some breach of the complex regulations of the law. Where imposed by a coroner, he would record the amercement, but the collection of the money would be ordered by the king's justices when they visited at the Eyre of Assize (qv).

APPROVER
An accused person who attempted to obtain mercy by implicating his accomplices, as in the modern 'turning Queen's

evidence'. He had to confess to the coroner, then challenge his accomplices to trial by battle; if he won, he was freed.

ARCHDEACON
A senior cathedral priest, assistant to the Bishop. There were four in the diocese of Devon and Cornwall, one responsible for Exeter.

ASSART
A new piece of arable land, cut from the forest to enlarge the cultivated area of a manor.

ATTACHMENT
An order made by a law officer, including a coroner, to ensure that a person, whether suspect or witness, appeared at a court hearing. It resembled bail or a surety, distraining upon a person's goods or money, which would be forfeit if he failed to appear.

AVENTAIL
A chain-mail armoured hood, similar to a balaclava, attached to the edge of the helmet and tucked into the neck of the hauberk (qv).

BAILEY
The outer enclosure of an early Norman 'motte and bailey' castle. An artificial mound was built and a wooden tower erected on top – the 'donjon' (qv), later called a 'keep'. Around the base, usually asymmetrically, a ditch and stockade demarcated the bailey, in which a hall and other buildings for living quarters, stables, kitchens, etc were erected, the donjon being used in times of siege. Later, more complex castles had inner and outer bailies, such as Exeter's Rougemont.

BAILIFF
Overseer of a manor or estate, directing the farming and

administrative work. He might also investigate manorial disputes and crimes and hold the manor court. He would have reeves (qv) under him, and himself be responsible to the lord's steward or seneschal (qv).

BALDRIC
A diagonal leather strap over the right shoulder of a Norman knight or soldier, to suspend his sword on the left hip.

BARON
Any major landowner, especially those powerful enough to have political influence. Often at loggerheads with the king, many barons, especially the Marcher Lords along the Welsh border, ran almost independent kingdoms.

BURGESS
A freeman of substance in a town or borough, usually a merchant or craftsman. A group of burgesses ran the town administration and elected two Portreeves (qv) as their leaders, later replaced by a mayor.

CANON
A priestly member of the Chapter of a cathedral, also known as a 'prebendary', as they received their income from a prebend, a grant of land or a pension. Exeter had twenty-four canons, most of whom lived near the cathedral, though unlike the majority of other cathedrals, the canons were paid a small salary and had a daily allowance of bread, candles etc. Many employed junior priests (vicars and secondaries) to carry out some of their duties.

CATHARS
People of south-western France in the 11th–13th centuries, who professed a 'gnostic' type of Christianity, also known as the Albigensian heresy, as they were centred around the town of Albi. They professed free-will and thought all material things were the produce of evil. They fell foul of the Roman Church

and though the Templars seemed to have some sympathy with them, they were ruthlessly exterminated by the Inquisition on the orders of Pope Innocent III in the 13th century.

CHAPTER
The administrative body of a cathedral, composed of the canons (Prebendaries). They met daily to conduct business in the Chapter House, so called because a chapter of the Gospels was read before each meeting.

COG
A crude building material made from clay, dung, ferns etc, supported between a wooden framework.

COMMANDERY
The main Templar establishment in a country, such as at Paris or the New Temple in London, now used by the legal profession. It would be headed by a Master, the Grand Master being at Acre in the Holy Land, until expelled by the Saracen onslaught, when he moved to Cyprus. Lesser Templar establishments elsewhere in a country were called Preceptories.

CONSTABLE
Had several meanings, but here refers to the military commander of a castle, sometimes called a 'castellan'. In royal castles, such as Exeter's Rougemont, he was appointed by the king, to keep him independent of powerful local barons. On a lower plane, in towns and some manors, a constable was a law enforcer assisting the bailiff or burgesses.

CORONER
A senior law officer in a county, second only to the sheriff (qv). First established in September 1194, though there are a few mentions of the coroner in earlier times. Three knights and one clerk were recruited in every county, to carry out a wide range of legal duties. The name comes from *custos placitorum coronae*, meaning 'Keeper of the Pleas of the Crown', as he

recorded all serious crimes, deaths and legal events for the King's Justices.

COVER-CHIEF
Head-dress of a Norman lady, more correctly called a *couvre-chef*. To Saxons it was called a 'head-rail' and consisted of a linen cloth held in place by a band around the forehead, the lower edge hanging down over the back and bosom.

CROFT
A small area of land around a village house (toft) for vegetables and a few livestock, used by the occupant (cottar) who was either a freeman (socman) or a bondsman (villein or serf).

CUIRASS
A short tunic, originally of thick, boiled leather but later of chain-mail or plate metal, to protect the chest in battle.

CURIA REGIS
The King's Court or Council, his tenants-in-chief, composed of the most senior barons and churchmen, who offered advice and devised national policy. From this developed the great Offices of State, especially the courts.

CURRAGH
A Gaelic word for a boat of similar construction to a Welsh coracle, but dinghy-shaped instead of round. Though flimsily constructed of tarred hide stretched over thin wooden frames, it was used extensively for voyages as far afield as Brittany.

DEODAND
Literally 'a gift from God', it was the forfeiture of anything that had caused a death, such as a sword, a cart or even a mill-wheel. It might be confiscated by the coroner and sold for the Crown, but was sometimes given to the deceased's family as compensation for the death.

DESTRIER
A war-horse, a large animal strong enough to carry an armoured knight. When firearms made armour obsolete, destriers became draught-animals, from whom carthorses are descended. Previously, ploughing and carting was carried out by oxen.

DONJON
The fortified tower on the motte in early Norman castles. Originally of wood, it was later replaced by masonry. The later word 'dungeon', meaning a prison cell, came from the lowest chamber in the donjon, where prisoners were incarcerated.

EYRE
A sitting of the Kings' Judges, introduced by Henry II in 1166, which moved around the country in circuits. There were two types, the 'Justices in Eyre', the forerunner of the Assizes (now Crown Courts), which was supposed to visit frequently to try serious cases; and the General Eyre, which came at long intervals to scrutinise the administration of each county.

FIRST FINDER
The first person to discover the corpse of a slain person had to rouse the four nearest households and raise the 'hue and cry' to give chase to the culprit. Then the bailiff had to be notified and then the coroner. Failure to do so resulted in amercement (qv) by the coroner.

HAUBERK
Also called a 'byrnie', this was a chain-mail tunic with long sleeves, to protect the wearer from neck to calf. The skirt was slit to allow him to ride a horse. A metal plate was often secured over the front of the chest to further protect the heart.

HIDE
A medieval measure of land, which varied from place to place,

but was usually 120 acres at the time of the Domesday survey, but later quoted at anything between 30 and 80 acres. A hide was supposed to be enough to support a family and was divided into four 'virgates'. Another land measure was the 'carucate', about 100 acres, the area one ox team could plough in a season.

HONOUR
A holding of land by a lord from the King, a baron or the church. It might be a large estate or a single manor and many honours consisted of numerous, separate holdings spread over many counties. A manor might be one village or several, under the same lord, but some villages were split between different lords.

HUNDRED
An administrative sub-division of a county, originally supposed to consist of a hundred settlements.

JURY
Unlike modern juries, who must be totally impartial, having no prior knowledge of the case, medieval juries included witnesses, local people who were obliged to gather to tell what they knew about a crime or dispute. The coroner's jury was supposed to be all the males over the age of twelve from the four nearest villages, though this was usually a practical impossibility.

JUSTICIAR
One of the King's Chief Ministers in Norman times. In the reign of Richard I, the most effective was Hubert Walter, Archbishop of Canterbury, who was his military second-in-command at the Third Crusade, before he returned home during the Lionheart's imprisonment in Austria and Germany, to raise money for his ransom. Richard made him Chief Justiciar and Hubert virtually ruled the country after Richard's permanent departure from England in May 1194, only two months after returning from captivity.

KIRTLE
A woman's gown, worn to the ankles, with long sleeves, wide at the wrists, though fashions constantly changed. The kirtle was worn over a chemise, the only undergarment.

KNARR
An early medieval merchant ship, generally like a Viking longship, but much broader in the beam. It was partly decked with a single hold, mast and sail.

MANOR REEVE
A foreman appointed in every village, either elected by villagers or by the manorial lord. He oversaw the daily farm work and though illiterate like the vast majority of the population, he would keep records of crop rotation, harvest yields, tithes, etc, by means of his memory and notches on tally sticks.

MARK
A sum of money, though not an actual coin, as only pennies were in use. A mark was two-thirds of a pound, or thirteen shillings and fourpence (now equal to sixty-six decimal pence).

MOTTE
The artificial mound on which the wooden donjon (qv) was erected in early Norman castles, surrounded by the bailey (qv). An excellent Devon example is at Totnes.

MUTILATION
A common punishment for all kinds of offence, as a lesser alternative to hanging. Removal of a hand was the most frequent, but feet, tongues, ears and noses were also cut off, as well as blinding and castration.

ORDEAL
There were many types of legal Ordeal, supposed to be a

test of guilt or innocence, such as walking over nine red-hot ploughshares, picking a stone from a barrel of boiling water or molten lead or being submerged in water. The 'Ordeal of the Bier' was to detect a murderer by making a suspect touch the bier on which the corpse laid, when the fatal wounds would begin to bleed again. This is mentioned by Shakespeare in Richard III, Act One.

OUTLAW
Literally, anyone outside the law, usually escaped prisoners or sanctuary seekers. They usually took refuge in the forests and lived by banditry, as in the tales of Robin Hood. Highway robbers were sometimes called 'trail bastons'. Outlaws ceased to exist as legal persons and were considered 'as the wolf's head', as they could be killed on sight by anyone, who could claim a bounty if they took the severed head to the sheriff or coroner.

OUTREMER
The four Christian kingdoms in the Levant at the time of the Crusades, including the Kingdom of Jerusalem.

PHTHISIS
Tuberculosis, rife in medieval times.

PORTREEVE
One of the two senior burgesses in a township, elected by the others as leaders. They were superseded by a mayor, the first mayor of Exeter being elected in 1208.

PRECENTOR
A senior canon in a cathedral, responsible for organising the religious services, singing etc.

PRECEPTORY
A Templar establishment (see Commandery).

PRESENTMENT OF ENGLISHRY
Following the 1066 Conquest, many Normans were covertly killed by aggrieved Saxons, so the law decreed that anyone found dead from unnatural causes was presumed to be a Norman, and the community was heavily punished by the 'murdrum' fine, unless they could prove that the deceased was Saxon. This was done before the coroner by male members of the family. This continued for several centuries, as a good source of revenue for the Treasury, even though it became meaningless so long after the Conquest, due to intermarriage.

SCILLY ISLES
A group of islands off Land's End, noted for pirates in the Middle Ages. In 1208, over 100 pirates were hanged there at Tresco.

SECONDARY
A young priest, junior to a vicar (qv), who may also be an assistant to a canon (qv).

SERGEANT
Also spelt 'serjeant', has several meanings. A senior-man-at-arms, or a law officer in early times, below a bailiff in a town; also the squire of a Templar Knight, who wore brown or black.

SHERIFF
The 'shire-reeve', the King's representative in each county, responsible for law and order and the collection of taxes. There was great corruption amongst sheriffs, and it was a much-sought-after appointment, large sums being paid for the post, due to the many opportunities for embezzlement.

SENESCHAL
See Steward.

SOCMAN
A freeman, as opposed to a bondsman. The latter consisted of villiens, serfs and slaves in descending order of servitude in the feudal system.

STEWARD
The senior servant of a lord, also called a seneschal. It could be a highly prestigious and responsible post, especially in a great house. The Stuart dynasty derived their name from being stewards.

SUMPTER HORSE
A pack animal, used for carrying loads rather than riding.

SURCOAT
Also called a 'super-tunic', it was worn over the tunic or over armour, where it protected the wearer from the sun on the metal and provided a site for heraldic emblems. The most famous was the white surcoat of the Knights Templar, with the characteristic broad red Cross.

TRAIL-BASTON
A highway robber, an outlaw (qv) who usually worked with a gang.

TUNIC
The main garment for a man, pulled over the head to reach the knee or calf. A linen shirt might be worn underneath and a cloak or mantle over it. The skirt was slit for riding a horse.

UNDERCROFT
The lowest level of a fortified building. The entrance to the rest of the structure was on the floor above, isolated from the undercroft, which might be partly below ground level. Removable wooden stairs prevented attackers from reaching the main entrance above.

VICAR
A priest employed by a more senior cleric, such as a canon (qv) to carry out some of his religious duties, especially attending the numerous services in the cathedral. Often called a vicar-choral, from his participation in chanted services.

WATTLE & DAUB
A common medieval building technique, where clay or plaster is applied over a woven framework of hazel withies.

PROLOGUE

March 1195

The disabled ship drifted rapidly towards the lee shore, a rugged coast seen dimly in the dusk. Although by the violent standards of the Severn Sea the weather was far from extreme, there was a strong north-westerly wind, sufficient to raise spume from the crests of the grey Atlantic rollers and partly obscure the towering cliffs with spray.

The short, stumpy vessel pitched and rolled at the mercy of the waves, having no steerage-way from the single sail, which lay collapsed on the deck. Neither was there a steering oar near the stern, both that and the steersman having been washed away. The little ship was now merely flotsam awaiting the inevitable impact with the northern coast of Devon. The great cliffs, where Exmoor abruptly tumbled into the sea opposite distant Wales, now loomed on the port beam of the derelict. Although all the land immediately ahead was lower than to the east, it still presented a jagged prospect of rocks, reefs and coves.

The knarr was a broader version of the Viking long-boat, with high stem and stern posts, but no dragon carvings ornamented it. The forward and after thirds were decked in, but the centre was an open hatch for the cargo. The canvas cover was gone, as was the cargo, and the hold was thigh-deep in water, which shipped over the sides each time the knarr broached the waves in its uncontrolled plunge towards the rocks.

Although it was dusk, there was still enough light for the sole survivor to see the corpse of one of his shipmates lying alongside him, his feet tangled in a rope, which had saved it from being washed overboard. Terrified, the young seaman clung to a fallen spar on the deck and stared ahead through the spray at the grey bulk of the shore, which seemed to race towards him. He knew most of the landmarks between Penzance and Bristol and, even through his fear, recognised to his left the Great Hangman, England's highest cliff, which towered more than a thousand feet above the end of Combe Martin Bay.

As the last few cable-lengths of open sea gave way to thunderous white surf, he glimpsed a dim yellow light high on the land, above the point where the vessel must inevitably strike. A few seconds later, with a shriek of terror, the youth felt a grinding crash as a roller lifted the hull on to a jagged reef at the foot of a cliff. The impact tore his feeble grasp from the spar and, as the vessel tilted almost on to her beam ends, he slid across the deck and was washed off into the surf by the advancing wave. The breaker rolled him up a narrow gully between the rocks and almost contemptuously spat him out on to a tongue of shingle that ended in a shallow cave. Sobbing with fear and only half aware of his surroundings, he scrabbled on hands and knees through the white foam that streamed back to meet the next wave and collapsed far enough up the tiny beach to escape being sucked back into the sea.

Wet through in the keen wind, he lay shivering for a while, then slipped into unconsciousness, unaware of the wavering gleam of a horn lantern and the scrunch of feet that came down a narrow path from above.

CHAPTER ONE

In which Crowner John mounts his horse

'At last, Gwyn! I can do it without that bloody box!'

Later, John de Wolfe thought how strange it was that he should be so exultant at such a little thing, which would never have crossed his mind two months ago. Yet, in Martin's Lane that morning, he was as pleased as a child with a new toy. The two men who watched him seemed just as delighted, but his servant Mary, who watched from the doorway of his house opposite, clucked under her breath at the infantile antics of three grown men.

The 'bloody box' was a set of crude wooden steps knocked together by Gwyn of Polruan. It had done sterling service for the past two weeks, in allowing de Wolfe to climb up on to his new horse, Odin. But this morning he had been able to discard Gwyn's invention and put his whole weight on his injured left leg to lift the other into the stirrup. Now he sat solidly on the back of the patient stallion, a grin spreading across his normally stern face.

'You'd better carry this crook for the time being, Crowner,' advised Gwyn, the shaggy red-headed giant of a Cornishman who had been his henchman for almost twenty years. He handed up a walking stick, which de Wolfe had been using since he threw away his crutch three weeks earlier, and the coroner pranced the stallion up and down the lane for a few yards, turning and weaving in pure pleasure. Although he had been riding for the past ten days, the fact that he could now mount his own horse without climbing steps made him feel independent at last.

Mary shook her dark hair in mock despair and vanished into the nether regions of the house to cook the midday meal. Secretly she was as pleased as the men outside that her master was not only almost back to full physical fitness but that he should have lost his snarling frustration at being housebound for so many weeks.

It was in early January that he had broken his leg on the tourney field at Bull Mead. In his dying moments, de Wolfe's beloved old horse, Bran, had pitched him to the ground. The coroner's shin-bone had snapped, but thankfully it was a clean break, and Gwyn's prompt action in lashing the leg to a plank with leather straps had kept it in a good position. The Cornishman had seen this done by the Knights Hospitaller in Palestine, and with the constant help of Brother Saulf, a monk from the little hospital of St John up near Exeter's East Gate, the leg had mended rapidly. De Wolfe's tough physique, hardened by years of soldiering, together with his wife Matilda's relentless if grim-faced nursing, had had him back on his feet in three weeks.

Now, two months later, he was riding his horse again. 'I'll take him up to the castle, Gwyn,' he called, and walked the black stallion up the narrow lane to the high street. His officer trotted alongside, his shaggy hair bouncing over the collar of his frayed leather cape.

As de Wolfe pushed his way through the crowded main street, thronged with people shopping at the stalls on each side and with carts and barrows jostling for passage, he was assailed by greetings, mostly congratulating him on his return to health. An early spring was in the air and, though it was cold, there was a clear pale blue sky overhead while the lack of rain for a week had allowed the usual slush of garbage underfoot to dry to a crumbly paste.

The houses and shops in the main thoroughfare were of all shapes and sizes, mostly wooden, but a few were now built in stone. Most were tall and narrow, crammed together like peas in a pod. Some had straw thatch, some crude turf, some wooden shingle roofs and others stone tiles. Hazy smoke filtered from under the eaves of most dwellings, only a few having new-fangled chimneys.

Suddenly, as he plodded sedately through the crowded street, he felt a prickling of the hairs on the back of his neck. Though not an imaginative man, de Wolfe knew from the experience of many an ambush that he was being watched. It was a sixth sense, an occult gift that had saved his life a few times in the French and Irish campaigns, as well as in Palestine. He had felt it yesterday when coming home from the tavern and had glimpsed a face peering around a wall, the man vanishing almost instantly as John turned in his direction. The features had seemed vaguely familiar, but despite racking his brains, he failed to recall who it might have been.

Now, again, he looked about him and once more the same face gazed fleetingly at him from the steps of St Lawrence. A split second later, the man, enveloped in a dark mantle, turned and vanished into the church. De Wolfe knew that if the fellow had no wish to be accosted he would have melted away by the time he slowly got himself down off Odin. He cudgelled his memory to recall the identity of that face so briefly seen, but still nothing came to mind. He shrugged and urged the stallion on again. It seemed unlikely that the man was an assassin – though there had been a plot against him a couple of months ago. Hopefully that was all over now.

A hundred yards short of the East Gate, John hauled his steed around to the left and walked him up the slope towards the castle, perched at the top corner of the city. From the ruddy colour of its local sandstone, it was always known as Rougemont, built by the Conqueror in the northern corner of the old Roman walls. Passing through an open gate in a wooden stockade, de Wolfe rode into the large outer ward, where the huts of the soldiers and their families half covered the slope to the inner fortifications. A few yards more and he came to the tall gatehouse where he had a cramped chamber on the top floor.

The solitary guard on the steep drawbridge saluted de Wolfe with a lift of his spear as he passed under the gateway and stopped opposite the low door of the guardroom. Immediately, a man-at-arms with a badge of seniority on his leather jerkin emerged, his craggy face softening into a grin of welcome. 'Glad to see you, Crowner! How's the leg today?'

De Wolfe looked down at Gabriel, the sergeant of the castle guard, an old friend and covert sympathiser in his running feud with the sheriff, his brother-in-law, Sir Richard de Revelle. 'Better and better, Gabriel! For the first time I can mount my horse from the ground.'

To demonstrate his prowess in reverse, John lowered himself carefully from the stallion's back and, with the stick in his left hand, limped resolutely into the guardroom and across to the foot of the narrow, twisting stairs that led to the upper storey. Gwyn and Gabriel stood behind him, looking anxious as he began the ascent. On the third step he slipped and only Gwyn's brawny arms saved him from falling backwards out of the stairway entrance.

De Wolfe swore fluently, including a few Saracen oaths in his frustration, but had to admit that he was not yet ready to get up to his chamber. 'It's this twice-accursed stick, it gets in the way!' he fumed. 'We'll have to have some other room at ground level.'

Leaving Odin at the guardhouse, he set off across the littered mud of the inner ward towards the keep that sheltered against the far wall. 'Stay and watch my horse, Gwyn,' he called over his shoulder. 'I'm off to badger the sheriff for a new chamber.'

With his stick prodding the earth at every step, his strengthening leg made good progress across the triangular area inside the high, crenellated walls. On his left was the bare stone box of the Shire Hall, the courthouse where he held most of his city inquests, and on his right, the tiny garrison chapel of St Mary. All around the inside of the walls were huts, sheds and lean-to shanties; some were living quarters for soldiers and a few families, others storehouses, stables and cart-sheds. The keep was a squat, two-storey building over an undercroft, which housed the castle gaol. The two upper floors contained the hall, and chambers for the sheriff, the constable, a number of clerks, servants and a few knights and squires.

Richard de Revelle lived here for much of the time, going home to his manors at Revelstoke near Plympton and another near Tiverton, where his sour-faced wife spent all her time, not deigning to reside in the admittedly Spartan quarters of Rougemont. John suspected –

indeed, he had had the proof of his own eyes – that his brother-in-law preferred the cold chambers of the castle to the company of his spouse: there, he could indulge his liking for ladies of the town when she was well out of sight.

De Wolfe clumped up the wooden steps to the door of the keep, the man-at-arms on duty giving him a smiling salute. The coroner was a popular man amongst soldiers, both from his reputation as a seasoned Crusader and for being a staunch supporter and personal friend of their king, Richard the Lionheart.

The guard watched him limp through the arched doorway at the head of the steps, a tall, lean figure, always dressed in black or grey. With raven hair down to his shoulders, thick black eyebrows and habitual dark stubble on his beardless face, the soldier could well believe that he had been known as 'Black John' by the troops in the Irish wars and the Crusades. With his slight stoop, head pushed forward and the long, lean face with the great hooked nose, he looked like some predatory bird of prey, a crow or raven.

Most of the middle floor of the keep was taken up by the hall, a jostling, bustling vault where clerks and merchants ambled about with their parchments, servants carried food to tables against the walls and others stood around the great hearth, gossiping and scheming. The coroner ignored them and stumped across to a small door, his stick tapping on the flagstones. Another man-at-arms stood sentinel, though this was mainly from the sheriff's need to show off his own importance rather than for security. Rougemont had not heard a weapon clashed in battle for over fifty years, since the siege in the time of Stephen and Matilda.

Nodding to the guard, John pushed open the door

and walked into the sheriff's office. De Revelle's private rooms were behind it, but this was his official chamber, where he conducted the business of being the king's representative for the county of Devon – which job that he was currently hanging on to by the skin of his teeth, since his recent exposure by de Wolfe as having been involved in the abortive rebellion by Prince John against King Richard.

Richard de Revelle raised his eyes from the parchments on his table and scowled when he saw who had entered. A slight, neat, rather dandified man, he was in no position to antagonize his brother-in-law who, together with the powerful loyalist faction in the county, was keeping a close eye on him. After a muttered greeting, which failed to include any enquiry as to the state of de Wolfe's leg, the sheriff threw a curled piece of vellum across the trestle towards him. 'What do you think of that, Crowner?' he snapped, his small pointed beard jutting forwards pugnaciously.

De Wolfe knew that the other had not the slightest interest in his opinion on the document and that he was merely trying to score a petty advantage: the sheriff could read and write fluently, whilst the soldier-coroner had never been to school. But for the first time, he was able to turn the tables on his unpleasant brother-in-law. He picked up the parchment with studied nonchalance and scanned it. Though half guessing, he was soon able to throw down the sheet and turn his deep-set dark eyes to the other man's face. 'Nothing new in that! They've tried before to take possession of the island, but were repulsed. No one can get a foothold there without an army, not even the Templars.'

The sheriff scowled again, his narrow face growing rather pink above his thin moustache. 'Well done, John!

I had heard you were having lessons from the cathedral canons,' he said patronizingly.

De Wolfe grinned. 'Being housebound for nearly two months gave my clerk the chance he'd been waiting for – daily lessons in reading and writing.'

De Revelle jabbed a ringed finger towards the parchment. 'You must have known these Knights of the Temple better than most when you were in Outremer. Are they going to let William de Marisco thumb his nose at them for ever? They've been granted Lundy for years, but the bastard repels them every time they try to land.'

The coroner sat on the edge of the sheriff's table, to take the weight off his leg. 'They're a mixed bunch, the Templars. Many are obsessional fighters, like the Lionheart himself, which is why he respects them so much. A few are mad, I think. They can be reckless to the point of insanity, just like some of the Muhammadans they admire, even though we're enemies.'

He shifted his stick on the flags, his mind far away in the dust of the Holy Land. 'I have seen them act as if they actually sought a glorious death, in suicidal attacks, sometimes unnecessary. Yet more and more of the Templars have become soft, especially those who remain in Europe and never venture to the Levant.'

On safe ground, away from the sensitive topic of Prince John, the sheriff nodded sagely. 'They've moved a long way from their origins as Poor Knights of Christ and the Temple of Solomon. Now they're the richest Order in Christendom, with huge estates and able to lend money to kings.'

De Wolfe shrugged, a favourite response: he was the most taciturn of men.

His brother-in-law picked up the document and read

it again gloomily. 'I hope they don't expect me to do anything about this. I don't fancy sending a few men in small boats to try to winkle de Marisco from his rock.'

'Let the bloody Templars do their own dirty work,' advised the coroner gruffly. 'If the king has granted them Lundy, it's up to them to install themselves.' He cleared his throat, another mannerism, which heralded a change of subject. 'I need another chamber, Richard, for my official business. I can't get up to the top of that cursed gatehouse until my leg improves even more. You must have space somewhere lower down.'

It took five minutes of arguing and demanding before the reluctant sheriff, pleading shortage of accommodation in the crowded garrison, conceded him a small storeroom in the undercroft, on condition it was strictly a temporary lease. The coroner's original room in the gatehouse had been as inconvenient as de Revelle could make it, a token of his disapproval of the introduction of de Wolfe's appointment six months before. Previously, he had had absolute authority over every aspect of the law in Devon, which had given him ample opportunity for dishonesty and corruption. Like most of his fellow sheriffs, he strongly resented having another senior law officer poking his nose into his business and taking away both part of his power and the financial pickings that went with it. But the coroners had been appointed on behalf of the Lionheart by his wily Chief Justiciar, Hubert Walter, for the very purpose of collecting every penny for the royal treasury, impoverished by Richard's costly wars. Much of this money-gathering was to be achieved by combating the rapacity of the sheriffs and de Revelle had had no choice but to accept the royal command. He had supported the appointment of his sister's husband, partly because of her nagging but also because he thought that he would be able to keep his relative-by-marriage under his thumb – a hope that proved very much in error.

De Wolfe hauled himself from the table and tapped his way to the door. 'I'll go down to inspect this closet you've so graciously offered me,' he grunted sarcastically. 'Gwyn and Gabriel can move my table and stool down there. It's all the furniture the King's coroner possesses for his duties!'

With that parting sally, he limped out of the chamber, leaving the sheriff smarting with annoyance, but impotent to protest, in his present fragile state of probation.

After telling the hairy Cornishman to get their chattels and documents moved to the miserable cell under the keep, John remounted Odin and walked him down through the town again. It was not yet mid-morning and the meal that Mary was preparing would not be ready for a couple of hours.

He decided to amble down to the Bush tavern and have a quart of ale with Nesta, his mistress and landlady of the inn. He knew that Matilda would be busy with her devotions for the rest of the morning at the little church of St Olave's in Fore Street. He suspected – almost hoped – that she was enamoured of the parish priest there, a fat pompous cleric. She visited there several times a week for various obscure Masses and this gave de Wolfe the opportunity for daytime visits to his Welsh lover.

The Bush was not far from St Olave's and, though it was unlikely that his wife would come out of the church during the service, he was cautious enough to work his way through the cathedral Close and then take the back lanes of the lower town to reach the tavern. As he came out of the Close through the Bear Gate and skirted the Shambles, where sheep, pigs and cattle were being slaughtered amid blood and screams, he again had the feeling of being watched. Perhaps sensitive to the proximity of his wife, he looked down from his stallion's back at the crowded street and, from the corner of his eye, momentarily saw a man staring at him from the end of a booth that sold hot pies. A second later he had disappeared amongst the crowd, but de Wolfe knew that it had been the face he had seen twice before, once yesterday and again an hour ago, when he went up to Rougemont.

Exasperated both at the antics of the man and also his own inability to remember the name, de Wolfe urged Odin down the slope of Priest Street,* where many of the vicars and secondaries from the cathedral lodged. At the bottom was the lane that ran around the inside of the city wall, with the quayside and the river Exe beyond, but the coroner turned right half-way down the street of irregular wooden houses, into Idle Lane. This took its name from the bare wasteground in which sat the Bush Inn, its steep thatched roof perched on a low stone building pierced by a doorway and four shuttered window openings.

John hitched Odin's reins to a bar at the side of the inn where several other horses were secured, and went round to the front door, into the large, low room, hazy with smoke from the fire in the wide stone hearth. He went across to his favourite table near the fire and, such was his prestige in the Bush, before he had even lowered himself to a rough bench, a stone quart jar of ale was

* Now called Preston Street.

banged down in front of him by old Edwin, the one-eyed pot man. Seconds later, the smooth form of the landlady slid alongside him and pressed affectionately against his sound leg.

Nesta was a redhead of twenty-eight years, with a high forehead, a snub nose and a body like an hourglass. The widow of a Welsh archer de Wolfe had known in the Waterford campaign years before, she was now his favourite mistress – although, as both she and Matilda well knew, she was not the only object of his considerable passionate appetite. Dressed in a green gown beneath a linen apron, her russet curls peeping from under her white headcloth, Nesta slid her arm through his and prodded his opposite thigh with her finger. 'And how is your lower member today, John?' she asked, with mischievous ambiguity.

He gave her one of his rare lopsided grins as he slipped an arm around her shoulders. 'A little stiff in the mornings, thank you – probably from lack of exercise during the night.'

They spoke in Welsh, as he had learned this at his mother's knee and had kept fluent over the years by talking to Gwyn in his native Cornish, which was virtually identical. After some affectionate banter, which only a woman like Nesta could have drawn from the normally grim coroner, the talk turned to more general matters. After telling her about his new cubbyhole of an office in the castle, and the rapid improvement in his 'lower member' which had allowed him to mount his horse, de Wolfe mentioned the annoyance of the face that kept peering at him from around corners. 'You hear of every single thing that happens in Exeter, madam! Do you know of any stranger recently arrived who might wish to stalk me?'

Immediately Nesta became serious, worried at anything that might be a potential danger to her man. Her big grey-green eyes widened as she looked at him in concern. 'Men are coming and going all the time, many of them through this tavern, John. Merchants, sailors, pilgrims, soldiers, thieves – must be scores every day. What does he look like?'

De Wolfe shrugged. 'I can't describe his face – he keeps it part shaded by a wide-brimmed hat – but it has nothing out of the ordinary, as far as I could tell from the instant it was on view. About my age, I would suggest.'

'Oh, you mean an *old* man – was he bent and tottery and used a stick?' she gibed, getting a hard pinch on her plump thigh for her impudence.

'I know that I have met the fellow, but I just can't place him,' he said testily, banging the table with a hard fist.

Nesta thought it best to change the subject, before his temper rose with frustration.

'How is your dear wife, these days? Does she still mop your fevered brow?' Nesta, though a kind and open-hearted woman, sometimes failed to conceal her jealousy of Matilda, who as of right shared house, bed and board with the dark man Nesta loved. The Welsh woman knew that her own station in life was far too distant from that of a Norman knight ever to dream of being more than his paramour, even though she knew that John de Wolfe had a genuine deep affection for her. Though it seemed that he and his wife were always at loggerheads, the rigid conventions of feudal and religious life had forced them into an indissoluble bond. Although Matilda had temporarily left her husband two months ago, his broken leg had driven them together again: Matilda had grimly announced her intention of nursing him back to health, and had done so with the icy determination of a Benedictine nun turned gaoler.

'She's drifted back to being the same old Matilda,' he admitted sadly. 'At first, she never spoke to me, except to tell me to sit or lie down or crawl to the privy pot. Then her old manner slowly returned and she treated me at first like a naughty schoolboy, then like one of Gabriel's new recruits.' He stared thoughtfully into the leaping flames in the hearth. 'But by God's white beard, she was efficient! She stuffed food down me like a fattening goose to mend my leg, and even suffered Gwyn in the house when it came to him helping me to stumble about to strengthen my limbs. She even put up with poor Thomas, whom she hates like poison, when he came to divert me with his reading lessons.'

Nesta hugged his arm, then reached over to take a drink from his earthenware pot. 'You sound quite fond of her, Sir Crowner,' she said, with a tinge of wistfulness.

De Wolfe shook his black locks vigorously. 'Fond, no! Sorry for her, no doubt. I did her a wrong when I let her be humiliated over you and Hilda – though that was no fault of mine. It was that sleek bastard de Revelle who took a delight in shaming his own sister. But I evened up the score when I interceded on her behalf for him.'

'It must have cost her pride a great deal, having to plead with you for him, especially at a time like that.' Nesta felt sorry for her rival, as she often did. Much as she loved him, she was realistic enough to know that being married to John de Wolfe would be no bed of roses.

The coroner swallowed the rest of his ale and waved Edwin away as he threatened a second refill from his big pitcher. 'I must get home and eat Mary's boiled pork and cabbage. And Thomas is coming afterwards with his parchments, I must get back to my duties as soon as I can.'

As he rode slowly home, he planned how to deal with the numerous tasks that a coroner had to carry out – tasks that had been largely neglected in the past two months, though for a few weeks now, he had managed to deal with some cases in the city and nearby villages. Further afield, deaths had had to remain uninvestigated, and assaults, a rape and numerous administrative tasks had gone by default. His brother-in-law had taken delight in pointing out that they had managed very well for centuries without a coroner until last September and that they could, no doubt, manage just as well in the future, which had made de Wolfe all the more anxious to get back to work.

He had no assistant or deputy, though the edicts of the Curia Regis had ordered that three knights should be appointed as coroners in each county. The duties were so onerous – as well as unpaid – that only one other had been found willing to officiate in North Devon, and he had fallen from his horse a few weeks later, then died of a broken back. As no replacement could be found, de Wolfe had the whole of the huge county, one of the biggest in England, to look after alone. It was sometimes physically impossible for him to travel the long distances to cover all of his multifarious duties, but until he had broken his leg at the New Year, he had managed to get to almost every suspected homicide and serious assault, as well as to most hangings and sanctuary-seekers.

He reached Martin's Lane and slowly dismounted, leaving Odin in the farrier's care. His left leg pained him as he walked across to his house, reminding him that he was not yet back to normal. Pushing open the street door of blackened oak, he went into the vestibule where he hung up his grey cloak and pulled off his riding boots. His old hound Brutus ambled through the covered passage to the back yard, where in one of the servants' huts Mary had her kitchen and her bed. The maid bustled after the dog, who nuzzled de Wolfe in greeting. Wiping her hands on her apron, she announced that dinner was ready. 'And she's back,' Mary added, with a jerk of her head towards the inner door.

A handsome woman in her twenties, Mary covertly sided with John against the grim Matilda and her acidulous French maid Lucille. In the past, he had shared her mattress on more than one occasion, but lately she had resisted him: Lucille was getting suspicious and Mary valued her job even more than the pleasure provided by the lusty coroner. 'Go in and make your peace,' she suggested. 'She'll probably have guessed where you've been this morning.'

As she vanished down the passageway, de Wolfe sighed and lifted the latch on the inner door to his hall. The house in Martin's Lane was a tall, narrow structure of wood, with a shingled roof. It consisted almost entirely of one high room, but with a solar added at the back of the upper part of the hall, reached by an outside stairway from the backyard. The solar was both their bedroom and Matilda's retreat, where she spent her hours when not at prayer or slumber in some indifferent needlework.

At the back of the hall, most of the wall was taken up by a huge stone fireplace, with the tapering cone of the chimney rising above it to the rafters. Two settles and a couple of cowled chairs stood in a half-circle around the hearth, and down the centre of the gloomy room a long oak refectory table took up much of the space. The heavy boards of the walls were hung with sombre tapestries that helped to keep the draughts at bay. The floor was slabbed in stone, another modern innovation of Matilda, who scorned the usual rushes or straw strewn on beaten earth.

When he entered, his wife was sitting at the far end of the table, waiting for her meal. Though there were benches along each side of the table, at each end was a heavy upright chair, used by de Wolfe and Matilda almost consciously for the purpose of staying as far apart as possible. He closed the door behind him and limped towards her.

Matilda lifted her head to glare at him, her square pug face devoid of any welcome. 'You've been overdoing it again, I suppose! I told you that it's too soon to be riding that great beast of a horse. God knows where you've been on it, but I suppose I can guess.'

The coroner threw his stick on to the table with a clatter and stared down at her. 'I've been up to Rougemont to see your damned brother, if you must know! I need a new chamber that's not almost on the roof of the cursed gatehouse, and all he would give me was a closet the size of our privy.'

He stamped to the fire and threw on a couple of logs from the stack, as Brutus sidled in behind him and lay down to bask in the warmth. The mention of the sheriff imposed an ominous silence upon them: she had never mentioned her brother's name since she had had to plead with her husband not to reveal him as a would-be rebel.

De Wolfe stood warming himself by the rising flames and looked across at the back view of his sullen wife. Though never pretty, sixteen years ago when his father had arranged their marriage into the well-known de Revelle family, she had been slimmer and had had a good complexion. Now at forty-six – half a dozen years older than de Wolfe – she had thickened into a podgy, short-necked woman, with coarse skin and thinning fair hair. She had loose flesh under her chin and her puffy lids gave her a narrow-eyed, almost Oriental appearance. John put this down to some internal disorder of her vital humours, though it did not seem to diminish her appetite for either food or wine.

'Now that you can sit a horse again, I suppose you'll be off about the countryside at all hours,' she complained to the opposite wall, not turning to address him.

'It's my duty, for Christ's sake,' he snapped. 'You were the one who was so keen for me to become the king's coroner here.'

'Must you blaspheme every time you open your mouth?' she retorted, still staring ahead of her. 'It would be fitter if you went to church more often, instead of the tavern.' Since the débâcle two months ago, she also avoided mentioning Nesta's name, though Matilda, like most of Exeter, was well aware of the attraction the Bush Inn held for Sir John de Wolfe.

'I've neglected the coroner's tasks for too long, though Gwyn and Thomas have done their best these past few weeks. I can't leave matters to them and the bailiffs much longer. I must get out and about as much as my leg will let me – it's strengthening fast, better each day.'

He paused, then added, almost reluctantly, 'Due in large measure to you, Matilda, for which I'm truly grateful.' He said this awkwardly, as even a hint of intimacy was foreign to their relationship.

She swung round on her chair, the heavy skirt of her

brocade kirtle swishing on the flagstones. 'You have your duty as coroner and I have mine as your wife. I wasn't going to allow some drab of a maid or a doxy from the lower town care for your injury. It was bad enough having that hairy Cornish creature or that pervert of an ex-priest hanging about the house most of the time.'

De Wolfe sighed, sensing that things were rapidly getting back to normal between them after their relative truce of the past two months. But a developing quarrel was blunted by the appearance of Mary with a tray bearing a large wooden bowl of broth and bread trenchers covered in pork and cabbage. She was followed by the emaciated form of old Simon, their yard servant who chopped wood and tended the fires and the privy. He brought a pitcher of hot wine with two pewter mugs, and the business of eating and drinking diverted the ever-hungry Matilda from her nagging.

After champing her way through a large meal, including the slab of bread that did service for a plate on the scrubbed boards of the table, and drinking the better part of a pint of mulled wine, Matilda abruptly broke her silence by announcing that she was going to the solar to have her hair brushed by Lucille, though de Wolfe suspected that she was going to sleep off the effects of her full belly.

She stalked out without another word and, thankfully, he took his mug across to the hearth and sank into one of the monk's chairs, which had wooden sides and a hood to keep off the draughts that came from the unglazed windows, covered in linen screens. Brutus came to lay his big brown head on his master's knees, and John stared absently into the fire as he fondled the animal's ears.

Mary appeared to clear away the debris of the meal

and scour the table. 'Thomas called earlier. He said he would bring some work at about the second hour.' She jerked her head in the direction of the nearby cathedral, whose bells for its many services told the city the time. 'I gave him some food, too. The poor man looks half starved,' she added, with a hint of accusation that de Wolfe underpaid his clerk. The little ex-priest received a penny a day from the coroner's own pocket, which – as he enjoyed a free mattress laid in a servant's hut in one of the canon's houses in the Close – should have been ample to feed him. It was certainly far more than he had had until last September: he had been virtually destitute since he had been thrown out of Winchester, where he had had a teaching post in the cathedral school. One of the girl pupils had accused him of an indecent assault. After failing to scratch a living by writing letters for merchants, he had walked to Exeter and thrown himself on the mercy of his uncle, Archdeacon John de Alençon. A good friend of de Wolfe, the canon prevailed on the new coroner to take Thomas as his clerk, for the little ex-priest was highly proficient with quill and parchment.

The coroner was almost dozing off, replete with food and warm wine, when the scrape of the door on the stones jerked him into wakefulness. He turned, expecting to see his clerk, but it was Gwyn of Polruan, named after his home village, a fishing hamlet on the Fowey river. The huge man poked his head inside first, wary in case Matilda was at home: she looked on anyone who was not a Norman as some sub-species of mankind, especially Celts. She hated the thought that her husband was half Welsh, from which stemmed much of her virulent dislike of her mother-in-law.

'It's safe, Gwyn, she's up in the solar,' said de Wolfe,

guessing the reason for his officer's hesitation. He kept his voice down as there was a narrow slit high in the hall that communicated with the upper room.

The Cornishman padded in and stood by the coroner's chair. De Wolfe was taller than average, but Gwyn more than equalled his height and had a massive body that made the coroner look thin by comparison. He had an unruly mop of wiry hair and a huge bushy moustache that drooped down each side of his mouth almost to his chest. Bright blue eyes shone out above a bulbous nose. 'I've shifted our belongings down to that festering hole in the ground that the sheriff so generously gave us,' he growled. 'I hope to God your leg mends even faster so that we can go back up to our proper chamber.'

'Anything new occurred today?' asked John. 'Any deaths or woundings?'

Gwyn shook his shaggy head. 'Nothing today. There are two hangings at the Magdalen tree tomorrow, which you should attend if you can.'

One of the duties of the coroner was to seize for the king's treasury, the chattels of condemned felons and to record the fact of execution and the profit – if any – on his rolls. This would be presented to the royal judges, along with every other legal aspect of life in Devon, when they eventually trundled to the county as the General Eyre. It was different from the Eyre of Assize, which was supposed to come each quarter to try serious cases, but which was often a year late.

'I saw that fellow again today – twice, in fact,' remarked de Wolfe. 'I'm sure he's following me, but with this leg I've no chance of catching him.'

Gwyn frowned. Anything that threatened his master, even remotely, was something to be taken seriously. Although the city was a fairly safe place inside its stout walls, with its gates locked from dusk to dawn, he knew that Sir John had quite a few enemies, most of them antagonistic to his fierce loyalty to the king. 'I must keep a sharper eye out for him,' he rumbled. 'I'll follow you when you're riding or walking the streets. If I see anyone, or if you give me the wink that he's there, I'll have the bastard, never fear!'

With this grim promise, he lumbered out, but de Wolfe had no chance to slide into slumber as he heard his henchman's voice in the vestibule and almost immediately the door opened again to admit Thomas de Peyne, who sidled through the wooden screens put up to reduce the draughts.

His clerk was a poor specimen of a man, short and scrawny, with a slight hump on his back and a lame left leg, both due to childhood phthisis, which had carried away his mother. Thin, lank brown hair, a slight squint, a long, pointed nose and a weak chin all conspired to make him the least attractive of men, which was emphasized even more by his threadbare clothes – a grey tunic under a thin black cloak. Though expelled from the clergy almost two years ago, he still hankered passionately after his old vocation, and those who did not know his history often assumed that he was still a priest. Living in the servants' quarters of a canon's house and associating with clergy every day, he kept abreast of all the ecclesiastical gossip, which was often useful to John de Wolfe.

However, for all his unprepossessing appearance, Thomas possessed an agile and cunning brain, and had a remarkable talent for penmanship. His knowledge of history, politics and the classic writers was remarkable, and though de Wolfe and Gwyn pretended to be contemptuous of his puny physique and timid nature, they were secretly quite fond of the little ex-cleric.

Thomas came across the hall in his customary tentative manner, his writing materials slung in their usual place over his shoulder. 'Are you up to date with your rolls?' demanded his master. The clerk lifted the flap of his bag and produced two palimpsests – parchments that had been reused several times: the old writing was scraped off and the surface rubbed with chalk to make it ready for new ink.

'These are the last two inquests, Crowner. And the names of the last two weeks' hangings, with a record of their chattels, such as they were.' He handed the rolls to de Wolfe, who stared at the first few lines of each and silently mouthed the Latin words Thomas had been so laboriously teaching him these past weeks. 'Will you read them aloud for practice?' suggested Thomas hesitantly. Sometimes de Wolfe was in no mood for reading practice and today seemed one of those occasions.

'Too damned tired, Thomas! Maybe my wife is right. Riding that horse this morning has taken it out of me.' In truth, several quarts of ale at the Bush and the wine at his midday meal were more the reason for his torpor. 'Anything else happening?' he asked. His clerk was the nosiest man in Exeter and often provided gossip that kept him informed of many of the city's intrigues.

Thomas shook his head glumly. He liked nothing better than to feel part of the coroner's team, and to have no titbit of scandal to pass on made him feel as if he had shirked his duty.

'Have you seen this damned fellow peering after me around corners these past few days?' de Wolfe demanded.

Thomas's bright, bird-like eyes flicked to the shuttered window. 'The man in the street Gwyn told me about? No, I've been up in the gatehouse writing these rolls. But I'll keep a look-out now, with Gwyn. Have you any idea who it might be?'

'Indeed not. I thought you might have heard of some new arrival in the city that might match this knave. About thirty-five, strong-looking, his face shaved and his clothing an unremarkable dun brown, with a wide-brimmed pilgrim's hat that shades his eyes.'

The little clerk looked worried, as if his inability to know of every transient passing through Exeter was a personal failing. 'Perhaps he is a pilgrim, then – or masquerading as one. Have a care, Crowner, you have enemies in this county.'

At that moment, the door grated open and Matilda marched in, refreshed from her nap in the solar. She was dressed in a heavy green mantle over her kirtle and a white linen coverchief was wrapped decorously around her temples and neck, secured at her forehead by a silk band. Behind her followed Lucille, her sallow face framed by a brown woollen shawl.

As soon as Matilda saw Thomas, the expression on her face changed as if she had just trodden in something left by Brutus. Without a word, the clerk scooped up his rolls and scuttled from the hall. 'You shouldn't let that little pervert bring his work here to tire you out, John,' she snapped.

'It's not his work, woman, it's my work!' retorted de Wolfe. 'Thank God I can get back to something approaching my duties.'

His wife ignored this and dropped heavily on to one of the settles near the hearth. 'Let's see that leg of yours, husband. Brother Saulf warned you to make sure it doesn't swell again by putting too much strain on it.'

'Damn it, woman, there's nothing to see now! It's almost as good as new.'

'Do as you're told, John. I've not cared for you all these weeks for my work to be undone now by your neglect.'

Reluctantly, he sat on the chair opposite her and, with the rabbit-toothed Lucille staring from across the room, he hauled up the skirt of his long tunic and pushed down his grey woollen hose to the ankle. 'There, I told you. You'd not know anything had been amiss with it.'

The leg certainly looked well, the last traces of redness on the shin having faded and the slight deformity almost gone. Matilda reached out a ringed finger and prodded it, but could feel no puffiness. There was nothing but a smooth ridge under the skin where the broken ends of the shinbone had knitted together.

'I told you, I'm back to normal again. You don't have to complain about me riding a horse. God knows, I've had worse injuries than this in my campaigning days.'

He hauled up his stocking again and stood up. 'Now that I've prised a makeshift chamber from your brother, I can get back to business.'

The mention of Richard de Revelle silenced her, as usual now since he had so narrowly escaped disgrace. After a moment, she abruptly changed the subject. 'It's high time the Justiciar, or someone in Winchester or London, filled these vacant coronerships,' she said. 'Walter Fitzrogo fell from his horse more than six months ago and has never been replaced. Even before that, the county was one crowner short – and then you go acting the fool and break a leg. Is that any way to run a country?' She might have added that it would be better for England if the king stayed at home and paid more attention to the affairs of his realm, but she knew that criticism of the Lionheart would stir her husband into a passionate diatribe of loyalty to his sovereign.

'Well, no one wants the job, so I've got to make the best of it,' he growled, tired of the same old complaints from his wife. He sensed that she was leading up to another tirade about his being away from home so much, neglecting her and failing especially to pander to the social life of the county aristocracy, which meant so much to her.

'You'll be forcing yourself on to that great horse every hour of the day just to defy me! You'll regret it – that leg is not yet fit for riding. You'll fall from the saddle like Fitzrogo, or get a purulent fever in the bone. I suppose you'd like to make me a widow, just for spite!'

Exasperated at the accuracy of his predictions, John moved towards the door. 'No fear of that, wife! I've not been outside the walls of Exeter these past two months. It's high time I began getting around more. And that's just what I'm going to do now. I've not been through one of the city gates since they carried me home on a cart from Bull Mead.'

He banged the heavy door behind him, and as he sat on the bench in the vestibule to pull on his riding boots, Mary appeared from the passageway. 'Did I hear raised voices in there?' she asked. A dark-eyed, attractive woman, she was the bastard daughter of a Norman man-at-arms whose name neither she nor her Saxon mother had ever known.

'Same old story, that I'm always away and neglecting her – she's getting back to normal, more's the pity,' he muttered. 'I'm going for a ride around the outside of the walls, if anyone wants me.'

As she handed him his mottled grey wolfskin cloak from a peg on the wall, Mary virtually repeated Matilda's caution. 'Watch that leg of yours, Sir Crowner! You're not as young as you think, remember.'

As he threw the cloak around his shoulders, he gave her a quick kiss. 'I'm still young enough to creep under your blanket tonight, if you'd let me!' She pushed him away with mock annoyance, fearful that Matilda or her maid might appear, but de Wolfe pulled open the iron-banded front door and stepped into the narrow street.

A few minutes later, he was riding Odin sedately through the Close around the cathedral, picking his way along the criss-crossing paths between the piles of rubbish and earth from new graves that made such an unsightly contrast to the soaring church with its two great towers. Urchins ran around yelling or playing ball and hawkers touted shrivelled apples and meat pies to the loungers and gossipers who stood or squatted around the untidy precinct. He came out through Bear Gate into Southgate Street and pushed his way past the throng around the butcher's stalls, where more hawkers squatted behind their baskets of produce. With almost a sense of adventure, he passed under the arch of the South Gate, with its prison cells in the towers on each side, and emerged from the city for the first time in many weeks. Ahead of him, past the small houses, huts and shacks that had sprung up outside the walls, the road forked into Holloway and Magdalen Street, leading to Honiton, Yeovil and, eventually, distant Winchester and London, which to most residents of Exeter were as remote as the moon.

De Wolfe turned right and followed the city wall steeply down towards the river, where a number of small vessels were beached on the muddy banks. A stone quay and some thatched storehouses lay at the corner of the walls, where the line of the ancient Roman defences turned towards the West Gate and the road to South Devon and Cornwall. He plodded along slowly, taking in the familiar sight of the broad, shallow river, which meandered through the swampy islands that carried the mean shacks of the workers from the fulling mills which processed the wool that was the prime wealth of England.

Reining in Odin at the edge of one of the broad reens of muddy water that separated Exe Island from the bank, he watched the traffic coming out of the West Gate. Those on foot or with small handcarts, even some on a donkey or pony, used the rickety wooden footbridge that spanned the river and the grassy mud to reach the further bank. Large vehicles, like the ox-carts with their huge wooden wheels, and anyone on horseback had to ford the river, which here was just at the upper limit of the tidal reach.

His gaze travelled to the stone bridge, the huge project still less than half finished. The builders, Nicholas Gervase and his son Walter, had completed seven of the eighteen arches needed to span the marshy river, but even though they were wealthy mill-owners, their funds had run out. Until they could raise more from the burgesses and churchmen of Devon, travellers would still have to clamber or wade across the Exe. Even though it was incomplete, the city end of the bridge already had a chapel built on it, with a resident priest, a token of Nicholas's beholdenment to his ecclesiastical paymasters.

As John de Wolfe sat taking his ease on the broad back of his stallion, watching life go by with almost lazy contentment, he became aware of another horse coming up behind him at a trot. Without needing to turn, he knew from the clip of the hoofs that it was Gwyn's big brown mare and a twinge of annoyance came over him at the idea that he needed a nursemaid on such a short jaunt as this.

Then he wondered whether the Cornishman had managed to seize his mysterious stalker, but as his officer stopped alongside, he found that he was wrong on both counts.

'Mary told me you'd be somewhere outside the walls,' grunted Gwyn. 'I thought I'd best find you now, in case you wanted to make some arrangements for the morning.'

De Wolfe's black eyebrows rose up his forehead. 'What arrangements?'

'A rider has just come to Rougemont from Oliver de Tracey's bailiff at Barnstaple to report a murdered man on a wrecked ship at Ilfracombe.'

John whistled through his teeth. 'A wreck and a killing? Both of those are crowner's business, Gwyn. Any more details?'

The big man shook his shaggy red head. 'The messenger knew little. He had been riding since noon yesterday. The body was found the night before, it seems.'

The coroner lifted a gloved hand to rub the bridge of his beaked nose, a mannerism he had that seemed to aid thought, much as Gwyn scratched his groin and Thomas crossed himself when agitated. 'A dead man on a ship means either mutiny or piracy. We must go and discover which.'

His officer looked concerned. 'The north coast is a long way on the back of a nag when you have a poorly leg, Crowner. Let me go in your stead.'

The coroner leaned across and slapped him on the shoulder. 'Not nearly so far as Palestine, man! We'll set off within the hour and take it easily. We can get to Crediton by nightfall, find a night's rest there and get an early start to Barnstaple in the morning.'

The Cornishman still looked doubtful. 'Your good lady's not going to like it, you being away for at least three days.'

But de Wolfe was rejuvenated by the prospect of a return to activity and was in no mood for Matilda's strictures. 'To hell with her grumbling, Gwyn! Go and tell that little turd of a clerk to meet us on his pony at the North Gate by the fourth bell.'

He touched Odin's flanks with his heels and wheeled him around, heading back for the walls. 'And bring some food and drink in your saddle pouch. It's a long ride to Ilfracombe.'

CHAPTER TWO

In which Crowner John inspects a corpse

All the next day the coroner's trio rode steadily across the county, following the main track north-west from Copplestone, about thirteen miles from Exeter, where they had spent the night bedded down around the hearth at the small manor house. The weather remained chill but dry, and the going underfoot was good. The winter mud had hardened, but not yet dried into the dusts of summer. The bushes and trees alongside the narrow road were budding into the first signs of spring, and a few primroses and violets lurked in the undergrowth on this tenth day of March.

Though he would not admit it, by midday de Wolfe's leg had begun to ache, from jolting incessantly in the stirrup, but he had suffered far worse after two major and countless minor injuries in past campaigns. Even so, he was glad when Gwyn suggested then that the horses needed a rest, some water and half an hour's grazing. They had been on the road since first light and even at the modest pace set by John's leg and Thomas's pathetic riding, they had covered almost twenty miles. Now in the valley of the Taw, they were well over half-way to Barnstaple.

In a clearing just before the forest gave way to strip-fields near the manor of Chulmleigh, they slid thankfully from their saddles and hobbled the horses, letting them crop the short new grass that was now appearing after winter. A stream nearby offered men and beasts the chance to slake their thirst. Thomas, who rode his moorland pony side-saddle like a woman, staggered about, holding his backside and complaining about long journeys, which he detested.

'Come on, dwarf,' teased Gwyn, grabbing the clerk by his waist and holding him kicking and yelling in the air. 'Forget your sore buttocks and get us some bread and cheese from that bag.'

They were soon seated on a tree-stump, eating heartily and drinking from a leather flask filled with coarse cider. Even if the little ex-priest hated travelling, the coroner and his henchman were glad to be out on the road again: they had shared thousands of leagues over the past two decades, in Ireland, France and the Levant.

'We've made better time than I expected,' growled de Wolfe, between mouthfuls of hard crusts, even flintier cheese. 'At this rate, we'll not need to stop on the road tonight. We can be in Barnstaple by dark and claim a bed from Oliver de Tracey.'

'And ten or twelve miles to Ilfracombe tomorrow,' added Gwyn, sucking cider from the sides of his luxuriant whiskers. Even keeping down to a brisk walk or occasional trot, they could cover four or five miles in an hour without overly tiring the horses.

All that afternoon the three moved steadily northward, passing slow ox-carts and flocks of sheep, then a number of pilgrims and pedlars, as well as journeymen moving between employment with their tools slung in a bag across their shoulders. De Wolfe forgot the cares of life in Exeter, especially the moody and grim Matilda.

He had even forgotten the mysterious face that had been peering at him around street corners.

As it grew dusk, they found themselves at the estuary of the river Taw, with the port and borough of Barnstaple on the eastern side, some five miles inland from the open sea. Thomas, who had an encyclopaedic knowledge of history, informed his uninterested companions that the burgesses held a dubious claim to the oldest charter in England, granted by the Saxon king Athelstan, although certainly the first King Henry had given them a new Norman one.

As the light faded, the trio rode thankfully through the gate, just beating the curfew, and made their way to the castle. This had a small tower on top of a motte, which in recent years had been rebuilt in stone, in place of the original timber donjon. Around it was a triangular bailey inside a curtain wall that stood not far from where the small Yeo stream joined the Taw. The hall was a wooden building inside the bailey, the tower being a place for defence, too small for peacetime living quarters.

It was here they found the seneschal, the chief steward to the lord, and learned that Oliver de Tracey was away on a tour of his manors. However, the seneschal, a wizened old man called Odo who had looked after his lord's affairs for a quarter of a century, made them welcome. De Wolfe had been to the town several times in his capacity as coroner since the premature death of Fitzrogo and had had dealings with Odo before. The old steward seemed impressed with this new legal officer, partly because he admired de Wolfe's reputation as a Crusader and his close acquaintance with the Lionheart.

Gwyn and Thomas were sent off to the kitchens for a

meal, with the promise of a pallet of clean straw in the servants' quarters, whilst John was offered a chamber in the hall, which had a low bed and mattress, luxury indeed for such a remote place as Barnstaple.

'As my lord and his family are away, we have no formality in the hall tonight,' explained Odo. 'But there are a few knights doing their service here with their squires, as well as the constable, the priest, some travellers and a few clerks, so you are welcome to sup with us in an hour's time.'

With a dozen men eating and drinking in the flickering lights of wall flares and tallow dips on the table, de Wolfe spent a pleasant evening listening to and telling tales of past battles, skirmishes and ambuscades. As the ale and wine went down, the stories became more adventurous and far-fetched, but this was a life that he loved, the companionship of strong men and witty minds. At intervals, they were entertained by a pair of travelling musicians, who had arrived by ship from Neath across the Severn Sea, on their way to Cornwall. They earned their meal and mattress by some accomplished playing on pipgorn and crwth, Welsh wind and stringed instruments.

John took the opportunity to catch up with events in Wales; seven years earlier he had accompanied Archbishop Baldwin around the country on his recruiting campaign for the Third Crusade – in which the Archbishop himself had perished outside Acre. Speaking in his mother's native Welsh to the minstrels, he learned that the endless feud between Welsh and Normans was in a quiet phase. He even had news of his friend Gerald, Archdeacon of Brecon, who had been with them on the famous journey around Wales and was now apparently writing a book on the events.

But the business of the day was not forgotten; it had been Odo who had sent the messenger to Exeter the previous day.

'The manor reeve from Ilfracombe came here the day before yesterday seeking my bailiff, as your new coroner's law demands,' Odo said. 'He had news of this dead man found aboard ship the night before.'

De Wolfe wanted details, but Odo had little more to tell him. 'It seems a wrecked vessel was driven ashore somewhat to the east of Ilfracombe. On it, lashed to the deck by ropes, was a corpse with undoubted wounds from a sword or knife – certainly not injuries from the shipwreck. That's about all he could tell us, so I sent word to you. We have been told that now the crowner must deal with all suspicious and violent deaths.'

'And wrecks of the sea, as well,' added John.

This was news to Odo, and as de Wolfe explained, the group of men around the table listened with interest. Some had never heard of the new office of coroner and the rest were hazy as to his functions. 'Last September, at the General Eyre in Kent, the royal justices proclaimed an edict from Hubert Walter, our Chief Justiciar and Archbishop of Canterbury, which had several purposes,' explained de Wolfe.

'The main purpose seems to be to screw more taxes from the population!' growled one of the knights, who was working off some of his annual service to Oliver de Tracey in return for his manorial holding.

De Wolfe shrugged, conscious that this was the general perception of Hubert Walter's harsh taxation regime. 'Better an honest coroner than a corrupt sheriff,' he grunted. 'I name no names, but it is common knowledge that most of the sheriffs in England are more concerned with lining their own purses than with upholding the King's peace in their counties. Why else would so many nobles pay large sums to secure appointment to that office?'

Heads nodded around the table, for they remembered the scandal in the time of old King Henry, when all the sheriffs were dismissed for corruption – though almost all had seemed to claw their way back into favour.

'But what has that do with dead bodies and wrecks?' asked one of the Welshmen. Apart from a few franchise coroners in Glamorgan and Pembroke, the Normans' rule of law did not extend to most of Wales.

'King Richard's ransom was a heavy burden on England,' explained de Wolfe. 'One hundred and fifty thousand marks were demanded by Henry of Germany to release the Lionheart. This, together with the expense of the Crusades and his present wars against Philip of France, creates a need for every penny that our Justiciar can raise. It is where the coroner comes into the picture, to raise what legitimately belongs to the king's treasury.'

'Just another bloody clutch of taxes!' grumbled another knight.

John took a gulp of his wine and nodded in agreement. 'Taxes, like death and our wives, are always with us!' he exclaimed. 'Yet there are other advantages. The coroners now divert many lawsuits to the king's courts instead of leaving them to the mercy of the sheriffs' and burgesses' courts, whose ideas of justice are primitive. We record all serious crimes and accusations for presentation to the royal judges when they arrive at the Eyre of Assize in each county. Our very title of coroner comes from *custos plactitorum coronae* – keeper of the pleas of the Crown.'

This was beyond one of the castle clerks, though perhaps the amount of beer he had drunk was slowing his wits. 'But what has this to do with dead bodies or wrecks?' he complained.

'There are many ways of raising revenue for the king. Any fault of the community in failing to report a sudden death, to raise the hue and cry, or the death of any who cannot be proven to be Saxon – as well as rapes, assaults and other felonies – these lead to amercements, all grist to the Treasury. I have to attend every execution and see that the property of the hanged felon is seized for the Crown. If there is a wreck of the sea, then this also belongs to the king, as do catches of royal fish, the whale and sturgeon.'

For another hour, there was endless argument, lubricated by wine, ale and cider, about the morality of taxation, but it was all good-natured and de Wolfe defended his monarch's right-hand man, Archbishop Hubert Walter, in his need to extract as much money from the population as was bearable. Eventually, the minstrels played another tune and sang another song, and as the rush-lights burned low, the audience staggered off to their various chambers or sought their straw palliasses around the glowing embers of the fire in the Great Hall.

After a good breakfast early next morning, Sir John de Wolfe thanked Odo for his hospitality and, with his officer and clerk, set out for Ilfracombe. The main road curved westward along the estuary until it struck north-east to the coast, but there was a shorter, more direct route over the hills due north from Barnstaple through the village of Bittadon. The seneschal recommended this: although it was sometimes plagued by roving outlaws from the fringe of Exmoor, it saved a few miles' riding. The coroner and his brawny henchman were veteran campaigners and had little fear of wayside ambush – their heavy broadswords and Gwyn's fighting axe were sufficient to see off anyone other than a substantial band of men. However, Thomas rode in a perpetual state of anxiety, his beady eyes forever scanning the roadside for attacking ruffians, but the journey passed without incident.

A few hours later, they had covered the ten miles to the north coast and were jogging down the hill into Ilfracombe. The little port nestled between jagged cliffs, the harbour hidden behind a rocky prominence. The north-westerly breeze was strong and a line of white breakers hurled themselves against the craggy, indented shore. Ahead in the far distance, the hills of Wales could just be seen in the haze.

'Who does this place belong to?' asked Gwyn, as they trotted down towards the twisted street that led to the beach.

'The Bishop of Coutances owns the land, as he does a great slice of the county,' piped up the clerk, anxious to display his knowledge, especially when it concerned churchmen. 'But he sub-let it to Robert of Pontecardon many years ago and then it passed to Robert Fitzroy's family as tenants.'

'Damn who it belongs to,' grunted de Wolfe. 'Let's just find the reeve. He was the one who sent to Barnstaple with the news of this corpse.'

A substantial village and port like Ilfracombe would normally have had a resident bailiff, a more senior servant of the manorial lord, but Odo had told them that he had recently died of an apoplexy, and until Fitzroy or his steward appointed a new one, the manor reeve was having to cope with the administration. As they trotted down the only street, a dozen curious villagers appeared to gape at the strangers. The harbour was a sandy cove protected on the seaward side by a long peninsula, called the Benricks, which at the highest tides became an island. The outer end rose to a hill, on which was a low tower carrying a signal brazier to direct ships into the harbour. A score of buildings clustered around the harbour, ranging from a few stone-built houses to rickety hovels made of turf. The roofs were mostly thatched, but the larger dwellings had heavy stone slates, better to resist the foul weather that blew so often into this Atlantic mouth of the Severn Sea.

There were a couple of storehouses and fish-sheds at the head of the beach and several fishing boats were drawn up above the tide-line. Leaning against the single quay, listing until the water floated it again, was a merchant vessel with a stumpy mast. A procession of labourers was filing across a plank to the shore, carrying sacks of lime on their backs.

A few yards from the quayside, de Wolfe halted Odin and called down to a young woman, who was gawping open-mouthed at the new arrivals. She had a baby at her breast, the infant naked in spite of the keen wind that ruffled the poor wench's rags. 'Where can we find the reeve, girl?' boomed the coroner.

Wide-eyed at the revelation that this great dark stranger from another world spoke her language, the young mother pointed wordlessly at a stone house directly opposite, then turned tail and ran away, the baby's lips still clamped to her bosom.

By now, more inhabitants had gathered to peer at the new arrivals, and from them, a stocky middle-aged man with a large moustache and a square brown beard

stepped forward. 'You must be the crowner, sir. I am
Matthew, the manor reeve. I've been expecting you.'

John recognised him for a sensible, reliable man,
which was more than could be said for some reeves,
who often seemed high-grade idiots. The manor reeve
was at the bottom of the pecking order of officials
in the feudal system, responsible for the day-to-day
organisation of the village farm work. Although all but
the stewards were illiterate, the reeves kept account of
village business – crops, stock, tithes and work rotas –
by means of notched tally-sticks and their memories.

With half the population following at a respectful
distance, the reeve led them across to the bailiff's house,
which he was occupying for the time being. A boy took
their horses to the backyard to be fed and watered and
they went into the building. It had the luxury of two
rooms, though they were bare of any comfort, apart
from a few benches and stools grouped around the fire
on the beaten earth floor in the centre of the smaller
room. Piles of bracken and hay lay against the walls,
forming the sleeping quarters for the reeve's wife and
four children. The other room was the kitchen and
dairy, which was shared with a cow and three orphaned
spring lambs.

Matthew's wife brought them bread, meat and ale,
and they sat around the clay-lined fire-pit where burning
logs threw a blue smoke into the atmosphere.

'The cadaver is in one of the fish sheds over on the
quay,' explained the reeve. He had a handsome face,
albeit scarred by cow-pox, with a moustache that almost
matched Gwyn's in size.

'How did you come by this corpse?' demanded the
coroner.

Matthew leaned forward, his roughened hands on the

knees of his serge breeches. 'A boy up on the headland above the harbour saw this derelict vessel out to the east, no sail upon her and obviously going to be driven ashore. A gang of us set out at once to find where she would beach, in case we could save any souls.'

Gwyn, who came from a fishing village himself, strongly suspected that they would have been more interested in saving cargo and gear than souls, but kept these cynical thoughts to himself.

'We went across the cliffs, but the vessel had been blown further up towards Combe Bay, and by the time we had walked that distance, she had struck on Burrow Nose, near Watermouth. It was almost dark, but we found her wedged in a gully. She was not too badly damaged, but by the next day, she had broken up with the pounding of the tide.'

'And this dead man?'

'He was on the deck, just astern of the hold. The mast had broken and the spars had come down, so that his legs were tangled in the rigging. Otherwise, we would never have found the body – it would long have been washed overboard, out at sea.'

De Wolfe downed the last of his ale from a crude pottery jar and stood up. 'Let's go and have a look at him, then.'

Pulling his pointed leather hood over his head, he made for the door and stooped to pass under the low lintel. Watched by the curious villagers, who followed the party at a distance, they were led across the street to the quayside. Matthew strode ahead to a small shed made of rough timbers, the turf roof held down against the winds by flat stones. As they entered the open landward end, an overpowering stench of decaying fish filled their nostrils.

Two elderly women and a boy were standing at a crude bench, gutting fish and dropping them into wicker baskets. The entrails were thrown on to the ground to add to a stinking heap, which would be shovelled into the harbour for the tide to remove. Thomas de Peyne, the only sensitive member of the team, shrank back, holding his threadbare cloak over his nose.

'He's in that corner,' declared the reeve, pointing past the women to the dark recesses of the shed. Gwyn walked across and pulled a tattered canvas from a still shape lying against the wall.

De Wolfe and the reeve joined him to look down at the pathetically small figure of a youth, huddled in death on the odorous earth. The young man wore dark trousers and a short tunic pinched in with a wide leather belt. His clothes were still saturated with sea water and he lay on his side, as if asleep, his face to the wall. Gwyn bent down and lifted him like a child, to lay him flat on his back.

'He's had a mortal wound, that's for sure,' observed Matthew, pointing down at the thin bloodstains that had not washed completely from the fabric of the man's hessian tunic.

At the upper part of his belly, there was an oblique rent in the cloth, surrounded by the sinister pink staining. John squatted on his heels alongside the corpse, undid the belt and pulled up the tunic.

'The head of a pike!' said Gwyn immediately, jabbing a massive forefinger towards a characteristic wound on the victim's upper abdomen. A two-inch-wide stab with bruised edges lay on the pale skin below the rib margin, while in line with it, and half a hand's breadth away, was an angry red graze on top of more bruising.

'How can you tell it was a pike?' asked the reeve, a man of no military experience.

'The spike went in here,' snapped de Wolfe, poking his finger deeply into the stab wound. 'And the side-arm below it made this mark here.' He indicated the abrasion.

'Can't have been more than sixteen, this lad,' observed Gwyn. 'Do we know who he might be?'

'Not a local fellow,' said the reeve. 'The vessel had no name, but several of our fishermen say it is from Bristol. It plies up and down the coast from the ports on the Severn down to Plymouth and sometimes across to St Malo and Barfleur.'

De Wolfe, though a soldier, was a reluctant sailor and marvelled at the bravery – or foolhardiness – of the shipmen who sailed their clumsy cockleshells around the violent waters of western Britain.

Thomas had overcome his revulsion at the stench of fishguts and was almost fearfully peering at the corpse under Gwyn's elbow. 'A drowned sailor?' he asked timidly, spasmodically making the Sign of the Cross.

'No, dwarf, a stabbed sailor,' grunted the big man. 'Skewered on a pike. This is murder.'

The coroner checked that the body had no other injuries, then motioned for the reeve to throw the canvas over him again. 'Was there any sign of anyone else aboard?'

Matthew shook his head. 'Nor any remains of a cargo. The hull had been sound until she crashed on to the rocks, but there was not a box, barrel nor bale aboard her.'

John thought he detected a note of disappointment in the man's voice and he suspected, like Gwyn, that the villagers had been intent on plundering the wreck. 'I had better get out there and view the vessel,' he decided. 'How far away is it?'

Matthew looked slightly evasive. 'Half an hour's walk, Crowner, but not worth the journey. She'll have broken up altogether by now – the sea was battering her to pieces and yesterday there was hardly anything left.'

De Wolfe glared at him. 'I have a legal duty to view the wreck, man.' He turned to Thomas. 'I'll hold an inquest when I get back, so round up everyone who knows anything about this – and a dozen more men above the age of twelve.'

Minutes later, the reeve was leading them on foot across the back of the cliffs to a track that passed down through the hamlet of Hele, with its water-mill, and across the shoulder of Widmouth Hill to rejoin the shore further east. Two miles from Ilfracombe, they crossed a deep, sandy inlet and scrambled across a warren to a low cliff. Below, the surf sucked and pounded remorselessly in a series of rocky gullies and narrow inlets.

'I said there was little left of her,' shouted Matthew, going down a muddy sheep-track ahead.

Looking down, de Wolfe saw that the reeve exaggerated somewhat, as the lower part of the fifty-foot hull was still jammed firmly between the jagged teeth of a reef. The tide was now almost at full ebb and it was easy for them to get to the derelict without getting wet, apart from the spray from an occasional large wave.

The stump of the mast still poked up at an acute angle, but all the gunwales and most of the deck planking had gone, timbers littering the small shingle beach immediately inland of the wreck.

'All you'll get from this one is some kindling for your winter fires,' cackled Gwyn, with a wink at the gloomy manor reeve.

'What would she have been likely to be carrying, Gwyn?' demanded the coroner, still suspicious that the villagers might have made off with some cargo, which should have been confiscated for the king's treasury.

'Depends where she came from. If it was Brittany or Normandy, then maybe wine and fruit. If she was outward bound, she'd have had wool, no doubt.'

De Wolfe nodded at that. He had a substantial interest in wool exports himself, having sunk most of the loot from his foreign campaigns in a partnership with one of Exeter's foremost wool merchants, Hugh de Relaga. He also shared in the profits of his family's estate at Stoke-in-Teignhead, where his elder brother, William, was a keen sheep-farmer.

'There's nothing to see, Crowner, as I told you,' said Matthew, virtuously.

De Wolfe had to agree, but Gwyn clambered the last few yards over the rocks and pulled himself on to the wreck, standing rather precariously on a surviving thwart, which had supported the decking. He looked around intently, determined not to miss any clues. Before taking up soldiering, he had helped his father as a fisherman in his home village of Polruan and was well used to the sea and ships.

As de Wolfe and the reeve watched him, Gwyn seemed particularly interested in the remains of the mast, a tree-trunk a foot thick, which had broken off about six feet above the deck.

He pointed to some marks at waist height and shouted back to the other men, 'Fresh slashes in the wood here! Been struck several times with a heavy sharp blade, fore and aft.' He hopped back ashore and came up to them.

'What does that mean?' grunted his master, who knew next to nothing about ships.

'The halyards were cut to bring the sail down, 'explained the Cornishman. 'No one in the crew would do that to their own vessel, so it must have been boarded and disabled.'

De Wolfe looked grim. 'So it was piracy, not mutiny – though that was unlikely from the start, for why would the crew of a dull merchantman want to mutiny?'

'How many men on a vessel like this?' asked Matthew.

De Wolfe looked at Gwyn for enlightenment.

'About five or six, usually. Two men could sail her in normal weather, but they need extras for sleeping, cooking and handling her at the ports.'

'So the rest are still floating around the Severn Sea until they get washed ashore?'

Gwyn shook his shaggy head. 'Many bodies never turn up. They either sink or get pulled out into the broad ocean. Or, in this channel, they may even end up near Gloucester.'

As if to confound him, at that moment there was a distant cry from above and a man appeared on the skyline, waving his arms.

The group at the wreck stood watching as he came rapidly down the narrow paths with the agility of a mountain goat. He was within a hundred yards before Matthew recognised him. 'It's Siward, a shepherd who lives up on the cliffs above here. What the devil does he want? He's a bit lacking in the head.'

From the speed of his surefooted descent, de Wolfe had expected some active youth, but when he got to them, Siward showed himself to be a gnarled old man, with a bent back and a face like a walnut, wrinkled and brown. He wore a rough woollen tunic, the skirt tucked up between his legs and pushed into an old rope wound around his waist. He was barefoot and his toenails were curled like ram's horns.

He had sparse grey hair, and although his eyes were as bright as a blackbird's, the lids were red and inflamed.

'You took the corpse, sirs?' Siward asked abruptly, in the manner of one who, isolated with his sheep, rarely conversed with his fellow men.

'When did you see a corpse, old man?' demanded de Wolfe.

Matthew opened his mouth to warn again that the octogenarian was more than a little simple, but Siward seemed quite able to speak for himself. 'When I took the other one away – the live one,' exclaimed the old Saxon.

The other four stared at him. 'What other one?' rumbled Gwyn.

Siward rolled his bloodshot eyes heavenwards. 'Almighty God spoke to me the other evening, and gave me a task. I looked across the sea from my dwelling and saw this vessel being driven ashore.'

'He lives in a turf hut on top of the cliffs,' explained Matthew.

'I lit my lantern and hurried down here. From the upper path, I saw the ship just before it hit the rocks. Then, there were two bodies on the deck, but only one by the time I had got down here.'

'What of this living man?' demanded the coroner.

'He was on the shingle, more dead than alive. I dragged him up on to the grass, then went up for my pony, which I ride to herd my distant flocks.'

'You got a horse down here?' said Gwyn incredulously.

'He is an Exmoor cob, he can go where any sheep can stray. I draped the man over the pony's back and took him up to my house. He began shivering, so I knew he was alive.'

'And where is he now?' asked the manor reeve.

'Still in my hut. His mind came back yesterday, but he is very weak.'

Since he had become coroner de Wolfe had ceased to be surprised by anything. 'Then take us to him at once. Lead the way,' he said.

Again with a remarkable turn of speed for an old man, Siward scuttled back up the cliff path, with the coroner, his officer and the reeve labouring behind him.

'Why didn't you know about this, Matthew?' panted de Wolfe, as they reached the top.

'He doesn't belong to our manor. He works under the reeve in Combe Martin – the sheep are from there. Siward has probably never set foot as far away as Ilfracombe.'

At the top of the cliffs, there was a rough grassy ridge, and tucked in a hollow out of the wind was a crude circular hut, the walls made of stacked turf reinforced with loose stones. The roof was also of turf, the grass growing as strongly on it as on the surrounding pasture. Blue smoke drifted from under the ragged eaves.

Siward pulled aside an unhung door made of drift-wood and beckoned them inside. In the dim light, they saw a single room floored with soiled bracken, on which two orphan lambs were bleating. Against the further wall, near a small peat fire confined by large stones, was an indistinct figure huddled under a torn woollen blanket.

'Can't understand a word from him,' complained Siward, whose only language was English, heavy with the local accent.

Gwyn and de Wolfe advanced on the man and bent

down over his hunched form. He looked up and they saw he was another young man, probably no more than eighteen, with a deathly pale face and sores on his lips. Before he could speak, he was racked by a bubbling cough and spat copiously into the ferns on the floor. His eye-sockets were hollow, and in spite of the ghastly whiteness of his face, two pink spots burned on either cheek.

Gwyn put a hand on his forehead. 'He's got a burning fever, Crowner.'

'Who are you, boy, what happened to your ship?' de Wolfe asked. He spoke in English and the youth looked blankly at him, shivering and hugging the rough blanket more closely around his thin shoulders.

'He doesn't understand a damned word,' explained Siward. 'I've given him some hot ewe's milk and a few herbs I have here to try to calm his fever.'

Suddenly, between a spasm of teeth-chattering, the shipwrecked sailor loosed a torrent of words. De Wolfe and his officer looked at each other in satisfaction. 'He's a Breton,' exclaimed the coroner and changed his questioning to his blend of Cornish-Welsh.

With a wan smile, the sick youngster responded in his own language and, within minutes, they had the whole story from him. The vessel was the *Saint Isan*, owned by a syndicate of burgesses from Bristol. It made regular voyages from the Avon to the Cornish ports and then across to Brittany. It had a master and a crew of five, two Somerset men and three Bretons. A few days ago, they had been coming from Roscoff via Penzance, back towards their home port, and were running before a brisk wind between Lundy and the mainland.

'Our old tub was always slow, even with a following wind. A couple of hours after noon, we were overhauled by a longer vessel that had half a dozen oars each side, though these were shipped as she easily outran us under her sail.' Alain, for that was his name, stopped for a prolonged bout of coughing. 'Before we knew what was happening, they were alongside and a dozen men scrambled over the side,' he continued, gasping for breath. 'I remember seeing them almost cut our master's head off with a sword and throw him overboard as they attacked all of us. Then one came at me with a club – I remember nothing more until I woke up on the deck, clinging for my life, with a dead man alongside me. Then the vessel struck and the last I recall was being thrown into the sea. I came to again in this hut, where this kind fellow has been doing his best for me.'

'You have no idea who these pirates were?' demanded Gwyn.

'I recollect very little. It was all confusion for the couple of minutes that I remember. They shouted in English, that's for sure.'

'What was their ship like?' asked John, standing over the man like a great black crow.

Alain shrugged under the blanket. 'Nothing special, though it was not a trading knarr like the *Saint Isan*. It was slimmer and faster, more like a longship – and it had a big sail, as well as a bank of oars on each side.'

'No name painted on the bow, nor any device on the sail?' grunted Gwyn.

'Nothing. Other than that they used your Saxon tongue, I've no idea who they were or where they came from.'

Gwyn pulled down the ends of his moustache, as if that would help him think. 'You are a shipman in these waters. Have you heard of any other vessels being attacked in this way?'

Alain shook his head wearily. 'It was never mentioned by the other men, God rest them.'

'What cargo were you carrying?'

'It was a mixture – some wine, casks of dried fruit, bales of silk, I don't know what else.'

'Valuable stuff, a good haul for pirates,' observed Gwyn.

After some more questions, it became obvious that Alain had nothing else useful to tell them. Although de Wolfe would have liked him to appear at the inquest to identify the corpse, it was obvious that the young Breton was far too sick to be moved at present. They described the dead man to Alain, who felt sure that it was a Bristol youth called Roger, of mixed Norman and Saxon blood.

De Wolfe felt in his waist pouch and gave Siward three pennies, with instructions to get some good food for the shipman and to tend him until he was fit to travel down to Ilfracombe, hopefully in a few days' time.

Leaving the old shepherd and his patient, they made their way back the several miles to the port, arriving in mid-afternoon. Their clerk was fussing outside the bailiff's dwelling, hopping about on his lame leg like a black sparrow, marshalling the reluctant crowd of about thirty men and boys whom he had coerced into a jury.

De Wolfe, conscious that the day was slipping away, led them across to the fish shed where the cadaver lay. 'Let's get this over quickly, Gwyn,' he growled. 'There's little we can do today – it will mean at least one other journey back here later.'

At the shed, he instructed Gwyn to pull out the body into the open, and the jury stood in a wide half-circle in the keen wind, the surf rumbling beyond the harbour and the seagulls wheeling and mewing overhead.

The Cornishman cut short his usual formal opening of an inquest and merely yelled at the motley throng, 'Silence for the king's crowner!'

With his arms folded across his chest, de Wolfe stood near the head of the corpse and addressed the jury. 'You men are representing the Hundred in this matter. I have to determine who this man might be and where, when and how he came to his death. The witness who can name him is too ill to attend but was also a member of the crew of that vessel. The name of the dead man was Roger of Bristol, that's all I know. He was part Saxon, but we cannot prove presentment of Englishry as there are no relatives here nor even the only witness who knew him.' He glared around the faces of the jury, as if daring them to contradict him. 'In the circumstances, I am not going to amerce this village as it is plain that he died before reaching your land.'

There was a murmur of relief from the older men and the few wives who stood listening in the background. At least they would avoid the heavy fine for being unable to prove that the dead man was a Saxon: the Norman laws assumed that, in default of proof, he was of the conquering race – even if that event had taken place well over a century ago.

'This witness I mentioned confirms that the vessel, known as the *Saint Isan*, was attacked by pirates somewhere between here and Lundy Island. We know of this death, and the survivor claims he saw the ship's master killed, so we assume that the rest of the crew were also killed or drowned.' He paused to look down at the shrouded figure at his feet. 'This man, Roger of Bristol, was most certainly murdered.'

He motioned to Gwyn, who pulled off the canvas

and displayed the corpse to the jury. As they shuffled nearer for a better view, the coroner pointed out the deep slash in the belly, livid against the whitened skin. 'A typical pike wound. There is no explanation other than murder.'

Again his dark face came up and his eyes slowly ranged across the villagers, brooding on each face in turn. 'Have any of you here any knowledge of who may have done this thing?' he boomed. 'Have you heard tell of any piracy in these waters?'

There was muttering and whispering and general shaking of heads, and the coroner, not really expecting any useful response, was about to carry on speaking when a quavering voice piped up from the middle of the crowd, 'I have heard tell, sir, that them Appledore folk are not above a bit of thieving at sea.'

This provoked a further buzz and another man, dressed in the short blue serge tunic of a sailor or fisherman, called out, 'I do know they've pillaged a wreck last year, afore the lord's steward could get to it. That was down Clovelly way.'

John de Wolfe spent a few minutes trying to get more concrete evidence than these rumours, but he ended with the suspicion that there was bad blood between Ilfracombe and Appledore, a small village on the other side of the river from Barnstaple. After he had ended the inquest, with the curt decision that Roger of Bristol had been killed against the king's peace by persons as yet unknown, he dismissed the ragged jury and turned to Gwyn and Thomas. 'What d'you think of these Appledore accusations, eh?'

'Village gossip, that's all,' grunted his ginger henchman. 'Any hamlet will strip a wreck, given the chance. This one was already pillaged or they would have stolen every last raisin.'

'But why Appledore? They might just as well have blamed Combe Martin or Bideford – or Lundy itself, which is more likely,' objected Thomas.

De Wolfe shrugged. 'Some local spite, no doubt. You have to live in one of these villages to fathom the petty disputes they dredge up.' He looked thoughtfully at the corpse. 'Though they may be right, of course.'

CHAPTER THREE

*In which Crowner John meets
an old acquaintance*

Another long day's ride meant that it was almost dusk when, on the following evening, they reached Exeter's North Gate. An early start from Umberleigh, a few miles south of Barnstaple, had enabled them to ride steadily, allowing John's leg and his clerk's backside to survive the many hours in the saddle.

When the coroner reached his house in Martin's Lane, he saw Odin settled in his stable opposite, then went wearily through his front door and took off his riding clothes in the vestibule. In the hall, his wife was sitting in her usual place before the hearth, partly hidden by the hood of her monk's chair. At the sound of the creaking door, she peered around its edge. When she saw him, she gave a throaty grunt and turned back to the fire. 'You've deigned to come home, I see.' It was her usual frosty greeting.

De Wolfe sighed. He was in no mood for a fight: he was tired and hungry. 'It's a long ride from Ilfracombe, in under a day and a half,' he muttered.

'You're a fool to attempt it, with that leg,' she retorted illogically. After complaining about the length of his absence, she was now implying that he should have stayed longer on the way back.

John ignored this and, sinking on to a bench at the empty table, gave a great yell for Mary. She had already heard him returning and soon bustled in with a wooden bowl of broth and a small loaf, which she put in front of him with a broad wink.

'Get that down you, master. I'll bring some salt fish and turnips afterwards.'

Brutus had ambled in after her and now sat between the coroner's knees under the table, with his big brown head on John's lap, waiting for some titbits of bread soaked in ham broth.

Matilda's brief conversation had dried up and now she studiedly ignored her husband. It suited him to have some peace, at least until he had finished the food that Mary brought in relays, including a jug of hot spiced wine.

Afterwards, he limped to the fireside and dropped into the other cowled chair, but his leg had stiffened up and was crying out for exercise. He decided that he would best get that by walking down to the Bush to see Nesta. However, he felt that he should try to smooth over relations with Matilda before he left her again.

His first efforts, telling her of the events in Ilfracombe, were met with curt derision. 'All that way to see a dead shipman and a half-drowned Breton! What business is that of a coroner? You should leave such petty matters to the bailiffs.' Matilda's ideas of the duties of a county coroner were modelled on those of her brother, who sat comfortably in his chamber and gave orders to minions whilst enjoying the social status of a senior law officer and administrator. Richard de Revelle was not a 'hands-on' person like de Wolfe; he was an aspiring politician – or had been until he had burnt his fingers over his support for Prince John's rebellion.

Tonight de Wolfe could not bring himself to argue the matter – he was tired of the old controversy, which seemed to be building up again after the respite that his accident and her grudging nursing care had provided. For the past two months, Matilda had been single-minded in her determination to bring him back to health and activity. She had held her tongue about his many faults and, though uncommunicative on anything other than his welfare, she had avoided any censure of his affairs with other women. Now, though, there were signs that the truce was over and that Matilda was slipping back to her old self.

He doggedly changed the subject in an effort to coax her out of her sulk, telling her of the curious persistence of the man who peered at him around corners. Thankfully he found that, for some reason, this tale seemed to catch her attention. 'Surely you can recollect the face?' she asked. 'You've not so many friends that his is lost in the crowd!'

Ignoring the gibe, he said, 'It's been niggling at my mind for a couple of days – and nights, when I can't sleep. There's something familiar about his features but for the life of me I can't put a name to him.'

'No doubt it's some old drinking crony – or a blood-thirsty acquaintance from your years of slaughter on the battlefield. But why should he not approach you?'

De Wolfe scowled into the glowing fire, his mind's eye seeing the mysterious fellow's face once again. 'I can't imagine what he can be up to – but if he appears once more, Gwyn will get him. He's to keep a special watch for the man. He only appears within the city, so he can't vanish over the horizon.'

The subject was soon exhausted and, as John had hoped, Matilda shortly left the growing darkness of the hall to go up to her solar, where Lucille would brush her hair and get her dressed for bed. As soon as she had gone, he left the house and, with Brutus sniffing contentedly at his heels, made his way slowly down to his favourite tavern to see his favourite woman.

Early next morning, the coroner decided to call upon the sheriff to tell him of the situation in the north of the county. Soon after a dawn breakfast, he walked up to Rougemont, giving his aching leg every chance to strengthen itself with more exercise. He called first at the cubbyhole in the undercroft, where Gwyn and Thomas were squeezed into a space a quarter the size of their usual chamber in the gatehouse. The Cornishman grumbled at the cold dampness of the room, caused by the wet sheen on the inner wall, whose stones were covered with green mould. Thomas was crushed against a side wall, trying to write on his rolls at their trestle table, which now half filled the tiny space.

'When I return, Gwyn, I want you to follow me into the town at a few paces distance,' de Wolfe commanded. 'If this accursed fellow appears, catch him and discover what he wants. Put your dagger to his throat, if needs be!' With this harsh admonition, the coroner stumped up the few stone steps to the churned turf of the inner ward and walked around the corner to the wooden stairway that gave entrance to the keep.

A few moments later, he pushed open the door to de Revelle's chamber and marched in without warning. This time, the sheriff was not at his table signing documents, but was standing, with his back to de Wolfe, in a small alcove at the further end of the room. A curtain hung on a pole across the entrance to offer some rudimentary privacy but it was pulled back to reveal his brother-in-law relieving himself down a stone shaft built into the thickness of the wall. This came out at the foot of the keep, adding further ordure to the mess in the inner ward.

Hearing footsteps, the sheriff dropped the front of his tunic and spat down the hole in front of him. 'Can't I even use the garde-robe without someone bursting in without a by-your-leave?' he snarled, without turning round.

'Don't worry, Richard, I've seen men having a piss before now,' grunted de Wolfe. 'When you've emptied your bladder, I'll give you some news that might interest you.'

De Revelle spun round, shaking the folds of his green robe back into place. 'It's you, John. I might have guessed that only you would barge in here unheralded. What news is this?'

He went to the table and settled himself behind it in his chair, his small, pointed beard jutting forward as if to defy de Wolfe to deliver anything that might be of the slightest import to him.

The coroner leaned on the other side of the table, his knuckles on the oak boards, hunched forward so that his big hooked nose was aimed at the sheriff like a lance. 'Piracy, that's the news! Murder and theft against the king's peace up on the coast around Ilfracombe.' He deliberately emphasised 'the king's peace': ever since he had been appointed last September, there had been a running battle between the coroner and sheriff about the prosecution of serious crimes. Now, after he had described the events of his visit to Ilfracombe, he bluntly demanded of de Revelle some action against the pirates. 'It's your county, as far as law and order are concerned,' he boomed. 'I'm charged with dealing with wrecks and dead bodies, but you are the king's representative here and it's up to you to keep his peace.' Again he emphasised the king, as a reminder that it was the Lionheart who was the sheriff's *raison d'être* and that he had better be single-minded about that fact.

But, typically, de Revelle tried to wriggle out of his responsibilities. 'I'm sheriff of the county of Devon, not of all the bloody sea around its coasts!' he blustered. 'Let the king's navy deal with any pirates.'

The lean, black form of the coroner bent even closer to the dandyish figure, who backed away slightly. 'When they murder subjects of the king and loot ships from one of his major cities, that's business for the enforcers of law in this or any other county!' he barked. 'Unless you have decided not to uphold the peace of your sovereign, King Richard?' This was a thinly veiled reminder that the sheriff's tenure of office depended on his behaviour, as far as loyalists were concerned – men like Lord Guy Ferrars and Reginald de Courcy, as well as de Wolfe himself.

De Revelle recognised the warning and grudgingly came to heel. 'Very well. What's the best way to go about this? From what I've heard in the past, we need look no further than Lundy. It was ever a nest of pirates, right back to the days of the Vikings.' It occurred to neither of them that their own Norman blood was only a few generations removed from those same Norse pirates who had settled in northern France.

When he saw that his brother-in-law was disposed to be more reasonable, de Wolfe relaxed and moved back from the edge of the table. 'I agree. It's quite possible that William de Marisco and his island stronghold might be the source of this trouble. But there was a hint that this particular outrage may have come from Appledore.'

The sheriff's fair eyebrows rose a little. 'Appledore? Seems unlikely that they would turn to piracy without de Grenville knowing about it – unless you're suggesting that he's party to it.'

De Wolfe gave one of his grunts: the de Grenville family held the lordship of Bideford, which included Appledore, but he wouldn't put a little piracy past them if the pickings were good enough. 'Early days yet. We need to find out more facts before we start accusing anyone.'

This was another dig at Richard, whose methods of detecting crime usually began in the torture chamber below the keep, rather than through seeking the truth in the town or countryside. De Wolfe carried on with his advice. 'Send a few men-at-arms up there for a start. I'll go with them and look around the ports there – Bideford, Appledore, Barnstaple, maybe even Bude. Shake the tree hard enough and maybe some fruit will fall out.'

With obvious reluctance, the sheriff agreed to let Sergeant Gabriel and four of his men go up to the north of the county with the coroner for a couple of days. As John was leaving, he called after him, 'It'll be Lundy, you mark my words! Those de Mariscos are evil bastards – they have no respect for human life. Or the king's peace.'

'That's rich, coming from you!' de Wolfe muttered cynically, and slammed the door behind him.

The coroner had no duties until noon, when he had to attend two hangings at the Magdalen Tree outside the city walls so he decided to pay a visit to his mistress. On the way, he put his head into his miserable office and warned Gwyn that he was going to walk through the streets and to keep a sharp eye out for his annoying mystery man. The shaggy-haired Cornishman gave him a few moments' start, then followed him at a discreet distance, keeping back to match the slow pace of his master, who still had a slight limp. They went out through the gatehouse of Rougemont and down Castle Hill, then turned into the main street.

Gwyn kept him in sight, pushing through the folk that thronged the narrow streets – shoppers, porters, loungers, pedlars and the rest. The coroner was an easy man to shadow, standing a head taller than most, his black hair bobbing over the collar of his mottled grey cloak.

Towards the end of the street, approaching Milk Lane that turned down to Butcher's Row, the officer saw him suddenly stop dead in his tracks and stare to his left. Then he waved an arm at something out of sight and Gwyn tried to close the distance between them. A porter with two great bales of wool hanging from a pole over his shoulder got in his way, just as a donkey with wide side-panniers tried to pass him. Cursing and pushing, the Cornishman lost a valuable minute in getting to de Wolfe's side, by which time the coroner had moved to the edge of the street, behind a stall selling trinkets and herbs. 'He was there, blast him!' fumed de Wolfe, pointing at a narrow gap between the side wall of a tall house and an adjacent storehouse. 'I can't move fast enough with this bloody leg of mine.'

Gwyn dashed into the gap, his huge shoulders almost filling the space between the two walls. 'I'll find him this time, never fear!' he yelled over his shoulder.

'If you do, I'll be at the Bush,' called his master and, with a snarl of disgust at his own infirmity, carried on down the street on his way to Idle Lane.

Not long afterwards, as the cathedral bell tolled for the morning high mass at about the tenth hour, Gwyn was bending his head beneath the low lintel of the tavern doorway, staring about in the smoky gloom for de Wolfe. There were only a few customers at that hour and Nesta was sitting with him at his customary table near the hearth, a jar of ale in front of him. The landlady beckoned to Gwyn, then yelled at the ancient potman to bring drink, bread and cheese for the coroner's ever-hungry henchman.

'I got him!' rumbled Gwyn triumphantly, as he dropped heavily on to a bench opposite the pair.

'So where is he?' demanded de Wolfe, looking expectantly at the doorway. 'Did you have to fight him? Or did you kill him, by chance?'

His officer shook his head, as Edwin banged a pot before him and placed a small loaf and a hunk of rock-hard cheese on the scrubbed boards of the table. 'No fight, no struggle. The man wants to meet you secretly, so I told him to come to your house at the second hour this afternoon. You'll be back from the gibbeting and had your meal by then.'

'But who is he, this mystery man?' demanded Nesta, her pert face quivering with curiosity as Gwyn stuffed his mouth with bread.

De Wolfe was accustomed to his bodyguard's relaxed attitude to communicating news, but even so he jabbed a forefinger across the table towards him. 'Swallow that quickly and tell us, or I'll pull that moustache clean off your face, damn you!'

Gwyn gulped down his mouthful and wiped the back of a huge hand across his mouth. 'He said his name was Gilbert de Ridefort and that he was sure you'd remember him.'

De Wolfe sat back in astonishment. 'Good God, of course I do! Are you sure that was the name he gave?'

'No doubt at all – he made me repeat it a couple of times. Said he daren't show himself too openly and he wasn't sure he could depend on you, now that you're a king's law officer.'

Nesta was looking from one to the other for enlightenment. 'So who is he? And why didn't you recognise him before, if you knew him, John?'

De Wolfe's face was drawn into a scowl of concentration. 'It was the beard and moustache – or rather the lack of them – that confused me. When I knew him, he had a faceful of dark brown hair. I'd never seen him shaven, as he is now. But, yes, the eyes and nose are Gilbert's.'

'So who is he? And why all this subterfuge?' asked the auburn-haired tavern keeper.

'He is a Knight of the Temple – or was.'

'Why "was"?'

'With no beard or moustache, something is amiss. They demand strictly that no Templar is shaven.'

Although everyone knew of the famous warrior monks, whose full title was the Order of the Poor Knights of Christ and the Temple of Solomon, most people knew little about them, except that they were now rich, powerful and ruthless.

Nesta's insatiable curiosity was now well and truly aroused. 'How do you know this man, John? And why should he seek you out?'

'I remember him now – at the siege of Acre in 'ninety-one,' broke in Gwyn, through a mouthful of cheese.

De Wolfe waved his empty ale pot at Edwin, who hurried to get a refill from the casks at the back of the large room. 'That's right. He was one of the crazy Templars who fought like demons alongside us in Richard's army. De Ridefort was one of the survivors and I met him a few times later, at the battle of Arsuf and again on the march towards Jerusalem.' His ale arrived and he took a deep draught. 'But I wonder what he's doing in Devon – and without his beard?'

'He's obviously hiding from someone,' opined Gwyn. 'He was forever looking over his shoulder and keeping his face under the brim of his big hat.'

'But who is he?' persisted Nesta. 'Is he an English Templar?'

'No, he's a French knight. I seem to remember that he was based in the Templar Commandery in Paris. The first time I met him was briefly at the castle of Gisors, in 'eighty-eight.'

'Where's Gisors?'

'A town in the Vexin, where that leering bitch Lucille comes from. On the borders of Normandy, north of Paris.'

'Ah, I remember him there, too,' said Gwyn. 'We were in the king's company, though he was Prince Richard then. We were at that big meeting between his father, old King Henry, and that bastard Philip of France.'

Nesta was impatient with this diversion. 'What's that to do with this Templar seeking you out, John?'

De Wolfe downed the rest of his ale and stood up, his gaunt frame almost reaching to the blackened rafters. 'I don't know, dear woman, but I hope to find out this afternoon. Meanwhile, we've got to attend to two felons dangling at the the end of a rope. Gwyn, go and find our poxy clerk and fetch him down to the gallows with his pen and parchment. Their exit from this world has to be properly recorded, even if they don't have two pennies between them for the king's coffers.'

Witnessing the execution of two petty thieves did not blunt John's appetite for his midday meal. Hanging and mutilation were as familiar to the population of England as bull-baiting, cock-fighting, eating and sleeping. Each Tuesday and Friday, those citizens of Exeter who had nothing better to do walked out through the South Gate and up the road to the gallows on Magdalen Street, where a pair of stout posts supported a long cross-bar which, on busy days, could dispatch three felons side by side.

The crowd came to watch the executions as a form of entertainment, a free diversion from the weary squalor of their existence. Many were old men and grand-mothers, with their urchins who ran around playing tag while pedlars hawked their pies, fruit and sweetmeats to the throng.

The coroner's task was to record the name and date of death of each victim, which Thomas de Peyne noted in his neat script on the coroner's rolls, with details of any land or chattels that the felon may have left behind, which was then forfeit to the Crown. The two petty crimi-nals gave up their sad lives with little protest and, his job done, de Wolfe went home, where he found Matilda already tucking into boiled fowl and cabbage. She was as uncommunicative as ever when he sat at the other end of the sombre table and waited for Mary to bring his food. However, her interest was awakened when he told her that they were to expect a visitor before long. 'It's a Knight of the Temple, one I knew slightly in France and Outremer,' he explained, unsure whether she would welcome the intrusion of a stranger into the house.

'Is this the man who has been peering at you around corners?'

'It is indeed – Gwyn caught him at it again this morning, but it seems he was unsure of whether I would greet him with open arms or throw him into gaol.'

'And which is it to be?' she demanded, staring at him over a chicken thigh grasped in her fingers.

'I can't tell yet – but something strange is going on. The man's shaved off his whiskers, which is forbidden by the Templars.'

'He can't be hanged for that,' she observed.

'I wouldn't be too sure – the discipline of the Templars is as hard as flint. Yet as as far as I recall, he was quite senior in the ranks of the order. When we left Palestine with the king, we sailed in a Templar warship and they mentioned that Gilbert de Ridefort was to go back to Paris to take up some important position at their Commandery there.'

Matilda put down the bone and wiped her mouth with an embroidered cloth from her sleeve. Automatically, she adjusted her hair, just visible under the white linen coverchief. 'A senior knight, you say? That means that this Sir Gilbert is an important man, I presume?'

John supressed a sigh, but he was glad that the interest sparked by her incorrigible snobbishness might give him an easier passage for a while. 'He is certainly well connected, as he is the nephew of Gerard de Ridefort, a former Grand Master of the Knights Templar – though that may be a mixed blessing. Gerard is notorious as the man who lost Jerusalem to the Saracens in 'eighty-seven.'

His wife, for all her posturing as a full-blooded Norman lady, knew little of what went on in the wider world and de Wolfe tried to explain a little more about that glorious, but somewhat sinister, order of militant monks. 'It was said to have been founded almost eighty years ago, when a French nobleman from Champagne and eight other knights offered their services to Baudouin, the king of Jerusalem, supposedly to patrol the roads of the Holy Land and protect pilgrims from the infidel.'

Matilda had stopped tearing at her food to listen to him – a novelty as far as her husband was concerned. 'Why d'you say "supposed"?' she asked.

'I doubt that nine men could do anything useful in Palestine – and no one has ever heard of them protecting anyone. They spent only nine years there, then suddenly returned to France.'

'So why are they called Templars?' she demanded.

'Because, strangely, for their residence Baudouin gave them part of his palace, built over the foundations of the Temple of Solomon. They were originally called the Poor Knights of Christ, resigned to poverty, obedience and chastity, though now many live in splendour and lend money to kings and emperors.' Matilda thought about this for a moment, but her mind slipped back to more immediate concerns than history.

'How old would this Sir Gilbert be?'

Her husband looked at her from under his bushy black brows. There was a note in her voice that he failed to recognise. 'About our age, I suppose – or maybe he looked younger with no beard.'

'And he's coming here, to this house, today?'

'I told Gwyn to fetch him – he is lodging in some house in Curre Street*.'

---

* Now Gandy Lane.

Matilda sniffed disapprovingly. 'What does a high-ranking Templar want, staying in such mean surroundings?'

'Maybe he wishes to be inconspicuous. We can ask him very soon.'

'Are there other Templars in Devon?' she asked, continuing to puzzle him with her unexpected interest in his affairs.

'Few compared to other counties. There is one of their Preceptories near Tiverton and I think they own more land elsewhere, but it is tenanted out to others. They were granted Lundy by the old king, but William de Marisco refuses even to let them land on the island.'

'How many Templars are there?' she asked.

'Many thousands, no doubt. The Grand Master controls them all from Acre, since this Gilbert's uncle lost the Holy City a few years ago, but under him there are Masters at their Commanderies in many countries, with lesser Preceptories controlling great estates. In England, they are based at the New Temple in London, where their round church was built a few years ago.'

Mary entered to clear away the debris on the table, and her master and mistress moved with their wine to sit by the fire. As she went out, the maidservant looked back at them with a quizzical expression. It was rare to see those two conversing like a normal man and wife.

'King Richard seems quite partial to them,' Matilda observed. 'You say he left Palestine in one of their ships?'

'Yes, he owes much to them, especially for their valour in battle at the Crusades. He has shown many favours to them, both in England and Normandy.'

'But do you share his admiration?' Matilda had a

shrewd mind, when it was not clogged with religious fervour or after social advancement. She had detected some reserve in her husband's attitude to the Poor Knights of Christ.

'I admire their discipline and their valour, which often bordered on the foolhardy.' He hesitated a moment. 'Yet I always felt there was something odd, almost sinister about them. We could see only their outward face – the one they turned to the world. They kept something hidden from all others.'

'But they are exemplary Christians, surely. Wasn't St Bernard of Clairvaux once their spiritual inspiration?' Matilda might have been hazy about political history, but she knew her saints.

De Wolfe gave one of his shrugs. 'Yes, he wrote the Rule, their strict code of behaviour, as far as I recall,' he answered thoughtfuly. 'But there are strange rumours about their beliefs. When they weren't fighting the Muhammadans, they were studying their religion with apparent approval. And some say that the Templars have a very different outlook on Christianity from the rest of us, even to the point of heresy. But I find that hard to believe – the Pope has given them a status above everyone, even the crowned heads of Europe. All very strange.' He stared pensively into the fire, his mind far away in the Levant, seeing again the ranks of mounted warriors in their long white surcoats emblazoned with the scarlet cross.

Matilda finished her wine and rose from her chair. 'I'll go up and have my maid attend to me,' she announced. 'Call me when Sir Gilbert arrives.'

As she left, he heard her yelling for Lucille, and exhaled in wonderment that the mere mention of a mysterious knighted monk should send her off, like some silly girl, to have her hair tweaked and her gown changed.

Outside, the day had turned colder and an early spring chill seeped through the shutters and under the doors. De Wolfe prodded the fire with an old broken sword kept in the hearth and threw on a few more logs. Half-way through his next cup of Loire wine, he started as Brutus suddenly hoisted himself to his feet and faced the door. He growled, but slowly wagged his long tail, so John knew that he had heard Gwyn arriving. The man was a favourite of every dog in Devon.

A tap on the door was followed by the whiskered face appearing cautiously in the opening, seeking out de Wolfe's wife. Then, with relief, Gwyn opened the door wide and stood to one side. 'Sir Gilbert de Ridefort, Crowner!' he announced.

De Wolfe got up and went to welcome the visitor, nodding to Gwyn to escape to Mary's kitchen for some food. 'And tell her to take word to the mistress that our guest has arrived,' he added.

Turning to the newcomer, he gripped his arm in greeting and waved him towards the fire. 'So it was you who was haunting me these past few days, de Ridefort!' he said. 'Now that I know your name, I recognise you, but until then your lack of a beard and moustache was a perfect disguise.'

'Pray God it remains so!' said de Ridefort fervently. 'Maybe if it fooled you, it will be equally effective with others.'

John sat him on a high-backed settle near the fire and dropped back into his own chair opposite. The knight declined the offer of food, but accepted some wine, which John poured from the jug into one of Matilda's best chalices, taken from a shelf on the wall.

As they drank to old times, the coroner surveyed his guest, wondering whether his visit would mean trouble. He saw a man almost as tall as himself, with an erect bearing, broad shoulders and a slim waist. With his pilgrim's hat removed, he had wavy brown hair down to the collar of his dark green mantle, another sign that something was amiss: Templars, though their faces were never shaven, were required to keep their hair short.

Gilbert had a rather long, aristocratic face with a straight nose set between large hazel eyes. His chin was square, below a firm mouth, now set in a rather sad smile. As John had guessed, he was on the right side of forty, a year or two younger than himself. A handsome fellow, thought the coroner, one who could easily turn a woman's head, though celibacy was strictly enforced by the Rule of the Temple – they were not allowed to kiss a female, even a mother or sister.

De Wolfe came directly to the point. 'What's all this mystery about, Gilbert? Why are you not dressed like a Templar and what happened to your beard?'

De Ridefort sighed and bent forward, his hands grasping the cup resting on his knees. 'I take you for an honest man, de Wolfe – and one who I have heard will not suffer injustice.'

John grunted: he could think of no better response.

'But I also know you are King Richard's man – you were often at his side in Outremer and you were with him when he was captured near Vienna.'

'I claim no credit for that,' snapped the coroner. He still blamed himself for failing to prevent the kidnap of his sovereign when they were trying to pass through Austria in disguise, after being shipwrecked on the way back from Palestine.

'I mention the king because he is so partial to the

Order of the Temple – and I wondered if your sympa-
thies were equally strong.'

Puzzled, de Wolfe replied, in a noncommittal fashion, 'I have nothing against you Templars – you were
undoubtedly the best fighting men in the Holy Land.'

Gilbert took a sip of his wine and looked uneasily
at John, as if undecided whether or not to confide in
him. 'I am no longer a Templar. In fact, I am a fugitive
from them.'

This remarkable admission left the coroner staring at
his guest. 'But a Templar is for life – I've heard that
they never allow abdication, except into an even stricter
monastic order.'

The other man nodded sadly. 'They do not believe
that I have left them. In fact, they are searching for me,
to take me back into the Order – in chains, if needs be,
or even a shroud.'

The coroner leaned over with the wine jug and filled
de Ridefort's cup. 'You'd better tell me the whole story,'
he said.

The handsome man opposite shook his head. 'Not
yet – not the whole story.'

John bristled. 'Do you not trust me, then?'

'It's not that at all. I have no wish to embroil you in
my troubles – certainly not until I know if you have any
sympathy with my cause. And I need advice, as well as
help, if you are willing to give it. Yet the devil of it is that
at present I cannot explain everything to you. Some you
must take on trust.'

The coroner took a deep drink and thought quickly.
This man smelt of trouble – he had an aura of doom
about him. Though de Wolfe had nothing against him,
their depth of friendship was not great. He had met
him across a table a few times at Gisors, and again

in Palestine, either during troop marches or yarning around an evening camp-fire. He was not a bosom companion for whom he would lay down his life – though, de Wolfe's nature being what it was, he would never stand by and see injustice done. 'Why were you so reluctant to make yourself known to me?' he asked. 'All that furtive peeping around corners – you're lucky my man Gwyn didn't throw a spear at you, as I'm not short of enemies, even in Devon.'

De Ridefort smiled. For the first time his worried face had relaxed and again John saw that here was a man who could bowl over the ladies with no effort whatsoever. 'I'm sorry for the skulking in alleyways, John, but I was anxious to see what sort of man you had become, since being elevated to your new judicial state – whatever a coroner is. I'm not at all clear on that.'

De Wolfe gave one of his throaty grunts. 'It's no great honour, I can tell you. You needn't stand in awe of my great power. Now, are you going to tell me what you want with me?'

The revelations were interrupted again as the door opened and Matilda came in. She was resplendent in her best kirtle of green silk, tied around her thick waist with several turns of a silver cord whose tassels swept the floor. Her sleeves were almost as long, the bell-shaped cuffs knotted into tippets to keep them off the ground. Her hair was now gathered into two coils above each ear, held in place by silver net crespines. She had obviously goaded Lucille into extra efforts to make her look her best for the visitor.

Gilbert de Ridefort rose to his feet as John introduced his wife. He bowed over her hand and led her courteously to his own chair before the hearth, before sitting between them on a hard stool.

'Sir Gilbert was just about to tell me of his reason for visiting Exeter,' grated de Wolfe, determined to manoeuvre his guest into some better explanation than he had so far offered.

'I'm not sure your charming lady wishes to be bothered with such matters,' said Gilbert smoothly. The coroner could not decide whether he meant this or was using it as another excuse to delay revealing his true reason for seeking him out. Then his eye strayed to Matilda and he saw that his wife was undoubtedly captivated by the errant Templar. Her eyes were fixed on his face and, though a stocky woman of forty-six can hardly simper, he saw that the expression on her face was unlike any she had ever bestowed on him. Far from being jealous, he felt annoyed that such an unattractive middle-aged woman should be so foolish as to display her instant infatuation.

It was all the more ridiculous as she knew he had taken the strictest monkish vows of chastity and, for a moment, he wondered if de Ridefort was on the run because he had committed some amorous or lecherous indiscretion. It would not be the first time that a Templar had gone astray, though the harsh regime of their Order prescribed dire punishments or ignominious expulsion for offenders who were stripped of all knightly honours.

For once, Matilda unwittingly supported her husband in his thirst for explanation. She almost cooed as she denied that de Ridefort's story would tire her.

'Very well. You must both know that I have been these past two years in the Commandery of our Order in Paris – the main centre of our activities outside Palestine. I was a fairly senior member of the Chapter, under our Master, who in turn was responsible only to the Grand Master in Acre.' He stared into the fire, with an expression that suggested he saw the flames of Hell dancing between the logs. 'I came into possession of certain information of which only a few of the highest in the Order had any knowledge. Though I was prominent in the hierarchy, even I was not supposed to be privy to the secret. It came to me by accident.'

'What was this secret?' asked Matilda, breathlessly.

'I cannot divulge that, certainly not yet, but it is a matter of the greatest import in our religious faith. I have still more soul-searching before I can decide what to do about this.'

'You make it hard for me to understand your problems, de Ridefort,' snapped de Wolfe. 'If you cannot give any inkling of what distresses you, how can I ever help you?'

Gilbert jerked himself to his feet and stood agitatedly before the hearth, his back to the fire, so that he could face them. 'I am torn between the ingrained loyalty to the Knights Templar, whom I have served faithfully for fifteen years, and my anguish at deciding to reveal what I know. I cannot let this knowledge loose at the moment. There is another who shares both the secret and my torment as to what should be done.'

Matilda was staring open-mouthed at this Norman Adonis, who had walked in and captivated her mature heart with his looks and his story of heartrending conflict of loyalties – even though she had not the faintest idea what he was talking about.

But her husband, with more worldly-wise cynicism, wanted far more disclosure than the Templar seemed willing to provide. 'Much as you are welcome in my house, as any knight would be, I fail to see what you want with me,' he said.

Restlessly, the visitor threw himself back on to his stool

and hunched forward, his gaze returning to the fire as he spoke. 'This other knight is an old and dear friend of mine, Bernardus de Blanchefort, who has been at a Preceptory of our Order in the southern part of France since we both returned from the Holy Land. He is from those parts, his family having estates in the Languedoc and on the slopes of the Pyrenees. We have met many times in the past two years and our concerns have grown as we realised that a great conspiracy has long been afoot, into which, as Templars, we have unwittingly been drawn.'

De Wolfe, though not an unintelligent man, was a practical, straightforward soldier and the man's words meant little to him. They went right over Matilda's head, but she was content to gaze at him and savour the dramatic, if incomprehensible, story he seemed bent on unfolding. John cleared his throat and waited for further enlightenment.

'I cannot tell you more. I must wait for Bernardus to come so that we may decide on what should be done. But at the moment I am in great peril from the Order, who suspect that I am a dangerous renegade and will do anything to prevent me staying at liberty.'

At last de Wolfe saw a glimmer of light. 'You want protection and a means of escape, is that it?'

'Yes, John, but how that is to be attained I cannot tell. I must wait for de Blanchefort to arrive.'

'But why choose such a remote place as Devon, when you fled from Paris?' asked Matilda, looking wide-eyed at this hero.

'I remembered your husband, both from Gisors and Palestine. I always felt you were a man who could be trusted, not always an easy person to find these days. You told me you came from Devon and it seemed a logical place to aim for, if I was trying to reach either Scotland or Ireland to get beyond the reach of my Templar brethren.'

The coroner gave a scornful snort. 'You should forget Scotland if you want to avoid Templars! The place is full of them, you must know that. Ireland would be far safer – much of the country is still under the wild tribes, though you may as well be dead as have to live outside the Norman domains there.'

De Ridefort nodded dutifully. 'Then we shall make for Ireland, when Bernardus de Blanchefort arrives. He should be only a few days behind me. He was going to take ship from Brittany, whereas I came through Harfleur.'

'Does he know where to find you?' asked Matilda solicitously, in a tone she never used with her husband.

'I have told him to seek out the coroner, lady. Everyone knows Sir John here, I'm sure he will bring us together.'

De Wolfe was still unhappy with this strange story. 'You must be in very deep trouble with your Order, de Ridefort. You have left their house, you have cast off the uniform so familiar throughout the known world – and you have shaved your face, which I know is forbidden to your fellow knights. You can never go back now, surely. Are you not beyond their forgiveness?'

De Ridefort shifted on his stool. 'Bernardus and I have crossed our Rubicon. If we live, it will be as outcasts in some remote place, like this Ireland you recommend. Even there, I suspect the long arm of the Templars will reach us eventually.'

'And you refrain from telling me what it is that is worth the price of this sacrifice?' demanded de Wolfe.

'I cannot at this time. The secret is too awful to be

revealed, unless de Blanchefort and I decide to take the plunge into the abyss and let the world know.'

The situation was beyond both John's comprehension and his patience. 'I always thought there was some strangeness about the Templars, if you will forgive my bluntness,' he said. 'What is it that seems to set your Order so much apart from others?'

For answer, the fugitive asked a question in return. 'You remember our first meeting at the castle of Gisors, some years ago?'

De Wolfe nodded. 'I was in the guard of Prince Richard, who accompanied his father King Henry. You were there with many other Templars.'

'That event was momentous – and not only for the confrontation between Henry and Philip of France.'

'That was momentous enough – we had a fight on our hands, over that damned tree that both Richard and Philip wanted to give them shade during the negotiations. The bloody French ended up chopping it down.'

'Yes, the so-called Splitting of the Elm. But, for the Templars, the meeting at Gisors was far more significant. The Order of Sion, which had secretly been responsible for founding the Templars in Jerusalem, divorced itself from us at Gisors – and even changed its name to the Priory of Sion. Much of the trouble arose from my uncle's misfortune in losing the Holy City to the Saracens in the previous year. His memory was vilified and, as one of his family, the shame has clung to me, like dung to a hoof.'

A little light began to penetrate John's mind. The Grand Master of the Templars, of whom Gilbert was a nephew, had lost a disastrous battle at Hattin, and soon afterwards, was driven from Jerusalem by Saladin's army. Perhaps a grinding resentment of the sneers against his family's honour had turned de Ridefort to seek revenge on the rest of the Templars, who blamed their impetuous leader for the devastating loss of Jerusalem. What better revenge could there be than to disclose some dark secret that they had jealously guarded for the better part of a century?

Matilda, who had listened enraptured to these obscure matters, brought the conversation back to a more mundane level. 'You cannot stay in that sordid Curre Street, Sir Gilbert. It is fit only for Saxon tradesmen, not the likes of you.'

'It suffices well enough, lady. I wanted to remain inconspicuous. I have a corner of a room with several others. Dressed like a pilgrim, I wished to behave like one, to avoid attention.'

She huffed and puffed her indignation then came out with a solution that brought a scowl to her husband's face. 'Why not stay here, then? We can have a comfortable pallet laid before the hearth, which would be better than sharing an earth floor with half a dozen stinking pilgrims.'

De Ridefort must instantly have caught de Wolfe's lack of support for the idea as he waved his hand in grateful but firm denial. 'I must distance myself from a law officer as much as possible, my lady. Not only for my sake, but for John's. It may be that powerful retribution will fall upon me and I would not wish your husband to be caught by it – especially as his sovereign lord is such a devotee of the Templars.'

De Wolfe weighed in with a counter-proposal. 'Certainly Curre Street is not a suitable dwelling for you – but why not take a bed at an inn? I suspect that the modest cost would not be a problem for you, for the short time you hope to be in Exeter.'

Matilda glared at him, tight-lipped. She knew very well which inn he would suggest and suspected that it would form yet another excuse for him to visit his Welsh whore, as she called Nesta. Her chances of keeping such a handsome man under her roof vanished when de Ridefort took enthusiastically to the idea and, as expected, de Wolfe promised to take him down to the Bush to settle him in.

Gwyn was dispatched to Curre Street to fetch the knight's pannier and get his pilgrim pony from a nearby livery stable, and within the hour, de Wolfe was introducing the stranger to the tavern-keeper, leaving an irate Matilda at home, fuming at the loss of her latest diversion.

CHAPTER FOUR

In which Crowner John visits the Shambles

Mindful of Matilda's infatuation with the handsome Templar, John was a little concerned that Nesta might suffer the same symptoms, but although her eyebrows rose a little when he walked in with de Ridefort, she showed no signs of falling for him. After de Wolfe had explained the need for bed and board, Nesta sent the newcomer up the ladder with one of her maids, to approve his accommodation and leave his roll of belongings. The large space under the thatch of the Bush's steep roof was divided into a number of sleeping spaces. Nesta had one corner, with the luxury of a door, while the rest of the boarded space was communal sleeping, with mattresses filled with clean straw, and a few open-ended cubicles, containing similar straw pallets.

While de Ridefort was up there, Nesta asked, 'Who is he, John? A good-looking man, but he speaks poor English. Is he French?'

De Wolfe explained a little of the situation, but refrained from saying that he was a fugitive. 'He is an ex-Templar, but whether he is still celibate I don't know – so watch your step, my girl!' His attempt at wit was half-hearted and Nesta knew him well enough to sense that there was more to this business than just a passing traveller wanting a bed for a few nights.

'This is the man who has been stalking you! Come on, Sir Crowner, you can tell me more about him than that.'

'I know little myself, except that he wants to remain incognito while in Exeter. He is expecting a friend soon, then they are off to Ireland. I knew him slightly in the old fighting days, and he has looked me up as he was passing through.'

Nesta sniffed peevishly. 'You know more than you let on, John. What's all the mystery?'

He was spared answering by the descent of de Ridefort down the rickety steps, and soon they were drinking ale and eating a pair of boiled fowls that Nesta had caused to materialise from the cooking shed behind the inn. Some other travellers had just arrived and she was dealing with them, so the two men had time for a low-voiced conversation, to the chagrin of Edwin, an incorrigible eavesdropper.

'I have been absent from Paris these past six weeks,' murmured Gilbert. 'By now, the Master will have sent urgent news about me to London.'

'How would they know you came to England?'

De Ridefort smiled sadly. 'John, you should know after all your travels that the Poor Knights of Christ have the best intelligence in the world. There are Templars or their agents in every town and every port of any size. Nothing happens but they know about it – they need information to conduct their huge business transactions. They fund most of the kings of Europe and lend money to anyone who pays a sufficient levy on it. They will know that I took ship from Harfleur to Southampton. Soon, they will be after me, and their efficiency is legendary. I should know – I have been one of them these past fifteen years.'

He looked around the room, searching the faces of the merchants, tradesmen, travellers and harlots who made up the customers of the Bush, as if a Templar might be hidden amongst them already. 'Sooner or later they will catch up with me, unless Bernardus and I can get abroad before they arrive.'

John was beginning to tire of this repetitive forecast of doom. 'If you have not revealed this great secret of yours, whatever it might be, then what have you to fear?'

'The very fact that we have left the Order and broken virtually all the rules laid down by St Bernard. That is enough. It may be a mortal crime, our lives may already be forfeit. Certainly, the best we can hope for if we are recovered by them is endless incarceration and penance.'

He tore at his chicken and as de Wolfe began thinking aloud. 'There are no Templars in or near Exeter, that I know. There is a small Preceptory beyond Tavistock, almost fifteen miles from here.'

'I know how they act, John. The main Commandery in London will send men to seek me out. They may well require any local Templars to assist them, but the thrust of the search will be from our New Temple on the banks of the Thames. The gravity of the secret is such that they will not entrust any great responsibility to rural knights or sergeants. It will be senior brothers who come after us.'

De Wolfe snorted with impatience. 'You keep on about this bloody secret, Gilbert! How does your Order know you have it and that you might broadcast it? And why should you wish to do that, anyway? Don't you have fifteen years of loyalty to consider?'

De Ridefort dropped the remains of his fowl and pushed the thick trencher of gravy-sodden bread away from him. 'It torments me all the time. Bernardus and I were too outspoken and argumentative about many things in Paris. We thought we were indulging in academic discussion with our fellows, but as the truth began to dawn upon us, after I learned of certain matters we should not have explored, we were cautioned then reviled. I had already had enough of whispered innuendoes about my uncle, whom the younger Templars now accuse of incompetence at best and treachery at worst in his calamitous behaviour in the Holy Land.'

'The sins of the uncles visited upon the nephews, eh?' misquoted John cynically.

'Not only did the brothers of the Order began to despise and suspect me, but the priests outside started murmuring heresy. There is great trouble brewing in France, John, especially in the south-west, where de Blanchefort comes from. Though generally the Templars have sympathy with the Cathars there, in their dangerously unconventional beliefs, the power of Rome and its army of priests are becoming both anxious and vindictive – and some of that is falling on Bernardus and myself.'

'So this great secret is a matter of Christian faith?' asked de Wolfe, trying to pin down this elusive tale more firmly.

'You could certainly say that,' agreed Gilbert cautiously. 'When the time comes, you will know it, along with the rest of the world, unless we are silenced beforehand.'

He would say no more, however much as John probed, and when Nesta came back to join them, the conversation was bent to other subjects. De Ridefort was particularly curious about the other's duties as coroner, for no such office existed outside England. As they finished their meal, and drank more ale and some wine, de Wolfe explained his functions to an attentive listener who had many searching questions. The red-headed Welsh woman sat and listened to the two men and John noticed that her gaze often strayed to the profile of the handsome Frenchman. Eventually, Nesta was called away to settle some shrieking dispute between her maids in the kitchen.

As soon as they were alone again, de Ridefort returned to his worries. 'I'll stay here in the inn for most of the day, John, and not show myself about the town.'

'No one here knows you, that's for sure,' said de Wolfe, to reassure him, 'but I'll keep an eye open for you. Both my officer Gwyn and my nosy little clerk know everything that happens in this city. So does Nesta, for that matter – her intelligence is county-wide!'

De Ridefort reached an arm across the table and gripped John's elbow with a strong hand. 'Let me know of any strangers who arrive. They need not be in Templar dress – we do not always wear it when necessity demands.'

'I know you do not wear a chain-mail hauberk, but surely you always have your white mantle with the red cross on the shoulder?'

'It is so claimed, John, but not always adhered to in travelling away from the Commanderies and Preceptories. And only the knights and chaplains wear the white mantle – the chaplains have it fastened in the front, but we must let ours hang loose. The lower ranks, such as sergeants, wear brown or black, but all with the red cross.'

De Wolfe sighed. 'White, black or brown, cross or no

cross, Gwyn and Thomas will watch out for you these coming days. Now I must get myself home, or my wife will chastise me.'

Somewhat uneasily, he left de Ridefort in the company of his mistress and made his way back to Martin's Lane. It was now late afternoon and he had nothing to divert him in the way of corpses, rapes or even a serious assault.

As he was passing through the cathedral Close, he saw a familiar figure coming towards him, enveloped in a full black cloak. The crinkled grey hair surmounted a lean, ascetic face from which a pair of blue eyes looked out serenely on the world. It was John de Alençon, Archdeacon of Exeter, one of de Wolfe's favourite churchmen, who lived in one of the dwellings in Canon's Row, along the north side of the Close. After they had greeted each other and passed the time of day, de Wolfe thought he might tap the senior cleric's knowledge of some of the things hinted at by Gilbert de Ridefort.

'I recently met an old Templar friend I knew at the Crusades,' he began, adapting the truth slightly. 'He caused me to become curious about their beliefs and the strange secrecy that seems to surround their order.'

The Archdeacon took his arm and steered him towards the line of prebendaries' houses. 'Come and talk with me a while, John. I've seen little of you since you let your warhorse fall on to your leg.'

The priest's asceticism did not extend to a rejection of good wine and soon they were sitting at a rough table in his bare room, the only ornament a plain wooden crucifix on the wall. Between them was a flask of his best wine from Poitou and each man held a heavy glass cup filled with it.

'Why this sudden interest in theology, Crowner John?'

he mocked gently. 'I've never taken you for a man who has much time for the Almighty, more's the pity!'

De Wolfe grinned sheepishly. It was true that his devotions were reluctant and perfunctory – he went to Mass occasionally, but only on High Feasts or when Matilda nagged him to accompany her to some dreary service at St Olave's. 'It was meeting this old Crusading companion again, who now belongs to the Templar establishment in Paris. Some of the things he mentioned intrigued me, that's all. The Order is said by some to have a rather different view of Christianity from the rest of us – is that true?'

He was fishing for information without wanting to give anything away, a difficult task with someone as astute as John de Alençon – but the cleric was happy to discourse on anything touching the Faith. 'I agree with you that their organisation is somewhat peculiar,' said the archdeacon. 'Though they are under the direct protection of the Holy Father in Rome, many in the Church have for long been uneasy with the favoured status of the Templars.'

'Why is this?' prompted de Wolfe.

'They are immune from orders by even the highest bishops, only bowing their knee to the Pope. They recruit not only devout men, especially rich ones with wealth or land to donate, but also attract excommunicate knights and persons with unorthodox views of religion,' he said disapprovingly.

At this the coroner's heavy eyebrows lifted. 'I have heard that some accuse the Templars of heresy – but how can that be, in a such a devout body of men so favoured by Rome and patronised by St Bernard?'

The grey-haired priest looked shrewdly over the rim of his glass at his friend. 'This is a strange conversation for you, John. You are usually full of tales about murdered men and mutilated corpses. Why this sudden interest in the Templars?'

De Wolfe sighed – he seemed to be transparent to his old friend.

'This man seems to have fallen out with his Order. I can say no more, but I wondered if his dispute with them is real, or whether he has some ailment of the mind that convinces him he is persecuted.'

The archdeacon looked puzzled. 'To fall out with the Templars would be very unusual – their brothers are bound to them for life. And it would be a very grave situation to fall foul of them as they are not known for their tolerance and forbearance with those who cross them.'

'Do they have any dark secrets that they would not wish spread abroad?'

'Rumours abound, John, but most are probably idle tittle-tattle. They have been accused of many things over the years.'

'Such as?' persisted the coroner.

'Idolatry, including worshipping a disembodied head named Baphomet – and even the denial of the crucifixion of Our Lord and spitting on the True Cross.' He shuddered and crossed himself as he uttered the words, reminding de Wolfe of his own clerk. 'But I think these must be foul slanders about an Order so favoured by Rome.'

John sensed that he was getting on to ground that might prove harmful to de Ridefort, if the established Church had some antipathy to the Order of the Temple. He let the conversation slide into less dangerous topics, though he knew that the priest was still intrigued by his interest.

He spent an hour with de Alençon and when the wine flask was empty, the archdeacon walked him to the door of his narrow house. As they parted, the cleric's last remark proved that he had not forgotten their earlier discussion.

'Advise your friend, John, that he had better keep a good watch over his shoulder, if he has become at cross-purposes with the Poor Knights of Christ. They possess a very long arm indeed!'

When he arrived near his own house, de Wolfe saw Gwyn hovering in Martin's Lane, talking to Andrew the farrier as he hammered a shoe on to a roan gelding. The Cornishman looked scruffier than usual, his tattered thick leather jerkin more frayed than ever and his serge breeches crumpled above his muddy boots. The only acceptable part of his outfit was the large scabbard that contained his broadsword, hanging from the diagonal baldric strap over his right shoulder.

'Have you been at war while my back was turned?' demanded the coroner as he approached his officer, whose flaming ginger hair and beard were as unkempt and tangled as if he had been through six blackthorn hedges.

Gwyn grinned amiably and patted the hilt of his sword. 'There was a riot down in the Shambles just now – you can barely have missed it if you walked up from the Bush.'

'Any work for us there? What was it all about?' demanded his master.

'One dead, two badly wounded,' replied Gwyn. 'One I injured myself, after he had killed the other fellow.'

De Wolfe was already striding off towards the meat

market, which was on the other side of the cathedral Close. 'Come on, man, tell me about it as we go.'

'A group of men came into the city, driving a score of pigs. They set up a booth on Bell Hill, half-way up Southgate Street, and began killing a few hogs, offering the joints at a price lower than the Exeter traders'.'

'They must have been fools – or desperate!' said de Wolfe, as they hurried along. 'It's not even a market day! The local butchers wouldn't stand for that.'

'They didn't – not for more than a few minutes. They started shouting at them, then overturning tables. The pigs were running wild, the traders were fighting and the customers were screaming in panic.'

'What about the portreeves and burgesses? Where were they with their bailiffs?'

'They soon arrived and it developed into a free-for-all. Then the cudgels came out and the knives, even a couple of old swords. It was bloody chaos!'

They hurried through Bear Lane and out into South Gate Street where the Serge Market lay slightly downhill from the Shambles, in the dip before the road rose again to the gate. There were plenty of people milling around, but no obvious fighting. 'It's gone quiet now,' exclaimed Gwyn, in a disappointed tone. 'All hell was let loose here half an hour ago.'

John de Wolfe pushed past a crowd of onlookers near an overturned stall to get to the middle of the road. He was carrying no sword, but kept a hand on the hilt of his dagger in case there was more trouble. Above the hub-bub of chatter and complaint, he could hear a familiar voice shouting a few yards away. 'Gabriel! What's going on?' he yelled, pushing through the crowd to reach the sergeant of the castle guard, who was shoving at the crowd with four other men-at-arms, clearing a space around some bodies on the fouled ground.

When John broke through, with Gwyn at his shoulder, he thought at first that there had been a massacre, as the mud was running with blood. 'It's not all from your customer, Crowner!' the sergeant reassured him, his lined old face creasing into a grin. 'Most of this is swine's blood – though these human swine here have added a few pints!'

De Wolfe cursed as two terrified black pigs crashed against his legs, before careering off into the throng. He stepped into the squelching pink mud and looked down at a still corpse, then at two men groaning on the ground. One had blood pouring from a large gash in his scalp, the other was doubled up in pain, clutching his belly. From between his fingers, oozed an ominous dark red clot.

'The dead 'un is a meat-hawker from Milk Street,' announced Gabriel. 'These other two are from the gang from the countryside.'

Gwyn bent over the man with the stomach wound. 'I fixed this bastard,' he said gruffly. 'He was one who ran through the Exeter man.'

Gabriel and his men were gradually restoring order, pushing back the gawping crowd and getting some to restore the fallen booths. Here there was a disordered mixture of serge and worsted rolls, lamb and pork – much had ended up on the ground and urchins and dogs were playing with the meat. A few surreptitious looters were picking up joints and offal, trying to wipe away some of the mud before making off with their booty.

'Where are the rest of the intruders?' snapped de Wolfe.

'I've got two of them pinioned over there, Crowner,' answered Gabriel, motioning towards the nearest house. 'The others have made a run for it. They're far beyond the gate by now.'

John looked down at the dead and injured. 'Better get the corpse taken to his home, if he's a local.'

Gwyn nodded. 'What about these other two?'

De Wolfe looked at the head wound on the first man. His hair was matted with blood, but the bleeding seemed to be slowing from the gash. He was sitting up, groaning, but conscious. 'This one will live, unless the wound suppurates later. Gabriel, take him to the gaol down there at the South Gate. Illegal trading is a city problem, not one that concerns the king.'

'I'm glad to hear you admit that, for once, John.'

Turning, de Wolfe saw the sheriff standing behind him, elegant in a short brown mantle over his long green tunic. He wore a close-fitting helmet of brown felt, tied under the chin, and his shoes were in the latest fashion, with long curled points at the toes.

De Wolfe pointed to the cadaver then moved his finger to the other man. 'These are within my jurisdiction, Richard.'

'But only one is dead, Coroner,' said de Revelle sarcastically.

'The other has a mortal wound,' stated de Wolfe bluntly. After a score of years on many battlefields, he considered himself an authority on violent injuries. 'He's losing blood clots from his belly, so he'll not last long. My officer put a sword into his vitals as he was killing this Exeter man.'

The victim about whom they were talking had slumped sideways and his face had taken on an ashen hue. A priest, a young vicar-choral from the cathedral, had pushed through the crowd and went to crouch by his side, cradling the dying man's head on his lap. He pressed the small cross from a chain around his neck against the victim's forehead and muttered a Latin absolution into now deaf ears.

'No point in trying to take this one to the gaol, Crowner,' said Gabriel, 'but I'll get the corpse moved and clap these other three in the gatehouse.'

'You'd better get an apothecary to look at his wound. We don't want him dying on us before he's hanged,' boomed a new voice. This came from a large warrior, with a forked grey beard, wearing a mailed hauberk and a round iron helmet. Ralph Morin, the castle constable, had come down with the sheriff and a dozen more soldiers to quell the disturbance. He took over from his sergeant and ordered the men-at-arms to get rid of the crowd. Grumbling and swearing, they dispersed gradually and the stalls were hoisted back into their places for trading to start again.

As the corpse was being carried away on a wattle hurdle, de Wolfe and his brother-in-law began walking back to the high street, Ralph Morin and Gwyn at either side. 'I can't see why they risk coming into the city, these out-of-town traders,' said the sheriff testily. 'They can set up their stalls a few hundred paces away outside the walls and no one can deny them.'

'The portreeves and the burgesses are rightly strict about the monopoly within the city for the freemen. They pay their taxes and have a right to expect the best of the trading,' said Ralph Morin. 'If every free cottar and runaway could come in and sell at a lower price because they pay no dues, the city would be ruined in no time.'

'I'll have to hold an inquest on those two in the

morning,' grumbled de Wolfe. 'For the other man will be dead long before then.'

'I'll hang the other three scum for you, John,' offered de Revelle. 'The County Court is held tomorrow and I'll delay it until after your inquest.'

De Wolfe shook his head stubbornly. 'Thank you, but no, Richard. If the killer lived, I would attach him for the next Eyre of Assize, but as he has no hope of surviving there's no need. The remaining offence, unless the inquest finds otherwise, concerns trading, not killing, and the burgess court can deal with that. It's not the business of either of us.'

Richard de Revelle clicked his tongue to convey his exasperation with de Wolfe's interpretation of the legal system but, on probation himself over the rebellion, he was unable to be as despotic as before.

As they walked briskly in the chill March wind, Ralph Morin turned the conversation into a less controversial channel. 'What about this problem up on the north coast? What are we doing about it?'

'I'm sending Sergeant Gabriel up there with a few men to get a feel of the problem, if organised piracy is afoot,' said de Revelle loftily.

John felt exasperated that the sheriff had appropriated his suggestion as if it was his own, but managed to bite back any protest. 'I intend setting off straight after the court tomorrow morning,' he said. 'We can get much of the way before nightfall and on to Ilfracombe the next day.'

'I thought it was Appledore you were interested in,' objected the sheriff.

'We are – and Bideford and, perhaps, Combe Martin. But I have to see this survivor again. He may have recalled something that would help to identify the attackers. He was too ill when we first saw him to be very helpful.'

They fell silent for a while and soon were in the narrow main highway of the city. As they passed the Guildhall, two figures hurried out of the arched doorway of the new stone building and accosted them in the road. They were the two portreeves of Exeter, Hugh de Relaga and Henry Rifford. They had been elected by their fellow burgessess to lead the civic organisation of the city, especially commerce, as the markets and fairs, the wool and cloth trades made Exeter one of the most thriving English towns. Hugh de Relaga, de Wolfe's partner in the wool enterprise, was a tubby, cheerful dandy, fond of good living and bright clothes. He was a complete contrast to Henry Rifford, a prosperous leather merchant but a serious, rather gloomy man above middle age. His beautiful daughter, Christina, had been brutally raped a few months ago, which had done little to improve his spirits.

'Is it over? What damage has been done?' demanded Rifford in agitation. The two men had been poring over municipal acccounts in a back room of the Guild-hall and had only just been informed of the riot in Southgate Street.

'Our clerk says a man is dead – is he a guildsman?' asked de Relaga.

Richard de Revelle took it upon himself to explain what had happened, never missing the chance to take credit for knowing everything and being the instrument of restoring order. Reassured, the portreeves calmed down, but decided to walk with their clerks to the Shambles and the Serge Market to show their concern to the citizens. 'We must visit the dwelling of the dead man and ensure that his guild-master is informed so that support can be offered to the family,' said de Relaga, with his typical concern for the more unfortunate of his townsfolk.

As they parted, de Wolfe reminded them of their other legal responsibilities. 'As the killer is dead, there will be no need to bring anyone before the king's judges – but the three men in your gaol are your problem.'

The sheriff could not resist having the last word. 'I could try them for causing an affray in my County Court tomorrow – but if you want them for illegal trading, you're welcome.'

With that parting shot, they walked on the few yards until de Wolfe came to the opening for Martin's Lane, leaving the others to continue on up to Rougemont. Giving a deep sigh, he pushed open his street door and prepared to meet the grim face of his wife when he told her that he would be leaving for another expedition to the north coast.

CHAPTER FIVE

In which Crowner John holds an inquest

In spite of his gloomy apprehensions, John found Matilda surprisingly tractable when he entered the hall. She had changed her garments again and wore a blue kirtle, which he knew was one of her best. He tried to open the conversation by telling her of the skirmish in Southgate Street, but she had no interest in that: her mind was on other things.

'Did you settle that poor man in a decent lodging? Not that there's anything decent about that low tavern.' Her active resentment of Nesta had been held in check since her husband had been disabled after breaking his leg, but she was starting to throw the old barbs at him once again.

'It's the best inn in the city – certainly better than sharing a room with sweaty pilgrims in Curre Street,' he countered gruffly.

'He should have stayed here. It's warm, quiet and more suitable for a man of his station in life,' said Matilda firmly.

'He said he wanted to move to an inn. It was his choice.'

'You did nothing to encourage him to take up our invitation, did you?'

He glowered at her as he took his chair on the opposite side of the fire. 'It may not be a very good idea to get too friendly with that particular man,' he muttered. 'If what he says is true, he's playing a dangerous game, not only with the Templars but with the Church generally and Rome in particular.'

Matilda made a dismissive gesture with a heavily ringed hand. 'You're just making excuses, John. I thought he was supposed to be a friend of yours.'

'Hardly a friend, just an acquaintance from the past. I owe him no more than any other man.'

'Well, we can't leave him to rot in that common hostelry, with half the scum of Devon around him.'

'What do you mean?' he said suspiciously.

'At the very least he must come to sup with us tonight. I've told Mary to prepare a decent meal, if she's capable of it for once – and to make it sufficient for an extra guest.'

'You want him to eat here?'

'Of course! We must make amends to him as you snubbed my offer to accommodate him under our roof. Send old Simon down to that tavern with a message for Sir Gilbert to come up here at dusk, to dine with us. I hope you still have some decent French wine in that chest of yours in the corner.' She pointed to a dark recess of the hall, where her husband kept a stock of sealed stone flasks purchased from a wine importer in Topsham.

He sat silently cursing the woman for interfering in his business: after hearing the archdeacon's views, he had a gut feeling that no good would come of this unexpected appearance of Gilbert de Ridefort. But his inertia was a futile defence, as Matilda continued to glare at him until he rose reluctantly and went out to the yard to summon Simon.

He dallied a while with Mary, sitting on a stool in her kitchen. It was a thatched hut with a cooking fire, a couple of rough tables stacked with pots, and in the corner the mattress on which he had once enjoyed an amorous hour or two.

'She's set her cap at this visitor, Crowner,' Mary commented, stirring a blackened iron urn hanging on a trivet over the fire. 'That poxy French girl has been brushing her hair and fiddling with her gowns for half the afternoon. I think she fancies the man, though much good it will do her if he's a Templar.'

John grinned as he watched Mary scowling into her cooking pot. 'I think he's more an ex-Templar, my girl. Not that it will make any difference to the mistress's chances with him.'

She looked over her shoulder at him. 'It's pathetic when a middle-aged married woman gets a passion for some man. Though I must say he's a good-looking fellow, enough to turn any woman's head. He was wasted as a warrior monk, or whatever you call those people.'

De Wolfe reached for a honey-cake but the platter was snatched away from his reach by Mary. 'Those are for the end of the meal so leave them be, sir! The mistress wants a special effort for tonight and I've had to go out and buy more pork and onions – not that there's much choice of food this early in the season. I can hardly give such an important guest the usual salt fish – the mistress would have me maimed, the mood she's in.'

De Wolfe was just about to ask her if she had seen the affray in the meat market when a long nose appeared around the door, followed by the face and hunched body of his clerk, Thomas de Peyne. 'Where did you spring from?' grunted the coroner. 'I thought you would be home anointing your backside with goose-grease, ready for the long ride to the north tomorrow.'

The little man groaned in anticipation of another full day in the saddle, but the news he brought overshadowed his problems. 'You asked me to keep a look-out for any important visitors to the city, Crowner,' he began, in his high-pitched quavering voice.

De Wolfe had impressed on Gwyn and Thomas earlier in the day that they should keep their ears to the ground to discover if anything unusual was going on in town or cloister. They knew nothing of de Ridefort's fears of pursuit, but the clerk was adept at ferreting out gossip amongst the ecclesiastical brethren and their servants.

'So what have you discovered, my master spy?' he chaffed.

'A foreign priest has arrived and called upon Bishop Marshal today,' chirped Thomas.

'What sort of news is that, eh? This city is always awash with priests.'

His clerk smirked. 'Not with envoys from the Vatican, Crowner!'

De Wolfe stood up suddenly, his head brushing the rough rafters of the hut. 'From Rome? How do you know?'

'The rumour is that he is a papal nuncio. So far, that's all that's known.'

'What the devil is a nuncio?' rasped his master.

'It's like a messenger – or a person with a particular task.'

'Is that the same as a legate?' De Wolfe was fairly ignorant of the hierarchy of the religious establishment.

Thomas, a fount of knowledge on it, shook his head vigorously, then crossed himself automatically. 'No, a legate is an ambassador to a royal court – a far superior person, almost always a bishop. There is talk that this man is an abbot.'

'Who is he, and where did he come from?'

Thomas shrugged, his humped shoulder rising unevenly to the left. 'No one knows yet. He arrived travel-weary on horseback, with two burly servants as guards.'

'Where is he staying? At the bishop's palace?'

The scribe shook his head again. 'He rode off after paying his respects to Henry Marshal and went out of the city, as far as I know.'

De Wolfe thought for a moment. Gilbert de Ridefort had left his French Commandery only six weeks ago, so it was impossible that Rome could have been notified and had sent this man after him – that would take at least three or four months. But he could have come from Paris or the Temple in London. Or he might be nothing to do with de Ridefort, which was the most likely explanation. 'Did you hear any description of this priest?'

Thomas tapped his receding chin in thought. 'The vicar I spoke with saw him. He was short in stature.'

De Wolfe clucked in exasperation. 'Short! That's no description. You're short, damn you, half the population is short.'

Thomas screwed up his face in concentration. 'He said something else ... Oh, yes, he had a strangely shaped nose.'

The coroner groaned. 'You have a strangely shaped nose too, you fool. It's like the sheriff's toe-cap, long and pointed! Is that the best you can do?'

'I never saw him, Crowner! I had two minutes' conversation with a passing vicar, that's all,' whined Thomas.

Reluctantly John accepted that his clerk had done his best.

'Well, try all you can to find out this abbot's name, where he came from, where he's lodging – and most of all, why he is in Exeter.'

A cunning gleam came into the clerk's eye. 'I can't do that if I'm in Ilfracombe or Appledore, Crowner.'

De Wolfe's dark face scowled at him. 'Very well. You only slow us down on that damned broken-winded pony of yours anyway. Stay behind and seek every morsel of information you can on this man. If there's anything to write on your parchments about our trip tomorrow I'll dictate it when I return.'

With a glow of satisfaction that his posterior had escaped days of punishment on horseback, the little ex-priest scuttled away to continue his espionage.

In spite of Matilda's scorn, Mary had made a good meal from what food was still available at the end of a long winter. Herbs added extra flavour to the pork, cabbage and onions, and after this, fresh bread, butter, cheese and honey-cakes were enough to fill any man's stomach, all washed down with wine and ale or cider.

De Wolfe sat silently through most of the meal, listening to his wife fawning and simpering over their handsome guest, who was as gallant with her as Matilda was foolish. He regaled her with stories of life in France and she responded by exaggerating her own Norman credentials. Though born and bred in Devon, living most of her life at Revelstoke and Tiverton, she had once spent a month or two with distant relatives in Normandy, from where the de Revelle family had come a century ago. On the strength of this, she proclaimed herself to be a first-generation Norman, bolstering this illusion by her contempt of Saxons and especially Celts. To a person of de Ridefort's perception, the silly deceit must have been patently obvious, but he went along with the charade, which heightened her infatuation. Only when they left the table and sat around the fireplace, with more wine brought in by old Simon, did the conversation turn to more immediate topics.

'There is no sign yet of your friend from France?' asked the coroner gruffly.

'Bernardus de Blanchefort? No, I had thought he would have arrived by now, but the Channel crossings are unpredictable. He may have had to wait for a fair wind.'

There followed a diversion, as Matilda, almost breathless with this mention of yet another French nobleman, prised from him all the details of the expected compatriot. 'He is a Templar like myself and fought alongside me in the Holy Land. Then he returned to a Preceptory near his ancestral estates at the foot of the Pyrenees for a year or so before being sent to Paris, where he was at the Commandery with me.'

Matilda's broad face creased into an admiring smile. 'I'm sure he must be another heroic person like yourself, defending the Faith in the Holy Land.'

De Wolfe, whose own crusading record was second to none, felt it was time to throw cold water over the mutual-admiration duet that was developing. 'I heard today of another visitor from France. Exeter seems suddenly to have become popular in that respect.'

Gilbert's manner changed at once and he looked warily at John. 'Who was that? Not a Templar?'

De Wolfe shook his head slowly. 'A priest by all accounts. Thought to be an abbot from Paris, who called briefly upon the bishop then went on his way.'

The other's face paled. Whatever it was he feared was no fantasy but a grim reality, thought the coroner. 'You must know something more about him, surely? What did he look like?'

De Wolfe took a long, slow swallow from his wine cup. 'I had third-hand information only – cathedral gossip, really. All I was told was that he was short and had a peculiar nose.' He set down his cup carefully on the flat arm of the monk's chair. 'And my clerk said that he was a papal nuncio, whatever that might mean.'

De Ridefort jumped up as if jabbed with a dagger, his foot knocking over a long fire-iron with a clatter. His lean face was ashen and his fingers were clenched. De Wolfe, who had seen him fight fearlessly in the heat of battle in Palestine, now saw him in near terror at the mention of a passing visitor to Exeter. 'They've traced me to this city – there can be no doubt,' he whispered.

Matilda looked in concern at her new idol, sensing his distress. 'Who is this priest that he worries you so much, sir?'

De Ridefort paced across the front of the hearth and back, then flopped down on to his stool. 'Worry is a gross understatement, dear lady,' he said, struggling to get a grip on his emotions. 'I do not know his name, but there was an abbot from Fleury who sometimes came to the Commandery to speak to our Master. He was small and had a singular nose. But whoever he is, the fact that he is now styled a papal nuncio can surely mean only that he is on my track.'

'What's a nuncio?' demanded Matilda.

'According to Thomas, who knows everything connected with the Church, it is a messenger from Rome,' supplied de Wolfe.

'And this singular nose?' persisted his wife, looking at de Ridefort.

'If it's the same priest that I recall, he had a nose completely without a bridge. It came down straight from his forehead, with no trace of the usual dip between the eyes.'

'A truly Roman nose, in fact!' commented John.

'This is no time for your stupid puns, John,' snapped Matilda. 'What are you going to do about it?'

Her husband felt it time to bring them all down to the earth of common sense. 'Wait, for Christ's sake! We have no reason to think that this man has anything at all to do with Sir Gilbert. He jogged into the city with two guards, paid a duty call on the bishop then jogged out again. Why should we think he has any interest in Sir Gilbert, whom no one knows is in the city, except us?'

Some of de Ridefort's colour had come back into his face, but he was still uneasy. 'Thank you for trying to comfort me, John, but the coincidence is too great. An envoy from the Holy Father arrives in one of the most remote cities in Europe a few days after a renegade Templar. Why else would he be here, if not to seek me out?'

They argued the matter for some minutes, de Ridefort being adamant that the search for him was getting closer. 'I must leave Exeter and hide somewhere more obscure until Bernardus arrives,' he exclaimed in agitation. 'Can you suggest some remote village outside the city?'

'What about a monastery or an abbey? There are plenty of those about the county who would be glad to offer you hospitality,' offered Matilda, desperate to play the part of a maiden of salvation to her hero.

But de Ridefort rejected this suggestion vehemently. 'Religious houses will be the first place they will search. They can depend upon priests, of whatever Order, to hasten to obey the command of Rome to report all travellers and strangers answering my description.' He had a sudden thought. 'I'll wager that was the message this abbot is distributing about the country – he would have taken it to Bishop Marshal to pass on throughout his diocese.'

'I can soon find out from the archdeacon if that is so,' said de Wolfe. Then he smote his forehead in realisation that he would be absent for several days, in which he had so far avoided telling his wife. 'I have to leave for Ilfracombe at dawn tomorrow, so there is nothing further I can do until my return.'

He caught a poisonous glare from Matilda, and knew that she would give him a piece of her mind as soon as their guest had left.

'I should stay at the inn and not venture out, except at night, if you have to. I still think that no one can be looking for you in the city – who would know what you look like? Especially now that you have no beard or moustache. I failed to recognise you myself.'

'When will you be back?' asked de Ridefort. 'I need to move to somewhere utterly remote.'

'I shall spend two nights away and be back at curfew on the third day. Then I will arrange somewhere for you. It's the best I can do.'

And with that, the errant Templar had to be satisfied.

In spite of the absence of Thomas, who was always a brake on their progress, the journey to Ilfracombe took a day and a half, partly due to heavy rain, which made the track a quagmire during the first afternoon. The coroner and his officer, followed by Sergeant Gabriel and four soldiers, rode as far as Umberleigh on the first day and spent the night in a barn. In the morning they rode on, straight through Barnstaple, reaching Ilfracombe by noon.

Here John found little that was new since his last visit, except that the wrecked ship had broken up completely, a few scattered planks in the rocky coves being all that was left. The sole survivor, Alain the Breton, had improved in health and had been brought into the little port from the shepherd's hut on the cliffs. He was now being looked after by the family of a ship-master in the town, until a vessel called that could take him to either Bristol or St Malo, where he would be returned either to his employers or his family.

The coroner interrogated Alain again, but the youth had no further recollection of anything that might identify the pirates, except that there had been a dozen oarsmen on board.

Gabriel asked the reeve what had happened to the dead body.

'We buried him behind the church – there are a dozen graves of seamen there, mostly without names, men who have been washed ashore over the years.'

Both the sergeant and the coroner questioned the reeve and a few others at the harbour about any tales of piracy in the area. Apart from some vague rumours that covered virtually every port and fishing hamlet from Minehead to Padstow, there was nothing concrete about their allegations, which seemed to arise mainly from personal animosity for the various villages.

There was little else to keep the coroner and his men in Ilfracombe, and after some food and ale in the reeve's house, for which de Wolfe gave the man's wife a couple of pence, the seven men set off for Appledore. The little port was on the opposite side of the river, where the Taw and the Torridge joined, and although as the crow flies it was only about twelve miles distant, they had to travel through both Barnstaple and Bideford to get there, almost doubling the journey.

It was twilight by the time they reached Barnstaple and again de Wolfe requested a night's lodging at the small castle of de Tracey, though the lord himself was still absent, this time at a hunting lodge somewhere out in the countryside.

Next morning, they rode to Bideford to cross the only bridge over the Torridge and then the three miles to Appledore. Here they unenthusiastically surveyed the huts along the shoreline and the few more solid houses set back on the slope above.

'Another poor-looking place, Crowner!' grumbled Gwyn, looking about him at the shabby dwellings and the rickety fish-huts with their nets hanging alongside.

'If they are pirates, they can't be very good ones,' added Gabriel cynically.

The village was built on a promontory jutting out into the sandy estuary of the two rivers, the open sea a mile away to their left, where wide dunes edged the ocean. There was no proper port, as in Ilfracombe, and vessels were beached on the sheltered side of the low peninsula. Four or five small fishing boats lay above the tide-line, but there was no sign of any deep-sea ship. The village seemed deserted at first, but as they trotted along the single track between the dozen dwellings, a few women, some with babies on their hips, came to the doorways to stare at them.

'There can be no pirate fleet working out of here, surely to God?' asked the sergeant, looking in disgust at the place they had ridden for almost two days to reach. 'They would be hard put to raise a crew for one decent vessel in a place this size.'

Gwyn was doubtful. 'I agree it seems unlikely – yet a dozen fit men, with a few weapons between them, could prevail against a small merchantman if they were better sailors and better fighters.'

De Wolfe glanced around him. Seeing only women and children, he said, 'Let's find someone we can question.' One of the men-at-arms dismounted and went across to the nearest thatched hut, where a fat woman was leaning against the doorpost. A moment later, he came up to the coroner's stirrup. 'She says all the men are either out fishing or at the manor court in Bideford. But there's a sick man two houses along.'

They moved a few yards down the sand-blown track and the soldier went into another dwelling. He came out with a middle-aged man hobbling on a single crutch jammed into his armpit. With recent memories of his own broken leg, the coroner slid from his horse and went across to meet the invalid. 'I'm Sir John de Wolfe, the county coroner,' he said courteously.

The man nodded, his bald head shining in the sudden gleam of sunlight from between the scudding clouds. 'Your soldier told me. What trouble have you brought to this poor vill?' The arrival of a troop of men-at-arms and a king's official could never be good news, but the man became less anxious when he learned that they were seeking news of pirates. 'Here, in Appledore?' He sounded incredulous at the suggestion. 'We scratch a living in the fields behind here, and some of the men catch a few fish for our lord and to sell in Barnstaple. We don't even have a proper reeve – the one from Bideford comes to boss us about.'

'That needn't stop you taking a boat out pillaging now and then,' challenged Gwyn, glowering at him.

'We don't have a sea-going vessel – nothing bigger than those.' He swayed as he pointed his crutch at the beached fishing boats, none of which were more than twenty feet in length.

Gwyn stared at them then agreed. 'That Breton lad said the boat that attacked them was rowed by six oars a side. So it would have to have that many sets of thole pins along the gunwales. It would be far bigger than those cockleshells.'

Gabriel had a suspicious nature and was not yet convinced. 'Those are only the boats here at the moment, fellow,' he growled. 'You must get larger vessels at other times?'

The villein shook his shiny pate. 'I tell you, we don't have a bigger boat! The traders all go up-river to Bideford. It's more sheltered and there's a quay and a proper town there. Sometimes a vessel from Wales or Cornwall will bring us a load of lime for the fields and take away some grain, but that's only a couple of times each year.'

'What's in that bigger hut?' demanded the coroner, pointing to a wattle-and-daub shed with a tattered thatch roof that came down almost to ground level.

'Part is a barn, with the winter hay, and a stock of lime and clamps of turnips for the winter. All gone now, we're living on fish.'

To be sure that the building was not stacked to the rafters with looted merchandise, the visitors went across to look, but the villager was right: the mouldering interior held only the remnants of the hamlet's winter stores.

De Wolfe dismissed the man and led the party away, trotting back along the west bank of the Torridge towards Bideford. 'If there is any piracy in this area, it can surely be carried out only with the knowledge of Richard de Grenville,' he said. 'The men of his various villages could never vanish to sea for days on end without him knowing.'

'Maybe his steward or reeves are in on the conspiracy without his knowledge?' suggested Gabriel. He and Gwyn rode at either side of the coroner.

The Cornishman, used to the ways of seaside villages, dismissed the possibility. 'Where would they get a vessel big enough to go out to sea without their lord knowing? They couldn't afford to build one or keep it without his knowledge. Either he is the architect of the piracy or we're barking up the wrong tree in thinking it may be Appledore.'

'What about outlaws?' asked Gabriel. 'God knows, there are thousands roaming England's forests and moors. Any at the coast could set up as pirates instead of as highway robbers and thieves.'

Gwyn pulled his fingers through his luxuriant moustache. 'Possible – but where would outlaws get a decent vessel? Only by raiding a village or port and stealing one, and there's no reports of such a crime in the West Country.'

As they rode, they discussed other possibilities. Perhaps the pirates had come across from Wales, Ireland or even Brittany, but Alain had been adamant that his attackers had spoken English, which ruled out any incursions from the Celtic countries.

A score of men and boys passed them in the opposite direction, going back to Appledore after attending the fortnightly manor court as witnesses, jurors and appellants. They gave curious and somewhat frightened looks at the party of armed strangers coming from their village, but apart from muttered acknowledgements and tugging at forelocks they trudged past as fast as they could.

'That lot doesn't look as if it could ambush a ship,' muttered Gwyn. 'Stealing a couple of pigs would be about their limit.'

By now they had returned to Bideford. The small town had half a dozen vessels grounded along its quayside and the rising tide was beginning to lift some of them off the muddy sand. Gwyn's nautical eye scanned each intently for six sets of oar pins, but they all seemed innocent of such additions.

The town's defences were an earthbank topped by an old wooden stockade, though the three gates had been rebuilt in stone. Richard de Grenville lived in a small castle, which was more a fortified manor house, but he was absent from his domains in Winchester, petitioning the Chancellor, Walter Longchamp, about some land dispute. His wife and family had gone with him, leaving his steward in charge, who had presided over the court that day. Now he pressed the coroner to food and drink and invited the party to stay overnight. While eating good bread and cheese and drinking some of de Grenville's best wine in the castle hall, John broached the matter of piracy with him.

A burly man of about de Wolfe's own age, with a black beard and moustache, the steward answered, 'We suffered the loss of a vessel last year. Some say it sank after leaving here for Bude, but we never found any signs of the wreck.'

'So why d'you think it was pirated?' asked John.

'One dead body was washed up on Braunton Sands a fortnight later. He had wounds that I'm sure were from an axe or cleaver. Some said they were due to being pounded on rocks by the waves, but there are no rocks

where he was found. And I say the injuries were from a
sharp-edged weapon.'

'That was before you had a coroner to look into it,'
said de Wolfe. 'Almost the same thing has happened
near Ilfracombe and we need to find who's responsible
– then hang them!' He told the steward bluntly, that
Appledore had been under suspicion, but this raised
a laugh rather than indignation. 'Those dolts couldn't
capture a coracle full of nuns, let alone a merchant
vessel! It's a wonder they can find the sea with their
fishing boats, they're that stupid. It's the in-breeding,
you see, in a place so small and remote.'

As half the hamlets in England were equally small
and remote, de Wolfe wondered why the steward had
such contempt for this particular village, but before he
could pursue it, de Grenville's henchman went back to
piracy. 'Don't waste your time looking at places like
Appledore, Crowner. I know damn fine who took our
vessel – and I'm sure the same goes for the one at
Ilfracombe.' He paused for effect, his dark eyes staring
into de Wolfe's. 'De Marisco, he's the man you want.
Not that you can ever get near him, stuck out there on
his rock of Lundy. He thinks he's not part of England
– nor does he take any notice of its laws. His men are
a bunch of bloody brigands and pirates. You need look
no further than them.'

His air of conviction was impressive and de Wolfe
began to think that he was probably right.

CHAPTER SIX

In which Crowner John visits his mother

Once again, the horsemen reached Exeter just before the gates closed at the twilight curfew, though this was getting later every evening as March progressed. Gwyn left them outside the walls to go to his home in St Sidwell's and the men-at-arms clattered away to the castle, leaving de Wolfe to stable Odin at the farrier's.

He crossed the road to his own house and, whilst wearily taking off his riding clothes in the vestibule, heard voices from inside the hall. Hungry and thirsty, he pushed open the inner door fretfully, far more interested in filling his stomach than dealing with a visitor. As he walked across to the hearth, he saw Gilbert de Ridefort was talking animatedly to Matilda. Clad in a plain brown tunic, a hooded cloak discarded across a nearby stool, he rose courteously as John entered. 'Your good lady has been entertaining me graciously until your return,' he said. 'I was anxious to hear if you had any more news, especially of somewhere where I might hide myself more discreetly.'

Instead of her usual grim welcome, Matilda gave her husband a weak smile and enquired solicitously after his leg following such a long ride. 'Supper will not be long, John,' she added uncharacteristically. 'I've told Mary to make a special effort, as I've invited Sir Gilbert to dine with us again.'

De Wolfe groaned inwardly at the prospect of having to entertain a guest, when all he wanted was to eat, then go down to the Bush to see Nesta. Even sitting at his own fireside with a pitcher of ale would be preferable to listening to his wife and Gilbert prattling on about the glories of Normandy.

He sank on to the seat just vacated by de Ridefort, who took the one opposite.

'Is there any news?' persisted the former Templar.

De Wolfe shook his head wearily. 'Nothing from the north of the county. It was a wasted trip.'

'But what about this priest? And is there any sign of strange knights in the city?'

'I've just set foot back in Exeter, so I have no means of knowing,' he said irritably. 'I must go up to the castle after the meal so maybe I can learn something then.'

'I think that tonight my brother is attending a feast at the Guild of Cordwainers,' said Matilda, with a return of her usual abrasive tone.

De Wolfe, however, was determined to fight for his alibi to visit the Bush. 'That won't be until later this evening – and, anyway, I have other business to attend to in my chamber, if you can call such a hole in the ground by that name.'

Mary came in to set places at the table, followed by Simon staggering under a basket of logs for the fire. He returned with more wine and ale, and for the next hour, the three ate and drank. De Wolfe sat mostly in silence, trying to stop his ears to Matilda's persistent attempts to extract details from de Ridefort of his life in France. He found it difficult to reconcile the stern warrior he had known in Palestine with this urbane and courteous fellow, who so obviously had a way with women when the need arose.

Yet de Wolfe detected an undercurrent of anxiety in de Ridefort, and was conscious of the regular worried glances that the visitor gave him whenever he could disengage himself from Matilda's importuning. Eventually the coroner took pity on him and disclosed his plans for settling him somewhere outside the city.

'I've decided to lodge you in my home village, where I was born and where my family still hold the manor,' he offered.

The younger man's face lit up and his relief was obvious, though Matilda's scowl gave away her feelings: she despised her in-laws as much as they disliked her.

'Are you sure they will accept me, John?' asked de Ridefort. 'And where is this place of yours?'

'Stoke-in-Teignhead, about fifteen miles south of Exeter, just inland from the coast. It's a few hours' gentle riding, as long as the tide is low enough to cross the river at Teignmouth.'

'Not much of a place, I can assure you,' sniffed his wife, 'but I'll admit that it's remote enough, if you really feel you should leave the amenities of the the city.'

'Apart from your gracious hospitality, I'm not seeing much of Exeter, madam,' observed Gilbert. 'I spend all day cooped up in the inn to avoid drawing attention to myself.'

John stood up and stretched his back, stiff after a day in the saddle. His leg seemed to have stood up to the journey remarkably well: it was pain-free and virtually back to normal. 'I must go about my business for a couple of hours. Are you staying here or going back to your lodgings?'

Matilda turned her eyes on the former Templar,

her beseeching expression making her husband cringe. 'You've just said you are imprisoned in that place, so stay awhile and sit at peace before a good fire. I'll get the servant to fetch more wine.'

De Wolfe was indifferent as to whether the knight might ravish Matilda on the cold flagstones, but he suspected that even the fearless Crusader was not equal to that challenge. As he made for the door, he promised to take de Ridefort to his new hideaway next morning.

'Be ready with your satchel and horse. I'll meet you at the Bush just after dawn.' With that, he vanished into the darkness of Martin's Lane, turning in the opposite direction from Rougemont and the sheriff.

It had been some time since the coroner had had the chance to bed his mistress and he took advantage of a slack time in the tavern to spend an hour with her in her small room on the upper floor. There were a score of customers in the smoky room that occupied the whole ground level, most of whom were well known to him, but none remarked on his ascent of the wide ladder in the corner: his relationship with Nesta was too familiar to them to be worth a comment.

Nesta's room had a proper bed with short legs, rather than the usual pallet on the floor. He had bought this for her a year ago, to keep them both up a little from the draughts that whistled across at floor level. It had seen a great deal of action in that twelve months, and it was a tribute to the French carpenters that its legs were still intact after their vigorous love-making.

Now they held each other quietly after this latest episode, contentedly snuggled under the coverlet of sewn sheepskins. Nesta enquired impishly after his aching back. 'It must be all this riding today, Sir Crowner – both on your horse and elsewhere!'

He pinched her bare thigh in retribution, but at the same time, buried his face in the auburn curls at the base of her neck. 'I wonder how Gilbert de Ridefort is dealing with Matilda at this moment? Has he managed to fend off her lecherous advances?'

The Welsh woman giggled. 'I can't imagine the poor woman having such a thought in her head – unless it's for the fat priest at St Olave's.'

The thought of his wife reminded de Wolfe that he was running out of time. 'I'd better get back before she has the poor fellow stripped of his tunic and hose.' He sighed, groping over the edge of the bed for his clothes.

Nesta slipped out the other side and dressed quickly in the gloom. 'And I'd better attend to my business or that old fool Edwin and those daft serving maids will have driven all my patrons away with their stupidity.' She opened the rough door and let in a dim light from a horn lantern left burning for the guests to find their way to their pallets. 'Come down for a last mug of ale before you go – my last brew was better than ever, though I say it myself.' As well as being a pretty woman and an enthusiastic lover, Nesta was an excellent cook and a talented ale-maker. De Wolfe often bemoaned the fact that both social barriers and his marriage prevented him from living with this jewel of a woman.

He hauled himself from the bed and pulled on his undershirt and long grey tunic, slit back and front for riding a horse. The long black woollen hose came up to his thighs and his pointed shoes and a heavy belt completed his garb. He had left his hooded cloak of grey wolfskin downstairs.

When he climbed down the wooden steps into the ale-room, lit by the flickering flames of a large fire and a number of tallow dips on the tables, he made out a familiar shape sitting near the door. As he reached the floor, Nesta bustled past, intent on chasing one of her harassed serving maids. 'Thomas has been waiting patiently for you these past ten minutes – he has some message for you, he says.'

She sailed away and he went over to the little clerk, who hopped to his feet and peered bird-like up into de Wolfe's face, his sharp eyes glistening in the candle-light. 'I've found out who the priest is – the one from France,' he squeaked excitedly. Eternally grateful to the coroner for giving him employment, which had saved him from penury and perhaps starvation, Thomas was always desperately anxious to prove his worth. Although de Wolfe and Gwyn usually treated him with scornful contempt, he had been inordinately useful to them on many occasions.

'So who is he?' demanded his master.

'An abbot from Paris, called Cosimo of Modena.'

'Modena? That's not in France.'

'No, he's from the north of Italy. I gather he is a Vatican priest, posted to Paris some time ago as a special nuncio. No one knows what his special duties might be,' sniggered Thomas.

'How did you discover this? And where is he now?' demanded the coroner.

'I was talking to one of the Benedictines from St James's Priory, who came up to a service for St Jerome today. He said that Abbot Cosimo has installed himself at the priory, much to the discomfort of the prior.'

'Why should he complain?'

'First, because Cosimo is a Cistercian – in their strictness they look down on these Cluniac Benedictines, even though their Orders have the same origins. Also it seems he arrogantly demanded accommodation and sustenance for himself and his two men on the authority of Pope Celestine, producing some letter from Rome that virtually overrides any reluctance, even by bishops.' Thomas crossed himself spasmodically as he spoke.

De Wolfe considered this, leaning against the inside of the inn door. 'And no one knows on what errand this Italian is engaged?'

The little clerk looked crestfallen. 'I couldn't discover this, Crowner. No one seems to know. The abbot is a very secretive person, it appears.'

John thoughtfully rubbed the dark stubble on his long chin. 'We got on well with the jolly prior at St James's, did we not?'

Thomas, delighted to be asked his opinion, bobbed his head eagerly. 'Prior Peter was very amiable when we were there for the catching of that fish a few months ago,' he agreed.

Just before de Wolfe's disaster, when his old horse both broke his leg and saved his life, they had visited the priory when the coroner had had to attend the landing of a sturgeon. The prior, a rubicund fellow with a taste for good wine, had made them welcome on that occasion.

'Be ready at dawn, Thomas, with whatever you need for a few days' absence from that flea-pit you stay in near the cathedral. I have a task for you that you may well enjoy.'

And with that the former priest had to be satisfied.

The coroner thought that at forty he must already

be getting old as he jogged on Odin through the early-morning mists alongside the river Exe. As an active soldier, he had woken as fresh as a daisy at whatever hour the trumpet sounded, but now he felt bleary-eyed and his brain remained sluggish until he could shake off the effects of sleep.

Behind him rode Gwyn on his big brown mare, and Thomas, sitting side-saddle on his moorland pony. Alongside him was Gilbert de Ridefort, sitting as tall and erect as a fence-post on his grey gelding. He looked every inch a Templar knight, even if the famous white cloak with the large cross was missing.

The quartet rode silently, each with his own thoughts, though every few hundred yards Gilbert would give a quick look over his shoulder, checking that no pursuing shapes were dashing after them through the morning fog.

They passed a number of peasants and traders making for Exeter, many carrying huge bundles or pushing handcarts with goods to sell in the city, others with laden donkeys or ox-carts full of produce. The road went due south from Exeter towards Topsham, the small port at the head of the estuary of the Exe. Between them was the tiny priory of St James, founded half a century before by Baldwin, the famous sheriff of the county. The small building was down on the slope, just above the floodplain of the river, and John told Gwyn to stay up on the main road with Sir Gilbert, out of sight of the priory, in case the mysterious Roman priest was abroad. He and his clerk went down to the building and, within a few minutes, de Wolfe had returned alone. 'As I hoped, it was an easy task,' he explained, as they set off more briskly towards Topsham. 'Prior Peter seems to have no real love for this Italian, who he feels has battened upon him like an unwelcome leech.'

'So what of your clerk?' asked de Ridefort.

'The prior is letting him stay there under the guise of a travelling brother on his way to take up a parish in Cornwall. Thomas is well suited to spinning such deceptions. He could probably make them believe he was the new archbishop!'

'Why should the prior agree to this?' grunted Gwyn.

'I told him that the secular authorities wanted to know why a papal nuncio was in England without announcing himself to the authorities. I don't know if it's true or not, but neither does the prior. Thomas is going to snoop about to try to find out why this Italian is here.'

'I have no doubt why that man Cosimo is here,' commented de Rideport bitterly. 'He was sent last year to investigate the Cathar heresy in the Albi region of France and to report back to his master in Rome. Now he has a similar mission to find me.'

De Ridefort had already confirmed that Cosimo of Modena was indeed the priest he used to see about the Commandery in Paris. He was now convinced that this abbot had been sent to deal with him, either by capture or elimination.

Presumably with the stimulus of the abbot so near, the Templar set a cracking pace and within half an hour were in the little port of Topsham, seeking the ferry that crossed the river to the marshes on the western side. From there, they trotted to Powderham then on to Dawlish, the first village on the open coast. As they passed through, Gwyn watched his master from the corner of his eye and, as he expected, saw him look longingly at a fine stone house in the only street.

Mischievously, the ginger-haired officer couldn't resist

some comment, which was lost on de Ridefort, though his thoughts were mainly on his own predicament.

'Quite a few vessels beached here, Crowner,' observed Gwyn, with a false air of innocence. 'Some of them real sea-going vessels – the Normandy fleet must be in.'

De Wolfe merely grunted – he knew what the Cornishman was hinting at. One of his favourite mistresses, the blonde Hilda, lived in Dawlish. She was wife to Thorgils the Boatman and with most of the cross-Channel shipping lying in the little creek, he was now probably at home with his young and beautiful wife.

With no chance of a visit the coroner kept his eyes on the track, and they continued along the coast for a few miles until they came to the wide valley of the Teign. At the point where it entered the sea, a sand-bar drastically narrowed the river so that at low tide horses could splash across. This morning they were in luck and could wade straight across with no delay. By noon the three riders were winding their way down a pleasant wooded valley into Stoke-in-Teignhead. The manor house was just outside the village, which consisted of a new church to St Andrew and a dozen houses and huts, of a better quality than in most other villages.

The coroner's father, Simon de Wolfe, whose family had come from Caen in the last years of the previous century, had been killed fifteen years before in the Irish campaigns. Though, like his son, he had spent much of his life fighting, he was also a careful and considerate landowner: his two manors at Stoke and at Holcombe near the coast were kept in good condition and the villagers were well treated.

Inside the bailey around the house, servants and freemen came running to greet their popular master, for now John de Wolfe, his brother William and his sister

Evelyn jointly owned the honour, with their sprightly mother Enyd enjoying a life interest in the manor.

Their Saxon steward, Alsi, came out to organise the stabling of the horses then effusively escorted de Wolfe and de Ridefort into the house. Gwyn made for the kitchen hut, where he knew from long experience that giggling maids would ply him with food and drink until he was fit to burst.

The house was solidly built of stone: one of Simon's last acts before he died had been to provide his family with a substantial home built to resist attack, though thankfully there had been no fighting around here for decades. The stockade, which encircled the bailey, was still sound, but the drawbridge over the small moat had not been raised for many years, a good indicator of peaceful times.

'Are the family at home, Alsi?' asked de Wolfe as they climbed the outer staircase to the entrance on the first floor.

'Your mother and sister are here, Sir John. Your brother is overseeing the cutting of new assarts in the West Wood.'

John grinned at the familiar tale. William, though he looked remarkably like himself, was no soldier. All his enthusiasms were for farming and managing the estate, which suited John well as he shared in the profits. Together with a steady income from his share in the wool-exporting business with Hugh de Relaga, he had a comfortable income without having to work for it.

In the solar, he introduced Gilbert de Ridefort to his mother and sister. Enyd de Wolfe was a still-pretty woman of sixty, with a little grey in her fair hair – de Wolfe's colouring came from his father. Enyd was pure Celt, which explained part of Matilda's antipathy to her. Her father was Cornish and her mother Welsh, and John's fluency in those similar languages had been learned in childhood at Enyd's knee.

Evelyn was a plump, cheerful woman of thirty-four, still unmarried. She had once wanted to become a nun, but her mother had rightly suspected that her daughter was too garrulous to settle under the constraints of the veil and insisted that she stay at home and help run the manor-house.

De Wolfe gave them an edited version of de Ridefort's problem, emphasising that the knight wanted somewhere quiet to stay until his companion arrived from France. His sharp-witted mother, who knew every nuance of her son's character, knew full well that there was more to the man's problems than a need for peace and quiet, but she said nothing and, with Evelyn, gave him a warm welcome. Gilbert became his usual charming self and soon had them eating out of his hand. He offered, with just the right amount of reluctance, to stay at the local inn to save them the trouble of boarding him, but they would have none of it.

'Not that the church hostel is uncomfortable,' said Evelyn, proudly. 'My father established it for travellers, instead of a rowdy alehouse. But you will be far better off here.' After her intuitive reading of the situation, she could have added 'and safer', but she held her tongue.

After a good meal, Gilbert was shown to a small chamber off the hall, the only other room apart from the solar and the ladies' sleeping chamber. He dropped the large satchel that held his possessions and looked with satisfaction at the thick straw mattress laid for him on the floor. As John prepared to leave for Exeter, de Ridefort begged him to keep him informed of any developments. 'Your clerk must find out what Cosimo of Modena is really engaged in,' he pleaded.

'One small priest cannot be any threat to you, surely,' said de Wolfe, reassuringly. 'Even his two escorts could hardly abduct a fighting Templar against his will.'

'Not personally, it's true,' replied de Ridefort. 'But he is an accomplished organiser and schemer. There will be other men to do any strong-arm work, you can depend on it. That's why I'm keen to know if any strange fighting men appear in the district. You will let me know that, John?' he ended, with an imploring look in his eyes.

With promises to keep him up to date with any developments, and especially to tell him when Bernardus de Blanchefort arrived, the coroner took his leave, with hugs for his mother and sister.

After collecting Gwyn, he rode via the West Wood, to greet his brother William. They could do this as part of their homeward journey by going through the band of forest that bordered the river and thence up to Kingsteignton, as the tide would by now prevent them from crossing back at Teignmouth.

They found William with his tunic pulled up between his thighs and tucked into a broad belt, serge breeches inside stout boots, swinging an axe with his bailiff and half a dozen villeins from the village. They were cutting down trees to extend the arable land and oxen were dragging away the larger trunks for timber and firewood, the smaller branches being burned on a large bonfire.

'There must be few lords of the manor who work alongside serfs,' muttered Gwyn, slightly disapproving of this degree of egalitarianism.

'He does it because he likes swinging an axe. So do I, but I prefer hitting a Saracen rather than a beech tree,' replied de Wolfe, gazing benignly at his brother.

When William saw them approach, he dropped his axe, and for fifteen minutes the brothers talked animatedly, the Cornishman going discreetly to the bailiff for a chat. John explained to William the situation concerning de Ridefort, more forthright with him than with the women. 'This threat against him seems real enough, but he sees an assassin behind every tree,' he concluded. 'I'll be glad when this other Templar arrives and the pair of them can clear off to Ireland or wherever they wish to go.'

Before they parted, his brother promised to do all he could to make his unexpected guest as welcome as possible. De Wolfe collected Gwyn, and they rode off along the narrow track into the forest that bordered the tidal part of the river. The sky was overcast, with the threat of rain, but it held off as they crossed the Teign where it narrowed suddenly four miles inland from the sea. At a steady pace, they expected to reach Exeter in the early evening, following the road from Kingsteignton through Ideford and Kenn.

The two men rode side by side, mainly in silence. They had covered thousands of miles together over the years, in snow and sandstorm, sleet and sun. Neither was talkative and, except when reminiscing over a quart of ale in a tavern, their conversation was confined to immediate matters, such as deciding which fork of the track to take or a suspicion of a lame horse.

Today their steeds were performing well, and de Wolfe was pleased with Odin, a worthy successor to his beloved Bran. At a steady trot, letting the stallion and the mare set their own pace, the pair could keep going for many hours. On a decent track in good weather, when the mud was dry, they could cover thirty miles a day. This particular route was not the main road between Exeter and Plymouth, that being further north, but it was well used and had many villages and patches of farmland between the stretches of forest. So it was something of a shock when the two riders came round a bend inside a mile of trees to find themselves confronted by half a dozen armed ruffians, obviously intent on highway robbery.

With bloodcurdling yells, the footpads rushed at their intended victims, wielding a variety of weapons. One ragged outlaw swung a long stave, trying to knock Gwyn from his horse. Two others converged each side of de Wolfe, one waving a rusted sword and the other jabbing with a broken lance, the lower part of its shaft missing. The other trio circled behind, armed with an axe, a long dagger and another staff.

If they had thought they were ambushing a pair of fat merchants, returning from Kingsteignton market, they were sadly mistaken. The coroner and his officer had been attacked a score of times in several parts of the known world and were well versed in defending themselves.

After the first few seconds of surprise, the reflexes of these two old soldiers snapped into action. Though de Wolfe wore no hauberk or helmet, his long sword swung at his hip and a mace and chain stood in a pocket on his saddle. Gwyn wore his usual battered cuirass of thick boiled leather with metal-studded shoulder pads. In addition to his massive sword, he had a long-handled axe slipped into a loop on his saddle-bow.

Almost as the yelling began, there was a rattling hiss as both swords were slid simultaneously from their scabbards. Gwyn, with an exultant howl that matched his almost manic grin of delight at the promise of action, hoisted his mare's forelegs high into the air and pulled her round, then let her drop on to the villain with the staff, who screamed with pain as her metal-shod hoofs struck him in the chest. As he staggered back and fell on to the track, Gwyn kept his steed turning to face the two men who had come up behind. The one with the dagger had frozen rigid at the realisation that they had picked the wrong pair to rob, and before he could gather his wits, Gwyn had swung his sword at his neck. He fell poleaxed into the road, already dying from the fountain of blood that shot from a main artery into the leaf-mould of the track.

Meanwhile, de Wolfe had his two bandits to contend with. The man with the lance, his face contorted into a broken-toothed snarl of rage, jabbed up at him. The coroner's sword was not long enough to reach the attacker and he felt the tip of the lance dragging at his riding cloak, although the wolfskin was tough enough to resist the thrust. As the second man came to his other side and attempted to hack at de Wolfe's leg with his sword, he dug both his prick-spurs into Odin's flanks. Indignantly, the stallion leaped forward, leaving the two outlaws facing each other across an empty space. Dragging on the reins, de Wolfe pulled Odin round and repeated Gwyn's manoeuvre, rearing the horse up to fall upon the most dangerous adversary – the man with the lance.

He managed to dodge the flailing hoofs the first time, but fell to his knees and was trampled by the big destrier when John ruthlessly pulled Odin round a second time. An iron shoe landed squarely between the ruffian's shoulder-blades and even above the shouting of the men and the neighing of the protesting horses, John heard the crack as the spine snapped.

Realising the fatal error they had made, the other four tried to make their escape. The one that Gwyn had first knocked to the ground was slowest off the mark and paid for it with his life. He made for the trees, but the big brown mare was upon him before he reached them. Gwyn had couched the bare sword under his left armpit to hold the reins with that hand, whilst he pulled his axe from its thong and slid his right hand down the shaft. As the mare came level with the fugitive, the wedge-shaped axehead whistled down to strike him on top of the head. The blade cleaved his skull almost down to the nape of the neck and the man fell twitching to the road in a welter of blood and brains. The momentum had taken the Cornishman almost into the trees, but he hoisted the mare round to see how his master was faring with his contest.

Two of the remaining outlaws had already reached the safety of the dense woodland, but de Wolfe was pursuing the last one diagonally across the track, his sword poised for a strike as soon as he was within reach. But the man was lucky: he shot between two beech trunks only inches ahead of the weapon. The trees and the thorny scrub between them at the edge of the road were too dense to allow a horseman to follow and Odin skidded to a halt with his nose in a tangle of brambles.

The two old Crusaders trotted back to each other and halted in the middle of the road, slamming their swords back into their sheaths. Gwyn, his wild carrotty hair poking from under his pointed leather cap, grinned with unashamed delight. 'We haven't done that for a long time, Crowner!' he growled, swinging down from his mare to wipe the mess from his axehead in the long grass at the edge of the track.

He walked over to the robber whose neck he had half severed and rolled him over with his foot. 'Dead already – most of his blood is on the ground.' As he checked that the other outlaw with the split head had also given up the ghost, the coroner slid from his saddle. He was suddenly aware that, contrary to his expectations, his damaged leg was still not quite restored to normal, especially when called upon to perform gymnastics upon a warhorse. He stroked Odin's neck and whispered into his ear, as the stallion was still quivering with excitement and exertion.

When his horse was calmer, John walked over to the body of the man he had felled with Odin's hoofs. He was lying face down and, expecting him to be unconscious or dead, he was surprised to see the fellow move as he approached. Futilely, he was trying to pull himself towards the trees on his hands, his legs trailing uselessly behind him, paralysed by his broken back.

After a few attempts, he sank hopelessly back to the dirt road, his face turned sideways towards de Wolfe, his hands beneath his body. As the coroner bent down to speak to him, he suddenly brought up his right hand and made a desperate attempt to stab upwards with the dagger he had drawn from his belt.

As de Wolfe stepped back in surprise, Gwyn, who had come across the road to join him, swore and began to pull out his sword but John put out a hand to stop him. 'Leave him be, Gwyn. He's going to die, anyway. Not much point in carrying him back to Exeter to be hanged.'

'He's an outlaw, Crowner, so he is as the wolf's head. Best kill him now, then I could claim the bounty.'

Anyone declared by the courts to be outside the law did not exist officially under the king's peace and any citizen was entitled to kill them on sight, as if they were a wolf. If the severed head was taken to the county gaol, a payment could be claimed from the sheriff as a reward for helping to rid the forests of the bands of armed robbers that plagued the countryside.

De Wolfe shook his head. 'I don't think it would be either legal or politic for a coroner or his officer to claim the wolf's head. And I would have to hold an inquest on it, anyway.' Gwyn, looking disappointed, indicated the two corpses. 'What about them? Will you hold inquests there?'

John considered for a moment. 'I see no point – we will never know their names nor be able to get presentment of Englishry. There are no witnesses except us and no one knows or cares what happened to them. Legally, they don't exist.' He turned to look down at the paralysed ruffian, whose head had fallen forward to press his face into the soil, in an attitude of final despair. De Wolfe wondered briefly what it would be like to know that death was soon inevitable. He was not an imaginative man and had only vague notions of the resurrection that the priests seemed to take for granted. Would he meet this robber in Heaven – or Hell? Would all the men who had ever lived be there? All the children, all the infants, all the unborn babes? It seemed an unlikely proposition, but he shrugged off this sudden introspection and bent down to speak to the doomed outlaw. 'What made you take to the forest, fellow? Are you a thief on the run – or an escaped sanctuary-seeker?'

Slowly the man lifted his head enough to turn it to face the coroner. 'Neither, damn you! I killed a man in fair fight, after he cheated me at dice in a tavern in Lyme. But the bailiffs gave false witness. The man I fought was cousin to a burgess and the court condemned me in five minutes.'

'So you escaped and ran for the woods?'

'My wife and my mother paid a bribe to the gaoler – it left them destitute and they lost their breadwinner, for I was an ironsmith. I've not seen them since – nor never will now.'

The story was too familiar to tug at anyone's heart-strings. The man was no more than twenty-five, by the looks of him, though he was filthy and dressed in little better than rags.

'What are we to do with him?' asked Gwyn, still fingering the hilt of his sword. 'It would be kinder to put him out of his misery, not leave him there in the road, paralysed with a broken back.'

While he was thinking of an answer, de Wolfe noticed that both their horses were wandering down the road, nibbling at choice clumps of new spring grass that were appearing along the verges. They both walked over to take their bridles and turn them to bring them back to the scene of the fight.

A sudden movement of the surviving outlaw drew their eyes back to him and they saw that he had solved the problem himself. The dagger that he had tried to stick in the coroner was lying near his outstretched hand. Seizing it in one hand, he used the other with one last despairing effort to lift himself off the road. Holding the knifepoint upwards against his breast, the hilt against the ground, he lurched downwards to force the sharp point into his heart. With a bubbling cry, which sounded almost like joy, he released himself from an intolerable life, dying in the dirt of the king's highway. Gwyn and his master stood holding their reins, their eyes meeting after they watched the last convulsive spasm of the body.

'That's settled that, then,' grunted Gwyn.

De Wolfe climbed on to Odin, his leg still giving him a twinge of pain. 'I'll call out the manor reeve from Ide when we pass through. He'll have to send someone to bury these corpses in the forest. They can't be left here to stink.'

Before riding off, he took one last look at the dead outlaw and again the fleeting thought came into his mind: where had the spirit of the man gone in the last few minutes? Was killing a man any different from sticking a pig? Or was there something extra that made a body, arms and legs into an ironsmith?

He cursed himself for foolishness – he must be getting old to start this wondering what secrets the grave held for him.

CHAPTER SEVEN

*In which Crowner John hears
much about Templars*

On his return to Exeter in the early evening, John rode straight up to Rougemont to see his brother-in law. Gwyn came into the city with him, instead of going to his dwelling in St Sidwell's, just outside the East Gate, as his wife and family were staying with her sister in Milk Street.

De Wolfe found Richard de Revelle in his official chamber in the keep, in discussion with the castle constable, Ralph Morin. A flask of wine was open on the table and the sheriff motioned John to fill himself a pewter goblet. It was a good red vintage from Aquitaine and the coroner relished taking something expensive from his notoriously mean brother-in-law. 'Our trip to the north produced nothing useful,' he began. 'The village of Appledore could barely raise a couple of rowing boats.'

De Revelle nodded languidly, as if already bored by the coroner's presence. 'I've already heard that from Ralph here, whose sergeant reported to him. I tell you, it's Lundy we should be looking at. They've harboured pirates for centuries.'

De Wolfe looked across at the constable, who stood

solidly in the centre of the chamber, his feet apart and his arms crossed as if he had grown out of the floor. His grizzled grey hair and matching forked beard, together with his chain-mail hauberk and massive sword, suggested that he had just stepped off a Norse longboat. 'Dressed for battle, Ralph?' he asked.

Morin grinned, his rough, weather-beaten cheeks wrinkling. 'No, John, there was no attack on the city today. I've been down at Bull Mead putting the garrison through some exercises. All these years of peace are turning them soft. We need a good war to sharpen them up.'

'We nearly had one a few months ago,' muttered de Wolfe, and there was an awkward silence in the room as the constable and the coroner avoided looking at the sheriff.

'Gabriel told me about the ride to the north coast,' said Morin, to cover the hiatus. 'He says there were no signs at all of any looted goods or ships that might have been involved in piracy.'

John nodded in agreement. 'That's right, though they might have concealed goods in any of a hundred barns around the countryside. But galleys with a bank of oars, as that young Breton described, can't easily be hidden out of sight.'

'There are scores of small coves and bays up there where a ship or two could be hidden off the beaten track,' objected Richard.

Morin grunted again. 'I'm no sailor, but that exposed coast gives no shelter except at known harbours.'

De Wolfe poured himself another brimming goblet of wine, ignoring a scowl from de Revelle. 'They may be from far away, of course,' he said, 'from Ireland, Brittany or Galicia in Spain. There have even been attacks from

Turks and Moors in the past. For centuries our Viking ancestors used to come from Scandinavia to terrorise the Severn Sea.'

'What about the Scilly Isles? The whole population down there seem to be robbers,' suggested Morin.

De Revelle poured himself some wine, taking the opportunity to move the flask as far as possible from his brother-in-law. 'Wherever they come from, they must have a base within striking distance – they can't stay at sea indefinitely. And they need somewhere to store their booty, so I still say Lundy is the place. Since the de Mariscos came there, there's been nothing but trouble – look at this business with the Templars.'

De Wolfe pricked up his ears at the mention of the Knights of the Cross. 'Is anything new happening over that matter?'

The sheriff shook his head. 'Not that I know of. But it's high time that that nest of vipers on the island was wiped out. If the king spent more time looking after his affairs at home, maybe something would be done about it.'

This time, the coroner suffered no awkward silence, but met the sheriff head on. 'Richard, forget any ideas about a new king doing a better job. Remember your own position in this – the king we have is the king we keep!'

Faced with this blunt warning, de Revelle reddened but left the sensitive subject of an absentee monarch and reverted to the problem of Lundy, which was within his jurisdiction of Devon. 'I will do something about it, never fear! Last year, my predecessor fined William de Marisco three hundred marks for failing to deliver up to the Templars – and I'll impose the same amercement this year!'

De Wolfe's lean face creased into a sardonic smile. 'For God's sake, what use is that? He ignored the fine last year and will ignore any you put upon him in the future. The only penalty de Marisco will heed is force of arms.'

Richard banged his empty goblet petulantly on the table. 'And that's damned difficult on an island like Lundy. Half the time, you can't get near the place because of the weather – and when it's calm, any invader can be seen coming from ten miles, unless there's a sea fog.'

De Wolfe became impatient with his brother-in-law. 'Make up your mind, Richard! The other day you said Lundy was none of your business. Now you claim you want to deal with de Marisco, so who has changed your mind? Then, in the same breath, you say it's impossible.'

The constable's deep voice asked a question. 'What's the story behind this Templar claim to the island? I know nothing of its history.'

The coroner perched himself on the corner of de Revelle's table. 'After the civil war between Stephen and Matilda, King Henry, back in 'fifty-five, declared that all royal lands granted away in Stephen's reign be handed back to the Crown – or so my knowledgeable clerk tells me. William de Marisco ignored this. It was rumoured that he was a bastard son of the first King Henry, so maybe he felt he had a better claim than anyone. But five years later the king granted the island to the Knights Templar as part of his contribution to their Order. Not that they needed any more possessions, they were so rich by then, but I suppose he wanted to keep in good favour with the Pope, who was partial to the Templars.'

'So what happened?'

'A party of Templars – knights, sergeants and servants – tried to take possession, but William prevented them from landing. They were lucky not to be drowned.'

'They tried several more times, but the same thing happened,' added the sheriff morosely. 'Then, instead, the Templars were given some land in Somerset belonging to the Mariscos, but they had to pay rent for it, so they still want to get their hands on the island.'

De Wolfe finished the last of the wine in his cup and stood up. 'But that doesn't solve our problem. Everyone knows that the Mariscos have carried on the old tradition of piracy from Lundy, but there's no evidence that this Bristol vessel was one of their victims.'

Richard de Revelle snorted. 'There's no evidence because we haven't looked in the right place yet!'

The coroner leaned his hands on the table to look de Revelle in the face. 'We? Since when have you rubbed your arse raw riding back and forth to Barnstaple and beyond? I've done it twice in the last week.'

Stung into a reaction that he later regretted, the sheriff then announced that he would lead a force there the very next week and ordered Ralph Morin to send a couple of men ahead to organise sea transport for two-score men-at-arms. 'As I declare this to be a foray on behalf of the king, send messages to de Grenville in Bideford and Oliver de Tracey in Barnstaple, that we need half a dozen knights from each to accompany our force.'

John's eyebrows climbed up his forehead when he heard his brother-in-law invoke the Lionheart as the reason for a somewhat rash expedition to Lundy. Knowing of de Revelle's crafty mind and his habitual duplicity, he decided the sheriff was trying to strengthen the fragile pardon he had been given by the royalist barons a couple of months ago. 'This I must see, Richard, so I'll come with you – there's sure to be deaths, so it will be fitting to have a coroner on hand!' he exclaimed, with a grin that was almost a leer.

'And if you're sending most of my soldiers, then I'll be with you as well,' boomed the constable. 'Let's hope that Exeter doesn't fall under siege while we're away, for the garrison will be down to a man and a boy!'

By the time they had finished discussing the details of travel and supplies, John could sense that de Revelle was already regretting his impetuous decision: he was no fighting man. A frustrated politician, he was best at delegating tasks, especially when it came to anything physical or dangerous. But it was too late now, the decision had been made, and his proclaimed admiration for the Templars was the main motive for his trying to gain their inheritance on Lundy – as well as some credit for himself in London and Winchester.

The meeting broke up and de Wolfe collected Odin from the inner bailey then jogged through the town to put his horse to rest in the farrier's stable. A quick look into his house showed that Matilda was out, and Mary appeared with the usual news that she had gone to an evening service at St Olave's. Declining the maid's offer to make him supper, the coroner trudged down to the Bush, feeling his leg stronger than ever, though it ached at the end of the day.

Nesta soon organised food for him and before long he was contentedly ploughing through a boiled knuckle of pork lying on a thick trencher of bread, a wooden bowl alongside filled with shredded onions fried in beef lard and a pile of boiled cabbage. It would soon be Lent and this might be one of the last meat meals he would taste for weeks – not even an egg was allowed by the strict adherents to the Faith, though many a fowl or joint disappeared in the solemn period before Easter, not all of it down secular gullets.

Half-way through his second quart of ale, Nesta left chivvying her maids to sit with him for a while. Between mouthfuls, he told her of the day's excitements, the transfer of Gilbert to his own manor, the outlaw's ambush and the proposed expedition to Lundy. The pert Welsh woman listened round-eyed as he described the fight with the trail-bastons, as highway robbers were often called. She sat clinging to his arm as he told of the rout that Gwyn and he had inflicted on the men, tendrils of her glossy red hair escaping from under her close-fitting linen helmet.

When he had demolished the meal, Nesta signalled to one of the maids to take away the gravy-soaked trencher – it would join the others from today's meals for Edwin to take to the beggars who clustered around the cathedral Close and Carfoix, the central junction of the main roads in the city. She brought him another pot of ale and also gave him a beaming smile, which earned her a kick on the ankle from her mistress.

'Brazen hussy, trying to give you the eye!' she snapped in mock jealousy, but John knew that she was fond of her girls and looked after them well, for both were orphans. As well as giving them a home, she guarded their morals until they could find husbands – unlike most town taverns, the serving wenches in the Bush were not part-time whores who paid a percentage of their earnings to the landlady.

He was giving an account of the proposition to land on Lundy next week – which caused Nesta anguish at the prospect of her man being either slain or drowned – when a huge figure came to hover over the table near the hearth. 'Gwyn! My favourite coroner's officer!' Nesta patted the bench alongside her and pushed de Wolfe along so that the ginger giant could sit down. With the two large men at either side, she looked like a robin between a raven and a red kite.

Almost before Gwyn could open his mouth, a quart jar of ale was banged in front of him by Edwin, whose leer was worsened by the whitened blind eye that was a legacy of the Irish wars. Nothing loath, he took a long swallow that sank the better part of a pint and wiped the back of his hand across his soaking moustache, before delivering his news to his impatient companions. 'There are Templars arrived in the city, crowner.'

This was about the last thing that de Wolfe had expected that evening. All along he had had a healthy scepticism about Gilbert de Ridefort's fears, and although the arrival of Cosimo of Modena lent some credence to his story, there were many other explanations for the abbot's mission. Was this new twist another coincidence, or was the Templar from Paris really a fugitive in danger of his freedom? He waited for his officer to enlarge on his story. He knew from long experience that it was futile to press him – Gwyn would speak when it suited him.

After some throat-clearing, another drink and a belch, he continued, 'I was in the aleshop at the corner of Curre Street just now, talking to a tanner I know. He said that he had seen a fine procession coming up from South Gate earlier in the day, three knights on destriers, with three squires behind and two packhorses led by a groom.'

'What was so fine about them?' demanded Nesta. 'There's nothing unusual about a few knights – they were probably on their way to their term of service at some castle.'

Gwyn picked up a crust of bread that the maid had left behind and stuffed it into his mouth. When he had chewed it sufficiently to speak, he carried on with his story. 'These men were in full chain-mail with aventails and helmets, as were their squires. They had swords but no lances nor shields, so there were no armorial emblems to identify them.'

'And no surcoats, presumably?' snapped the coroner. The long cloth garment worn over the mailed hauberk prevented the glint of metal signalling their approach and also kept off the sun, which might roast some-one inside a hauberk padded with a gambeson. It was also a convenient place to display the wearer's heraldic motif.

'No surcoats, so no red crosses of the Knights of Christ,' agreed Gwyn. 'But it seems they all had full beards and moustaches and cropped hair.'

'That's common enough, even though it may be against the present fashion,' objected Nesta.

The Cornishman grinned at her, though in deference to his master he avoided a playful pinch to her bottom. 'There was one sure way to find out, lady – ask! Though the knights and their squires ignored the common crowd in the street, one cheeky lad ran alongside the groom and asked him where they were going. He said to the priory of St Nicholas and added that they were Templars, come all the way from London in less than a week.'

Gwyn went back to his ale while de Wolfe digested this news.

'What in hell do they want here at this time?' he muttered. 'Is it just coincidence that Gilbert claims he's being hunted? And now this business of the Templar claim to Lundy.'

The thought suddenly came to him that perhaps his dear brother-in-law had been keeping something from him. His change of heart in his uncharacteristic willingness to mount a campaign to Lundy might not have been as spontaneous as it appeared. He turned to Gwyn, speaking over Nesta's head. 'In the morning, get yourself down to St Nicholas's and see what you can find out about them. If they are lodged in a priory, they must have a mandate from the Church for some purpose. The closest Templar land is near Tiverton, so whatever their business may be, it has to do with Exeter.'

'And perhaps to do with their fellow Templar, Gilbert de Ridefort,'said the officer ominously, putting into words what John already feared.

'Unless they are going to join our invasion of Lundy next week,' said the coroner sarcastically. 'But to know of that, they'd have to be necromancers, to read the thoughts of our noble sheriff a week in advance!' He paused. 'Unless that crafty bastard up in Rougemont knew they were coming.'

Though the next day was a Wednesday, the sixteenth day of March, de Wolfe was dragged unwillingly by Matilda to the morning mass in the nearby cathedral. 'Every Christian should attend mass at least once a day,' nagged Matilda, but she managed to force him to church only twice a month at most. He resented every minute they stood in the huge, draughty nave of the cathedral, listening to the distant gabbling of a junior priest, or else in the tiny church of St Olave, suffering the unctuous tones of the fat priest his wife so admired.

After the service, he walked up to the castle and waited in the clammy chamber under the keep for

Gwyn to return from the priory. He spent the time practising his Latin, mouthing the phrases written for him by Thomas. He was improving all the time, able to read better than he could write but making much more progress with his little clerk than he had previously under the tutelage of the cathedral priest.

Someone darkened the low doorway and, looking up, he saw that it was Thomas himself, his cheap shoes and hose spattered with mud for it had rained during the night. He had just ridden his pony the couple of miles from St James's Priory and was bursting to tell his news to his master. 'I stayed in the priory as you arranged, Crowner, and tried to find what brought Abbot Cosimo to Devon.' He crossed himself fervently as he mentioned the Italian's rank. 'I could discover little, except that he came from Paris some weeks ago and rode here via London, where he stayed in the New Temple near the Fleet river.'

'How did you find that out?' grunted de Wolfe, interrupting him.

'The priory stable-boy was talking to one of the guards the abbot brought with him. They were not very talkative, especially to me, but the priory servants seemed to get more out of them.'

'Are they also foreign, these guards?'

'No, they are English Normans, and I suspect they are also from the Temple in London, though they don't belong to the Order. They are more lowly servants.'

'We already knew he was from Paris and visited the Templar headquarters there – so what's your real news?'

'Yesterday he rode off on his fine mare, with the two men behind him. They are still away, they didn't come back last night.' Thomas shrugged his lopsided shoulder and looked more furtive than usual. 'After he'd left, I slipped into his cell and had a look around. They must mean to return, for some of his belongings were still there, including a writing-bag, like this.' He pulled forward his shabby satchel, in which he carried his quills, ink and parchments.

'And you got a good look inside it, I trust?'

The little clerk nodded vigorously. 'You said it was important, so I risked my immortal soul by searching the pouch of a papal nuncio, God forgive me.' Guiltily, he made the Sign of the Cross.

'And what did that tell you, my trusty spy?' demanded John.

'There was a letter there, dated about five months ago, from a Cardinal Galeazzo in Rome, giving Abbot Cosimo authority to seek out and report on any and all forms of heresy in France and neighbouring countries. And, also, there was a more recent missive, about six weeks old, from Hugh, Bishop of Auxerre, ordering him to pursue any renegades from the True Faith, wherever they may be found, even including the Isles of Britain.'

De Wolfe considered this for a moment. 'Did these parchments name any particular heretics or renegades?'

Thomas wiped a dew-drop from his thin nose with the back of his hand and sniffed. 'No, they were general directions to the nuncio – but this is typical of the Inquisition against the Cathars and Albigensians in the south-west parts of France.'

John knew next to nothing about heretics in France or anywhere else, but the fact that Cosimo of Modena's mandate seemed mainly to concern religious problems in southern France, where de Ridefort's expected fellow-fugitive came from, was yet another coincidence that was hard to swallow. 'Did anything else emerge from your delving through his belongings?'

Thomas wagged his head from side to side. 'No, that was all that was in his satchel, apart from a religious tract and some writing materials. But it is surely enough to prove that he is on a special mission to seek out heretics. The orders from both Rome and France come from persons of great ecclesiastical standing.' Thomas paused for a quick tapping of his forehead, chest and shoulders, then continued. 'Both letters had heavy seals, one with emblems of the Holy See and the other from Hugh of Auxerre, who is well known as the head of the Inquisition in France. So Abbot Cosimo is certainly not in Devon to enjoy the air and the scenery – he is on the prowl!'

De Wolfe relaxed his usual stern manner sufficiently to compliment his clerk on his efforts at espionage and Thomas glowed with the praise, which was all the more valuable because of its scarcity. His master sent him off to buy breakfast at one of the stalls in the outer ward, while he sat in his damp cubbyhole and pondered the significance of the information.

The appearance of a papal nuncio, charged with seeking out those who rebelled against the strict tenets of the Church of Rome gave credence to Gilbert de Ridefort's fears, about which until now de Wolfe had been very dubious. He had half suspected that the man suffered from some paranoid state of mind, maybe rooted in some personal wrong-doing he was trying to blame on the Templars, but unless the arm of coincidence was very long indeed, Abbot Cosimo's mission confirmed the story.

But what was the Italian priest intending to do? Was he here to persuade de Ridefort to see the errors of his ways and to take him back into the fold? Or was he here to denounce him to Bishop Henry Marshall – who was probably too concerned with his own affairs to worry about some foreign backslider? Or was the knight to be dragged back to the new Temple in London or even across the Channel to face the Inquisition in France? And how would that be achieved? A seasoned Templar warrior was no easy prey, even for the two strong-arm men that Cosimo had brought with him.

And what of this Bernardus de Blanchefort, who was allegedly on his way, like the Second Coming? Was the abbot here to trap him as well? Or maybe Bernardus was the prime quarry and de Ridefort was irrelevant.

And, anyway, what was this 'awful secret' about which de Ridefort made such oblique hints? All these questions and not a single answer made de Wolfe impatient for some action and, with a muttered curse, he stood up and promptly struck his head on the slimy stones of the low arched ceiling. His muttering turned into a bellow of profanity and, rubbing his scalp, he stepped out into the castle yard. Turning to look with loathing at the tiny cave his brother-in-law had foisted on him, de Wolfe decided that enough was enough: he would go back to his old chamber even if he had to be hauled up by a rope and tackle.

Striding across the mired bailey, dodged by passing men-at-arms, self-important clerks and porters pushing barrows, he made for the gatehouse, his grey cloak streaming out behind him in the cold wind. Within the guardroom, which lay just inside the raised portcullis, he found Gabriel yelling some admonishment at a young soldier, who scuttled away thankfully when the sergeant turned to greet the coroner. 'Good day, Crowner. I hear we're going back to the north again next week.'

'Yes, you had better pick some men who don't get seasick, if the sheriff is set on going to Lundy.' De Wolfe looked at the bottom of the staircase to his chamber. 'I fell down those damned steps last week, but my leg is much stronger now, after all the exercise. Stand behind me, Gabriel, and catch me if I collapse.'

With a somewhat apprehensive sergeant close behind, he began to climb the narrow, winding stairs. To the silent relief of both, he did far better than he expected and reached the top without so much as a stumble. As he pushed aside the sacking that did service as a door, he found Gwyn sitting in his accustomed place on a window-sill, eating bread and cheese with a pot of cider in his hand. He rose and pulled forward a rickety stool, the only furnishing in the office since the trestle had been taken below.

De Wolfe dropped heavily on to it, his back against the rough stones of the wall. The climb had taken more out of him than he expected, though his leg had held up well. 'Give me some of that bread and ale first, man, then tell me what's new.'

Gwyn handed him some victuals, then passed on to his master what he had learned of the three unknown knights who had arrived in the city the previous day. 'I toured the alehouses last night, seeking gossip, but apart from many people seeing them ride through the town, no one knew anything about them. Several had heard the groom say they were Templars, but we knew that already.'

'Nothing else?' asked de Wolfe. He knew that Gwyn often kept the best bits until last.

'This morning, I went into Bretayne and walked up to St Nicholas's.'

Bretayne was the poorest quarter of Exeter, named

after the Celtic Britons who had been pushed there when the Saxons took over the city centuries earlier. It was a slum of narrow lanes and miserable huts in the north-western corner of the walls, the small priory of St Nicholas lying at its edge.

'There was a farrier in the yard, shoeing a big war-horse, one almost the size of your old Bran,' continued Gwyn. 'It was no monk's nag and obviously belonged to one of the Templars. I got talking to the farrier and he said they needed the job done quickly, as they would be riding out of the city shortly. I asked him where and why, but he couldn't tell me.'

'Did he know the name of the horse's owner?'

Gwyn scratched his head. 'He did and it sounded familiar, though I can't place it in my mind. Not to put a face to.'

John valiantly concealed his impatience. 'The name?'

'Brian de Falaise – I remember it, for it's where William the Bastard came from.'

De Wolfe ignored the Conqueror's origins and concentrated on the name. 'There was such a Templar at Acre. A big heavy man.'

'That applies to many men – especially Templars!' observed Gwyn.

'What about the other two?' demanded the coroner.

His officer shook his head. 'No sign of any of them, and the farrier knew no more. I called to a monk who was hoeing the garden and asked him who his visitors were, but he told me to mind my own business, the miserable sod.' He swallowed the last of his cider. 'If you want more information, best send that evil little gnome of ours down there. He has a way with priests, with his Signs of the Cross and his Latin speech.'

De Wolfe agreed with him, and told him what Thomas had discovered in the other priory. 'If all else fails, I'll go up to St Nicholas's myself and ask these fellows why they're here. I can play the old Crusader act, if Brian de Falaise is one of them.'

Gwyn hauled himself to his feet, half filling the chamber. 'Well, they'll not be here all day, according to the farrier. He was told to return at curfew, to check the shoes on the other horses after their journey from London.'

De Wolfe rose with him and moved to the stair-head. 'I'll try to visit them tonight or tomorrow. Meanwhile, when that miserable clerk of ours returns from his breakfast, I'll send him to snoop around at St Nicholas's.' Pulling aside the sacking, he stood back to let the Cornishman through. 'You go ahead of me, Gwyn. If I fall arse over beak, then at least I'll land on you!'

That morning, fifteen miles away, John's sister was attending mass at the church in Stoke-in-Teignhead, as she had almost every day since she was a child. Although her ambition to become a nun had long since faded, she remained very devout, though this never affected her amiable and outgoing nature. Today she was accompanied by the tall, handsome guest at their manor, Gilbert de Ridefort.

It was her mother who had pressed him to go with Evelyn – Enyd herself was less conscientious in her church-going, thinking that twice a week was sufficient for her soul's welfare. She had an ulterior motive in sending him with her daughter: both women knew that there was more to de Ridefort than John had admitted. Though not in open conspiracy, they wished to wheedle as much of his story from him as possible and a sedate walk to and from the church, a quarter of a mile away, might be a good opportunity. Strangely, de Ridefort seemed rather reluctant to attend divine service, and as Evelyn sensed he enjoyed her pleasant company well enough, she had to conclude that it was the devotions themselves that were not attractive to him. This seemed strange for a Templar or even an ex-Templar, as he would have been accustomed to spending hours each day in church.

But Enyd's persuasive tongue vanquished his reluctance and, with a maidservant little older than a child trailing behind, they walked leisurely to the church of St Andrew, rebuilt in stone by Simon de Wolfe shortly before his death. On the way there, they talked of many things and Evelyn, listening to his tales of travel in France and the Holy Land, was captivated by his charm.

However, she had learned nothing new about his presence in Devon by the time they reached the church and she resolved to be more forthright on the way back. During the service, they stood before the chancel step, with the half-dozen villagers who were not at work placed respectfully behind the daughter of their manorial lord.

The portly and rather jolly parish priest rattled through the Office rather less quickly than usual as he sensed that Evelyn's guest was someone special, even though he had no idea that he was a former monk of the Temple. Evelyn watched de Ridefort covertly during the short service and noticed that though he went though the motions required of him it was with an almost mechanical familiarity, devoid of any apparent spiritual enthusiasm. His face remained set in a wooden expression, and his lips were unmoving where responses were called for during the ceremony. She felt that, though he was there in body, his mind was deliberately closed to the religious content of the service. At the church door, when the priest obsequiously ushered out the lady whose family was responsible for the easy living he enjoyed, Evelyn briefly introduced her guest as Sir Gilbert de Ridefort, but took him away before any further explanations were needed.

As they began to walk back, Gilbert was subdued at first, but she soon had him talking again. 'You seemed unimpressed by our priest's abilities, sir?'

He gave a rather sad smile at this. 'Your amiable cleric did all that was required of him. It is just that I have come to have so many doubts about the Faith he professes.'

John's sister suddenly felt she had tapped a vein that might satisfy her curiosity. 'I have heard that most men of God suffer crises of faith at some time.'

He laid a hand gently on her shoulder as they strolled down the churchyard path between the yew trees. 'This is not a crisis of *my* faith, but of the Faith itself,' he said enigmatically.

'I don't understand,' she said truthfully.

'Your brother told you that I am – or, rather, I was – a Knight of the Temple?'

She was puzzled at this oblique reply. 'Yes, but surely they have a faith stronger than most? You are the soldiers of Christ.'

De Ridefort smiled down at her as if humouring a child's belief in fairy-tales. 'The Templars are a strange Order. We are certainly strong guardians of the Faith, but perhaps we exist mainly to guard it from criticism and enquiry.'

Evelyn raised her face to look into his face. 'Are you

suggesting that our faith needs such protection from doubts?'

At the gate, he turned and looked back. The few villagers from the congregation were talking to the priest at the church door and no one was within earshot. 'Yes, it has been so protected for many years. Rome is a jealous and powerful guardian, which suffers no competition. A thousand years ago, St Paul took Christianity away from its origins and transplanted it into that city. But there were other branches of Christianity, in Palestine, Egypt and elsewhere, gnostics who would not accept the rigid doctrines of Rome.'

This was bewildering to Evelyn, who had known nothing other than conforming to the unyielding despotism of the Church and was almost unaware that any other view could exist. 'Are you speaking of heretics?' she asked, almost in a whisper.

Gilbert took her arm and they walked on slowly, the young girl trailing behind them, more interested in the spring flowers by the wayside, than the unintelligible conversation of her elders. 'Heretics? That's a wide and varied description. You had your own heresy here in these isles, centuries ago, when Pelagius claimed free will and free thinking for all men. And now, especially in southern France, there are the Cathars, the Albigensians who desire to pursue their faith in their own way – a way that I fear will soon bring down the wrath of Rome upon them, with disastrous results.'

Evelyn felt a flutter of alarm in her breast and, like Thomas de Peyne, an irrational desire to cross herself. Was this man, with his hand upon her arm, a dangerous heretic, an anti-Christ?

But she had a strong will and decided to take the bull by the horns. 'What has that to do with the Templars

– and with you coming so far away to Devon, after leaving the Order? I thought that being a Templar was for life.'

'It should be, Evelyn. But I and few others have seen traces and fragments of a different truth that we were not supposed even to suspect. When the Order was founded early in this century, something had been discovered in Jerusalem that had to be suppressed at all costs. I am not privy to the whole story, which is known only to the Grand Master and to a few cardinals in Rome. It is not clear whether the first Templars actually found this secret or whether they were rapidly established by the Order of Sion to investigate further and then conceal something that had already been discovered.'

Evelyn was bewildered. 'Are you saying that you are now a fugitive because you came into possession of forbidden knowledge, even within your own community?'

'Exactly that – and they fear that I and those with me will divulge this intelligence to the world.' A gleam came into his eye and his voice quivered a little – so she thought he might be a little crazy.

'How did the early Templars come by this secret? And what is it, anyway?' she asked, almost fearful that the answer would provoke a thunderbolt from the skies.

His face twisted into a grimace of pain, as mortification and indecision racked him. 'I am torn between my vows of obedience and the right of all men to have a free mind, untrammelled by blind faith. Part of me is seized in the grip of the rigid dictates drummed into me since childhood, yet increasingly I see the merits of the gnostic way of thought – as do many other Templars in France, who are sympathetic to the Cathars. I should have the courage to tell the world the truth – and yet I am afraid.'

Evelyn began to feel that his responses to her questions took her further away from any real understanding. 'But what did they find, these first Templars?' she persisted.

'They were given part of the palace built over the ruins of the Temple of Solomon, destroyed by the Romans when they dispersed the Jews. The first few spent several years excavating further in the underground passages that were said to have been Herod's stables – and what they found there they transported back to southern France, in conditions of the greatest secrecy. Nine years after their foundation, the original nine Templars returned to France for good.'

Again he had managed to answer her without imparting any relevant information, so she tried again. 'Southern France seems to feature greatly in all this, sir,' she observed. 'That is where these Cathars you speak of live – and where this Templar friend you are awaiting has his estates. I once heard from an indiscreet monk that there was even a theory that Joseph of Arimathea and Mary Magdalen visited the area after the death of our Saviour, as it was a haven for many Jews fleeing from the Holy Land.'

De Ridefort gave a dry laugh. 'Visited? She did more than that! She came to live there, bearing the Grail within her! The Languedoc is the new Holy Land, which makes it all the more tragic that nemesis will before long fall upon thousands of those who live there.'

She still failed to follow his leap-frogging replies, but as they neared the entrance to the manor-house bailey, Evelyn made one last effort. 'But how could something taken from the foundations of a temple possibly rock the foundations of our Holy Church?' she asked in trepidation.

De Ridefort took his hand from her arm to point backwards towards the little church. 'What did we just do during the Mass?' he asked sternly. 'We partook of the body and blood of the resurrected Christ, the ceremony that is the core, the very heart of the Holy Roman Church. If that most sacred belief is shattered, then the thousand years since Paul made Rome the centre of the Christian universe crumbles into dust.'

They turned into the gateway and Evelyn, uneasy almost to the point of being frightened by this strange, enigmatic man, slipped away to report to her mother.

CHAPTER EIGHT

In which Crowner John hears some awful news

Next morning, Thursday the seventeenth day of March, was cold and blustery. Yesterday's promise of spring had been a mockery, typical of the western parts of the Isles of Britain.

Odin was having his hoofs checked in the farrier's forge, so after an early bowl of hot broth with bread, de Wolfe went up to the castle on foot. A gusting west wind whipped at his worn cloak and threw occasional spots of rain at his face as he loped up to Rougemont. The covers over the street stalls rattled against their frames, the pedlars and tradesmen huddling inside their mantles and capes as they waited for their customers to brave the elements.

As he walked, he welcomed the absence of complaint from his leg, which now seemed virtually back to normal, both in strength and lack of the nagging ache that had been there for so many weeks. He ruminated on the previous evening, when he had spent a dull, but uncontroversial few hours with his wife, in front of their hearth. For once, she had no religious devotions to attend and they ate their supper in relative peace. He had no desire to go down to the Bush as he knew that Nesta was attending some meeting of Exeter inn-keepers at the Guildhall, to discuss the rising cost of barley and its effect on their ale prices. Since the poor harvest of the previous year, and the huge demand for grain made by the king to supply his army in France, the price of many staple foods was increasing. This added to the disgruntlement of the already overtaxed population, which de Wolfe feared might encourage Prince John to start plotting again against his absentee royal brother.

The rising cost of living was one of the topics of a rather stilted conversation between Matilda and himself, as they sat in front of the fire after their meal. He opened a jar of wine and, under its influence, they relaxed a little – lately, Matilda had seemed increasingly partial to a few drinks. The talk inevitably turned to Gilbert de Ridefort and John had told his wife of the discoveries of Thomas about Abbot Cosimo and the arrival of the three Templars the previous day. She appeared genuinely concerned for the knight's safety and had admitted grudgingly that de Wolfe had been right in hiding him away down in Stoke-in-Teignhead. Not only that, but she added some information of her own, gleaned that day from the inquisitive parishioners of St Olave's, which was within a few hundred paces of the priory of St Nicholas.

'You say that one of the knights was Brian de Falaise,' she said, 'and I was told that the others are called Godfrey Capra and Roland de Ver.'

John had never heard of this last knight, but he had a slight recollection of Godfrey Capra, who had been at the big meeting in Gisors. This was the so-called 'Splitting of the Elm', which seemed to have had some profound effect on the organisation of the Templars and at which Gilbert de Ridefort had also been present, something John could not now believe was a mere coincidence.

Now, as he walked up the last few yards to the gatehouse of Rougemont, de Wolfe sighed as he failed to put all these diverse bits of information into some sort of pattern. It was clear that he would have to make a frontal attack on these Templars, to try to discover what had really brought them to Exeter. He turned into the guardroom, but instead of tempting fate with another assault on the winding staircase, he put his head into the lower entrance and yelled up to attract Gwyn's attention. There was an answering bellow from above and his officer came clumping down, followed by Thomas de Peyne.

'We have to attend this week's mutilations at the eighth hour,' he told them. 'Thomas, did the sheriff's clerk give you a list?'

The bent little clerk scrabbled in his shapeless satchel and pulled out a scrap of parchment, which he consulted. 'There are three, Crowner, and you have to take a confession from one.'

De Wolfe frowned. 'A confession? Why?'

'It seems he also wants to turn approver, to save his neck, if not his right hand.' An approver was a criminal who wished to save his life by informing on his accomplices, when he might be allowed to avoid the death sentence, perhaps abjure the realm or even be set free altogether.

The coroner grunted and led the way across the inner ward towards the basement of the keep, which was half below ground. This dark, damp undercroft was part-prison, part-storehouse and part-torture-chamber, ruled by Stigand, a grotesquely fat gaoler with the intelligence of a woodlouse. Half the crypt was divided off by a stone wall, in which a rusted iron gate led into a passage lined with filthy cells. The rest was open space, dimly lit by the light from the small doorway and a few rush-lights on the walls. It was floored by wet earth and in one corner, Stigand lived in an alcove, sleeping on a straw mattress. Outside this was a fire-pit, which served both for his primitive cooking and for heating branding irons and other instruments of torture. At the moment, an iron pot of wood-tar, obtained from charcoal-burning, was bubbling ominously on the logs.

As the coroner's trio came down the few steps from the level of the inner bailey, a dismal procession emerged from the iron gate of the gaol. Led by Gabriel and a man-at-arms, three prisoners, dressed in rags and wearing heavy wrist and ankle fetters, stumbled across the uneven floor, prodded along by two more soldiers. Stigand locked the gate behind them, then waddled across to his fire, where a low bench held a selection of implements. Already in the centre of the cellar stood a small group of observers, including a priest from the garrison chapel of St Mary, in case one of the prisoners should die during the proceedings. The others were Ralph Morin, the castle constable, Henry Rifford, one of Exeter's two portreeves, and Sheriff Richard de Revelle, with one of his clerks from the County Court, which had convicted the miscreants.

The soldiers pushed and dragged the three men into a line facing the officials, so that the clerk, a portly man with over-inflated ideas of his own importance, could begin reading out the details of the sentences.

'Firstly, Robert Thebaud, butcher from this city, you are convicted of repeatedly and perversely giving short weight and of having manifestly tampered with your weighing scales to your own advantage.' He turned over a leaf of parchment and referred to some earlier record. 'You were fined ten marks by the burgess court of this city on the eighth day of June last year. And you were warned then that a second offence would lead to hanging or mutilation.'

The sheriff, resplendent in a short cloak in his favourite green thrown carelessly over one shoulder, waved a glove at the clerk. 'Is anything else known about this villain?'

Rifford, a paunchy, middle-aged man with a short neck and prominent eyes, was the portreeve representing the burgesses and guilds. He pointed an accusing finger at the wretched Robert, a burly man with a normally florid face that was now pale with fear. 'He was warned by the Butchers' Guild last year that if he transgressed again he would be ejected and no longer able to continue his trade in this city. That will happen now, though in any case, he'll be in no condition to fell cattle and chop meat with one hand!'

Thebaud fell to his knees and began to blubber for mercy, but no one took any notice of him: they were too familiar with such supplications from the condemned.

The clerk moved on to the second case, a sullen young Saxon with yellow hair hanging down his back. 'Britric of Totnes, you were apprehended in the Serge Market trying to pass off clipped short-cross pennies. In your lodgings, the city bailiff found a bag of clippings and iron shears for trimming the coins.'

The irregular silver pennies were of many types as some had been in circulation for a century or more from different mints around the country. Clipping the edges and melting down the silver for its value was a common but serious crime. Most coins had a cross on one side, and in later mintings, the arms of the cross were made longer, reaching to the edge in an effort to make clipping more obvious. Counterfeiting money was a hanging offence, but passing clipped coins was almost as heinous.

Britric seemed unmoved by this accusation and the clerk moved on to the last culprit, a shifty-looking youth with crooked, projecting teeth. 'William Pagnell, you were convicted of associating with known thieves who haunted the fair of St Jude two weeks ago. Three other men made off with goods to at least the value of five marks from various booths, but you were the only one caught. As the stolen goods, a candlestick found on your person, was of the value of only ninepence, you have avoided hanging on that charge.'

The clerk's droning voice was interrupted by the coroner. 'Is this the fellow who wants to turn approver?'

'Yes, Crowner. If the others are caught and confirm that this Pagnell was equally one of them, then they may all hang, whether he has his hand struck off now or not.'

Pagnell joined his fellow prisoner on his knees in the damp earth, his chains rattling as he wagged his clasped hands in supplication to de Wolfe. 'Sir Crowner, I wish to confess my small guilt and earn your mercy by confessing the names of these other men who led me astray,' he whined.

The distant bell of the cathedral tolled faintly in the distance and Richard de Revelle slapped his gloves in impatience. 'Come on, clerk, get on with it. I have more important work to do.'

The pompous official turned to the coroner with a questioning look. 'Will you accept him as an approver, Crowner?'

'Yes, if it means that by his confession we can catch the greater thieves,' he grunted.

Pagnell gabbled his thanks then ventured a little further. 'And if I confess every syllable I know and make promises in the name of the Holy Mother and every saint never to trangress again, may I keep my limb? Without it, I and my family will starve, for I am a wood-carver. I have had no work for two months and I only took that trinket to buy bread for my children.'

Richard de Revelle gave an exasperated snort. 'Every evil wretch that comes here spins the same lying excuses and promises to reform, only to steal or slay the moment he is released.'

As much to confound and aggravate his brother-in-law as from any feeling of compassion, de Wolfe gestured at the guards and the gaoler. 'Take him back to his cell. I'll hear his confession and then decide on what is to be done with him.'

'What right have you to interfere with the decision of my County Court, Crowner?' snapped the sheriff.

'The duty to take confessions of approvers was laid on me by the Article of Assize last year,' retorted de Wolfe, glaring across at de Revelle. 'And maybe you remember that that Article was promulgated by the royal justices – the judges of our lord king!'

With a barely concealed grin at his master's loss of face, Gabriel gave the order for one of the guards to take the prisoner away and when Stigand had slouched back to stand near his fire, the grisly proceedings went ahead. They were rapid and efficient, with none of the ceremony that attended an execution. Two men-at-arms grabbed the blond Saxon and one unlocked his arm fetters with a crude iron key. The obese gaoler rolled a large log across the floor, stained an ominous ruddy-brown, and set it on end to form a block about two feet high. The victim was forced to his knees, Stigand grabbed his right hand and pulled it across the block. Reaching for a cleaver, he spat upon the blade and sent it whistling down to sever the wrist with one blow.

In spite of his previous impassive mien, Britric gave a high-pitched scream and fainted as the arteries in his arm spurted across the block, the hand falling to the muddy floor. Wheezing with the effort of delivering the blow, the gaoler pulled a rag from the wide pocket of his soiled leather apron and slapped it over the end of the wrist to staunch the haemorrhage temporarily. The Saxon had fallen to the floor, but one of the soldiers held up his arm, whilst Stigand turned to the pot of tar on the fire. He stirred it with a piece of stick, which he then used to lift a large dollop of the sticky brown mess. Pulling away the cloth, he slapped the tar on the raw flesh and bare bone ends, spreading it over the stump, where it rapidly set solid as it cooled. Then he picked up the hand nonchalantly by its thumb and threw it on to his fire where, as it hissed and blackened, the fingers contracted to form one last agonal fist.

The official party watched all this indifferently, with the exception of Thomas de Peyne, who although he had seen it many times since entering the coroner's service, still felt nauseated at the sight of blood and the severed hand being so casually treated.

Two soldiers dragged Britric back through the iron gate and came back to repeat the performance on the whimpering butcher, Robert Thebaud, who began screaming as his chains were released and did not stop until he was hauled back to his cell.

Anxious to be off to his chamber, Richard de Revelle

started for the doorway but, almost as an afterthought, turned to speak to de Wolfe. 'The expedition to Lundy is arranged for Monday, John. We shall leave at dawn and hope to get to Barnstaple that night.' With a last flourish of his gloves, he vanished about his business, with his constable following reluctantly behind, leaving the coroner to enter the gaol, where the thief's confession could hardly be heard above the screams and moans of the two mutilated men.

An hour later, de Wolfe made the climb up to his chamber in the gatehouse and joined Gwyn and Thomas in their customary bread, cheese and cider.

Thomas had nothing new to report about the Italian abbot from his eavesdropping in the cathedral precinct. Cosimo had not visited the bishop again and he had no means of knowing if he had yet returned to St James's Priory.

'What about you, Gwyn?' growled de Wolfe. 'Did the taverns provide any more news than the cathedral?'

Before replying, his officer peeled a strip of hard green rind from his cheese with his dagger. 'Not a lot, Crowner. You said your wife already told you the names of these other two Templars. I went to a couple of low alehouses in Bretayne last night and spoke to an ostler and a porter from St Nicholas's. It seems the leader of the three is this Roland de Ver, who comes from the New Temple in London, though before that he was in Paris. He has reddish hair and beard, says the porter, but little else is known of him.'

'What of the others? One is that Godfrey Capra, whom we saw at Gisors when the great aggravation took place between Prince Richard and that bastard French king!'

'I just recall him. He was a thin, dark fellow, with a sour face. He was born in Kent, I was told – he never went to Palestine with us.' He bit off a chunk of his rock-hard cheese and champed on it. 'The other one we both know of is this Brian de Falaise. The ostler said he also came from the Templar Commandery in London, though he is really from Normandy.'

Thomas had been listening quietly to this from his stool at the table, where he was writing out a précis of the approver's confession that John had so recently heard in Stigand's foul prison. 'When I was in Winchester, there was a priest in the train of the Bishop of Rouen who had been at Gisors at this meeting in 'eighty-eight that you keep talking about. He told me that though it was mainly a political wrangling between old King Henry and Philip of France, something else went on there that affected the Templars.'

'Do you know what it was, dwarf?' grunted the Cornishman.

Thomas's lazy eye slewed from the coroner to his officer. 'It seems that when the Templars were founded, they were really controlled by some obscure religious organisation in Jerusalem called the Order of Sion. It was supposed to have been founded by Godfrey de Bouillon several years before he captured the Holy City from the Saracens. He then installed the Order in the abbey of Notre Dame de Mont Sion, just outside the city walls.'

'What in Hell has this got to do with Gisors?' demanded Gwyn irreverently.

'At that meeting there in 'eighty-eight, at which you were present, the Order of Sion fell out with the Grand Master of the Templars so that they each went their own way after that, the Order changing its name to the Priory of Sion.'

The little clerk paused to give emphasis to his dénouement.

'The point is that the so-called "Splitting of the Elm" is really a cryptic reference to the final schism between the Order and the Templars and is nothing to to do with that silly squabble of whether the English or French sat in the shade of the tree. And what might matter to your current problem with Gilbert de Ridefort is that the meeting at Gisors was only a matter of months after his uncle, Gerard de Ridefort, lost Jerusalem again to the Muhammadans, in what some called treasonable incompetence!'

This was all beyond Gwyn of Polruan, who went back to his bread and cheese in disgust, but de Wolfe pondered Thomas's words for a while. 'So in Exeter now we have a priest from Paris associated with the Inquisition, a senior Templar from the Paris Preceptory and a Templar who was at Gisors – all of whom arrived within days of the nephew of a disgraced Grand Master!'

At the coroner's words, the clerk lifted his humped shoulders and gave his master a leer to show that he believed that these events were inescapably linked.

'The sooner we get rid of this errant knight, the better!' growled the coroner. 'But he won't go until this other fellow de Blanchefort joins him.'

Gwyn finished his food and took a giant swig from his cider pot. After a gargantuan belch, he wiped his moustache and spoke. 'At least it's not crowner's business,' he said, with no notion of how soon he was to be proved wrong.

The cathedral bell was tolling for the terce, sext and

nones services when de Wolfe got back to Martin's Lane to see how the farrier was getting on. At the livery stable he found Odin tethered by a head-rope to a ring in the wall. The large stallion was contentedly munching oats from a leather bucket; his hoofs had been trimmed and a few loose nails fixed back into his shoes.

The coroner began a conversation with Andrew, the young farrier, and they were deep in discussion about rival types of battle-harness when a figure hurried across from de Wolfe's front door. It was Mary, her fair hair flying loose from under her cap, the strings of which were untied in her haste. 'Sir John, come quickly! The mistress is in a terrible state – Alsi, the steward from Stoke, is here.'

As he followed her hurriedly across the lane, she explained that she had not known he was at the stables and had already sent Simon up to Rougemont to look for him.

Inside the hall, Matilda was sitting in one of the monk's chairs, bent forward and sobbing uncontrollably, whilst Alsi was hovering over her helplessly.

'What in the name of God is the matter?' said John, going to his wife and laying a hand gently on her shoulder. 'Has something befallen my mother?'

Instantly, Matilda stopped her keening and jerked up her head to glare at him. 'It's all your fault, you heartless man!' she yelled, getting up on her stocky legs and beating her hands against his chest.

Her husband pushed her down on to her chair and she subsided into sobs again. He turned to the steward, a man he had known since childhood. 'Alsi, what's going on? Why are you here?'

The thin, greying Saxon, still in his riding clothes, raised his hands in supplication. 'I should have found

you first, Sir John, and told you before Lady Matilda.
I am mortified to have caused her this distress, but I
didn't know it would affect her so profoundly.'

'What, man? What's happened?'

'Your guest at Stoke, Sir Gilbert. He's dead – murdered!'

Though violent death had been part of de Wolfe's
life for more than two decades, both as a soldier and
now a coroner, this news was particularly shocking.
De Ridefort's fears, and the increasing confirmation
that they might be well founded, had climaxed in
tragedy.

With Matilda still rocking herself whilst she moaned
her grief for her lost hero, John dropped heavily into
the other chair and stared up at the steward. 'When did
this happen – and how?'

Alsi fiddled agitatedly at the large clasp that held his
heavy brown riding cloak in place. 'He went out for a
ride late yesterday afternoon, Sir John. He fretted that
he was tired of skulking indoors, so he borrowed a mare
from the stables and rode off, saying that he would stay
within the manor lands. But towards dusk when he had
not returned your mother sent some stablemen out to
search for him, in case he was lost in the woods between
Stoke and the river.' He paused and gave a trembling
sigh. 'Just before dark, they found him – or, at least,
they first found the mare wandering. Then, within a few
hundred paces, just inside the tree-line on the banks of
the river, they discovered him lying dead on the ground
with blood upon him.'

'Could he not have fallen from his horse, or struck a
low branch?' As he uttered the words, de Wolfe knew
they sounded futile: any Templar knight, especially one
who had fought in Outremer, would hardly let himself

fall to his death on a gentle afternoon trot.

Alsi soon confirmed this. 'It was no accident, as you will see when you look at his wounds. He was deliberately slain, sir – and in a most bizarre manner.'

chapter nine

In which Crowner John is referred to the Gospels

'Even though he was your friend and a guest, John, you are still the coroner and I thought we had better observe the rules. We left the body where it lay.' William de Wolfe spoke sadly, conscious that a man who had been left at his house for safety had ended up dead within two days.

His brother tried to reassure him that he need feel no guilt over the tragedy. 'He should not have ventured out alone, especially in a place that was strange to him, William. In Exeter he was more than nervous, but he seems to have assumed that the wilds of the countryside held no risk.'

They were trotting their steeds along the track that led from the manor-house towards the river Teign, with Gwyn, Thomas, Alsi, a reeve and two grooms from Stoke following behind. De Wolfe had left Exeter as soon as he managed to calm Matilda, who blamed him incessantly for not ensuring that de Ridefort was guarded night and day. He suspected that she was using the tragedy partly as a weapon to accuse his family of being negligent in failing to protect de Ridefort.

Simon had brought Gwyn and Thomas down from Rougemont to the house in Martin's Lane and within an hour they were on the road to Stoke-in-Teignhead, covering the sixteen miles in four hours, having to wait a little for the tide at the ford at Teignmouth. Arriving in the afternoon, they rode straight to the scene of the death, which was guarded by two of the village freemen, set there the previous night by William. 'I sent our steward as messenger to Exeter, rather than a bailiff as you say the law demands,' explained his brother, as they rode. 'He set out a few hours before dawn with one of the ostlers, going by the inland road as we knew the tide would be high then. There seemed no point in raising a hue and cry in the middle of a forest at nightfall.'

John agreed. 'Neither do we need to seek present-ment at the inquest I'm bound to hold – his identity as a Norman is obvious. My concern is how he came to his death.'

'I feel responsible in great measure, whatever you say, John. I should have insisted that someone went with him, but I did not even know he was gone. I was selling sheep in Kingsteignton when he left.'

'At what time was he found, brother?'

'The light was fading, so it must have been after the sixth hour at this time of year. If the mare had not been seen, I doubt we would have discovered the body until this morning at the earliest, as he is hidden from view.'

When they arrived at the scene de Wolfe saw why this was true. A bridlepath split from the track alongside the Arch brook, which ran through low hills from Stoke to the river. It struck through the woods towards Coombe then turned to the water's edge. There was dense woodland all along the banks of the river, which was wide and tidal for about two miles upstream from the ford at Teignmouth. After some rank grass and bushes above highwater mark, the trees began abruptly and were thickest at the forest edge where there was plenty of sunlight. Less than fifty paces from the bridlepath, and a similar distance from the edge of the trees, Gilbert's body lay in a small clearing, where a large beech had fallen in a storm.

'He is just as we found him, though we covered him with a cloak as a mark of respect,' said William sombrely, as they all slid from their mounts at the edge of the clearing. The two freemen had been sitting on the fallen trunk and now rose expectantly at the arrival of their lords.

The coroner, his brother and Gwyn walked forward to the spot where a still figure lay under a riding cloak. Thomas hung back with the servants for a moment, then plucked up courage to edge nearer.

One of the socmen lifted the cloak and they saw that de Ridefort lay face down on the weeds between two scrubby elder bushes that had colonised the gap in the tall trees. The undergrowth was beaten down in a circle around the body and two tracks radiated away from it through the new spring grass into the trees. Dark blood was congealed on the leaves immediately to one side of the body and, though the face was hidden in vegetation, more blood was spattered in front of the head.

Before they touched the cadaver, Gwyn and his master stared carefully around the tiny clearing. 'There's been no horses in here. Whatever was done was carried out on foot,' declared Gwyn.

'There are many hoofmarks in the mud inside the trees, leading from the bridlepath,' volunteered one of the guardians of the body, pointing away to one side.

'He's fully clothed, though he has no mantle in this cold weather,' observed de Wolfe.

'That was his own cloak we threw over him, Crowner,' said the same freeman. 'It was lying twenty paces away, towards the mess of hoofmarks.'

De Wolfe dropped to one knee alongside the corpse. He realised what a tall man de Ridefort had been, as he lay stretched full length on the ground.

A quick inspection at close quarters soon dispelled any lingering hope that this had been some accident, for the knight's over-tunic of dark red wool was rent along a four-inch line just above his belt on the left side. The cloth was soaked in blood all around it, though because of the colour of the material, it had not been obvious from a distance.

'There seems no other body wound than this at first sight,' reported de Wolfe, 'But he has had a blow upon the head.' He could feel a swelling at the back of the cranium, and when he parted the hair, there was a large discoloured graze on the scalp.

'What about the blood near his face?' asked William, his face pale with the unaccustomed proximity of violent death. He was a farmer, not a man of action, and these things disturbed him more than most.

'That almost certainly came from him coughing blood – it is pinker and more frothy than the dark flow from his side. That means the wound in his chest was inflicted while he was still alive and has penetrated his lights.'

'Though he may have been without his wits from the blow on the head,' reasoned Gwyn.

The coroner rose and motioned to his officer to turn the dead man over on to his back. The handsome face was red-purple in death, except for pallor of the nose and chin.

William stared in horror. 'His face is blue! Has he been strangled as well?'

His brother shook his head. 'That is merely blood settling after death – the white nose and chin are where the face lay hard against the ground.'

The eyes were closed, but from the mouth a trickle of frothy blood emerged. Gilbert's hands had been out-stretched before his head when he was on the ground, but now that his body was turned, they stuck stiffly upwards in a grotesque parody of supplication.

'Ah, I was wrong about there being no other injuries!' exclaimed the coroner. He grasped one of the wrists to examine the hand. 'He's stiff, yet that is to be expected if he died last night. But look at these!' He pointed with a long forefinger at the palm of each hand, where there was a ragged wound in the centre that did not penetrate to the back. With Gwyn's aid, he removed de Ridefort's belt, which carried a sheathed dagger, and pulled up the over-tunic and tunic to expose the skin beneath. He rubbed away much of the smeared blood on the skin to expose a clean vertical incision slicing across the rib margin in the line of the armpit, just above the waist.

Thomas had been edging forward, forcing himself to look at the body, his left hand over his mouth to contain his revulsion. After staring at the exposed wounds, he crossed himself rapidly and gabbled in Latin.

'For God's sake, hold your tongue!' snapped Gwyn. 'What are you babbling about?'

'The Blessed Gospel of St John, chapter nineteen!' squeaked the clerk.

De Wolfe stared at him. 'What the devil do you mean?'

'The spear wound in the side – and the marks on the palms!' he said, in a melodramatic hiss.

William, who was a more ardent churchgoer than his brother, nodded vigorously. 'The crucifixion – the final spear in the side and the marks of the nails in the hands!'

John's gaze dropped from William to Thomas with dawning understanding. 'Are you suggesting that he was crucified?'

Gwyn, for all his antagonism to religion, bent to examine the feet of the corpse. The dead man wore calf-length riding boots, but there was no sign of any damage to the leather. To make sure, he pulled them off, together with the long woollen hose. 'Nothing on the feet – and the marks on his hands do not come right through,' he objected.

Thomas glared up at him indignantly. 'It's symbolic, you ginger oaf!' His tremulous excitement made him bold enough to insult his colleague.

The coroner wiped the blood from his fingers on the grass and stood up. 'We can do nothing more here. Have the body taken back to the church in Stoke where he may lie decently, until I can examine him more closely.'

As they walked away from the body, de Wolfe said that he would have to open an inquest that afternoon and ride back to Exeter at first light in the morning. 'There are people there I must see urgently. Beginning with a clutch of Templars and an Italian priest.'

It was a melancholy procession that made the journey from Stoke-in-Teignhead to Exeter the next day. De Wolfe had held a perfunctory inquest the previous afternoon, Thomas writing down the details of the men who had found the body and a brief account of its injuries. The blow on the head might have been inflicted by any blunt object, from the flat of a broadsword to a piece of timber. The wound in the side was clean and deep and might have been made either by a sharp-pointed sword or a spear. The ragged, somewhat superficial wounds in each hand had been caused by the point of a knife being turned in the flesh, these being the sum of the injuries. The bleeding from the mouth was attributed by de Wolfe to a deep puncture of the left lung, and there was nothing else to discover.

'Could not the cuts in the hands be due to the poor man trying to defend himself?' suggested William afterwards. De Wolfe had discounted this, as they were unlike the usual defence wounds and were identical on right and left palms. They had decided to take the body back to Exeter, rather than have it buried in the church of St Andrew at Stoke. De Wolfe's stated motive was that a Templar knight should lie at least for a time in a cathedral and preferably be buried there, if there was no Templar church within reach – but he had an ulterior motive, which he kept to himself for the time being. As an ox-cart would have severely delayed their journey back to the city, he decided to have the body wrapped in hessian and slung across the back of a sumpter horse led on a head-rope by Gwyn.

The journey back took five hours, de Wolfe being unsure which was the slowest, the gelding with the corpse or Thomas side-saddle on his pony. When they reached Exeter in the early afternoon, he prevailed upon his friend the archdeacon to accept the body and have it laid before one of the side altars in the base of the cathedral's north tower. He was careful not to describe or expose the strange injuries on Gilbert's corpse, in case John de Alençon probed more deeply into the matter and refused to accept a possible religious renegade with blasphemous wounds.

Matilda was not at home and Mary told him that she had spent almost all day praying in St Olave's for the soul of Gilbert de Ridefort. De Wolfe left his house and, with Gwyn at his side, strode through the streets to the priory of St Nicholas.

'We're in luck this time,' exclaimed Gwyn, as they walked through the archway into the small courtyard. Three superb horses were tethered there, attended by the priory grooms.

De Wolfe looked at the large stallions, which were almost as big as destriers. 'You can see that the Templars are never short of money!' he observed cynically.

A porter appeared from the gate lodge and directed them to the guest rooms, a small extension from the little priory at the end of the courtyard. These were just a few cells opening off a narrow corridor, with a larger common room at one end. Knocking on the open door, the coroner found the three knights sitting on benches around an open fire. They looked up questioningly, as he introduced himself. 'I am John de Wolfe, the king's coroner for this county. I believe that I have met two of you gentlemen in the past, both in the Holy Land and in France.'

Brian de Falaise rose to his feet, a man of about forty, almost as big as Gwyn with hair cut to a shelf around his skull to fit under a helmet, heavy beard and moustache of a dark brown colour. His face was weathered and ruddy, his nose large and pitted, his whole appearance that of an intolerant, aggressive tyrant. 'I remember you! They called you Black John at Acre and Ascalon,' he said gruffly. 'You were close to King Richard, as I recall.'

The second Templar was a slightly younger man, tall,

thin and bony with black hair and moustache and a thick rim of black beard around his chin. Just as de Falaise was pugnacious, Godfrey Capra appeared morose and stern. He also recognised de Wolfe from a previous encounter. 'I am sure that I have seen you, but I cannot remember where,' he said, in a voice that was rather too high-pitched for a tall man.

'It was at Gisors, at the Splitting of the Elm, when we had such trouble with the French,' replied de Wolfe.

The third knight, the leader of the group, could claim no such memories of the county coroner. He introduced himself as Roland de Ver, in a quiet and somewhat offhand manner. Probably in his mid-thirties, he was also tall and slim with light brown hair, and high cheekbones above the obligatory beard and moustache of the Templars. His blue eyes seemed wary and gave John the impression that he was suspicious of everything and everyone.

With Gwyn waiting back in the courtyard, de Wolfe was invited to sit with them whilst they exchanged some cautious reminiscences of Palestine and France. Then they enquired about his business.

'I had intended to visit you in any event, as I knew I had been acquainted with at least two of you in the past,' he began. 'However, today I bring you sad news concerning one of your fellow knights.' He watched their faces intently to see if this produced any reaction, but the three soldier-monks stared back without a flicker of emotion.

'And what might that be?' asked de Ver, quietly.

'Gilbert de Ridefort was murdered the night before last, way out in the countryside, some sixteen miles from here.'

There was a silence and de Wolfe felt that it was not

from shock or surprise, but was a pause whilst each decided on the best way to react.

'He was the nephew of our disgraced former Grand Master,' announced Brian de Falaise eventually. His voice was flat and unemotional and he did not ask what a French Templar was doing in Devon.

'We are sorry to hear that he has died a violent death. But that has come to many Templars – perhaps the majority, for we are soldiers of Christ,' observed Roland de Ver, in calm, measured tones.

Presumably feeling that he must also contribute a comment, Godfrey Capra added, with a scowl, 'Though he was no longer a Templar – he had reneged on his sacred vows.'

The other two shot him a look of angry caution, which was not lost on de Wolfe. 'You knew he was here, then?' he said.

'We had heard that he was in England,' replied de Ver, cautiously.

There was another silence and, as if they sensed that their lack of curiosity was suspicious, the burly de Falaise and Capra both spoke at the same time.

'How did he die?'

'So what happened, Crowner?'

Something told de Wolfe to be circumspect with details as he might need to keep something up his sleeve with these formidable men. 'He was ambushed when riding in the woods. His killers must have known where he was staying and followed him.'

There was another uneasy silence and Roland de Ver shifted on his bench. 'We cannot pretend that we are desolated by this news, de Wolfe. He was no longer one of us and his family have stained the name of our Order.'

'It must have been in the blood, uncle and nephew both,' snarled Brian de Falaise, his chronic ill-nature revealing itself.

The three looked up at de Wolfe with arrogant defiance.

'I am the King's appointed coroner, and though I opened an inquest on the body early this morning, that is by no means the end of the matter. I have to record all investigations for the royal justices when they next come to Exeter – and those investigations are by no means complete.'

Roland de Ver shrugged. 'Good luck to you, Crowner. It's none of our concern.'

His insolent dismissal of the matter incensed de Wolfe. 'He was a Templar – or an ex-Templar, at least. You are three senior members of that Order, who just happened to have arrived in this county just before he was foully murdered. I think it reasonable for me to ask some questions of you, if only to eliminate certain possibilities.'

De Ver jumped to his feet, his face reddened with anger. 'You will ask nothing, Coroner! Or, at least, you'll get no answers from us. Our presence in Devon is none of your business. We are above the law. You know our Order well enough to realise that the Holy Father in Rome has granted us immunity from the rule of all kings and princes in Christendom – most of whom are beholden to us for both money and military support.'

De Wolfe fumed at this, but he knew that they had the dispensation they claimed. Even his beloved monarch, Richard, was a staunch ally of the Templars and would hear nothing ill said against them. He said, more pacifically, 'Surely, sirs, you would be concerned to aid in the unmasking of whatever villain killed one who, at least in the past, had an honourable record in your Order. I know, from my own experience of De Ridefort in Palestine, that he fought long and valiantly in the Crusade.'

Flushed with anger, Brian de Falaise slammed a big hand against his bench. 'Both I and de Ver also fought in Outremer, as did you. Yet we stayed steadfast in our faith afterwards, not having the perverted blood of the de Rideforts in our veins!'

John stood his ground in the face of this trio of furious men. 'I am a law officer in this county and I have a slain man to deal with. I must ask you, why are you in Exeter? And where were you all two days ago? I know you were absent from these lodgings.' He expected a storm of abuse at this, but he was met with silence. Two of the Templars looked at their leader, de Ver.

The thin, almost haggard Knight of Christ addressed the coroner coldly. 'We will not deign to answer your insulting questions, Crowner. You have no authority to question anything we do – nor even enquire as to our mission. I know that your superior law officer, Sheriff Richard, has more respect for the Templars and we will complain forthwith to him about your behaviour, so that he may forbid you to pester us again.'

Hunched like a great black crow, de Wolfe wagged a finger at the three knights. 'The sheriff is by no means my superior. He has no authority to govern my investigations. I defer only to the king!'

De Ver waved a hand indifferently. 'I care not, man. If it pleases you better, I will complain to the king about you when I return to France.' His voice hardened to a sibilant hiss. 'But you will no doubt allow that the authority of the Pope is paramount over any petty official such as yourself. Now, get yourself gone, Sir Crowner, and don't bother us again. You are dabbling in great matters that you cannot conceive of.'

De Wolfe, insulted and exasperated, could not resist one last verbal thrust as he moved to the open door. 'Perhaps one of these great matters concerned the "awful secret" of which Gilbert de Ridefort spoke to me.'

That brought them all to their feet and the pugnacious de Falaise felt impotently for the hilt of his sword, only to find that he had left it in his cell whilst they were taking their ease in the common room.

'What do you know of that? What did de Ridefort tell you?' It was de Ver who snapped out the question.

The coroner stepped out into the grey daylight. 'Like you, gentlemen, I do not answer questions. I am a law officer and I only ask them.'

'Have a care, John de Wolfe,' snarled Godfrey Capra. 'You are an insignificant servant in a godforsaken part of a remote island. But the long arm of Rome can reach anywhere and squash you like a beetle.'

De Wolfe ignored his threat and left one last message with them as he left. 'If you have any sympathy or respect for the passing of one of your number, he is to buried in the cathedral Close tomorrow morning.' Then, fuming internally but keeping a stony outward appearance, he walked back to the archway of the priory to join Gwyn and out into the lane beyond.

CHAPTER TEN

In which Crowner John is furious

It was now late afternoon, and on leaving the Priory of St Nicholas, de Wolfe thought it politic to tell the sheriff of the murder of a Norman knight in his territory – and to discover his attitude to these arrogant Templars. At the gatehouse of Rougemont, he sent Gwyn up to their chamber to tell Thomas de Peyne to get himself down to St James's Priory on the river to see if he could discover anything new about the movements of Abbot Cosimo and his sinister henchmen, especially their whereabouts during the past two days.

Then he went on to the keep and marched in on his brother-in-law, who was deep in discussion with two of his tax-collectors. The sheriff had soon to make his twice-yearly journey to Winchester for his accounting of the taxes raised in Devon during the past six months. This 'farm', as it was called, was a sum fixed in advance by the king's exchequer and if a sheriff could screw more out of the population he could keep the balance for himself. This explained why the office of sheriff was greatly coveted and competed for. In Richard's reign, a 'shrievalty' – the post of sheriff – was sold by the king for a huge sum, most of the purchasers being barons and even bishops. Some even managed to become sheriffs of three counties simultaneously.

De Wolfe waited impatiently while de Revelle harangued the taxmen from Tavistock and Totnes for being late with their collections, threatening them with dire penalties if they did not come up with the loot by the end of the month. Eventually, the chastened men escaped and John left his seat in the window embrasure to hover over his brother-in-law as he sat at his parchment-cluttered table.

'We have a murdered Norman knight to deal with, Sheriff,' he began, and was gratified to see that those words ensured the other man's immediate attention.

As de Revelle presumably knew nothing of Gilbert de Ridefort's presence in his county, he had to explain the whole story from start to finish, and by the end, the sheriff had become quite agitated. Rising from his chair, he paced up and down before his fireplace. 'A Templar heretic! What next, by God's bones? And what was this secret he claimed to possess?'

The coroner shrugged. 'I don't know – and I don't care. It died with him, presumably, so it's quite safe. But, as the chief law officers in this county, we are keepers of the king's peace, so our task is to discover the culprit. It was a foul killing, an ambush, a blow on the head and then a ritual stabbing.'

The sheriff was not concerned with the details or the need to make an arrest. He was more worried about his standing with certain parties of great influence. 'You say there is a papal nuncio in the city, and three senior Templars?'

De Wolfe looked at him with contempt. 'Come on, Richard, don't act the innocent with me. You know damned well they are here – you went to a meeting with the bishop a few days ago to meet this Cosimo of Modena. And I don't believe that the spies you have planted all over the city and county would not have told you of the arrival of three Knights of Christ, even if they had failed to tell you themselves, which now seems unlikely.'

The sheriff stopped his pacing and looked out of the window slit. 'I had heard something about them, yes,' he admitted shiftily.

'So what are they doing here? For I know why Cosimo is here! He has a writ from the Vatican to seek out heretics.'

De Revelle ignored this last, but seized upon the matter of the Templars to upbraid John. 'Those three important knights are in the county to purchase properties for their Order,' he snapped. 'They have the Chancellor's blessing to treat with any baron – or the bishop – for the purchase of profitable lands from any honour that wishes to sell.' He marched back to his folding chair and dropped into it. 'They already have estates at Templeton, near my own manor at Tiverton, but desire something further west, perhaps near Torbay or Plympton. Again, my other manor at Revelstoke lies in that direction and I might be able to help them find land nearby.'

'That's what they told you, was it? Strange that they should arrive just as one of their renegade members, pursued by an emissary of the Pope, is found slain in the county!'

De Revelle glared at his sister's husband, regretting for the thousandth time that she had ever married this persistent meddler who was wrecking his comfortable life. 'They are here to reconnoitre for new Templar lands, I tell you! You are well aware of the great wealth they possess, and they need to invest it in the land, to the benefit of all of us.'

De Wolfe lowered his head towards de Revelle, as he stooped across the table. 'Why would their leader, this Roland de Ver – until recently a senior member of the main Templar house in Paris – concern himself with buying a few hides of Devon soil?'

The sheriff waved a hand with assumed airy nonchalance. 'You had better ask him yourself, John.'

'I have just asked him – and was told to mind my own business. Why should they be so sensitive and secretive if all they are doing is negotiating for the purchase of some land?'

De Revelle's face flushed above his trim beard and moustache. 'You mean you've been pestering them already? You have no right, John. The Templars have immense power and influence!'

'Especially with you, no doubt,' said de Wolfe tartly. 'Will you receive commission if you help them buy land in your county?'

'The business transactions I carry out are no business of yours, Coroner.'

John gave one of his rare, lopsided grins. 'You'll get little commission out of a dead heretic, Richard. For that's what I'm certain these knights are here about.'

'They are attending to Templar interests, I tell you!' shouted de Revelle furiously.

'I can believe that, though their present interest is not land! If they are concerned with their investments, you had better invite them to come with us on Monday. Maybe they can at last succeed in winning their allotted land on Lundy!' With that parting shot he left, convinced that his devious brother-in-law knew a lot more about the visitors than he was admitting.

It was dusk when he left the castle and walked home. Matilda was out, presumably still praying for the soul of Gilbert de Ridefort, so John took the opportunity to visit the Bush and spend an hour with Nesta in her room upstairs. After a satisfying dalliance with her under the sheepskins, he came down and continued his enjoyment with a boiled fowl, onions and cabbage, washed down with her best ale.

As he sat at his favourite bench near the hearth, the comely tavern-keeper kept him company, sitting opposite with her elbows on the table, looking affectionately at the lean, brooding man she loved. They talked of inconsequential things for a while, as de Wolfe had already told her everything about the strange death of the run-away Templar.

Eventually, he pushed aside the pile of chicken bones and the soaked trencher to concentrate on his quart of ale.

'You are off to Lundy, then?' asked Nesta, concern on her pretty face. 'Be careful, John, both of the sea and the men who live there.' At the hub of gossip related by travellers and mariners passing through the inn, she was on top of every piece of news in Devon and well knew the bad reputation of that lonely island set a dozen miles off the north coast.

As he was reassuring her of his safety, which would be ensured by the large party of knights and soldiers going on the sheriff's escapade, the old potman Edwin limped across to the table and addressed him by his old military title. 'Cap'n, someone was seeking you, when you were . . . well, upstairs earlier on.' He leered at the coroner, his collapsed whitened eye slewing horribly in its socket.

Nesta scowled at his innuendo. 'Who was it, you old fool?' she snapped.

Edwin twitched his thin shoulders under his frayed

woollen tunic. 'Never saw him before. A gentleman, no doubt, dressed in riding clothes, booted and spurred. He asked for the crowner, but he didn't say who he was or why he wanted him.'

'What did you tell him? That he was upstairs with the ale-wife?' she said, threateningly.

The old soldier grinned, showing the blackened stumps in his gums. 'No, I said the crowner would almost certainly be in here within the hour. He said nothing and walked out.'

'What did he look like?' demanded John.

'Big, tall fellow, no moustache or beard. Couldn't see his hair, he had a leather cap tied around under his chin. Looked about thirty or more years.'

'Not another bailiff come to report a sudden death?'

'Didn't look like any bailiff. More likely a soldier.'

De Wolfe looked at Nesta. 'I wonder if this is our long-expected Bernardus de Blanchefort? If it is, he's got a nasty shock awaiting him.'

Someone else marched up to the table, no rogue Templar but Gwyn of Polruan. 'A couple of messages, Crowner. First, that little toad Thomas has seen this Italian priest down at the cathedral Close. He turned up before I could send him down to the priory, saying that this Cosimo has come back to the bishop's palace with his two strong-arm men. Bishop Marshal is still away, but he has met two of the Archdeacons and the Precentor.'

'Has Thomas any idea of where they have been these last two days?'

'None at all – but their horses were tired and mud-spattered so they've covered some distance lately.'

De Wolfe gave a loud grunt, his usual means of responding when he had nothing constructive to say. 'And your other news?'

'Sergeant Gabriel was sent down to the gatehouse by the sheriff to tell me to command you to attend on him as soon as possible.'

'What about?'

'I don't know – but Gabriel said that two of the Templar's squires had been up there within the last hour.'

De Wolfe rose wearily to his feet. 'I'd better be off, I suppose. Maybe the Knights of Christ have thought better of refusing to speak to me.' And with Gwyn in tow, he began trudging back up to Rougemont.

If John de Wolfe had thought that the three Templars might have softened their attitude, he was very much mistaken. When he reached the castle keep, he found de Revelle's room almost filled with the Templars and their sergeants. Unlike their previous appearance in Exeter, all three now carried the large red cross of their Order on the shoulder of their mantles. Brian de Falaise and Roland de Ver wore the famous white cloaks of celibacy and, as a previously married man, Godfrey Capra was in black. Though they wore no armour or helmets, nor the surcoats with the red cross on the breast, the knights had long swords buckled to their baldrics. Their sergeants, grim-looking men who were much older than most squires, stood in the background, dressed in sombre brown that also carried the broad cross.

As John entered and stood by the door, the beefy Brian de Falaise glowered at him. 'Here he is, de Revelle! Tell this man to mind his own business, or it will be the worse for him!'

With this unpromising start, a cacophony of recrimination and protest began, some of it contributed by de Revelle. De Wolfe began shouting back and nothing was achieved above the din for several minutes. Then Roland de Ver rapped the pommel of his dagger upon the table and, in a steely voice, called for quiet. 'Let us all regain our tempers! I wish for no personal quarrel with you, Coroner. I realise that you have been charged with certain duties by the king and I respect your fidelity in wishing to carry out your legal functions.'

Somewhat mollified by this sensible statement, de Wolfe advanced to the table and nodded to the leader of the group. 'When a man is killed against the king's peace, especially a Norman knight, it cannot be ignored.'

'God will not ignore it and that is what matters,' said de Ver piously. 'Pope Eugenius long ago made the Templars independent of archbishops and you well know that Rome has decreed to all states in Europe that our Order is to be exempt from all national laws. Thus, you have no jurisdiction over us and cannot interfere with our activities.' He paused, then his tone changed to accusation. 'Not only do we deny you the right to question us, but we wish to question you. We are concerned at your apparent intimacy with Gilbert de Ridefort, especially your insinuations that he imparted certain information to you. De Wolfe, did he or did he not expound on his crazed heretical beliefs?'

'He did not – and I would have scant interest if he had. I am concerned with one thing only, and that is the manner of his death and who caused it.'

Roland de Ver patently disbelieved him and again repeated his firm intention of not answering any questions on any subject.

The coroner scowled at the calm features of this slim soldier-monk. 'Are you confessing that you had something to do with the death of your fellow Templar, but are refusing to let me question you about it?' he thundered.

'Watch your tongue, de Wolfe,' yelled Brian de Falaise, but de Ver held up his hand for silence.

'The last part of your question is true. You may not question us about anything. The first part is unanswerable, as we say neither yea nor nay to anything you might ask. We do not – we cannot – forbid you to investigate this death. You are welcome and have a duty so to do, as long as you do not try to ask us anything about that or, indeed, any other subject that we choose not to discuss.'

De Wolfe shook his head in exasperation. 'Well, do you choose to discuss Templar land-holdings in Devon? That seems an innocuous subject.'

His brother-in-law spoke up. 'I have already told these good knights about our expedition to the north on Monday and they have agreed to accompany us. We would welcome the support of six seasoned warriors, especially as they have a specific interest in the rightful claim of their Order to the island of Lundy.'

There was a silence, which allowed frayed tempers to simmer down. De Wolfe could see that the will of the Templars remained intractable and, having respect generally for their organisation, he had to admit defeat in any frontal attack upon them, though he remained highly suspicious of their involvement with the death of de Ridefort. His eyes roved over their faces, including those of the grimly silent squires, and he felt that any one of them might have slain de Ridefort, if their fanatical devotion to their Order demanded it. But there seemed no way of pursuing it now, though he resolved to continue investigating by any other means he could devise.

They took his silence for defeat and the atmosphere relaxed a little, as Roland de Ver obtained more details from the sheriff of the departure on Monday morning, and the arrangements for accommodation, food and fodder *en route* for Barnstaple. The coroner remained silent throughout these exchanges and stood aside as the six Templars filed out, the knights giving him a cursory nod as they left for the priory of St Nicholas.

He was left alone with Richard de Revelle, who breathed a deep sigh of relief. 'John, why is it that you seem to antagonise every person of authority with whom you come in contact?' he asked wearily. 'The Templars are the most powerful force not only in England but in the whole of Christendom – and yet, within the blinking of an eye, you manage to incense them with your accusations!'

'The dead man was also a Templar, but no one seems concerned about him,' retorted de Wolfe.

'He was a renegade of some sort, so Roland de Ver informs me,' replied the sheriff. 'Who are we to probe the mysteries of that occult Order? Keep out of it, John, it's none of our business.'

De Wolfe had his own ideas on that, but knew that it was useless arguing with de Revelle. He cared only about deferring to the most powerful men in the vicinity, men who even if they could not advance him would at least not hinder him in his eternal search for preferment. 'Why are they willing to join our expedition on Monday?' he asked, trying a slightly different tack.

'As I told you, they say that their purpose in Devon is to seek new Templar holdings – so what more natural than that three tough fighters and their hardy squires should take the chance to investigate how their long-established grant of Lundy has been frustrated for so many years?'

De Wolfe had to admit to himself that this seemed

reasonable, given the long history of defeat that the Templar claim to the island had suffered. Cynically, he thought that maybe now that their task of eliminating Gilbert de Ridefort had been successfully completed, they felt that a few days' diversion in the service of their Order might be appropriate.

De Wolfe pushed himself upright from the table edge and the sheriff pointedly picked up a quill and a parchment, ready to continue his work. 'So what is to be done about this dead knight? Is he to be pushed into a hole in the cathedral grounds and forgotten?'

De Revelle brandished the feather of his pen at the coroner. 'I would suggest doing just that. I don't want to know about him, now that three senior Templars have warned us off. Forget it, John. Go on to your next case – it's safer that way.'

With a snort of disgust at his brother-in-law's apathy, John stalked out and went home, but he was fated this night to have no peace. Outside his front door, he found his clerk hopping from foot to foot in impatience, with a summons from the archdeacon to visit him immediately at his house in Canon's Row.

Uneasy, but glad of another excuse to postpone sitting in his wife's company, the coroner beckoned Thomas to accompany him and strode along the few yards of Martin's Lane and into its continuation along the north side of the cathedral Close. Many of the twenty-four prebendaries of the cathedral lived here, together with their vicars, secondary priests and male servants, for theoretically no woman was allowed to reside in the Close.

John de Alençon was Archdeacon of Exeter; the other three holding that rank in the episcopal hierarchy were archdeacons of other parts of the diocese. He was

John's special friend, a staunch supporter of Richard the Lionheart, which was more than could be said for the Bishop, the Treasurer and the Precentor. A thin, ascetic Norman, he nevertheless had a dry sense of humour, but tonight it was not much in evidence when de Wolfe entered his bare study in the narrow house facing the cathedral.

'I have had a visit from this abbot from Italy, John,' he began, without any preamble. 'As the bishop has left for Canterbury, I had to receive him in the Chapter House and listen to his orders from France and Rome.' He sounded bitter at what must have been a traumatic meeting with such a powerful emissary.

'What orders were these, John?' asked de Wolfe mildly.

'That this corpse you brought back from somewhere is not to lie before an altar in the cathedral – and that it is not to be buried in the graveyard outside.'

The coroner stared at his friend. 'And what is to happen to him, then? A stake through his heart, then buried at midnight at the crossroads? Good God, man, the deceased was a monk, a follower of the Rule of Benedict. He can't be consigned to an unmarked grave like a suicide!'

The thin priest, enveloped from neck to toe in a black robe, looked saddened but resolute. 'Those were my orders and, after being shown a signed authority from the Vatican, I had no option but to obey.'

Thanks to Thomas's spying, John knew that this letter existed and was genuine. 'But why? A few hours ago you allowed him to rest in the North Tower.'

'That was before this Cosimo came to inform me of certain matters, John.'

'What matters would they be?'

John de Alençon shook his head sadly, the tight grey curls at the sides of his head lifting. 'I cannot tell you that. He forbade it. Suffice it to say that, given the damage that this Gilbert might have done, I am not surprised that he came to a dreadful end. It is a wonder that he was not cloven in two by a lightning flash from heaven.'

There was a moan from behind, and looking round, the coroner saw that his clerk was crossing himself in an almost frenzied way. 'And you can tell me nothing more, old friend?' he asked softly.

'Not even you, John. Like the confessional, some things are inviolate, and the command of a messenger from the Holy Father is one of them, much as we may dislike its content.'

'So what is to happen to Gilbert's body? Are you going to eject it from the house of the God he served all his life?'

The archdeacon's blue eyes were stern. 'I am not sure that latterly the man was much concerned with serving his God. But it is late and I am conveniently going to claim that nothing can now be done until morning.'

'And what then?'

'There is a small burial ground behind the church of St Bartholomew. I have prevailed upon the parish priest to have this body interred there in the morning, with the minimum of ceremony. The ground is consecrated and no doubt Abbot Cosimo will not be pleased, but I am willing to endure his displeasure in order to place this Templar in hallowed ground, even if the devil had entered his soul in his last days.'

De Wolfe realised that his friend had gone out on a limb, probably as much to please him as for the repose of de Ridefort's soul.

'I dare not officiate, but the priest of St Bartholomew's, William Weston, will put him in the ground with some appropriate words. I failed to tell him the whole story – indeed, I could not after the direct orders of Cosimo – so he will not be aware of the extent of the problem.'

With that, de Wolfe had to be satisfied, and late in the evening, he took himself home to meet Matilda's red-rimmed eyes.

CHAPTER ELEVEN

In which Crowner John attends a funeral

Putting Gilbert de Ridefort to rest next morning was a quick and almost furtive exercise. Soon after dawn, two grave-diggers carried the shrouded body on a bier from the cathedral to St Bartholomew's, a church in Bretayne, which had a burial ground against the north-west stretch of the town wall. Just after the ninth-hour bell, a few people straggled through the cold rain to stand briefly around the newly dug grave-pit.

Uncoffined, but wrapped securely in his clothing, with a linen shroud stitched over the top, the former Knight Templar was lowered into the hole by the two labourers, whilst the gaunt parish priest, himself shrouded against the rain by a long leather cape, mumbled some unintelligible version of the Mass for the Dead. The spectators – for, with the exception of Matilda, one could hardly call them mourners – stood well back from the muddy pit, as if to distance themselves from the deceased. Apart from John de Wolfe and his wife, they consisted of the three Templar knights, with their impassive squires standing in the background, Gwyn, Thomas de Peyne – and Abbot Cosimo of Modena, also with his two grim retainers lurking behind him. A couple of heads were visible over the stone wall that divided the churchyard from a narrow lane, curious at such goings-on early on a Saturday morning.

John had the strong impression that all those inside the graveyard had come solely to confirm that this dangerous and heretical renegade actually was buried in the earth and had not resurrected himself in a puff of sulphurous smoke.

There was an almost palpable air of relief when the grave-diggers began shovelling sticky mud down on to the body, and within minutes of the congregation coming into the churchyard, the grave was filled in and they began silently dispersing.

De Wolfe was surprised at the presence of the 'opposition', as he thought of them. All were suspects in his eyes, the only problem being that, with nine potential murderers, it was impossible to hazard a guess as to the real culprit or culprits: the way that Gilbert had died meant that either a single assailant or several might have killed him.

The coroner's original plan had been frustrated by the denial of burial in the cathedral: he had hoped to attempt the 'ordeal of the bier' while the body was lying there. He had brought it back from Stoke partly because he had hoped by some subterfuge to get the Templars and the abbot to view the corpse before it was buried to see if de Ridefort's injuries might bleed again in the proximity of the killer. He was not sure in his own mind whether there was any truth in this mystical procedure, but it was approved by the Church and he had heard tales in the past that when suspects had been made to touch the bier, the corpse had bled. Now the three Templars ignored him, though Roland de Ver managed a moderately courteous nod in the direction of Matilda, before hurrying out of the small graveyard.

De Wolfe was more interested in Abbot Cosimo, on whom he had never laid eyes until now. As Thomas had described, he was a short, slight man of middle age, with a strange facial profile, his forehead coming down in an absolutely straight line with his prominent nose. His hair was black and his complexion sallow, with a marked Mediterranean look about it. His small black eyes and thin lips over projecting teeth, gave him a rodent-like appearance. As the outspoken but perceptive Gwyn said later, he was the sort of creature you wanted to tread on when it crossed your path.

As he passed to go to the gate, the abbot looked right through de Wolfe as if he didn't exist, making no acknowledgement of him whatsoever. His two sour-faced acolytes closed ranks behind him, and the trio vanished rapidly into the rain, following the Templars. The abbot's henchmen, who de Wolfe learned later were men-at-arms from the Temple in London, were heavily built men in sombre tunics and mantles, who seemed rarely to speak and certainly never smiled. He never discovered their names and they seemed to view anyone who approached Cosimo with suspicion, fingering their swords or daggers as if they expected an assassination attempt at any moment. As John came through the gate and stared after them, he saw that Cosimo had caught up with the knights and was talking animatedly to them.

Matilda curtly expressed a wish to go to St Olave's and, in such an unsavoury neighbourhood as Bretayne, demanded her husband's company as escort, though the church was only a few hundred yards distant. The lanes were lined with hovels of board and cob, mostly roofed with turf or thatch, much of it tattered and disintegrating. Many of the dwellings were little better than ramshackle huts, tilted and leaning against each other. The narrow alleys were barely the span of two arms and the ground ran with sewage, rubbish and mud, amongst which dogs, cats, rats, fowls and a few pigs vied for space with urchins and toddlers, all seemingly oblivious of the filth and the rain.

With Gwyn and Thomas trudging behind, de Wolfe chaperoned his wife to her favourite place of worship and then, with some relief, suggested to the others that they adjourn to the Bush for discussion and refreshment.

As they crossed Fore Street, Gwyn looked several times over his shoulder, before stopping dead and staring back. 'Who's this following us?'

De Wolfe swung round and experienced a momentary *déjà vu* sensation, harking back to de Ridefort's early antics. A man in a wide-brimmed pilgrim's felt hat was behind him, enveloped in a soaking cloak of nondescript dun colour. De Wolfe recognised the hat as having been on one of the heads looking over the graveyard wall a few minutes earlier. 'What is it, fellow? Do you want me?' he challenged.

The man, tall and powerfully built, came up close to him and Gwyn stepped forward, his hand going to his dagger. The coroner had made a few enemies and, like Cosimo's men, the Cornishman was ever on his guard. But his caution was unnecessary, if the fellow's first words were true.

'Sir John, I am Bernardus de Blanchefort. I think you may have been expecting me.'

With his cloak steaming over the wattle screen near John's favourite table, the new arrival sat before a trencher of salt bacon and onions, a quart of ale by his elbow. Whether or not the man was still a Templar, he was allowed to eat the meat of four-legged animals, unlike the usual monk: the philosophy of the warrior-monks was that a fighting man needed to keep up his strength, which was also why the Order forbade its members to fast. Certainly, this warrior was eating Nesta's viands with a gusto that suggested he had had little food that day. The coroner and his assistants sat around the table, each with a more modest meal than the famished newcomer. Nesta and Edwin hovered nearby, the nosy old pot-man concealing his avid curiosity less successfully than his mistress as they fussed with supplies of food and drink.

'I arrived here from Weymouth yesterday, after a terrible passage a sennight ago from Caen,' explained de Blanchefort, between mouthfuls. 'I stayed last night in some fleapit tavern not far from here, whose landlord was a mean fat bastard who overcharged me.'

'Willem the Fleming, at the Saracen!' said Nesta indignantly, from where she stood at the end of the table. 'He gives our inns in Exeter a bad name, the way he runs that hovel.'

Bernardus had already been told by the coroner of the demise of his Templar friend. He said that he had gone to the funeral at St Bartholomew's not because he knew the deceased was Gilbert de Ridefort but because he was seeking John de Wolfe to make himself known. He had been told by someone at the castle gate that the coroner was at the burial ground, but when he saw the Templars there and Abbot Cosimo, he had been shocked and kept clear of de Wolfe until the others had dispersed. 'At first, I had no idea who the dead person might have been, but the sight of those wolves from the New Temple and Paris soon made it clear that it could only have been de Ridefort who had died.'

As he spoke, de Wolfe studied him from close quarters. Whereas Gilbert had been a handsome, elegant man, this southern Frenchman was a blunt, tough fellow with a direct, almost pugnacious manner. A few years younger than John, he had a square face, dark brown hair and thick eyebrows. The upper part of his features was tanned but his chin and lips were pale where he had recently shaved off the obligatory Templar beard and moustache. De Wolfe suspected that he was far more enthusiastic about matters of faith than de Ridefort had been, perhaps even to the point of obsession.

'They will kill us both if they can,' he said finally, having finished his food and pushed aside the trencher to take up his pot of ale. 'Now that Gilbert is silenced, I will be the next target. But I care not for them, this secret must be told, to dispel the myth that has plagued the world for a thousand years!' An evangelical tone had crept into his voice, though he kept it low and accompanied his words with furtive glances about the room. There were only a few other customers in the Bush at that early hour, all locals whom de Wolfe recognised as tradesmen and merchants.

'Are you going to tell us what this mystery is?' he demanded. 'De Ridefort seemed reluctant to divulge what was at issue – even though it seems to have cost him his life.'

'I will indeed – and that very soon. But I want to do it in a way that cannot be smothered by the forces against me.'

Though John frankly had little interest in whatever theological revelations these Templars wished to make, his clerk Thomas was hanging on every word. Crouched at the end of the table, his peaky face was fixed on de Blanchefort and his mouth was hanging open with expectation. 'Does this concern the Cathars and the Albigensian diversion from the holy teachings?' he squeaked, clutching his small cup of cider tightly as if to hang on to some remnant of security in the face of burgeoning heresy.

'It is not unconnected, but compared with those beliefs, it is as massive as the Alps compared with a molehill,' proclaimed de Blanchefort ominously. This sent Thomas into a paroxysm of crossing himself, as if to ward off the devil himself.

'So why have you come to Devon – and what are you going to do now that you are here?' enquired the ever-practical coroner, whose priority was still the discovery of Gilbert de Ridefort's killer.

'Like Gilbert, I come in flight, to escape the wrath of the established Church. I have no particular desire to be a martyr as I enjoy the only life I am likely to have. But if I need to die for the truth, as de Ridefort did, then so be it. We both sought to escape to a land more tolerant of revised beliefs, such as Scotland. He suggested that we made our way there from France, which is so dangerous for anyone who diverts from the rigid dictates of Rome.'

'So why Devon? This is a backwater in the mainstream of Europe.'

'Gilbert suggested it as a route to Scotland, perhaps via Ireland. To reach that northern land direct from France would be very hazardous with the full length of England between, containing many Templar Preceptories and endless Roman dioceses stretching the length of the country. And he remembered you for a fair-minded man and had heard that you were from

Devonshire. Like him, I trust that you can see your way to helping me.'

'What is it you want from me?' asked de Wolfe, rather suspiciously. His attempts to help de Ridefort had ended in disaster and he was not keen to repeat the process.

'I came here only with the intention of procuring assistance to journey onwards. I wanted to know how best to go about getting a passage from the many ports you have along these coasts, in an area where I fondly thought the long arm of the Order and the Inquisition would be unlikely to reach. But obviously I was wrong. Somehow, they must have discovered where Gilbert was heading, possibly by torturing some poor wretch in Paris to whom he had mentioned his destination.'

De Wolfe's great beak of a nose came closer to Bernardus' face. 'You put all those words in the past, as if you now have different desires?' he rumbled.

The former Templar shrugged. 'I still wish to save my skin if I can – mainly to stay alive and active to help my message on its way. There are others of our Order still in France, and elsewhere, who are unhappy with the status quo, but they do not yet seem ready to come out into the open as Gilbert and I have done.'

He stopped for a long sup at his ale pot, then continued. 'But now that Gilbert de Ridefort is not with me, I am willing to risk proclaiming this secret to all who will hear it and be damned to the consequences,' he declared harshly.

'What do you mean by that?' asked de Wolfe, apprehensive that this determined hothead was likely to make more trouble for the law officers of the county.

'The time has come to stop skulking about the country with this knowledge. I intend proclaiming it as publicly as possible – and the best place to do so would be on the cathedral steps tomorrow morning!'

Even Gwyn stopped in mid-swallow at this – and Thomas looked if he was going to faint. Of all of them, apart from Bernardus, the little ex-priest knew best the gravity of what the latter was proposing, if it had any connection at all with the heresy rampant in the Languedoc of southern France. Just as Gilbert had lectured Evelyn on the day of his death, Thomas knew of the rising concern of Rome against those who held gnostic views of Christianity and was aware of the increasing wrath of the ecclesiastical establishment against the Cathars and others in the French lands.

'A sermon on the cathedral steps!' barked de Wolfe, incredulously. 'The bishop will have some views on that – or he would have, if he was in the city.' He thought that the archdeacons and the other senior canons would more than compensate for the absence of Henry Marshal when it came to the prospect of a renegade monk preaching heresy from the West Front of the cathedral.

'Who d'you think would come to listen to you?' grunted the agnostic Gwyn.

'I shall wait until the end of Nones, Terce and High Mass to catch the congregation as they come out of the building,' said Bernardus, a joyful glee in his bright brown eyes that, in spite of his earlier protestations, suggested to John a willingness for martyrdom.

'You wouldn't last five minutes,' he objected. 'The canons would soon have the proctors on you.'

'Five minutes would be all I need to sow the seeds of doubt – and maybe the ears of the cathedral priests would be more fertile soil than those of the common people.'

De Wolfe was beginning to think that this man was mad, but the fact that Gilbert de Ridefort had had the same convictions – and de Blanchefort claimed that there were others still in France and even the Holy Land who agreed with them – weighed against this being some individual mental abberation. As he thought about de Blanchefort's plan for a heretical sermon, it occurred to him that this might be a way to smoke out de Ridefort's killers. If the former Templar tried to go ahead with this crazy idea, then similar means could be tried to silence him and the perpetrators might be unmasked.

As the man began some earnest theological debate across the table with the apprehensive Thomas, the coroner weighed up the risk of getting him killed with the chances of identifying the killers. He decided that if the damned fool wanted to stick his head into a noose – or more likely get burned at the stake – then that was his affair, but to reduce the likelihood somewhat, it would help if his intention to preach heresy was bandied about in advance. Then the opposition might take action before de Blanchefort committed some fatal indiscretion.

'You will be assured of a bigger audience if it is known about beforehand,' he said, with wily insincerity. 'We can put about the news quite readily. Thomas here is especially well placed to noise it abroad amongst the clergy and all those in the cathedral Close.' He looked at Gwyn with a lop-sided grin. 'And my officer here could broadcast it in almost every alehouse in Exeter, although maybe the patrons of taverns are not too concerned with new concepts of religion.'

De Blanchefort accepted this advice with a readiness that almost made de Wolfe ashamed at his own duplicity, but he salved his conscience with the thought that he might be saving the man's life, if not his liberty, in ensuring that he would be arrested before he committed some ecclesiastical treason.

Now de Wolfe changed the subject. 'These three Templars you saw at St Bartholomew's – do you know them?'

'Godfrey Capra is a stranger to me,' answered Bernardus. 'But I certainly know the other two. Roland de Ver was prominent in the Paris headquarters until a year ago. I think he was sent to the new Temple in London to stiffen their sinews with the same discipline demanded by the Master in France. And Brian de Falaise is also known to me from Outremer, where I knew him for a courageous, if reckless warrior.'

'They claimed to me to be in this part of England only to seek new estates for the Templars.'

'I find that very hard to accept,' said Bernardus scornfully. 'That's a task either for old members well past their fighting age – or, even more likely, for their sergeants. It is ludicrous to believe that three senior knights would be sent on such a mundane mission.'

'And what of this Italian abbot? Do you know of him?'

De Blanchefort banged his empty mug on the table and Edwin hurried to refill it from a large jug. 'Cosimo of Modena? Yes, I know him – who in France does not? He is a creature of Rome, though based at a priory near Paris. He has a roving commission to spy out heresy, supposedly being a servant of Hugh, Bishop of Auxerre, and William of the White Hands, Archbishop of Reims, who have taken it upon themselves to root out any form of dissension against Catholic orthodoxy. But he is widely thought to answer only to Rome itself.'

De Wolfe glanced at Thomas, who leered back smugly,

to confirm that this was what he had already discovered.

'And who is the most dangerous of all these?' persisted the coroner, doggedly seeking the likely killer of de Ridefort.

'Cosimo is most poisonous of them all, though I doubt that physically he is dangerous. That is why he travels with those two retainers who can protect his skin from the thousands who would like to flay it from his miserable bones – and to carry out any mischief he orders.'

'And the Templars?'

'Most of our Order are honourable men, unaware of the great secret that the Poor Knights of Christ have guarded for three-quarters of a century. Only recently has there been some leakage of the truth that is beginning to unsettle the consciences of a few knights such as myself.' He paused for a drink. 'These three are probably blind adherents to the Rule, who will carry out any mission directed by the Masters of a country or Commanders of Houses. This Roland de Ver ranks as a Commander of Knights, a step higher in the hierarchy of the Order, which again makes it ridiculous to think that he is on a mission to buy land.'

A distant bell tolled from the cathedral and de Wolfe downed the last of his ale and rose to his feet. 'If you are set on this rash sermon of yours, you have a day to prepare, but I suggest you keep out of sight in the city, as did Gilbert de Ridefort when he was here. You could stay at this inn – it is far better than the Saracen.'

De Blanchefort looked around the big ale-room of the Bush, but shook his head. 'I agree it is superior, but my horse is in their stable and my saddle bags in their loft. Also, I think it may be a less obvious place to find me, as I understand this is well known as the best inn in Exeter.'

Nesta beamed at this compliment, even though it meant that she lost a few pence in trade.

John murmured to her as they left, 'Get Edwin and the maids to put it about that there will be a revelation on the cathedral steps after the morning services tomorrow – I want the news to get around.'

The Saracen tavern was only a few yards away, on Stepcote Hill leading down to the river. At the end of Idle Lane, de Wolfe waited until he saw the figure of Bernardus reach the door safely, his floppy hat pulled well down over his face.

Then he gave instructions to Gwyn, and especially Thomas, to spend the rest of the day advertising de Blanchefort's proposed sermon, before walking back to his own house. He considered telling his friend the archdeacon of the man's intentions, but could not bring himself to commit such obvious treachery against him, even though it might conceivably save his life.

However, when he arrived home he did tell Matilda. He found her in a subdued mood after the funeral and had no idea how she would take the news that yet another heretic had arrived in town. She listened in silence from her usual cowled chair by the hearth.

'Sir Gilbert told us he was coming,' she said, in a dull monotone. 'Is he to suffer the same fate?'

When de Wolfe described how the new arrival intended to give a public declaration of the Templars' awful secret, she roused herself from her apathy and became increasingly incensed. 'Though I thought so highly of Gilbert de Ridefort, I have to accept now that it was God's will that caused him to be struck down for his blasphemous thoughts – but at least he kept them to himself. Now this other man comes, full of the devil's intentions. What is the world coming to, John? Is the anti-Christ now on earth and are we soon to witness Armageddon?' Her voice rose stridently as her anger gathered pace. Her infatuation with Gilbert seemed to have died with him. As usual, she turned her sharp tongue in the direction of her husband. 'You have been an instrument in this, John,' she chided, leaning forward in her chair to bristle at him. 'You should have sent de Ridefort packing from the county as soon as you realised that he was possessed of such heresy. The devil must have been within him, too, to make me feel warmly towards him, when all the time he was a wolf in sheep's clothing.'

De Wolfe failed to follow her logic but wisely kept silent as she continued to vent her spleen on him. 'And as for this new intruder, you should denounce him to the Church at once – and to my brother. He should be arrested and turned over to those who can close his blasphemous mouth.'

Her husband thought that Matilda would make the perfect candidate for leading the Inquisition in the west of England, but again kept his peace and instead went along with her mood. 'That's just what I am doing, in a way,' he said artfully. 'I am deliberately spreading the news of his intended revelations so that by the morning the cathedral authorities will know of his intentions. If they take him at all seriously, they will prevent him from speaking – and, no doubt, either these Templars or that abbot from the Inquisition will persuade him to leave the city. But neither your brother nor I has any jurisdiction over him. He is intending to commit no secular offence.'

Matilda was far from mollified. 'He should be hanged,

John. If anyone speaks against your precious king, you are outraged and instantly cry, "Traitor," but you seem unconcerned with this greater treachery against our Heavenly King!'

He bit back his desire to argue with her about the different jurisdictions of the ecclesiastical and civil powers: when it came to matters of faith, Matilda's arguments were based mainly on the loudness of her voice and her conviction of the infallibility of the priesthood and the Gospels. 'Well, I've done what I can in the matter. I'm the coroner, not the bishop. It's really none of my business – except that the killer of de Ridefort remains my concern, in spite of Richard's warning for me not to get involved.'

Matilda became morose and uncommunicative again, which John found more unnerving than when she was ranting at him. After a while, the silence became oppressive and he left for his chamber in Rougemont, with the excuse that he must make arrangements for his journey to Barnstaple in little over a day. That fanned the smouldering embers of her bad temper into flames again, as she upbraided him for leaving her alone for so long: the expedition to Lundy would take at least five days. The only factor in his favour this time was that the foray had been suggested and organised by her own brother, which de Wolfe was at pains to point out when he retaliated to her complaints about the endless neglect he showed her.

With a sigh of relief, he stalked out of the hall, grabbing his grey cloak to ward off the thin drizzle that was again falling on the city.

CHAPTER TWELVE

In which Crowner John witnesses an arrest

John de Wolfe spent a quiet couple of hours in his small, bleak room at the top of the gatehouse. Even the damp cold of the unheated chamber was preferable to the frigid company of his wife. He used the time to practise his reading of Latin, running a finger slowly along the lines of Thomas's perfect penmanship and forming the words silently with his lips.

The text was on the rolls that his clerk had written for current cases, pale cream parchment stitched together in long lengths, which would be presented to the king's justices when they eventually came to Exeter for the next Eyre of Assize. They were long overdue, but rumour had it that they were in Dorchester and might perambulate as far as Devon in the next month or two to hear any civil disputes and serious cases of crime that de Wolfe had managed to wrest from the sheriff's Shire Court.

John's ability to read the rolls was improving weekly, and now he stumbled through a recent case of rape to refresh his memory. The woman, a young widow, claimed to have been waylaid in the backyard of her own house in Goldsmith Street. She had been allegedly beaten and ravished, and had produced a bloodstained rag, the almost obligatory evidence required to substantiate such a charge. Certainly when examined by de Wolfe, she had had bruised cheeks and arms, a black eye and a couple of loose teeth. There was no doubt about the assailant, a local carter who had been living with her for some months. The bailiff to the burgesses and one of his constables were called by the woman and her sister, who had raised the hue and cry, though in fact the man needed no chasing, as he was sitting in the house drinking ale when the bailiff arrived. On the accusation of the two women, the carter was arrested on the spot and dragged away to the gaol in the tower of the South Gate. If de Wolfe had not been notified by the bailiff, the carter would then have been hauled off to the sheriff's fortnightly court and would most likely have been hanged, even though he loudly insisted that all he had done was give the widow a thrashing because she had stolen some money from his pouch when he was sleeping. As for the coupling, he claimed that that had been at least a daily event and had been enthusiastically received!

Against the equally loud protestations of Richard de Revelle, John insisted that such a serious charge as rape be referred to the king's court, so he examined the woman himself, chaperoned by the old hag who did service as the midwife in that part of the town. There seemed little evidence of actual rape, but the coroner knew that in a previously married woman that by no means excluded forceful ravishment, even though the injuries to this one's face were more in accord with a common assault. He decided to record all the facts and leave it to the king's judges to decide who was telling the truth. As it was a hanging offence, de Wolfe could not attach the man with a heavy bail payment and he had to stay in prison until the Eyre of Assize, much to the annoyance of the burgesses and sheriff who had to pay a ha'penny a day for his keep. It was common for the prisoner in such cases to escape, usually by bribing the gaolers, but the only future for him then was either to run for the forest and become an outlaw or to seek sanctuary in a church and then abjure the realm.

De Wolfe pushed the roll aside, having strained his eyes and his brain enough for one day. He pulled his mantle more closely around him as he saw the rain sheeting down outside the window slit and thought about this latest complication, Bernardus de Blanchefort. He heartily wished him a thousand leagues away for he was no concern of a coroner as long as he stayed alive. Due to Gilbert de Ridefort's tenuous claim to friendship, both he and this Bernardus had been thrust upon him and he seemed to be burdened with their safety, which he had spectacularly failed to ensure in the case of de Ridefort. 'To hell with him! Let him give his damned sermon!' muttered the coroner to himself, huddled in his bare attic. 'If he wants to commit suicide, so be it. Those Templars or the Italian rat will put paid to him if he utters more than two words in front of the cathedral tomorrow.'

His dismissal of de Blanchefort was short-lived, however. Just as he was thinking of walking down to the Bush for an early-evening drink, there was a familiar uneven tapping of feet on the stairs and Thomas appeared through the hessian curtain. He looked worried and agitated. 'Crowner, you must come down to the cathedral at once to see the archdeacon. He has sent me to fetch you.'

'What's the urgency, Thomas?'

'As you told me to, I put word about concerning this sermon tomorrow.' He crossed himself at the thought of it. 'I told several vicars, a few secondaries and one canon while I was walking about the Close and later having my dinner at the house where I lodge. Within the hour, there was a buzz of interest in it and several more priests and monks came to ask me about the time and place, some of them already angry. Then, not long ago, two canons appeared and almost blamed me for encouraging heresy, though I told them I was only passing on gossip I had heard.'

'Get on with it, man! What about the archdeacon?'

'John of Alençon sent his own vicar-choral to me just now, with a demand that he speak to you urgently about this affair. He wants to see you in the Chapter House straight away.'

'How did he know that I was connected with this?'

'Your involvement with the dead Templar led him to assume that you were behind this new man.'

'I'm not behind anything!' snapped de Wolfe irascibly. 'I wish I'd never heard of either of the damned fellows. But I suppose I must come down with you. What about Gwyn?'

'He has been around the alehouses with the gossip – no hardship for him, I'm sure!' the little man added wryly. 'And I saw him just now, talking to some of the men-at-arms downstairs in the guardroom, so he's probably telling them as well.'

The result of Gwyn's publicity was even more rapid than that of Thomas's. By the time John and his clerk had reached the gateway to Rougemont, Sergeant Gabriel was hurrying towards them from the direction of the keep. 'The sheriff wants to see you, Crowner. Something about a new Templar giving a sermon tomorrow. He seemed in a high temper about it. Wants you to go to his chamber right away.'

De Wolfe sighed a great sigh. 'Can't be done, Gabriel. I have to see the archdeacon urgently at the Chapter House. Tell the sheriff that if he wants to talk about it he had better join us at the cathedral without delay.'

Determined not to be at the beck and call of Richard de Revelle, de Wolfe waved the sergeant away and, with Thomas clip-clopping behind, he strode away down towards the high street and the Close.

He found John de Alençon waiting impatiently in the Chapter House. This was a square wooden structure outside the South Tower in which the daily chapter meetings of the canons and lesser clergy were held. It had bare benches around three sides and a lectern on the other, where a chapter of the gospels was read at each session, giving the assembly its name. A wooden ladder in the corner led to the cathedral library above. The archdeacon's spare frame was pacing up and down, his cassock sweeping the floor in his agitation. Sharp grey eyes looked out worriedly from his thin face, accentuating his ascetic appearance. 'John, what am I hearing about tomorrow? Is there no end to this?'

De Wolfe sank on to a front bench and turned up his hands in exasperated supplication. 'It is not of my doing. Another ex-Templar has appeared, this time intent on delivering some religious truth. I have no control over him, so what do you expect me to do?'

De Alençon slumped on to the wooden seat alongside the coroner. 'I wish the bishop was here. This should be the responsibility of someone with a higher authority. I have been visited by Cosimo and the Templar knights, who told me of their concern that serious heresy is afoot.'

The outer door banged and in marched Richard de Revelle, green cloak flowing in the wind and an expression of outrage on his narrow face. 'You're treading on thin ice, John,' he began, without any preamble. 'I have heard that some foolishness is to be to be perpetrated here tomorrow and it seems that you are linked to it in some way.'

De Wolfe jumped to his feet. 'For God's sake, it's none of my doing! Some religious fanatic appears in the city and immediately everyone thinks he is my protégé.'

'This cannot be allowed to continue!' shouted the sheriff. 'I'll have three senior Templars on my back like a ton of quarrystone. When they hear of this, they will demand that he be arrested.'

'Do you know who we are talking about?' grated de Wolfe. 'You want him arrested and yet you don't even know his name.'

'So who is he?' demanded de Revelle.

'He's another Templar – or perhaps former Templar would be more accurate. No doubt he has already been ejected from the Order,' observed de Wolfe.

The archdeacon, who disliked the sheriff as much as de Wolfe did, could not resist putting a brake on his autocratic manner. 'Forgive me, de Revelle, but I have to point out that not only do you have no jurisdiction in the cathedral precinct, except upon the roads, but that I fail to see how you can arrest anyone for threatening to give a religious address, sacrilegious or otherwise. Both those matters are strictly within the authority of the Church and its Consistory Courts.'

Richard de Revelle tried to bluster his way around this. 'Possibly true, Archdeacon, but if the outrage at heretical preaching leads to a public disturbance or even a riot, which could spread beyond the Close, then it most certainly is a breach of the king's peace and falls within my remit.'

The two Johns couldn't resist exchanging cynical smiles at this, coming from a recognised supporter of the prince's treason.

'I am very glad to hear you upholding your sovereign Richard's peace, Sheriff, and I will bear it in mind,' said the priest sweetly.

'Are you going to do nothing to prevent this obscenity, then?' fumed de Revelle.

'There is no way that we can allow anyone to preach publicly from our own cathedral steps,' said the Archdeacon decisively, 'especially when it is rumoured that he is fostering some heresy, presumably that of the Cathars, as he is said to come from that part of France.'

Once again the Chapter House door creaked open and this time a whole crowd of men jostled inside. The three Knights Templar ushered in Cosimo of Modena and their five retainers came in after them to stand ranged around the back of the room.

'Gossip travels fast in this city,' observed John de Alençon mildly, looking at the group of damp souls who stood dripping water on to the flagged floor, for the rain had begun again in earnest outside.

The small Italian priest moved to the centre of the floor, in front of the much taller archdeacon. He began speaking in a high pitched whine. 'It has come to my notice that we have yet more sacrilege amongst us! It is my duty to know of such dangerous men, especially from France, and I tell you, this Bernardus de Blanchefort may present a serious threat to our Mother Church. He must be taken and sent home to be taught the error of his ways.'

'What are these errors, Brother Abbot?' asked the archdeacon gravely.

Cosimo looked evasively from him to the coroner and back again. 'It is the usual foul nonsense, the perverted beliefs of those in the Albi region of the Languedoc. They are so evilly fanciful that, though they make no impression on educated men such as we, if preached openly to the public some of the weaker-minded may be influenced.'

'He must not be allowed to open his mouth,' roared Brian de Falaise, from a few feet away. His bull neck and rugged cheeks were almost purple with anger and de Wolfe suspected that if he hadn't left his broadsword at home to visit a church the blade would be whistling through the air at this point.

'Where is this accursed fellow, anyway?' demanded Richard de Revelle. 'Has anyone seen him? How did we hear that he was in Exeter and intended on this madness tomorrow?' He glared at his brother-in-law, as if suspecting that he was behind this new problem.

John decided that part of the truth was better than a complete denial. 'He accosted me in the street today, after the burial of his fellow Templar.'

'They are no Templars!' snarled Brian de Falaise. 'They would have been ejected from our Order with ignominy had they been found before they fled from us.'

'So you were searching for these men, then, and not just looking for land to purchase?' observed de Wolfe, with a hard edge to his voice.

Roland de Ver slid smoothly into the exchange. 'We are seeking new estates, indeed we are. But on our journeying we were also told to look out for our two wayward brothers, who were thought to be in this part of England.' He looked reprovingly at de Falaise, who glowered back. De Ver continued, 'My friend here is not quite correct in his harsh judgement of them. If we had come across them in our travels, we were to persuade them to return with us so that the error of their ways could be explained to them, and every effort made to bring them back into the paths of righteousness.'

At this, Godfrey Capra and Brian de Falaise looked at each other as if this was the first they had heard of it, but they wisely held their peace.

The archdeacon came back into the discussion, privately most concerned – as was his friend the coroner – about Gilbert de Ridefort's bloody end. 'Abbot Cosimo, I am not at all clear about your mission in Devon. Did you come because of these two Templars?'

The Italian's strange profile slowly turned up to the taller priest. 'I regret that I cannot discuss such matters, Archdeacon. As you know, I am a papal nuncio and as such have complete authority to conduct myself in any way that seems beneficial to the Holy See. But I can tell you that I am charged with the rooting out of heresy, wherever it may be found.'

After being told to mind his own business, John de Alençon stared stonily at de Revelle. 'What is to be done about this, Sheriff? Though I have pointed out to you that the precinct is outwith your jurisdiction, I take your point about not wanting a riot. Already, several of my priests and some monks have protested to me about the rumours concerning tomorrow.'

Richard threw back his cloak over one shoulder in a dramatic gesture. 'I will arrest the man the moment he shows his face. I will soon find some suitable charge.'

In spite of an icy glare from Roland de Ver, Brian de Falaise cut across de Revelle in a loud voice. 'Let us take him! We need no legalistic excuse, he is a renegade member of our Order and as such is subject to our discipline. As our leader says, we need to remove him to the New Temple so that he can be readjusted.'

De Wolfe wondered if 'readjustment' included tearing de Blanchefort's arms from their sockets on the rack, but the priest from Modena was now entering the verbal fray.

'What matters is that this troublemaker must not be allowed to open his mouth in public,' he hissed. 'In five minutes before an audience of dull-witted but impressionable folk, he might begin something that could do incalculable damage to the Holy Church. I don't care if the sheriff hangs him or the Templars drag him back to London, as long as he is not allowed to remain at liberty where at any time he might begin to spread this heresy.' With a face that momentarily reminded de Wolfe of a snake, he threw a poisonous look at the coroner. 'I hold you responsible in part for all this trouble. You seem very bound up with these two men – I trust you yourself have no leanings towards their perverted ideas.'

He looked over his shoulder to where his two glowering retainers stood menacingly near the door. 'I intend to have a presence in the cathedral Close tomorrow, as a safety measure in case you others fail in your duties.' With that, he pulled up the pointed hood of his black habit, glided towards his men and vanished with them into the night.

Now the Templars, the archdeacon and the sheriff all turned to the coroner. 'So where is he, John?' snapped de Revelle. 'You seem to know most about him. In fact, we have only your word for it that he actually exists!'

'De Blanchefort exists all right, as did de Ridefort,'

growled Brian de Falaise. 'I saw them both in Outremer – they were strange then. De Ridefort had strangeness in the blood, for his damned uncle proved that!'

John de Alençon held his hands as if in prayer. 'Do you know where he is now, John?'

'I have no idea where he is,' said the coroner, almost truthfully. 'I presume he is still in the city, as the gates are now locked, though he may have left since this afternoon, when I last saw him.'

De Wolfe satisfied his conscience with the evasion that he did not know exactly – to a few hundred paces – where Bernardus was at that moment, for as soon as he had known that he was going to the Chapter House for an inevitable grilling about the fugitive, he had seized Gwyn in the castle guardroom and sent him down to the Saracen to get the Templar out and hide him somewhere until the morning.

One of the brown-cloaked Templar sergeants moved forward and whispered to Roland de Ver. The knight nodded and pulled thoughtfully at his right ear. 'It is pointless trying to find this de Blanchefort tonight. I have never met him, but both my brothers here know him slightly by sight, and in the morning can patrol the streets around the cathedral to seek some sign of him.'

De Ver pulled his white mantle with the bold red cross more closely around him in preparation for leaving. 'Whatever happens, this man must not be allowed to climb the cathedral steps, let alone open his mouth to say even as much as "Good morning",' he declared. Turning on his heel he stalked from the bleak chamber, followed by the sheriff, then his fellow Knights of Christ and their sergeants.

The two Johns were left alone, apart from the rather

overawed Thomas lurking near the lectern. 'You have a talent for becoming involved in desperate situations, John,' said the archdeacon, with a twinkle in his eye even at this serious moment. 'A few months ago it was the murder of that silversmith, then it was the business of Prince John. Now you bring international heretics into our city and cathedral! What will it be next?'

De Wolfe gave his friend one of his rare grins. 'I'll think of something, John, never fear!'

CHAPTER THIRTEEN

In which Crowner John plays a trick

The services of Terce, Sext, Nones and High Mass took place in the choir of the cathedral from about the ninth hour of the morning. The first three were short devotions, mainly sung psalms. Once the main mass of the day was over, the clergy, who had already been at Prime and then the Chapter meeting since about the seventh hour, were usually more than ready for their dinner at about the eleventh.

But this Sunday morning, even empty stomachs were not enough to keep many of the canons, vicars, secondaries and choristers away from the West Front, attracted by the rumours that had been circulating since the previous day. The prospect of a break from the tedium of the endless round of services, the same faces and the same surroundings of the episcopal city-within-a-city, drew a considerable crowd into the Close and the number of clerics was swollen by scores of citizens.

The mood was one of curiosity rather than a desire for enlightenment, though a few of the older people, both lay and clergy, were either indignant or incensed that someone might have the effrontery to try to preach heresy from the cathedral steps.

As the black-robed clerics streamed out of the door
from the nave into the weak sunshine – for it had
stopped raining at last – they slowed down into a
sluggish pool of humanity surrounding the broad West
Front of the huge building. Some, whose desire for food
was greater than for dramatic diversion, walked slowly
towards their lodgings, determined that if nothing excit-
ing occurred before they reached the edge of the Close
they would go home. But many others milled about the
foot of the steps, gossiping and staring around, eager
to get a glimpse of the renegade who had promised to
reveal some awful secret.

Amongst this fluid throng were a number of solid
rocks, in the shape of sentinels determined to prevent
any such sabotage of the Faith. The three Templars
and their sergeants were spaced out across the width
of the building, within easy reach of the steps. In the
centre, Abbot Cosimo stood, closely flanked by his silent
henchmen who stared around them with suspicious
hostility. Further back, in an arc at the edge of the
open space before the West Front, stood the sheriff,
with Ralph Morin, the castle constable and half a dozen
men-at-arms under Sergeant Gabriel.

Near the small wicket-gate set in the closed centre
door to the nave, Archdeacon John de Alençon stood
with the coroner, though for once neither of de Wolfe's
assistants was with him.

Every moment or two, a ripple of anticipation ran
through the crowd, as someone saw, or fancied he
saw, a stranger appear in the Close. Several times, this
rolling murmur came then faded, and each time there
was a tensing of muscles and shifting of feet amongst
the guardians of truth.

'Did you see this man de Blanchefort last night to

warn him off?' asked the archdeacon, as another false alarm died down.

'I've not set eyes on him, apart from that one meeting,' said de Wolfe, truthfully as he had used Gwyn as an intermediary. 'If he's got any sense, he'll stay well clear of this ambush, unless he wants to risk the same fate as his friend.'

Suddenly there was a stir at the further end of the front of the cathedral, towards the corner facing Canon's Row. Heads turned, fingers pointed, and a surge in the murmur and chatter sent several of Gabriel's men pushing forward through the crowd. But they were outpaced by one of the servants of the Italian priest and also the sergeant of Brian de Falaise, closely followed by the Templar knight himself. They converged on someone who had walked around the corner of the building from the north side, keeping close to the wall until he reached the edge of the half-dozen long steps that stretched below the three big doors. Once the movement began, it was almost alive in its self-generation and a wave of people surged forward, the sentinels pushing and thrashing to get to the front.

The archdeacon stretched his thin neck to see better and began to move forward too, but John de Wolfe stayed where he was, a faint smile on his saturnine face. The first to press up to the new arrival was Cosimo's familiar, who seized him and swung him around. The man wore a wide-brimmed hat pulled well down over his head and a long grey cloak with a hood, which lay in concealing folds around his neck and face. He was a big man, tall and wide within the folds of his mantle.

De Falaise was the next to reach him and, with a cry of triumph, grabbed him by the arm. Simultaneously, the sheriff and Cosimo pressed through to form a tight circle in the midst of the confused throng of clerics and townsfolk.

'They seem to have got him, so pray God he cannot begin his devilish oratory!' cried the archdeacon, but the coroner remained impassive, assured that there would be no attempt at any seditious speech. He watched as the man pulled away angrily from the grip of several who were now pawing at him, amid shouts of 'Heretic!' and 'Anti-Christ!'

A second later, his hat was pulled off and his cloak ripped open, which provoked a great roar from the man. 'Get off me, damn you! Can't a fellow have a Sunday morning walk without being assaulted?' The bright red hair, wild as a hayrick in a gale, and the luxuriant moustache revealed the presumed heretic as Gwyn of Polruan, doing his best not to laugh at the chagrin of his would-be capturers.

'Who the hell are you?' roared de Falaise, who had never seen the coroner's officer before. Ralph Morin and Gabriel enlightened him, themselves suppressing grins. Although they had had no foreknowledge of Gwyn's appearance, they knew instantly who had instigated the jest. The sheriff also knew, but he was by no means amused. 'You great oaf! What do you think you're doing?' he snapped, confronting the Cornishman.

De Wolfe felt it was time he gave his officer some support and pushed his way to his side. 'Ah, there you are, Gwyn,' he said loudly. 'You're late, as usual.'

Abbot Cosimo and Roland de Ver demanded to know what was going on, as both realised that this was not Bernardus de Blanchefort.

'This fellow has been making fools of us!' blustered Richard de Revelle.

The coroner fixed him with a steely eye. 'Since when

is it forbidden for a citizen to walk peacefully in the cathedral Close, Sheriff?'

Richard de Revelle glared at his brother-in-law. 'Don't play the innocent with me, John. When did your lout of a man ever wear a pilgrim's hat and a grey cloak? Tattered leather and a sack around his head is his usual attire.'

'Then we should be pleased that his tastes are improving, Richard,' countered John sarcastically.

The crowd sensed that the fun was over and most realised that no heretic was likely to appear now. But Cosimo remained suspicious and looked around in every direction, with jerky movements of his head. 'Can we be sure that this is not some trick, some diversion to allow de Blanchefort to slip past us?' he hissed to Roland de Ver. He prodded his two retainers hard in their ribs to send them hurrying to each end of the West Front to stare about for any other stranger, who failed conspicuously to appear.

'Come on, Gwyn, we have work to do,' barked de Wolfe, with a wink at Ralph Morin. They walked away, leaving the three Templars glowering suspiciously after them and an exasperated sheriff protesting again to the archdeacon, who now could hardly conceal a smile of relief that no challenge to his beloved Church had been made.

Outside his house in Martin's Lane, de Wolfe retrieved his hat and cloak from Gwyn and asked him about Thomas de Peyne. 'Did they get away as we arranged?'

Gwyn nodded, still pleased with his role in the little play-acting they had devised. 'Soon after dawn he collected the Templar from the Saracen and rode with him out of the North Gate. Even at that little dwarf's riding pace, they should be past Crediton by now.'

'Where are we to meet them on Tuesday?'

Gwyn dragged thoughtfully at one end of his moustache.

'It's difficult if we are with all those others. I told Thomas to hide de Blanchefort away somewhere well outside Bideford, then to come and meet us at the bridge at noon. We should be there by then.'

After Gwyn had gone about his business, de Wolfe entered his house where he had a silent meal with Matilda. She enquired shortly as to whether the heretic had appeared and he told her equally shortly that there had been no sign of Bernardus de Blanchefort. He made no mention of Gwyn's mischievous masquerade, not wanting to give his wife another opportunity to castigate him.

Simon tottered in with a jug of wine, which Matilda seemed to relish far more than the salted herrings, turnip and cabbage that Mary provided from the kitchen. De Wolfe watched covertly as his wife drank a mug of the red Poitou and immediately refilled it. Since the shame of her brother's involvement in the abortive rebellion in the New Year, he had noticed that Matilda sought solace not only from her religious devotions but also from the wine flask.

Following the miserable meal, she called for Lucille, who helped her up to the solar to lie on her bed until it was time for her next pilgrimage to St Olave's.

John took the opportunity to go down to Idle Lane, where he also went to bed – in Nesta's little room on the upper floor of the Bush. They made love energetically and repeatedly until they lay side by side in delicious exhaustion, his arm about her shoulders. As the thumping of his heartbeat subsided almost to normal, he stared up lazily at the rough roof beams, his eyes tracing the twisted hazel withies that supported the thick straw thatch above them. He told her about the scene in the cathedral Close that morning and Nesta wanted to know why he gone out of his way to help de Blanchefort.

'Like de Ridefort, he was both a Crusader and a Templar, for whom I have always had admiration for their bravery and fighting prowess,' he explained.

'You old soldiers always stick together, eh?' she said, in a gently mocking tone. He pinched her bare belly with his free hand and she squirmed under the sheepskin that covered them. 'Not only that, but I had made a promise to Gilbert to help them both get away – and as I feel partly responsible for his death, I had to keep my word.'

She turned her head impulsively to kiss his black-stubbled neck. 'It was not you who killed him, John. Someone else wielded that club and spear. Do you have any idea yet who it may have been?'

His gaze dropped to the rough boards that partitioned off this corner of the loft. Though it was a crude chamber, he had enjoyed more pleasure within its walls than anywhere else on earth. He shook away the thought and answered her question. 'It must be either one of the Templars or their squires – though I would prefer it to be this poisonous abbot or his men. Not that I have any chance of discovering who it was now,' he added regretfully. 'I had hoped to use Bernardus as a tethered goat to tempt the killer to try again, but it could never have worked in the middle of Exeter. I had to smuggle him out for his own safety.'

The landlady of the inn snuggled closer into his armpit, her copper hair flowing over his chest, wide green eyes looking up at the stern profile of his long face. 'How do you intend getting him out of the country, then?'

'Thomas has ridden on ahead with him and I will see if we can find a ship in Bideford or nearby that can take him to Wales or Ireland.'

'What if he is seen by any of the others who are hunting him?'

'I must try to keep them apart, but they have never seen him without the Templar profusion of whiskers, so hopefully he would not be recognised.'

'Could you not have found him a passage more easily from the ports around here – Topsham or Brixham?'

Perhaps his mind was too relaxed by the pleasant sensation of wallowing in a warm bed alongside a naked woman, but in this unguarded moment he made a serious slip. 'I had thought of it. Maybe Thorgils the Boatman in Dawlish would have taken him off, but he only sails back to France, which is the last place that Bernardus wants to be.'

He felt Nesta stiffen against him. Though at the time of his foolishly heroic battle on the tourney field in January, Nesta and Hilda, wife of Thorgils, had come together in common concern for his life, they still looked upon each other as rivals for his affection and his body. True, Nesta was fairly confident that she had priority in terms of being cherished by him, but she well knew that the willowy blonde could easily seduce him into a quick tumble whenever the opportunity presented, and she could not suppress the jealousy that welled up within her at the mention of Dawlish.

De Wolfe cursed his own insensitivity and pulled her to him, as if to squeeze her back into his body, but Nesta lay inert and distant. Perversely and against his will, the image of Hilda crept into his mind. He had not spoken to her since the day he had broken his leg and had not lain with her since just after Christ Mass, but now a picture of her supple body and beautiful face flooded unbidden into his mind's eye. He had known her since she was a child and they had been sporadic lovers since she was fifteen, but as the daughter of one of his father's manor-reeves, she could never have been his wife.

With a groan of frustration, he screwed up his eyes to blot out the vision, and rolled on his side and clutched Nesta in an almost violent spasm. He kissed her eyes, neck and mouth in a desperate attack and felt her suddenly melt against him, returning his kisses and pressing herself to him with an urgency that told him the present battle was won.

They were too satiated to make love again and remained hugged together without speaking for a long time, John revelling in the feel of her body touching his from lips to breast to belly to thigh. In an effort to banish the hovering image of Hilda, he forced himself to think of Matilda, and in the way that a mind wanders in that sleepy dreamland after love-making, he recalled the early days of their marriage, sixteen years before. It had been a loveless match engineered by his father, who saw the advantages for his son of an attachment to the wealthy de Revelle family. Matilda had never relished her nuptial obligations and their night-time relations had soon wilted, especially as de Wolfe spent ten months of the year away on some fighting campaign.

Since he had given up being a professional warrior a year or two before, their enforced cohabitation had not seen any revival of passion. His mind's eye now saw her again at their midday meal, drinking red wine as if it was ale, and recalled with some shame that the last time they had attempted to make love had been when she was drunk many months ago. The episode was a dismal failure and ended in bitter recrimination from his wife and a resolve on his part never to repeat the fiasco.

Now that Nesta had recovered from her dark mood, her natural curiosity revived and she asked him about the Templars' involvement with the mission to Lundy next day.

'Their excuse is that they wish to test William de Marisco's will in keeping their Order from his island,' explained John. 'But I suspect that they don't trust me over de Blanchefort and wish to keep me in their sight.'

'And they're right, you crafty man!' she teased. 'But have you any real hope of making progress with this lord of Lundy?'

De Wolfe scowled at the roof. 'Almost none, from what I hear of him. There's no doubt that he runs a nest of pirates from his island fiefdom, but whether it was one of his ships that slew most of the crew of the vessel that was wrecked near Ilfracombe, I cannot tell.'

'What made our dear sheriff agree to this expedition, then? He's not usually one to put himself at risk.'

'He has a reverence for the Templars, for some reason. I suspect he thinks that by ingratiating himself with them, he may advance his own ambitions. They are so powerful a force in this and every other land. Even King Richard is partial to them, so maybe de Revelle hopes that by showing them assistance, he can gain favour with the king after his fall from grace at the New Year.'

She slid a hand on to his stomach and stroked small circles with her fingers. 'Why should you be involved in this, John? It sounds a hazardous mission and not one that involves a crowner's interest.'

'It does, you know. There was a wreck, which is my

business, and there was a slain corpse there, as well as a good history of the killing of the rest of the crew. That alone makes it my concern.'

He pulled his arm from under Nesta as his fingers were becoming numb, and continued his lecture. 'Although there's been no time to inform the king's justices and get a reply, any coroner can be sent a special commission from the Justiciar or the royal judges to become involved in almost any aspect of the law or administration. I'm sure that if the Curia Regis knew of a revival of piracy in the Severn Sea and that Lundy may be its nest, they would demand some action such as we propose tomorrow.'

Nesta's voice was sleepy. 'What's this Curia Regis you talk about?'

'The king's court – the nobles about him who give him advice and counsel. Now that he's in France, in practice the Chancellor and the Chief Justiciar run the country, but the major barons and the archbishops also have a say in what goes on.'

But Nesta had slipped into slumber, and before long, he had joined her, their heads together on the pillow.

The next morning, John de Wolfe recaptured some of the excitement of former days when he rode up to Rougement and saw the preparations for their journey to the north of the county. He felt a surge of the anticipation of battle, when he rode Odin through the gateway to the inner ward and saw well over a score of armoured soldiers jostling with their mounts. The smell of many horses and the clatter of harness, shields and swords brought back nostalgic memories of a dozen campaigns.

He watched as Ralph Morin and Sergeant Gabriel

harried their men-at-arms into a column. They were all in battle array, with chain-mail hauberks and round basin-like helmets with long nose-guards. Each man had a rectangular iron plate slung across his breast with leather thongs, to protect his heart from a lance thrust, and each had a long oval shield slung on his saddle-bow. As they were mounted for a long ride, they did not carry lances or pikes like foot-soldiers, but every man had either a heavy sword or a battle-axe.

Standing apart from the troops were the three Templar knights, not yet mounted but resplendent in their own armour, with long hauberks slit at front and back to sit astride their horses and polished metal-link aventails hanging from their helmet brims to protect their necks. Each had a huge sword hanging from a leather baldric, and over their armour they wore their white or black surcoats with the scarlet cross of the Order on the chest. Their sergeants waited attentively in a group behind them, holding the bridles of the beautiful palfreys. They were dressed in brown surcoats over similar armour, battle-axes or spiked maces hanging from their saddles.

In front of them strutted the sheriff, a groom holding his horse whilst he inspected the line of men-at-arms, to the ill-concealed irritation of Ralph Morin. De Revelle was kitted out in immaculate chain-mail, which, unlike that worn by de Wolfe and the Templars, was free of the scratches, dents and bent links of former combat. Over it he had his own white surcoat, emblazoned with a red griffin, which was repeated on his shield in the new fashion for displaying a family crest. The coroner walked his horse to the foot of the curtain wall of the inner ward, where Gwyn stood inconspicuously, holding the reins of his own big brown mare. Dressed in his usual thick jerkin of boiled leather, he had made a token gesture to possible fighting by donning a leather helmet with battered metal plates riveted around the crown and over his ears. He stared at the sheriff with scorn, as de Revelle fussed up and down the line of men-at-arms. 'You'd think he was preparing to storm Jerusalem! I wonder if he knows which end of the sword to hold?' he grunted scathingly.

The coroner, though no admirer of the sheriff, felt he should give him what little honour he deserved. 'Come, man, he was in Ireland for a year or so at one time.'

'Yes, in the company of Prince John. It would be hard to know which of them made the worst mess of it.'

It was true that, back in 'eighty-five, King Henry had given his younger son the responsibility of subduing Ireland, with catastrophic results due to the prince's incompetence – it had been during this time that Richard de Revelle had become one of his sympathisers.

There was further flurry of activity in the bailey as Morin and the sheriff mounted their horses, the group of Templars following suit. Gwyn hauled his great body aboard his mare and pulled her round to come alongside his master. 'This will be a slow journey with all the weight of armour on their horses,' he grumbled. 'They should have sent it ahead in carts or on sumpters.'

John agreed, but suspected that the sheriff wanted to make the best impression both on the citizens and burgesses of Exeter and on his Templar guests. Like Gwyn, the coroner had not worn chain-mail but also sported a leather cuirass with metal shoulder plates and had a round helmet hanging behind his saddle.

Playing the part of the great leader, the sheriff took his frisky horse to the head of the column, with the castle constable close behind. They began moving towards the gatehouse, when suddenly de Revelle held up his arm and came to a stop. Under the raised portcullis came three more riders and the coroner cursed when he saw the leader. 'What in the name of Holy Mary is he doing here, Gwyn?'

The Cornishman glowered as Abbot Cosimo and his pair of familiars clattered across the cobbles of the entrance on to the softer ground of the bailey. De Wolfe tapped Odin with his heels and moved over to hear what was being said between the newcomers and the sheriff.

'I decided that it might be interesting to visit the north of your lands,' explained Cosimo, in his thin, high voice. 'I have never been to England before and would see as much of it as I can whilst I am here. Also, not speaking English, it is more pleasant for me to remain with the Norman-French tongue for as long as possible.'

At this somewhat unconvincing excuse, Ralph Morin spoke up from behind the sheriff. 'There may well be some fighting, if we meet up with pirates – or if the lord of Lundy opposes our will.'

The abbot's thin lips rose slightly in a smile. 'Never fear, sir, I shall keep well clear of any such adventures.' As the papal envoy had previously made clear that he had the unlimited authority of the Vatican behind him for whatever purpose he chose, the sheriff bowed to the inevitable and courteously invited him to join their cavalcade. John knew full well that his brother-in-law was so thick with Bishop Marshal – another of the Prince's men – that he would never say nay to any senior churchman. He also strongly suspected that, like the Templars, the Italian was more concerned with even the slightest possibility of his missing heretic turning up in the north than with any interest in the Devonshire scenery. He realised, too, from the suspicious glances that all these parties flashed at him, that they felt he himself still had some connection with de Blanchefort – especially since Gwyn's antics outside the cathedral the previous day. He guessed that they still suspected he knew of the man's whereabouts and might even have him hidden somewhere – which, of course, he did.

The column began moving again and the papal trio fitted themselves between the tail of the soldiers and the six Templars, who formed the rearguard until the coroner and his officer tagged themselves on the end. They all trotted out of the castle and down the high street, scattering children, dogs and the occasional beggar as they made their way out of the city. Most townsfolk stopped their work or marketing to look with curiosity at this band of armed men, as in those days of relative peace, it was uncommon to see so many soldiers and knights on the move within Exeter. In the early-morning light, they clattered under the arch of the North Gate and settled down to the forty-mile ride to Bideford.

Though a herald or king's messenger could cover fifty or even sixty miles in an average day, using changes of horse, the usual distance for unburdened riders was about thirty, so it was about noon the next day when the posse reached Bideford, the little town on the banks of the river Torridge. They had spent the previous night at a manor near Great Torrington, the soldiers sleeping in two barns of a small manor belonging to the local lord, Walter FitzGamelin. As seasoned old campaigners, the Templars, with de Wolfe, Gwyn and Ralph Morin, were content to lie out in the hay with them, as did the abbot's sinister attendants, but the Italian and Richard de Revelle enjoyed the rather reluctant hospitality of

FitzGamelin in the hall of the manor-house. Sudden inflictions of visiting officials were never welcomed by manors and villages, especially when food for two score men and beasts had to be provided without recompense, but it was not nearly so bad as when a cavalcade of royalty or a major baron passed through, which might bankrupt a small community. Nevertheless the local manorial tenant had to provide hospitality without protest, even if with ill grace.

The same applied to Richard de Grenville at Bideford, but at least he knew in advance of their coming and of his further obligation to provide some of his own knights and men-at-arms. As with all honour holders, he held his lands from the king, either directly or through a baron, bishop or abbey, and as a condition of his grant, he was obliged to provide services and men in time of conflict or when otherwise needed.

As it happened, de Grenville was not particularly put out by the visitation. His little empire was quite affluent, with the dues from the port, the town markets and his several manors, so he could easily afford to assist the sheriff for a few days. Also he had little love for William de Marisco, who was one of his nearest neighbours, though separated by twenty miles of sea. His maritime customers had lost many ships in past years, and this was never good for trade. Although some had been taken undoubtedly by a whole range of pirates, from Turks to Welsh, he was convinced that Lundy had been responsible for a few and the hope that de Marisco might be brought to heel caused him to contribute willingly to the expedition.

When the party from Exeter arrived at the simple motte and bailey castle of Bideford, the troops were settled in some of the outhouses and sheds built against the inside of the stockade walls, whilst the knights and the abbot enjoyed the better accommodation in the hall. This was not the small keep on the mound at one end of the bailey, but a larger wooden building at its foot, where de Grenville and his family resided.

He was a pleasant, rather jovial man, middle-aged and running to fat. His red nose and pink cheeks suggested a partiality to wine and ale, which was confirmed by his generosity when the jugs and flasks circulated to his guests. His wife, a buxom, motherly woman, appeared briefly to greet them with her husband, then retired to her solar, leaving the men to their meal and ample drink, even though it was early afternoon.

'Two ships are prepared for us, but the tide will only be suitable early tomorrow morning as we cannot embark tonight in the dark,' de Grenville announced, as they all sat around the long table waiting to be served.

'Will there be enough room aboard for the whole company?' asked Ralph Morin. 'We have forty men and you have your own troop.'

De Grenville stood at the head of the table and waved a pewter tankard reassuringly. 'We will be six knights including myself, and half a score men from the castle guard. The vessels will easily carry us – we have no horses or equipment other than what we carry ourselves. The crews are local men, who know these treacherous waters and also Lundy – as well as anyone can, for Marisco never allows any but his own men to land there.'

They settled down to eat, but discussion concerning the expedition punctuated their meal. 'What do you know about piracy in these waters, de Grenville?' asked de Revelle. 'We have a death and a lost crew to investigate from Ilfracombe, as you must know.'

'There are so many possible culprits,' replied the

lord of Bideford, taking a capon's leg from his lips to reply. 'As much as I would like to think Lundy was responsible, so many other possibilities exist. There is a nest of pirates in the Scillies, and though the Bretons from St Malo operate mainly south of Cornwall, they sometimes find rich pickings from the Bristol trade up here. Then the Welsh come across from Swansea, Flat Holm and Porthclais near Menevia, and the Irish from Wexford and Waterford.'

'I have heard that some marauders come from as far away as Spain,' growled Morin, his grey forked beard wagging as he spoke.

'And further yet! Moorish galleys from the Barbary coast have been seen off Hartland, and it is said that some even come from Turkey.'

De Wolfe fixed his host with a suspicious eye. 'Yet I am told that we need not look that far away for many of our pirates. Our own coast may harbour them, from Cornwall to Somerset.'

De Grenville shrugged. 'I'm sure that may be right. Who is to tell what any vessel and its crew does once it leaves its own port? Weapons can be concealed in the hold and a few extra crew to outnumber the victim. The home village is not going to advertise the fact, if their men bring home a free cargo in these hard times. As long as they leave no shipmen alive to tell the tale, how can they ever be accused?'

'You know of nothing like that in this river?' persisted the coroner, though he knew that de Grenville would hardly admit to it.

Even this direct question failed to blunt de Grenville's good humour. 'I know you heard some tale about Appledore, when you came recently. But of all the places who are likely to be involved, that poor vill is the least likely. They have no safe anchorage and no vessel bigger than a miserable fishing boat. I cannot speak for Barnstaple, but no pirates sail from Bideford or I would know of it – and they have no need as commerce here is good enough. You should look to smaller havens, more remote and with a need to prey on others.'

The talk drifted on to other matters, and as soon as he could decently quit the table, de Wolfe quietly made his way outside. He checked quickly that Odin was well watered and fed and that Gwyn was happily eating and drinking his fill outside the kitchen with the other men. Then he left the castle gate, with an awkward salute from the somewhat overawed guard, and walked along the track by the riverbank into the small town.

The market was almost immediately outside the castle, and though it was late in the day for trade, many stalls and booths were still open. As he passed by to reach the bridge, a miracle play was being performed on a curtained stage, and a small crowd had gathered in front of the platform to watch. Most were women and children, but there was a sprinkling of men. De Wolfe recognised Thomas amongst them, his small hunched body next to a larger, muffled figure, who must have been de Blanchefort, though no part of his features was visible beneath his cloak collar and big hat. De Wolfe moved around until he was plainly in view of his clerk and waited until Thomas noticed him.

When he did, de Wolfe beckoned and, sensibly leaving the former Templar to continue watching the drama, Thomas came casually across to his master.

'I thought we were to meet at the bridge?' growled the coroner.

'I was there at noon, but there was no sign of you, so eventually we came nearer.'

'The journey was slower than I expected. We had that damned priest to hold us up. Have you had any problems?'

'Only that de Blanchefort keeps wanting to declare his awful secret to the world at large. I dissuaded him by pointing out that Bideford is such a remote town that it must be the least effective place on earth to reveal some great truth,' he added drily, crossing himself as a precaution against contamination from the man's heresy. 'Otherwise nothing. We have found a lodging out of the town, with an ale-wife in a village a mile or so away. No risk of being recognised there.'

'Have you tried to find a passage out for Bernardus?'

Thomas looked abashed. 'I spent the morning doing that, Crowner, but there is no vessel leaving, except to go to other harbours along this coast. The only two bigger vessels have been commandeered by Lord Richard for your expedition tomorrow.'

De Wolfe considered this, but no other plan came to mind. 'Keep trying, then. Our Templar says he has plenty of silver to buy a passage, so that should be no problem. All we need is a ship going to Wales or Ireland.' He arranged with his clerk that he should be at the bridge at two hours after dawn on Thursday, and if there was no sign of the expedition returning by then, at a similar time each day until they met. With a covert wave at Bernardus, he returned to the castle and brought Gwyn up to date with events.

He spent a couple of hours with Ralph Morin and Gabriel, checking the readiness of the soldiers for the morning. Everyone had taken off their mailed hauberks, which were hanging up on wooden poles thrust through the sleeves from side to side. The men were rubbing the steel links with handfuls of hay daubed with beef fat, to preserve them against rust, especially as they would be exposed to salt spray on the morrow. De Grenville was also out in the bailey, marshalling his armed men and knights. They had a motley collection of armour and weapons, but looked tough enough for the task ahead.

That evening, the hospitable lord of Bideford put on a good meal, which though hardly a banquet was a liberal entertainment, especially in the quantity of drink provided. A pair of minstrels at the bottom of the hall and two jugglers diverted the guests between courses. De Grenville's lady and their two eldest daughters attended for the meal, then tactfully retired before the serious drinking began. As well as the sheriff, coroner, constable, Templars and abbot from Exeter, there were the Bideford knights, chaplain, steward, treasurer and several others from the borough seated along the long table, with de Grenville at its head.

John de Wolfe found himself placed next to Cosimo, sharing with him a trencher, which was kept liberally loaded with food by attentive servants. Though the coroner had grave suspicions of the Italian, he had little option but to be civil to him out of deference to their host, though he would have preferred his room to the Italian's company. However, he was unable to be anything but blunt with the priest when conversation was inevitable. 'In spite of the confidential nature of your business in England, which you so firmly put to us, I feel little doubt that those two errant Templars were your prime concern,' he said.

The sly eyes in the olive face rolled up to meet his. 'You may think what you will, Crowner. I'll not deny that they formed at least part of my reason for venturing across the Channel from France. And I would dearly like to know the truth about Bernardus de Blanchefort.'

De Wolfe struck the point of his dagger into a slice of salted pork on the slab of bread between them and carried it towards his mouth. Before it vanished between his lips, he replied, 'I told you the truth, that he waylaid me and told me he wished to make some kind of public declaration before the cathedral. Obviously he thought better of it and is now on his way to a safer haven somewhere.' All of which was true, he thought, as he chewed on the pig meat – though not the whole truth.

Cosimo picked more delicately at the food with a thin silver poniard. 'So where is he now, I wonder? He is a dangerous madman, who should not be loose in Christian kingdoms.'

John, though not over-concerned with religion or the future of his immortal soul, had, like most people, an ingrained wariness of priests, instilled in childhood by family and chaplains. He avoided outright lying to them but was willing to prevaricate a little. 'I have no knowledge of where he might be, Abbot,' he said, salving his conscience with the thought that Thomas had not actually told him in what village they were lodged.

The priest sucked at his food for a moment then spoke to the trencher, rather than to de Wolfe. 'The whole edifice of civilisation in Europe depends on the stabilising influence of the Holy Roman Church. Without that framework of uniformity and constancy, the warring nations and tribes would tear themselves asunder inside a year or two.'

He nibbled at his meat, and, almost against his will, de Wolfe waited for the conclusion to this profound but obscure statement. 'Anything that could damage that stability threatens the very structure of life as we know it in these western lands and could plunge us into the barbarism of Africa and Asia. And that stability rests on the basic beliefs of Christianity, of which the Roman Church has been the guardian for more than a thousand years.'

The sly eyes looked up, to lock with those of the coroner. 'I will do anything to preserve that stability by preventing the serpent seed of disbelief from being planted in the minds of common folk. You may well bear a heavy responsibility on your shoulders, Crowner, for which you may have to answer in the next world, if not in this.'

With that barely veiled threat, the abbot turned back to his dinner and said not another word to de Wolfe for the rest of the meal.

CHAPTER FOURTEEN

In which Crowner John goes to sea

With an almost full moon the previous night, the tide was high along the banks of the river and the knights and men-at-arms filed aboard the two knarrs on gangplanks that were almost level. The long wooden bridge across the river was immediately upstream to the stone quay that had been built to serve Bideford, and all vessels with fixed masts were obliged to moor on its seaward side.

The grey light of dawn was filtering through broken cloud and the wind was slight and south-easterly, ideal for getting out of the Torridge into its confluence with the Taw, which flowed from Barnstaple to the open sea beyond Appledore. The waterways were tortuous and ever-changing, the banks of sand and mud altering with every flood and storm, but with this spring tide the flat-bottomed boats had no fear of running aground within the next couple of hours.

The lord of Bideford was aboard the first knarr with his own men and half the Exeter soldiers, as well as the abbot. The remainder were with the sheriff, Templars and coroner on the second vessel. As soon as the men were aboard, the ship-masters cast off and the sails filled to press them seawards for three miles up the river.

De Wolfe stood with the other knights on the left side of the stern, leaving the opposite deck clear for the seaman grasping the steerboard, a large oar lashed to a post on the bulwark. In the centre was the ship-master, a scruffy individual in half-length breeches and a tattered short tunic. Bare-footed, like the other four of his crew, he kept looking up at the sky and muttering foul language under his breath. Every now and then, he would bark some almost unintelligible instruction to the steersman or the crew holding the sheets secured to each lower corner of the single square sail.

Within half an hour, the lively breeze had taken them to the main channel and as soon as they rounded the promontory of Appledore, they felt the swell coming in through the entrance to the open sea. Soon half of the land-lubber soldiers were ill and many hung over the rough fence of the bulwarks, retching their breakfast into the turbid sea.

'Bloody fine fighting force we're going to be!' rumbled Gwyn contemptuously, standing like a rock, feet apart and hands behind his back. He was as much at home on water as on land and had little sympathy for those who were not.

De Wolfe himself, though not a bad sailor, disliked the rhythmic motion as they ran up to the bar between the final sand dunes. He was glad when the ships were in open sea, where the shorter, sharper pitching was less troublesome to his stomach. The sheriff was almost as green as his favourite tunic, but pride prevented him joining his men puking at the rail. Two of the Templars seemed immune, though Godfrey Capra became pale and noticeably silent.

Once outside the estuary, the two little ships ploughed on westwards, with a little northing to reach Lundy.

Above them, the early-morning clouds were breaking up and patches of blue sky appeared and increased as the hours went by, a low pale sun gleaming intermittently in the east. Though de Wolfe considered the weather kind, the ship-master frequently looked to the west and scowled at the open ocean. He muttered now and then to the steersman and pointed to the far distance.

'What's bothering him?' the coroner asked Gwyn.

The former fisherman had also been following the master's concern. 'There's bad weather coming – but not yet. See that cloud on the horizon?'

John squinted to see a bank of solid grey far away, stretched low down in the western sky. To him it looked innocuous and he turned away when the ship-master again began gabbling in his thick local accent.

'It's Lundy already. See it ahead there?' interpreted Gwyn. The air was clear and the dark line of the island rose like a distant whale on the horizon.

'It's three mile long, but less than one wide,' explained the shipmaster. 'We see it side on now from the east, but as we come to it from the south, it will foreshorten.'

The two knarrs hurried along with the brisk fair wind and the ebb tide, which was emptying the channel. In a couple of hours, Lundy was close enough to see the detail on the cliffs, which rose over four hundred feet at the southern end. Most of the men had now recovered from their *mal de mer* and were staring at this huge rock that rose out of the entrance to the Severn Sea. As they came even closer, the tip of the island was seen to hook out towards them in a broken promontory.

'That's Rat Island. The only good landing place is just around the corner from it – and Marisco's castle is above it on the cliffs, at the highest point,' explained the ship-master, pointing at the grey rocks. As the steersman leaned on his great oar and the crew adjusted the square sail, the knarr came round to weather the jagged promontory so that they could see the landing beach, a stretch of pebbles with a steep path winding up behind it. On the top of the cliffs, a low stone fortification was visible, but this sank out of sight as they got nearer.

The sea was fairly calm around the point and they glided towards the beach until the ship-master yelled at his crew once more. The yard rattled down the mast and lay on the untidy folds of the sail, as the knarr lost way. Pointing, the ship-master made it clear why he was keeping well off the shore. A line of men, several dozen in number, was spaced out just above the tide level and more were coming down the steep path from the settlement above. Even at that distance, the knarr's company could see the glint of the weak sunshine on spear-heads and swords.

'It looks as if we have a welcoming party already!' growled Ralph Morin, looking like one of his Norse ancestors with an old conical helmet and his jutting grey beard. De Wolfe, who had been studying the landing site, raised an arm to point high up on the cliff. 'Don't worry too much about them yet, Ralph. Look up there instead.' On a rocky spur above the path, they could just make out a contraption of wooden beams, with a few dot-like figures moving around it. All the fighting men knew what it was and their faces showed that they viewed it seriously.

'A trebuchet – that could indeed be a problem,' observed Roland de Ver. He spoke to the shipmaster and soon the other vessel came alongside. Their rails were roped together so that Richard de Grenville could join in the council of war.

'Are these men on the beach going to oppose us?'

asked Brian de Falaise truculently. 'If so, we should land in force and give them a thrashing.'

'Easier said than done,' retorted de Grenville. 'We cannot beach the knarrs on a falling tide in case we wish to make a rapid retreat. And using the curraghs to land mailed soldiers is fraught with hazard. If they are tipped out, they'll sink like stones!'

'So why the hell did we come?' demanded de Falaise harshly. He was itching for a fight but his lack of concern for his own safety was not shared so enthusiastically by the others.

Further discussion was interrupted by a loud splash and a fountain of water erupted from the sea ahead of them. It was many yards short, but the message was clear. The ships had been drifting towards the shore in the breeze and now the masters were hurriedly casting off the lashings that held the two knarrs together and setting men to haul at long oars over the sides. Though hopelessly inefficient, this halted the drift towards the cliffs and imperceptibly inched the boats back out to sea.

'What range does that thing have?' the sheriff demanded of John.

The coroner shrugged. 'Impossible to tell, other than finding out the hard way, Richard! It's high up, so its range will be greater and the fall of missiles more powerful.'

The trebuchet was an engine for hurling projectiles a considerable distance at an enemy. A long beam was pivoted vertically in a massive frame and a heavy weight fixed to the lower end. A large bowl at the upper end carried either one large rock or a collection of smaller stones. Several men hauled on ropes fixed to the top of the beam until it was horizontal, when it was released, the weight fell violently and the beam jerked back to the vertical, hurling the missiles forward over the edge of the cliff to fall on targets far below. Both the range and direction could be adjusted to cover all the approaches to the beach.

Frustrated, the knights stood on the decks of the two vessels, while the crews dropped two large anchor stones to prevent further drifting into danger. 'We must at least try to parley with these swine to see if they'll at least let us talk to de Marisco,' snarled de Falaise. 'And I'll go if you wish, de Ver.'

John mischievously suggested an alternative. 'Lundy is part of the county of Devon, so falls directly under the jurisdiction of our sheriff here. He must have the prerogative, as well as the honour, of going ashore first.'

De Revelle gave his brother-in-law a look that should have dropped him dead him on the spot and limped away from the rail, rubbing his left thigh. 'Of course I would, but this old wound I suffered in the Irish wars makes it difficult for me to get down into one of those small boats.'

De Falaise, well aware of the coroner's strategem, clapped de Revelle heartily on the shoulder. 'Never fear, sheriff, I'm sure our ship-master here has some rope and tackle that will let us lower you over the side – and I'll come with you.'

In the event, it was Roland de Ver who accompanied de Revelle, saying that, as leader of the Templars, it was his obligation to try to deal with William de Marisco over the rejected grant of land to his Order.

The crew and soldiers hauled one of the light skin-covered boats from the hold and dumped it over the side. The sheriff had been trapped into playing the hero and, albeit with ill-grace, got himself over the low gunwale into the curragh with no sign of a disabled leg. He held aloft a spare oar with a grubby white tunic, taken from the crew's shelter, tied to the top as a flag of truce. While de Ver was climbing in after him, there was another shot from the trebuchet, but it fell far short.

One of the crew took the short oars, set in thole pins on the boat's flimsy frames, and began rowing. Even with the added weight of two passengers wearing chain-link hauberks, the curragh was so light on the water that it sped across the few hundred yards to the shore. Another rock plunged into the sea many yards away, though the ripples from it made the boat dance about on the low swell.

'They've little chance of hitting a moving target so small,' said Godfrey Capra.

'Then let's hope they stick to single missiles,' grunted de Wolfe. 'If they fire a bucketful of pebbles, it needs only one to punch a hole through the bottom of that cockleshell.'

'If those men on the beach pissed in it, it would probably sink,' added Gwyn.

They watched as the little craft neared the shore, when the line of men began to congregate at the point where it would land. They could faintly hear a series of yells and could see swords and spears being waved threateningly. In the curragh, the sheriff was sitting rigidly on his thwart, waving the white flag with increasing desperation.

'Now they're throwing stones from the beach!' yelled Gwyn, who had the best eyesight amongst the anxious watchers.

Suddenly, they saw de Ver grab the flag of truce from de Revelle and bend forward, almost vanishing from view, with only his backside sticking up above the rim of the curragh.

'Surely he's not cowering down!' roared de Falaise in disgust, fearing that his leader was breaking the Templar tradition of reckless bravery in battle. The seaman could now be seen pulling the cockleshell around and rowing back towards the ship as if the devil was after him. Small splashes around the boat showed where a final fusillade of pebbles was landing, but in a minute or two, the craft was out of range and speeding for the ship. Roland de Ver was still hiding below the gunwales and de Wolfe wondered whether he had been hit by a stone or even a spear.

Gwyn's sharp eye was the first to detect the truth. 'They're sinking!' he yelled, pointing at the curragh, which was now noticeably lower in the water.

The sailor pulled at his oars like a man demented and came alongside the knarr with the little boat half full of water. Willing hands were thrust over the bulwarks to pull aboard de Revelle and the seaman. De Ver, with his face almost under water, stayed bent double until they had clambered out, then hurriedly followed them, still clutching the balled tunic, which he had been jamming into a hole punched through the tarred-leather bottom by a sharp stone. The damaged curragh swirled away and sank, as the damp heroes gained the safety of the deck.

'Bastards! We could have been killed!' snarled the sheriff.

De Wolfe grinned at this stupid remark. 'That's the general idea of fighting, Richard – kill or be killed!'

They all stood looking in frustration at the distant beach, where some of the defenders were now capering about and waving their weapons derisively at the two ships. John noticed that two sailing vessels, about the same size as the knarrs, were beached on the pebbles. Beyond them lay two longer, slimmer boats with a row of thole pins along each side for oars. 'Those are their pirate galleys, by the looks of it – so you *can* get ships safely on to that beach. If it wasn't for that damned trebuchet, we could make a run for the shore and jump off into the shallow water.'

The shipmaster grunted. 'As it is, we'd be sitting targets, giving them plenty of time to get the exact range. And we couldn't get off until the tide came in again.'

De Wolfe looked thoughtfully across to the other knarr, a hundred paces away, where he could see Richard de Grenville talking to Abbot Cosimo. An idea germinated in his mind and he shared it with the sheriff, de Ver and Ralph Morin.

'If we could only talk to de Marisco, maybe we could get some idea of his terms for letting us have perhaps even part occupancy of the island,' said the senior Templar hopefully.

John shook his head. 'I don't think anyone wearing the broad red cross has any chance of getting ashore. But if we could use Cosimo as a godly shield, maybe they would let me ashore as well to talk about piracy, as long as I don't accuse him outright.'

The two boats came together again and further discussion went on across the rails. Eventually, the Italian priest agreed to take part, confident that his papal immunity from every contingency would keep him safe, even from wild island buccaneers.

Another curragh was dropped into the sea and this time Gwyn offered to be the oarsman. With the abbot in the bow and de Wolfe in the stern, they set off again for the beach. 'None of us is wearing chain-mail, so at least we've got a chance of swimming for it,' observed the coroner cheerfully, as his officer's brawny arms sent them skimming across the water.

The trebuchet remained silent this time, and as they reached the half-way point, de Wolfe saw that the men on the beach were quietening, perhaps puzzled at this second futile attempt to storm the island with three men. Then Cosimo raised himself somewhat precariously on to his knees on the triangle of wood that braced the bows of the boat-frame and held up the large wooden crucifix that normally dangled from a thong about his neck.

As they got into the shallows and the boat bounced on the breaking waves, the men on the shore moved forward to meet them, some with raised weapons and a few with large pebbles ready to cast at the boat.

'I am Abbot Cosimo, an emissary from Rome,' screeched the priest, waving his cross as the sheriff had wagged his white flag.

Gwyn shipped his oars and hopped over the side, rocking the curragh dangerously and almost pitching Cosimo into the surf. He grabbed the bow and dragged it until the keel grated on the stones, then bodily lifted the abbot and set him on his feet on the beach.

A dozen men crowded around him suspiciously, but clearly the small black-robed priest was no threat to anyone. De Wolfe joined Gwyn alongside Cosimo and gazed at the men edging forward on the pebbles. Many were rough-looking peasants, carrying a spear or even a sickle, but about half appeared to be soldiers of a sort, with a varied mixture of mail or leather jerkins, some with helmets and most with a sword or mace.

'We wish to speak to your lord William at once,' he shouted, over the babble of voices. 'Who amongst you is leader on this beach?'

'Who's asking?' grated a tall, thin man with a wispy black beard around his chin. He wore a metal-plated leather tabard and a helmet with a nasal guard.

'The king's coroner for this county, Sir John de Wolfe, that's who.'

'Then you're not welcome. We only let this priest land because it's a mortal sin to drown abbots.'

There was a coarse cackle of amusement at their leader's wit, but de Wolfe walked up to the man and jabbed a finger into his chest. 'I said I'm the king's coroner. Are you telling me that you don't acknowledge Richard the Lionheart as your rightful sovereign? Maybe you're one of those Prince John traitors, eh?'

There were a few sniggers from the men standing nearby but the man's face coloured. 'I'm no Prince's man – I fought with Richard in Aquitaine in 'eighty-seven!'

The coroner whacked him on the shoulder. 'I was there too – and my man Gwyn here. A good year for fighting, that was.' Suddenly the mood lightened, as old warriors shared common cause.

'You want to see Sir William? It's a bloody long climb, begging your pardon, Abbot.'

Leaving most of the men on the beach to discourage any more landings, the black-bearded man, who said his name was Robert of Woolacombe, led them up the beach to the track, which was part earth, part rock and had stretches of crude steps at the steeper sections. It wound up interminably and Cosimo was panting and wheezing long before he reached the top. They passed the trebuchet, and de Wolfe noticed piles of large, rounded missiles and heaps of small stones, ready to devastate anything that came within range.

Four hundred feet above the sea, the path flattened out on top of a grassy plateau. At the southern tip of the island, Marisco's castle was built on the edge of the cliff, and in the other direction, several farmhouses dotted the bleak fields, the narrow island cut across at intervals by dry-stone walls. The view was tremendous, and the two knarrs looked like toys far below.

The group was led by Robert and three other armed men towards the entrance to a thick stone wall running around the landward side of the castle, creating an outer ward, inside which they could see the upper part of a two-storeyed keep. The outer wall had heavy gates set in an arch, but they never saw the inside, as three men marched out at their approach. From his confident bearing, the one in the lead was William de Marisco, lord of Lundy. He was a burly, red-necked man of about forty, with pale, protuberant eyes and a full beard and moustache. His wispy brown hair looked as if all the winds of the island had blown through it for most of his life. His cloak and tunic were frayed and slightly soiled, as if personal comfort was of little consequence on this remote island.

De Marisco strode up to the newcomers with a scowl on his face. 'Who the hell are you? Why did you let them land, Robert?'

'This one's a priest. I could hardly beat his brains out.'

'We've already got a priest, drunken sot though he may be. And who is this other one?'

De Wolfe returned his scowl, head thrust out. 'Sir John de Wolfe, the king's coroner for this county. I'm here to investigate a wreck and a murder.'

De Marisco stared at the coroner, hands on hips displaying a heavy sword hanging from his belt. 'I've heard of you. You were with the king in Outremer,' he declared, his truculence fading slightly. 'But what do you want with me? And what are those bloody Templars doing down there?' He turned to Cosimo. 'What are you doing here, Father? We already have all the religion we need on this island.'

The Abbot of Modena gave one of his strange smiles. 'Look on me only as a sightseer, my son. I was required to help these men get ashore, to prevent your servants slaying them.'

De Wolfe felt obliged to distance himself from the Templars, if he was to gain anything from this visit. 'I have nothing to do with the claim of their Order to Lundy. If you wish to discuss that with them, they are out there.' He waved a hand towards the sea.

'To Hell with them! I'll not waste my breath. But did they seriously think that a handful of men-at-arms could drive me from my rightful honour, granted to my kinsmen back in 'fifty four?'

'The soldiers are not there to aid the Templar's claim, de Marisco,' replied John. 'The sheriff is down there also and we are seeking pirates who have taken ships along this coast and murdered the crew of one recently. Your name has been mentioned more than once in such activities.'

The lord of Lundy burst out laughing. 'Pirates! The damned sea is swarming with them. Every third vessel in these waters pillages and kills when they think the pickings are good enough.' He swept an arm expansively around the horizon. 'From here I have seen two different pirates competing for the same victim, they are so thick in the water – Turks, Moors, Irish,

Welsh and Bretons, to say nothing of our local villains!'

'Which includes you, I take it?' suggested de Wolfe, with reluctant admiration for Marisco's openness.

The island chief leered at him. 'I'll say nothing that one day might be used against me, Crowner. But tell me of this particular crime you are investigating. Why come to me as a suspect?'

De Wolfe related the tale of the capture and wrecking of the *Saint Isan*, and the inquest on the corpse found on board. 'The survivor says a galley with six oars a side was responsible, similar to those two drawn up on your beach down there.'

'God's teeth, de Wolfe, there are hundreds of boats like that, especially amongst folk with a fondness for piracy. They can be rowed against the wind to catch a sluggish merchantman. But we've not used those in many weeks – in fact, one is holed, having run against Mouse Rock, which stove in a few planks.'

'You may say that, but how do I know it's true?' snapped de Wolfe. 'You have two galleys on your beach, the whole of Devon alleges Lundy is a nest of pirates and you have not denied it.'

De Marisco coloured with rising anger. 'I don't give a damn what you think, Crowner! Are you going to cart me off to Bideford in chains to await trial, eh? Have a care! You are here only on sufferance because of this priest.'

De Wolfe stepped forward a pace and the two men each side of de Marisco put their hands on their sword hilts in a warning gesture. 'If we are bandying questions, are you threatening the life of King Richard's coroner in this county? I have already pointed out to your man Robert that Lundy is no sovereign state. It is part of England and you hold your bleak island from the Crown. Deny that or threaten the king's representatives and you make yourself a traitor, de Marisco.'

The two big men eyed each other aggressively but de Marisco was not one to back down. 'Hold my island, you say! Yes, until old King Henry granted my estate to those self-righteous men who carry the red cross on their breasts. What have they to do with an English island? Let them stay in Palestine where they belong. They'll not throw me from my birthright, just to add to their possessions – I'll die first!' he added.

De Wolfe, who secretly had sympathy with his views, shrugged. 'That's none of my business, but the time will come when London or Winchester will send an army against you that can't be repulsed by one trebuchet and a handful of ragged soldiers. In the meantime, are you denying that one of your galleys took the *Saint Isan* and slew most of its crew?'

De Marisco looked at his thin henchman, Robert, who shook his head emphatically. 'We made no such attack then, I swear to it.'

De Wolfe noted the word 'then', but the man sounded sincere about not having taken that particular ship.

'You have your answer, Crowner. That's all I have to say to you, so look elsewhere for your culprits. Any port from Tunis to Dublin may harbour them, so I wish you joy of it!'

With that de Marisco turned and marched back to his rocky stronghold on the cliff. There was nothing else to be gained, so John, Gwyn and the silent Cosimo, who seemed slightly amused by the whole episode, followed their guards back down to the beach. The ragged army of de Marisco watched them with curiosity as they refloated the curragh and Gwyn rowed them back to the knarr, still anchored outside the range of the trebuchet.

On board, de Wolfe reported the futile visit to the sheriff and the other knights. De Grenville laughed cynically when the coroner described de Marisco's attitude. 'Typical of the arrogant bastard! He sits on this great rock and defies the world to do anything about him.'

When the three Templars heard de Wolfe describe the lord of Lundy's contemptuous dismissal of their claim to the island, their determination to do something about it was strengthened, especially in de Falaise, who seemed almost apoplectic with fury at the defiance to their great Order by an insignificant tenant on a remote island.

Roland de Ver turned in exasperation to the ship-master. 'Is there no other landing place further along the coast where we can avoid this damned trebuchet?' he demanded.

'There are several poor beaches along this east side of the island, but they are more difficult and dangerous – and I don't like the look of the weather.'

However, after much discussion and persuasion, the two ship-masters hauled up their anchor stones and moved further out to sea, watched intently by the crowd on the shore who again began yelling and waving in triumph at the apparent retreat of authority. When the two knarrs turned north and began to sail up the coast, the defenders tracked them along the shore, but because of the cliffs they had to climb almost to the top to find a path. A mile further on, the ships again came in closer and another stretch of pebbles, just past a small waterfall, was visible under the cliffs. Already a few of de Marisco's men had arrived, but most were still scrambling along the steep paths towards them.

'Get in as close as you can, master,' commanded the leader of the Templars and, reluctantly, the two knarrs came within a hundred paces of the beach before dropping anchor.

The ship-master kept looking up, and though the cliffs obscured the western horizon, the long band of cloud that had been so distant earlier on was now visible across the sky, and the wind had dropped to an ominous calm. It was early afternoon: the tide had turned from its six-hour ebb and was rising again.

'You could get the bows right against the beach now,' suggested Gwyn. 'A pair of sweeps would keep them nose-on to the shore whilst the troops jumped into the shallows.'

Again, the masters of the two vessels protested, mainly because they feared damaging the hulls on the stones, but also because of a sudden change in the weather.

Roland de Ver assuaged their fears with promises of more money, and the first knarr moved towards the shore, its bows crowded with men, the Templar knights crouching against the stem-post, shields up and swords in hand. In the other boat, Richard de Grenville led his own men, together with Ralph Morin and the rest of the Exeter soldiers. On the beach itself, a score of defenders were spread out thinly, looking rather hesitant as these formidable raiders in their impressive armour came towards them.

As the keel of the first ship crunched on to the pebbles, the Templars slid over the bulwarks into thigh-deep water and stumbled up the beach, followed by their sergeants and a dozen men-at-arms. A few spears were thrown at them, but they were deflected harmlessly by the shields of the experienced warriors. De Wolfe and Gwyn were behind the press of men in the bow, waiting to get ashore. Alongside them was the sheriff, looking decidedly unhappy as he spoke to his brother-in-law. 'Are we going to get ourselves killed for a few acres of barren Templar land?' he asked.

De Wolfe gave him a twisted grin. 'Yes, why not? A pity not to use that nice new armour of yours, Richard. Come on!'

He put his legs over the side and dropped into the cold water, a low wave gliding past to soak him up to the waist. Gwyn splashed beside him and, with a roar, waded happily through the surf, waving his sword in the air. Reluctantly, the sheriff followed them and they stumbled up the bank of stones.

Immediately, the line of Lundy men congealed into several groups, as hand-to-hand fighting began. The defenders had the advantage, as they were higher up the bank and the wet attackers were not too steady on their feet until they got out of the water, the pebbles rolling and sliding under their feet.

Yelling and clashing of steel began in earnest, and although the Templars and Gabriel were taking the brunt of the conflict, de Wolfe and Gwyn were soon parrying and thrusting at a couple of de Marisco's men. The coroner received a heavy blow on his shoulder, which dented one of the steel plates on his cuirass, but he returned it with such violent force to the side of his assailant's head that the man's helmet flew off and he dropped, as if poleaxed, on to the beach.

In the second's respite that this allowed him, de Wolfe saw that many more men were clambering down the cliff paths and that before long the invaders would be well outnumbered. To his left, he saw Gwyn and the sheriff fighting side by side and, grudgingly, he had time to admit that de Revelle's reluctance to expose himself to danger seemed to have worn off.

Though the islanders were losing ground as the new-comers fought their way out of the surf, the situation suddenly took a turn for the worse. A wave bigger than usual caught the second knarr and washed it broadside to the beach, momentarily heeling it over. The soldiers who were clambering over the bow at that moment were pitched into the surf and several sank under the weight of their chain-mail. Their comrades rescued them and none was drowned, but the errant wave turned out to be the first of many and almost immediately the two ship-masters yelled and pointed up at the darkening sky. A sudden squall whistled across the sea and, even under bare masts, the ships began rocking with the gusts of wind. The previously placid sea was already chopping up, and further out, the waves were crested with white horses.

Gwyn was the first to acknowledge the danger. 'We must get off at once! Those vessels cannot stay there – they'll be wrecked!' he roared at his master. De Wolfe took a swing at a ruffian who was waving a mace at him and cut the fellow's arm to the bone. Then he turned and knew instantly that they must retreat or be marooned.

He ran to Roland de Ver, then to the sheriff, and with shouts and gesticulations made them realise the situation. The Templars bellowed orders at the men-at-arms and formed a rearguard while everyone retreated to the knarrs, clustering around the bows. Some clambered aboard, while others pushed them off the pebbles, as the succession of waves and the rising tide got them afloat. As de Wolfe backed down the slope behind the fighting Templars, he stumbled over the groaning body of the man he had felled earlier. On a sudden impulse, he motioned to Gwyn and they tipped the inert islander unceremoniously over the ships' side, before clambering in themselves.

The Templars, in a tight semi-circle around the bow, made a last slashing attack on their adversaries, felling two and driving the rest far enough back to allow them to get aboard. They were helped in by willing hands, as the knarr slid into deeper water, pulled by four men on the long sweep oars. De Wolfe glanced across at the other boat and saw the last of their men being hauled aboard.

As the vessels were backed off the beach, the defenders hurled insults and a few stones, but within minutes the knarrs were well out, their sails hoisted. The wind was now gusting hard and the sky was dark grey, with spots of rain beginning to fall. As they looked back, they saw several bodies lying on the beach and a few men being carried or helped to their feet by comrades.

'What a pitiful fiasco! We should all be ashamed of ourselves,' snarled de Falaise, rubbing angrily a deep cut on his cheek where he had been hit with a ball-mace.

'God obviously did not wish you to conquer this time,' said Abbot Cosimo, who with his two had remained on board and watched the jousting with apparent amusement.

'But for this sudden storm we could have won the day,' snapped Roland de Ver, looking ruefully at a slash across his white surcoat that almost cut the red cross in half.

'We were fortunate that we left when we did,' said the sheriff. 'There was a legion of men coming down that path, who would have eventually outnumbered us two to one.'

'Templars are supposed to fight on even at three to

one,' snapped Godfrey Capra. 'It is a disgrace to leave the field at less than those odds.'

De Wolfe looked back at the shore as the knarrs began to roll and pitch as they left the shelter of the cliffs. 'Have we lost any men, Ralph?' he asked the castle constable.

'Two dead and left behind, and three with wounds but none serious. We must have felled a few of theirs, but I didn't have time to count them.'

Gwyn walked back from the bow, rock-steady on the swaying deck. 'What about this fellow we threw aboard? I can't get any sense out of him yet. He's got a bruise on his head the size of an onion where you hit him.'

The coroner had forgotten him. 'We'll throw him into de Grenville's cells when we get back to Bideford. Maybe he can tell us something useful, if he survives.'

He held on tightly to the rough wooden rail, his stomach telling him that the sooner this trip was over the better.

ChAPTER FIFTEEN

In which Crowner John rides to Exmoor

However else fate had been against them that day, in the matter of wind it was kind. The southerly breeze of the morning turned into a westerly blow when the horizon-wide cloudbank rolled in. The wind, together with the flood tide, gave them a fast if uncomfortable passage back to Bideford Bay, the spray constantly whipping across the decks and the knarrs pitching like unbroken horses as they dug their blunt bows into the whitened waves.

It was almost dark when they reached the entrance to the estuary and it took all the considerable skills of the ship-masters to get them safely into the channel, but the relief of entering calmer water caused a cheer to be raised amongst the cold and sodden warriors. They made passage around Appledore and up the Torridge in the dark, though the diffuse moonlight above the clouds and a few feeble lights from dwellings on either riverbank was enough to allow the shipmen to feel their way back to their berth against Bideford bridge.

At de Grenville's castle, his steward and servants raced around banking up fires to dry out their men-at-arms and to prepare hot food. Within a couple of hours, everyone had settled back to drink ale and spin ever-improving yarns about the day's events.

In the hall, afterwards, they all sat around a roaring fire set in a hearth in the middle of the floor, the smoke making eyes stream and lungs cough, but the blessed warmth was more than worth it, after the rigours of the ocean.

De Wolfe sat on a bench next to Richard de Grenville. After a time his mind wandered from the tale-telling and boasting to wonder what he was doing there. He was no further towards spotting either the killer of Gilbert de Ridefort or the origin of the pirates that had killed all but one of the crew of the *Saint Isan*. He ran through the possible suspects for the Templar's murder. Of the potential killers, he would have liked to make the abbot the prime suspect, perhaps using one of his acolytes for the deed – he doubted that Cosimo was capable of wielding the necessary weapons. Failing him, he favoured Brian de Falaise, as the most aggressive and short-tempered of the Templars, always looking for real or imagined insults. But then he wondered if the type of injuries inflicted on de Ridefort was not too subtle for the blunt de Falaise, and his musings turned to either the more enigmatic Godfrey Capra – or the leader, Roland de Ver. Perhaps the fatal head injury could have come from someone like de Falaise, but the biblical allusion of the wounds in the side and hands may have been added, perhaps even after death, by either of the other knights. Somehow, he did not consider any of the Templar sergeants as candidates, although logically there was no reason why they should not have taken part in the killing.

He shrugged off the profitless grinding of the problem in his mind and drank the last of his quart of cider. Then he realised that de Grenville was asking him something.

'That fellow you brought back with us, the one we threw into my gaol in the gatehouse. What are we to do with him? Do you want to take him back to Exeter?'

'No. Richard de Revelle would hang him the day he arrived there. I have no proof that he has done any wrong, save fight for his lord as he was ordered.'

'That surely is enough to hang him! He resisted the forces of the law on the soil of Devon – even against the county sheriff and the coroner. He tried to kill you – your shoulder plate still bears the mark.'

John held out his tankard to a passing servant for a refill. 'I suppose so, though I bear him no ill-will for that. It was in fair fight and I certainly did him more damage when I clouted him across the head than he did me.'

'So why did you bring him back?'

'I suppose it was an impulse – I had some vague idea of getting information from him about Lundy.'

The amiable lord of Bideford got up and clapped him on the shoulder. 'I must stay and entertain my guests here, but you are welcome to see if you can get anything from him.'

A little later, the coroner sought out Gwyn, who was sitting around a similar fire in the bailey, drinking and telling tales with Gabriel and his men-at-arms. They went to the cells, two small, foul-smelling rooms opposite the guardroom. The night guard brought a tallow dip and unlocked a door in its flickering light. On the dirty straw inside, the man from Lundy was slumped against the wall, conscious but holding his head and groaning. A filthy bucket was the only furniture, but half a loaf and a jar of water stood untouched just inside the door. He

lifted his head as they entered, screwing up his eyes at
the poor light they carried. He was in about his thirtieth
year, his weatherbeaten face suggesting he spent much
of his time at sea. 'Have you come to hang me?' he
muttered thickly, in a tone that suggested he cared little
if they had. His bloodshot eyes focused on the coroner,
and he recognised him as the man he had struck with
his sword just before his memory failed.

'You may surely hang, fellow,' said de Wolfe, 'but
I have no great desire to see you on the gallows, so
it depends on whether you have anything useful to
tell us.'

'What can I tell you? I am nothing but a serf to my
lord William.'

'Doing what, man? I am the county coroner and have
some power to save your neck, if you can be useful
to me.'

'I labour on the manor farm on Lundy for much of
the time, but am also a ship-man when required. We
run back and forth to Clovelly or the ports here.'

'And a little piracy when needed?' grunted Gwyn.

The man gave a cynical laugh. 'It would certainly put
my head into the noose if I said yes to that, eh?'

'I am not much concerned about piracy in general,
but about one matter in particular.' De Wolfe explained
about the vessel *Saint Isan* and the evidence of the
Breton lad. 'Your lord William denies that he was
involved and bids me look elsewhere – but as he claims
that half the boats between Cardiff and Constantinople
are pirate vessels, that's not much help to me.'

The man's eyes took on a little more life as he saw a
hope of saving his neck. 'If I can help you in this, will
you speak for me?'

'If you are very helpful, I may just forget to have that

door locked in the morning. Maybe then you could even find your way back to that godforsaken island.'

'I never wish to see it again, sir. I have no family there. If I could lie low in one of these boroughs, I could even gain my freedom.'

A villein who managed to escape from his hamlet to a town and survive for a year and a day was entitled to become a freeman. From the prospect of the gibbet a few moments ago, the islander now saw a better future, if only he could satisfy this black hawk of a man who hovered over him.

'What can I tell you? I know something of the sea and ships along this coast.'

'Which ports have a reputation for piracy? Are some more active than others?'

The fellow nodded vigorously, ignoring the pain it provoked in his neck. 'Some are free of it, like Ilfracombe and these towns up-river here. It is the smaller places that harbour them, where most of the village is involved in the enterprise and where everyone stays silent about it.'

'Such as where?'

He considered for a moment. 'Watchet and Minehead in Somerset, then Lynmouth and Combe Martin in the east of this county. Down west there are plenty – Clovelly, Hartland Quay and Bude are the nearer ones. But other marauding ships come from far and wide to prey on merchant vessels using the Severn Sea.'

'Had you heard anything of the seizing of this particular ship, making for Bristol? What about the cargo? Would that end up somewhere to be sold?'

De Wolfe and Gwyn stood over the man as he thought again. 'When did this occur?' he asked.

'Towards the end of the first week of this month.'

'Then it certainly wasn't from Lundy. We had no ships afloat then.' He thought again. 'Something comes into my mind ... gossip from seamen that came over to Lundy from Combe Martin about then. It wasn't them, though they're not averse to taking a small boat or two occasionally. Something in my head, even through the hurt you gave me, Crowner, tells me that Lynmouth may be involved.'

'Lynmouth? It's a tiny place. Could they put a big enough vessel to sea?' asked de Wolfe.

Gwyn wagged his hairy head confidently. 'A few cottages are enough to raise a crew – ten or twelve men to row and wield swords or pikes. Nowhere is too small for that.'

The coroner looked down again at the prisoner. 'Tell me more.'

'I know Lynmouth, I have sailed into there many times.' He looked sheepishly at his hands. 'De Marisco has more than once sent certain goods he acquired from other ships into there so that they could be carted to Taunton and Bridgwater for sale, with no questions asked.'

De Wolfe felt that at last he was getting somewhere. 'So in Lynmouth, can you say who might be responsible for running a galley out of there?'

'I'm no traitor to my mates, Crowner.'

'It's your neck that will be stretched, if that door stays shut.'

This persuasive argument removed any vestiges of loyalty between thieves. 'I know some names, but not who is the leader – it might be their lord himself, for all I know. But there is Eddida Curt-arm, a strange fellow with short limbs, who is supposed to be a fisherman.

Another who works with him is Crannog, a Cornishman, with an accent like your man here.'

Gwyn grunted, unsure whether this was a compliment or an insult.

'And Adret Picknose, that's another name I know. Other faces would be familiar, but I cannot put names to them. They certainly have at least one vessel with six pairs of oars in Lynmouth. It is masted, but narrow in the beam. They keep it on the beach around the west side of the river mouth, out of sight as much as is possible.'

A few moments more proved that the man from Lundy had nothing else useful to tell them. True to his promise, de Wolfe told him that he would be quietly released in the morning, as the castle gates were now firmly shut until dawn. In any case, after the buffet on the head he had received, he needed a few more hours to fully recover his senses.

'The sheriff won't be happy about you letting him free,' said Gwyn happily, as they walked back across the bailey. 'He would have liked someone to string up as a token of his successful exploits.'

'We won't tell him, then. Let him think the man remains incarcerated. And if this information about Lynmouth turns out to be true, maybe he will soon have some better villains to hang!'

Early next morning, the billeted knights rose from their pallets around the embers of the fire in the hall and, after seeing to their men and beasts outside, came back to a breakfast served by de Grenville's servants. De Wolfe related what he had learned from the solitary prisoner taken from Lundy, omitting to mention that the man had slipped away into the morning mists. 'Now that we are here in the north, it seems obvious that we should see if there is any substance in this tale of pirates working out of Lynmouth,' he suggested to the sheriff.

Richard de Revelle muttered about a wild-goose chase, but after the fiasco at Lundy, he was easily persuaded that it would save their faces if they achieved something elsewhere. 'This need not concern you, Sir Roland,' said the sheriff, to the leader of the Templars. 'You have no stake in this matter. It concerns local crimes only. Maybe you would wish to travel straight back to Exeter today, and perhaps act as escort to the good Abbot here?'

The senior Templar looked at his two companions and they shook their heads. 'Thank you, but we can go directly back to London via Taunton, which would take us near your possible nest of pirates. Having come this far, we would like to stay with you – and maybe our swords will be of some help if it comes to another fight like yesterday.'

The Italian priest, hunched at the table in his dark robe, also seemed keen to stay with the Exeter contingent. 'I will be glad of the company and added protection of these Knights of Christ, as my destination is Winchester. Like them, there is no point in my returning the long way round through Exeter.'

Though their reasons seemed sound, de Wolfe felt instinctively that they still did not trust him to have lost track of Bernardus de Blanchefort, which was so obviously the *raison d'être* for both parties to be in Devon. He wondered if it was safe for him to keep his rendezvous with Thomas at the bridge in an hour's time and decided to take precautions in case they set a spy on him.

When he had eaten, he wandered out into the bailey, saying that he wanted to check his horse's legs before the day's ride. Finding Gwyn, he went through the motions of examining Odin, whilst he gave his officer instructions. 'When I go to meet Thomas, follow me at a distance and keep a strict look-out for anyone from our party. It would likely be one of the Templar squires or one of Cosimo's brutes. Give me a signal if they appear and I'll keep clear of our clerk and de Blanchefort.'

Soon afterwards, he wandered casually out of the castle gate and strolled up the riverbank to the market-place, which was busy with early morning traders selling their goods to the folk of Bideford. He kept an eye on Gwyn, who loitered along the water's edge, then made his way to the bridge. This was a long, rather spidery timber construction. As at Exeter, there were plans to replace it in stone, but nothing had yet been started. He saw two figures, one tall, one short, leaning on the wooden parapet where it abutted the bank. Checking that the distant Gwyn still seemed unconcerned, de Wolfe beckoned them down to the muddy grass on the further side of the abutment. Here they were out of sight of the marketplace and the castle, but he could still see Gwyn by looking under the bridge.

De Blanchefort, in his bulky mantle and large hat, looked anxiously at the coroner. 'Have you managed to arrange anything yet? It seems impossible to get a passage from this place. They have only coastal vessels berthed here.'

De Wolfe explained the situation and said that they would have to move on to Lynmouth that day. 'There may be a better chance of a ship straight across to Wales from there. The channel is narrow and several ports lie on the other side where there will certainly be vessels going on to Ireland. And you would be safer there whilst waiting than on this side of the channel where your presence is well known.'

'And if there is no passage from this Lynmouth?' persisted Bernardus.

'Then you will have to make your way back here or to one of the southern ports.'

De Blanchefort still looked unhappy, yet he had no choice but to agree. De Wolfe studied him as Thomas asked about the practicalities of the onward journey. The former Templar looked drawn and haggard, compared with his appearance when he first arrived in Exeter. It seemed that the life of a fugitive was wearing him down and de Wolfe fervently hoped that he could board a ship out of Lynmouth – and out of his life. Bernardus stared under the worn timbers at the marketplace, bustling with people. The stage used for the miracle plays was still there and he pointed at it. 'Perhaps I should abandon this craven desire to escape and get up there.'

De Wolfe's eyes followed his finger. 'What do you mean?'

'I should mount that platform and tell the people the truth. My life is nothing, but for how long can I carry this burden of the secret? Let me stay and be done with it, Crowner!'

Thomas crossed himself and de Wolfe sighed. 'We have been through all this before, de Blanchefort. What use would it be for you to speak for five minutes to a few dumb townsfolk, who would understand little and care even less? Before you could explain or impress even that poor audience, you would have half a dozen Templars and a mad abbot leading a troop of soldiers to seize you and silence you for ever. For God's sake – if you still believe in Him – get yourself somewhere where you can plan in safety, whatever it is you feel obliged to do.' He grasped the man's arm and shook it. 'You know better than I what would happen if either de Ver or Cosimo dragged you away to London or Paris. Is self-destruction what you desire?'

De Blanchefort seemed to sag like a pricked bladder. His hands came up to his face in an agony of indecision. De Wolfe looked at them and prayed that the palms would not end with jagged stabs like de Ridefort's.

He heard Thomas speaking to him urgently and pulled his mind back to his clerk. 'Where do we next meet, Crowner, and when?'

'We leave the castle within the hour and should be at Lynmouth this evening. It is something approaching twenty-five miles distant. Follow well behind us and meet me at Lynton church at noon tomorrow.'

'I know nothing of these places. How will I find the church?'

'It's in the village on the hill above the valley that shelters Lynmouth. But be alert for any signs of the others, though I hope by then all our business will be completed, one way or the other.'

With a last look at de Blanchefort, who was still staring fixedly at the marketplace, de Wolfe shrugged in exasperation and, after checking that the distant Gwyn was still making no warning signs, he climbed the riverbank and made his way back to Bideford Castle.

The party that left Bideford was now smaller, as the hospitable Richard de Grenville and his men remained behind. The sheriff's expedition was four fewer than when they had left Exeter – two had been left dead on the beach at Lundy and two others, slightly wounded, would remain in Bideford until they were fit to travel home.

With the sheriff and Templars in the vanguard of the

column, Cosimo and his silent minions in the centre and Ralph Morin, John and his officer bringing up the rear, they left Bideford by the long bridge and travelled across the well-beaten track to Barnstaple. They did not enter the town, but continued north-east through the wooded valleys then on to the higher, more bare ground sloping up to Exmoor. They passed the villages of Shirwell and Arlington, then crossed the moor to Parracombe, the smell of the sea reaching them as they turned north to Martinhoe. One of Gabriel's men had been born in this area and was able to guide them as the settlements became sparse on the lonely stretches of heathland.

The journey was a silent one, apart from some gossip between the men-at-arms. The sheriff attempted conversation with Roland de Ver, but their common interests were so few that it petered out before many miles were covered. The abbot appeared to be sunk in contemplation as he trotted his mare, whilst the coroner and his man were so used to long periods of silence when on the move that any talking would seem to them like aimless chatter.

However, every few hours they stopped to rest and refresh themselves from provisions carried in their saddle-pouches and to feed their horses. Here they found their tongues to some extent, again mainly ribald badinage between the soldiers, but also some rather strained conversation between the leaders. As they neared the coast again in the early evening, de Wolfe felt it was time to make some plan of action. When they stopped just outside the tiny village of Martinhoe, just inland from the high cliffs, he broached the matter with Richard de Revelle, who was nominally the leader of the expedition.

'It will be almost dark by the time we reach Lynmouth,

so I suggest we camp overnight somewhere well short of the place where we can remain unseen. Then in the morning we can come upon them unexpectedly to see if there is truly any sign of piracy.'

The sheriff could find no reason to object to this, and Ralph Morin called across to the soldier who knew the area well to ask his advice about a suitable place.

'Sir, there is a rocky valley further along from here, a mile or so short of Lynton. After dusk, it is unlikely that anyone would come there to discover us, if we camped on the western end of the defile.'

They continued until they reached the edge of the sea, where steep wooded slopes and bare cliffs dropped into the line of surf below. The track wound along the sides of several bays, then climbed up to moorland again and soon entered a trough-like valley, where the grass and bracken were dotted with jagged rocks, which appeared on the skyline like broken teeth. The man-at-arms with local knowledge saluted Ralph and said, 'Lynton village is at the other end of this coombe, sir. If you wish to stay concealed, I would go no further – and light no fires.'

The constable sent three men back half a mile with the horses so that they could be tethered without fear of their neighing being heard in the nearby village. The rest spent an uncomfortable night wrapped in their cloaks and horse blankets, eating cold food, mainly hunks of meat and dry bread supplied by de Grenville before they left Bideford. At least no rain fell on them, but a mournful breeze whistled up the valley all night.

De Wolfe woke a few times – his body had become used to a bed after his years of tough campaigning and even the pile of dead ferns on which he lay failed to ease the ache in his limbs from the hard ground. The moon sped in and out of scudding clouds and lit up the eerie landscape, the fang-like rocks silhouetted against the sky. For those of a more imaginative turn of mind than John de Wolfe, such as his clerk Thomas, it was a place to conjure up illusions of evil spirits and the unquiet souls of the dead, but no such visions kept de Wolfe awake. He thought only of the soreness of his hips against the turf, and hoped that Thomas had managed to bring the difficult Bernardus along without too many problems.

Grey dawn came at last and everyone stretched, cursed and crawled to their feet to seek the small stream where they could drink and splash water in their eyes to awaken themselves. They ate the remainder of their provisions and the horses were brought back for all to remount and prepare for whatever the day might bring.

'Abbot, there is no need for you to put yourself at risk any longer,' said Richard de Revelle, with false solicitude. He was as anxious as the rest to see the last of the strange priest and his taciturn servants. 'Once we get to the village you could carry on along the well-marked track towards Taunton.'

Cosimo smiled his enigmatic smile. 'Thank you, Sheriff, but I will wait for my fellow-travellers, the Templars. It will be more reassuring to ride in their company.'

The six men from the Order had already announced steadfastly that they would ride with the law-men into Lynmouth, both from curiosity and a desire to help in keeping the king's peace. However, de Wolfe still felt that both parties were determined to keep him in view until the bitter end, to make sure that he had not deceived them over the renegade Templar. Again, he decided that he would have to be cautious about meeting Thomas later in the day.

Once they were mounted, Ralph Morin suggested that they make all speed down to the port, to avoid giving any warning that might allow evidence of piracy to be hidden, so they set off at a brisk canter, the rested horses eager and frisky. As they thudded through the small village of Lynton, the villagers gaped open-mouthed at the sight of these troops, who seemed to have appeared from nowhere so early in the morning.

Lynton was perched above a deep glen, which dropped sharply down from Exmoor, the little river Lyn rushing through it. At the end of the village, past the small wooden church that de Wolfe intended to use as his rendezvous with Thomas, the track turned sharply down to the left into the glen and followed the stream as it tumbled towards the sea a quarter of a mile away. The cavalcade slowed as it navigated the steep slope and John found he had to avoid deep ruts if Odin was to keep his footing.

Gwyn, alongside him, pointed down with a finger. 'Plenty of wheels pass up and down here! Can that all be for fish?'

Within a couple of minutes, they had reached the bottom of the glen, where the track flattened out on to a widening area above the beach, high wooded headlands rising on each side. Before it seeped through the pebbles, the river formed a large pool, filled at every high tide. A few small boats and curraghs lay on its banks, but beyond, on the wide, stony beach, a couple of bigger vessels were awash on the rising tide.

On either side of the track, between the river and the left-hand hill, stood a few small shacks and cottages, mostly of cog or wattle and daub. At the further end, almost on the beach, was a longer building, roofed with flat stones, which appeared to be an alehouse. A few surprised men came out of the buildings at the sound of hoof-beats, and after one look at the mailed soldiers, two turned tail and ran towards the sea. A few women and small children peered from doorways, fearful to come out at the sight of these menacing strangers.

The troop halted outside the tavern and the sheriff sent Gabriel and two men to run after the fleeing villagers.

De Wolfe trotted his horse up to de Revelle and the constable. 'I think the beach holds the key to this,' he said, sliding off his horse. 'We can't ride on pebbles, so let's take to our feet.'

Cosimo and his two men stayed well back on their steeds, whilst the rest hurriedly tied their reins to some bushes that lined the bank of the stream. Then, running as fast as their mailed hauberks would allow, they followed Gabriel to the beach, where the muddy earth of the village street merged into the pebbles.

Around the left-hand corner of the valley, the beach widened until it reached a rocky headland further along, and on this extension of the strand, two long, narrow vessels were lying side by side, pulled up high and dry. Each had a series of thole pins for oars fixed in the bulwarks and a short, stubby mast.

'Galleys, just as that captive said!' howled Gwyn, as he stumbled over the oval grey stones that formed the beach.

Ahead, more than a score of men streamed out of a long, ramshackle wooden shed built well above the high-water mark at the base of the wooded slope. At the sight of the helmeted soldiers coming towards them, most ran back inside, but a few others sped away towards the steep, tree-covered cliff behind.

'Into that building, at once!' yelled the sheriff, who

seemed to have gained courage since his escapade on Lundy two days before. Holding up his sword in both hands, he trotted towards it, with the constable and the six Templars in a line on each side of him.

Sure that they were able to look after themselves without further help, de Wolfe diverted, Gwyn close behind him, to look quickly into the two galleys that lay on the beach. The first was empty, having no decking to provide any cover, but when they looked into the second vessel, he saw two men crouching below the gunwales. As soon as they saw that they were discovered, they leapt up with a yell, one brandishing a rusty spear, the other a long dagger.

De Wolfe still had his sword in its sheath and jumped back to gain time to slide it out, but Gwyn, with a chain-mace in his hand, swung it at the spearman and knocked the weapon out of the fellow's hands as he jabbed with it. The man leapt out of the galley on the other side and ran for the cliff, followed by his accomplice, who did not wait to try his dagger on the coroner.

'Let them go, Gwyn. We're missing the party over there.'

They turned and ran towards the wooden building, from which almost a score of men had emerged, all now armed, to face the Templars and the sheriff's soldiers. There was much yelling and screaming, but within five minutes it was all over. The local bandits were not only outnumbered but had no armour. Three were felled in the first few seconds, the Templar knights and their sergeants standing shoulder to shoulder forming an efficient killing team. Morin and the sheriff wounded two more, who collapsed bleeding on the stones, then chased three more away. The locals, mostly dressed in short seamen's tunics and worsted breeches, fought valiantly: they knew they were in it to the death, either at the end of a sword or a rope. But their cause was hopeless and, after being gradually forced back and almost encircled by the soldiers, they suddenly broke rank and began to run away, dropping their weapons on the stones.

With no armour or swords to slow them, a couple made it through the closing ring of attackers and joined their comrades at the base of the cliff, where some had already vanished into the trees. The rest were seized by Gabriel's men and thrown roughly to the pebbles, sword points at their throats or ribs.

The coroner and his officer, distracted by the scuffle at the galleys, arrived too late for any fighting, which the sheriff was quick to notice. 'Maybe old age is slowing you up, John! Or are you losing your stomach for fighting, these days?'

The remark was too puerile to merit an answer and de Wolfe ignored him, addressing himself to Ralph Morin. 'Half these rogues have got away across the beach. We should try to catch at least some of them, surely.'

Morin called to Gabriel and some men were sent lumbering across to the cliff to seize some of the fugitives. The soldier who knew the locality panted across to the constable. 'Sir, they can get back to the village at Lynton up that bank. Shouldn't we ride up there and catch them at the top?'

'I'll do that with a few of your men, Ralph,' offered the coroner. With Gwyn, he began to trot back to the horses, Sergeant Gabriel and five men-at-arms behind them. But when they reached the alehouse and looked up what passed for the village street, he saw that they had further problems. One of the abbot's men was hanging off his horse, one foot caught in a stirrup, his body on the ground. An arrow was sticking out of his neck and a large pool of blood was soaking into the soil.

'Where the hell is Cosimo?' shouted de Wolfe, staring around. The priest's horse was still tied to a bush, but the saddle was empty and there was no sign of his other acolyte.

'In there, Crowner!' shouted Gabriel, pointing at the low doorway of the alehouse.

Figures were moving inside the dark interior and De Wolfe raced for the entrance, sword in hand and Gwyn at his back. He skidded to a halt on the threshold, looking at the tableau in the bare room. In the further corner, Abbot Cosimo was crouched against the whitewashed wall, kneeling on the earthen floor, whilst immediately in front of him, blood streaming from his left hand, was the second of his bodyguards. He held a sword and was waving it slowly between two ruffians who were crouched in front of him, one with a dagger, the other with an axe.

Only as de Wolfe darkened the doorway, did the two attackers realise his presence. The one with the axe began to turn, but the coroner gave a two-handed swing of his heavy sword, level with the floor, which took half the breeches off the man together with a considerable part of his right buttock. He screamed and dropped to the floor, his blood mingling with that which was running down inside the guard's sleeve and dripping off his fingers.

The other man turned and jumped with his dagger at Gwyn, who had come in alongside his master. Almost casually, the red-haired giant spitted him with his sword through the centre of his chest, with such force that the point came out under the man's right shoulder-blade.

The guard turned and, with his sound hand, lifted the abbot gently to his feet, without a word to anyone.

'Thank you, Sir John, that was most timely,' shrilled Cosimo. 'With only one arm, I fear that even this man of mine may not have able to protect me much longer.'

'What happened, Abbot?'

'We were waiting with the horses when, without warning, an arrow felled one of my men from his horse. The other was struck in the arm, though he plucked it out. When these two appeared, he ran me in here for shelter. But these two swine cornered us – perhaps they thought they could use me as a hostage to bargain for their own safety.'

'Now that you are safe, I have to go up to the village above – some other villains are escaping,' explained de Wolfe. 'The sergeant here will do his best for the wound in your servant's arm.'

He took with him Gwyn and the soldiers, they found their horses and galloped back up the glen, slowing to a brisk walk on the steepest gradient towards the top. Once on the flat, they stared at the score of crofts that was Lynton, scattered around an open area through which the track passed. There was no sign of anyone, for no doubt the inhabitants were hiding fearfully in their houses.

'Those cliffs must come up behind the village – in those woods towards the sea,' said Gwyn. They wheeled round to the right and passed between two huts and their tofts – the gardens and strips of land that made up the personal estate of each occupant. There were no fields on this side of the village, as it was too near the cliffs. Scrub and trees lay behind the dwellings, and spreading out, the riders pressed on as far as they could, until the undergrowth and the steep drop forced them to a halt.

'There's one – and another!' yelled Gwyn, spurring his mare sideways to cut off a man who was crouching in the bushes.

Within minutes, they saw half a dozen figures creeping out of the trees. One was cut down by a soldier, and another was seized by the other men-at-arms, who leaped from their horses and grabbed the fugitive, who was exhausted after his frantic climb up from the beach far below.

Gwyn and de Wolfe pursued another pair, but they vanished between the crofts.

'We've missed a few, damn it,' snarled de Wolfe. 'There were more than seven who made a run for that cliff.'

Leaving two of the soldiers to deal with the captives and the corpse, the coroner and his officer rode back into Lynton's village street, but there was no sign of anyone. They cantered to the far end, almost to the start of the valley of rocks, but the track was deserted.

'They must be hiding in the houses – maybe their own, for many of those shipmen must live up here. There are too few dwellings down in Lynmouth.' John was annoyed that they had not been able to account for all the miscreants – it seemed as if most of the men in the two villages were involved in crime, from the way that they had fought or run before even knowing why the sheriff's expedition had come.

Leaving the other men-at-arms to patrol the village, he and Gwyn rode back down to the port where Richard de Revelle and Ralph Morin, together with the Templars, had rounded up all the prisoners. They were tied hand

and foot, sitting in a dejected circle outside the ale-house. A small crowd of women, old men and children had emerged and were wailing and weeping, both for the few dead men laid out on the riverbank and the soon-to-be dead prisoners, whose fate must surely be hanging.

'What was in that shed on the beach?' demanded de Wolfe of the sheriff.

'Goods of all sorts, none of which could possibly be afforded by this miserable vill,' answered de Revelle complacently. 'Undoubtedly looted from passing ships – to be carted away to Bridgwater or Taunton or even Bristol to be sold.'

'I'd better look at it all later, to record it on my rolls,' muttered de Wolfe. He saw a chance to let Thomas appear without arousing any suspicion. 'I told my clerk to follow us from Exeter when he could. He had an attack of the bloody flux, but was recovering when we left, so I hope he finds us soon. I could do with his penmanship.' He looked up at the sky and, though the sun appeared only fitfully, reckoned it was still about four hours to noon, when he had arranged to meet Thomas. 'What do we need to do here now?' he asked the constable.

'I'll set fires in those two galleys to stop them being used again, though this village will be without many men for a few years to come, if we hang all this lot.' He indicated the bedraggled prisoners sitting in the mud, but was interrupted by a shout from one of the soldiers, who stood with outstretched arm, pointing at a sea-going knarr that had just appeared close inshore, having come around the eastern headland.

The tide was now just past its top and there was enough water for the knarr to enter the mouth of the little river before it ran aground. The ship-master and one of the crew splashed ashore and came to the village, looking in astonishment at the scene.

The sheriff was suspicious of this new arrival, but it became obvious that a vessel of this type was no pirate and it was soon established that it was the *Brendan*, out of Bristol, bound for Falmouth. The shipmaster had instructions to call at Lynmouth to pick up ten hogsheads of wine to take onward to Falmouth.

'Obviously part of a looted cargo,' snapped the sheriff. 'Where else would that much wine come from in a place like this?'

The man shrugged, indifferent to the source of the cargo. 'I do what I'm told,' he said. 'I don't own the vessel, I just sail it.'

'Well, you're stuck here until tomorrow's tide, that's for sure,' said Gwyn. 'Unless you want to leave in the dark tonight.' Philosophically, the master went back to his vessel to cook, eat and sleep until the morrow, while John decided it would soon be time to try to keep the appointment with his clerk.

Before he went, he became involved in another argument with his brother-in-law over jurisdiction. The sheriff announced that he intended trying the captives at a special Shire Court set up here today and hanging them straight away, but de Wolfe instantly objected.

'Piracy and murder are pleas of the Crown. They must be arraigned before the king's justices at the next Eyre of Assize!'

'Impossible! We are fifty miles from Exeter and it would take almost a week to march these men all the way back. Then they would have to be kept in prison until the judges condescend to come to Devon. God knows when that will be!'

'The Eyre is due next month, you know that.'

'They said that last month, but they've not been to the city since October. We can't guard and feed all the rabble in the West Country indefinitely – and the result will be the same. They'll be hanged.'

They argued back and forth, but de Revelle was adamant. For once, Ralph Morin sided with him, as a matter of practicality, the captives being so far from the only town where the judges would sit. Though the Shire or County Court, run by the sheriff, was normally held in the Moot Hall in Rougemont, there was no legal reason why it could not be held anywhere in the county, as long as the sheriff was present.

Reluctantly, de Wolfe had to agree, mainly because of the geographical problems, but on condition that the details of the accused and their property were recorded by him for forfeiture. This was another reason for having Thomas present, though he could hardly admit to knowing that his clerk was already in the neighbourhood.

The coroner spent more than an hour inspecting the contents of the shed on the beach. It was a veritable treasure house of goods, even though much must have been carted away already for illicit sale in the big towns of Somerset. Bales of silk, rolls of worsted, cheaper russet cloth and hessian were piled on casks of wine. There were small barrels of raisins and other dried fruit from the South of France and even a pile of green cheeses from Mendip. He was not sure if the coroner's duties ran to making a complete inventory of the looted cargoes, but hoped that they would have time for Thomas to make a list, not least to prevent it being spirited away by the villagers or even the manorial lord. If it could not be recorded, some soldiers must be left behind to guard it until trustworthy bailiffs could be sent from Barnstaple to have it carted out to safety. He doubted that the rightful owners would ever see any returned, but at least it could be sold for the king's treasury – if the hands of people like the sheriff could be kept off it.

He walked back to the alehouse, guessing that by now it could not be far off noon. Outside were twelve fishermen-turned-buccaneers squatting dejectedly in their bonds, with Morin's soldiers now searching for more looted goods in the houses and fish-sheds.

De Wolfe walked Odin away unobtrusively, leaving Gwyn to keep an eye on the Templars. He wondered if they still fancied stalking him on suspicion of con-cealing de Blanchefort somewhere, though with both of Cosimo's strong-arm men virtually out of action, he felt that the Italian was no longer a threat.

Lynton was still deserted, apart from the three sol-diers, who were burying the body of the slain fugitive at the edge of the village. Short of a house-to-house search, which might be necessary later, there was no way of discovering where the men who had escaped from the beach had hidden. De Wolfe thought that they might have taken to the woods or moors, to keep well out of sight until the sheriff's men had left the district. There was no manor-house anywhere near and he did not know who the local lord was – or whether he knew or cared if his subjects were part-time pirates.

He stopped Odin in the centre of the village to look around and decide what to do next. The church was on his left, a small timber Saxon building. It had no tower and looked little different from a barn, apart from the plain wooden cross nailed to the gable at one end. He sat for a moment in the silent hamlet, looking around him. Then a movement caught his eye further up the track, at the edge of the village. A pony moved out from behind a thicket and he saw that sitting on it side-saddle was Thomas de Peyne, small and black in the threadbare mantle that still gave him the air of a priest.

Cautiously, the clerk trotted down to his master, looking right and left all the time in his usually furtive manner. 'I said meet at the church!' snapped the coroner. 'And where's the Templar?'

Thomas glanced apprehensively at the nearby building. 'There are men in there – I looked just now and they all shouted at me to get out.'

Light dawned on de Wolfe. Now he knew what had happened to the escaped Lynmouth men. 'Are they claiming sanctuary?' he demanded.

Thomas gulped. 'I didn't wait to ask them, but certainly they were rough men in rough clothing. I doubt they were there for their devotions.'

The coroner stared up the road again. 'What have you done with de Blanchefort?'

'I hid him in a small wood, just off the road outside the village. After finding those men, I thought it better to leave him there until I had seen you.'

John nodded his agreement. 'This may be to our advantage, but he must keep out of sight, at least until tonight. Has he some food with him?'

'Not much, but enough to survive a day.'

'As an old Templar, he should be used to roughing it. Now, ride up and tell him that he must stay there until dusk, when we will fetch him. Then come back. There is work for you down below.'

As the clerk hurried away, de Wolfe dismounted and tied Odin to the rough gate in the thorn hedge around the churchyard. He walked through the circle of yew trees and pushed open the church door. Immediately there was a scuffle at the far end and five men crowded together to put a hand on the altar, a plain table with a tin cross and two candlesticks. The rest of the building was empty, the narrow window openings throwing a dim light on to the bare floor of beaten earth. They watched with apprehension as the menacing figure stalked up the nave towards them, a tall, dark, hunched figure in an armoured jerkin and metal helmet, with a huge sword swinging from his baldric.

'We claim sanctuary!' shouted one tremulously, and the cry was taken up by the others, as they shrank back from the approaching apparition.

'Sanctuary! Sanctuary!'

The coroner stopped a few yards away to study them. Three were fairly young, another middle-aged and the last was a short, misshapen figure, with a large head and short arms and legs. De Wolfe remembered the captive from Lundy mentioning the name Eddida Curt-arm, which would fit this one very well.

'I am Sir John de Wolfe, the king's crowner,' he boomed, in a voice that instantly silenced their cries. 'I respect sanctuary and, indeed, if you persist in claiming it, you will need me to save your necks, as all your accomplices look as if they will hang today.'

He looked at the group, all dressed much the same in tattered, faded fisherman's tunics and short breeches. All except the dwarf had tangled hair and bushy beards and moustaches.

He was round-faced, with a high forehead, his little eyes glinting with a cunning that de Wolfe marked down as dangerous. 'What do we do now, Crowner? Surely we have forty days' grace?' asked Eddida.

The coroner stood, arms folded, glaring at the men. 'First, you are murderous scum, and if you had not gained the safety of this consecrated place, you would be hanged like the rest. But now you have several choices. You can give yourselves up to the sheriff and stand trial today down in Lynmouth. Or you can stay here for forty days, when you will be fed by your village folk, who must guard against your escape on pain of heavy amercements. At the end of the forty days, if you have not confessed your guilt and agreed to abjure the realm of England, you will be shut up in here without food or water and allowed to die. If you try to escape from here, you are deemed outlaw and any man can cut off your head without penalty. Finally, at any time from this moment forth, you can confess to me and abjure the realm.'

After this long speech, he stepped back a pace and waited as they murmured amongst themselves. As they did so, Thomas came in through the door and rather nervously came to the coroner, jerkily bending his knee to the altar and making numerous signs of the Cross. 'Bernardus will stay where he is until tonight,' he murmured, looking apprehensively at the gang of rough-looking men clustered around the altar. Then their spokesman, Eddida, broke away and came to the single step that separated the rudimentary chancel from the body of the church. 'We will all confess and abjure, Crowner.'

'Then I will return later today. You are safe both here and in the churchyard – there's no need for you to clutch at that altar. There will be soldiers at the gate to prevent your escape.' He turned and walked towards the door, calling over his shoulder, 'You should get outside and cut some wood from the yews. You'll each need a rough cross to carry, and I'll see if I can find sackcloth robes for you.' With that he shooed Thomas out of the church and slammed the door behind him.

CHAPTER SIXTEEN

In which Crowner John takes confession

Richard de Revelle was far from pleased when de Wolfe informed him that some of the pirates had sought sanctuary in Lynton church. He was in the process of setting up his Shire Court in the alehouse when the coroner rode back to the lower village. The sight of Thomas behind him seemed to arouse suspicious interest in the three Templars, and John noticed them in deep conversation with Abbot Cosimo. Soon afterwards, Godfrey Capra rode away and de Wolfe was sure that he had gone up to Lynton to check on the village and look in the church to confirm the identity of the five sanctuary seekers.

The prisoners had been marched to another barn-like shed just behind the tavern and locked in, with guards at the door. Outside, the womenfolk were gathered, crying and keening, or shouting through the flimsy walls to their doomed men inside.

The sheriff had taken over the single large room of the alehouse, bringing in a trestle table and a few rough benches. A quantity of fresh fish, from this morning's catch, had been commandeered and some of Gabriel's men were cooking it over a fire at the back. Bread had been taken from the nearest houses, over the protests of the owners, and soon a scratch meal was being put before the leaders in the tavern, while the soldiers ate around their fire.

The prospect of a mass execution had no effect on anyone's appetite, but as they ate Richard de Revelle went back to complaining about the men in the church. 'Why should they escape a hanging, just because they were craven enough to leave their friends to fight, and because they could run faster than our men?'

De Wolfe pulled the meat off a grilled herring with his knife and waited for it to cool. 'Don't ask me. I didn't make the law.'

Abbot Cosimo, his fish on a slice of bread in his hand, looked up with a frown. 'Sanctuary is one of the sacred traditions of Christianity. In fact, it existed long before Our Saviour – the Hebrews had six Levitical cities of refuge and the Greeks and Romans also recognised the concept.'

The sheriff voiced his disapproval of anyone being able to escape the noose and cost the community money for his keep while doing so. 'I've a mind to go into that church and haul the bastards out!' he muttered, but the alert Cosimo heard him and was shocked.

'I forbid you, Sheriff! You would bring damnation upon yourself for such sacrilege – and I could excommunicate you.' As with many others, de Revelle's religious beliefs were a matter of habit rather than conviction, and the prospect of exclusion from the Church did not weigh too heavily upon him.

De Wolfe knew this, so added a more practical discouragement. 'The laws of the first Henry stipulate penalties for laying violent hands on fugitives in sanctuary – a hundred shillings for a cathedral or abbey and twenty for a parish church.' Still muttering, de

Revelle abandoned the subject, but for once, de Wolfe was thankful for Cosimo's presence as any violation of sanctuary would upset his plans.

When the meal was finished, the room was rapidly converted to the Shire Court, though still smelling strongly of grilled fish. The sheriff sat in the middle behind the crude table, with de Wolfe on one side and Ralph Morin on the other. The Templars and the abbot formed an interested audience on a pair of benches at the side.

In the absence of a court clerk, Thomas was sat at one end of the table, with his bag of parchments, quills and ink to make a brief record of the proceedings, a copy of which de Wolfe intended to place before the king's justices when they eventually came to Devon.

The twelve captives were marched in two at a time by Gabriel and two soldiers, their wrists roped together behind their backs. De Revelle demanded their names and a statement as to whether they were Saxon, Norman or indeterminate. So much intermarriage had taken place in the century since the Conquest that mixed blood was common, especially when stray Celts arrived from Cornwall or even from Wales, just across the water.

Then he accused them of piracy and murder, which they all denied. He yelled 'Liar!' at the top of his voice, and pointed out that each man had run away and seized arms to fight the king's law officers. Furthermore, they had two galleys and a shed full of goods that could only have been acquired by either piracy or smuggling, both of which crimes were a felony and a capital offence.

The reactions of the men varied: some defiantly admitted it, some denied it, others said nothing, and a few collapsed to their knees in sobbing heaps, pleading for mercy. Whatever their demeanour, de Revelle's decision was the same for each: he declared them guilty of piracy and murder, and sentenced them to be hanged later that day. The whole proceedings lasted barely half an hour and soon the condemned were back in their hut under guard.

De Wolfe was uneasy about the summary justice, and if it had been in or near Exeter he would have fought the sheriff tooth and nail to commit them to the next Eyre. But in this case, he saw the practical difficulties – and also had to admit that there could be no realistic alternative to a guilty sentence, given the circumstances. His only contribution to the proceedings was to ask each pair of captives if they recalled attacking the vessel *Saint Isan* a couple of weeks before and if they admitted to slaying most of the crew. Two of the most brazen rogues admitted that this was the last ship they had attacked and also confessed to dispatching the seamen. But they had no idea who killed whom, reasonably pleading that in the heat of a fight no one recalled details of their victims. However, this was good enough for de Wolfe, as he could now get Thomas to tidy up the inquest record on the corpse from Ilfracombe and eventually deliver a firm verdict to the Eyre.

The afternoon wore on, and as the fitful sun showed itself just before it slid behind the high western rim of the glen, the condemned men were led out to death. The parish priest was conspicuous by his absence, even with fugitives in his church. When de Wolfe enquired where he was, he was met with evasion from some older men of the village, but eventually one said that they had had no parson for the last three months, though no one had yet told the archdeacon of Barnstaple that the parish was bereft of pastoral care. Discovering what had happened to the priest was even more difficult, but it seemed that he had been found dead at the bottom of a cliff.

Gwyn's explanation was as likely as any: 'He was either drunk and fell off or they threw him off for threatening to inform on their crimes.'

John thought that perhaps the parson had fallen out with the villagers over his share of the loot, but speculation seemed futile. In any event, he was not here to shrive the condemned men in the hour of their death, but Abbot Cosimo agreed to say the appropriate Latin words over them. Thomas would gladly have volunteered, even though long unfrocked, and was greatly disappointed that the Italian denied him even such a dismal task.

As the sun set, the men were dragged out of their shed by the soldiers, who in truth were not unsympathetic to these poor people who made life a little less frugal by stealing from passing ships. But duty was duty and, one by one, they were pushed up a ladder propped against the branch of a tree at the bottom of the cliff. A noose secured to the branch was dropped over each head, and as the abbot muttered and made the sign of the Cross in the air, they were shoved sideways off the ladder.

The drop was the height of a man and some died instantly, their neck broken or its arteries hammer-blowed, though they still jerked and twitched for a few minutes in full view of those still waiting their turn. Others went blue in the face, eyes bulging and tongues protruding, and danced obscenely for long minutes, until a soldier dragged on their legs to end the agony.

As the grotesque ceremony went on, the wives and families of the victims stood sobbing and screaming in the background, some fainting and many yelling obscenities at the sheriff and his men. A line of men-at-arms kept them away from the hanging tree, using staves to whack them back when emotion drove them to desperation.

But the executions went on with grim efficiency and, as with the trial, were all over in half an hour. The bodies were laid in a row on the riverbank with those killed in the fight, and the families were allowed to take their dead for burial.

In the twilight, de Wolfe sought out his brother-in-law to talk to him again about the men in sanctuary. They had taken over the tavern for the night and were eating more bread and fish, though some enterprising soldier had also 'acquired' a few scrawny fowls for roasting.

The Templars and the abbot were there as usual, still regarding the coroner with some suspicion, though John knew they could have no inkling that de Blanchefort lurked less than a mile away.

De Revelle again began a tirade against allowing the men in the church to escape, but John held up a hand peremptorily. 'It's no good going on about it, Richard. They are entitled to abjure the realm and the sooner the better. I have no intention of staying in this godforsaken village for any longer than I need to see them depart.'

He explained that he had spoken to the shipmaster of the *Brendan*, who was leaving – without his casks of wine – on the morning tide. Though bound for Falmouth, he was willing for a fee to add a day to his voyage and cross to Swansea to drop off the abjurers.

'Where's the money coming from?' snapped the sheriff.

'The fugitives say they can scrape together a few marks, with the help of their families, if it will save their lives,' lied de Wolfe, as he intended de Blanchefort to pay for the passage – he seemed to have ample funds to sustain his travelling.

The sheriff rapidly lost interest in the matter, though the abbot seemed to approve this most Christian of acts and the Templars, devout monks that they were, nodded assent.

'As soon as I've eaten, I must go up there and take their confessions, getting my clerk to record such details as are needed,' said de Wolfe. He saw Roland de Ver exchange glances with Godfrey Capra and Brian de Falaise.

'An interesting process, sanctuary,' said de Ver easily. 'We would like to see it at first hand, never having encountered the coroner's role in this.'

De Wolfe cursed them under his breath – they were intent on making matters more difficult for him. This was compounded when Cosimo too invited himself to attend, allegedly 'to see the compassion of the Holy Church being applied in practice'.

Before they left, the coroner managed a covert word with Gwyn, ordering him to find Bernardus in the wood beyond the village and bring him to the church at midnight.

In the last of the twilight, they walked their horses up the glen to Lynton. Earlier, when he had examined the pirated contraband in the shed on the beach, de Wolfe had noticed a roll of hessian and commandeered it. Now he carried it on his saddle to the church and threw it down on the altar step. The five anxious fugitives had lit the stumps of the altar candles to produce a dim light and looked down at the roll of sacking with puzzlement. 'You can tear that into five lengths and make yourselves long tabards. Rip a hole in the centre and put them over your heads. Did you make those crosses?'

They mutely produced sticks broken from the church-yard trees, crudely lashed together.

John pulled Thomas forward and pushed aside one of the altar candles. 'Here's your writing table – you even have light near at hand.'

The clerk seemed reluctant to put the sanctified board to such a mundane purpose, but he had little choice. Tentatively, with much genuflecting and crossing himself, he spread out his parchment and prepared his pen.

De Wolfe was conscious of the Templars and the Italian watching the process keenly, scanning the five men for any sign of recognition. The dwarf seemed to fascinate Cosimo, who licked his lips as he stared at the strange figure with the peculiar limbs. At least there was no way that Eddida Curt-arm could be de Blanchefort, but the coroner could see that the other men were subjected to close scrutiny.

'You can act as a jury of witnesses, sirs, as the law demands, when I take the oath and confession of these men.'

De Wolfe made the abjurers kneel on the chancel step and each one in turn repeated his words. Each gave his name and village, then confessed to having been a pirate and murderer against the king's peace. The oath of abjuration was a problem, as it should have been sworn on the Gospels, which neither de Wolfe nor the priestless church appeared to possess. However, Cosimo came to the rescue by pulling a small breviary from the folds of his cassock. Holding this each man had to say, 'I swear on the Holy Book that I will leave the realm of England and never return without the king's permission. I will hasten by the direct road to the port allotted me and not leave the King's highway under pain of arrest or execution. I will not stay at one place more than one night and will seek diligently for a passage across the sea as soon as I arrive, delaying only one tide if possible. If I cannot secure such passage, I will walk into the sea up to my knees every day as a token of my desire to cross. And if I fail in all this, then peril shall be my lot.'

After they had all sworn, John instructed them formally about the procedure next morning, extemporising as he went. 'You should have cast off your own clothing, which would be sold, but because time is short you cannot make proper garments of this sackcloth so drape it over your clothes. You will go bareheaded and you will have your hair and beard shorn off. You will carry a cross in front of you and not leave the pathway, and you must never set foot in England again, or you will be outlawed and may be treated as the wolf's head, to be beheaded by any man who can lift a sword. Do you understand?'

There was a mumbled chorus of agreement.

'Then before dawn I will come again and take you down to a vessel below, which will sail on the high tide for Wales, as I told you earlier.'

He made sure that Thomas had written down a summary of the facts then that the men had a sharp enough knife to hack off their hair and beards and attempt to shave their chins.

Their business done for the night, the party left, leaving two soldiers on guard, and went back to the alehouse. On the way Cosimo queried part of the ceremony he had just witnessed. 'Sanctuary is common to all Christendom and I am more familiar with Italy and France. But I never heard of the hair and beard being shorn as a requirement.'

As de Wolfe had just invented it, this was not surprising, but he felt that the priest's question came of curiosity rather than suspicion. 'This is part of the abjuration process, not sanctuary,' he said gravely. 'England is different from your continental countries in that we are an island and therefore abjuration has to be by sea. Our formalities vary from other lands and this shaving of hair is to further mark out the abjurer as outside the pale of ordinary men.'

The explanation meant nothing, but Cosimo seemed to accept it as yet more evidence of the peculiarity of the people of this damp island.

Later, everyone settled down in their cloaks on the floor of the tavern, the soldiers having brought in hay and dry ferns from a barn up the glen. John was hopeful that, at last, the Templars and the abbot were satisfied that Bernardus was nowhere near, as their inspection of the five sanctuary seekers confirmed that they were genuine locals.

The most delicate part of his plot was now to be put into motion. When his sense of time suggested that midnight was not far off, he got up quietly and went outside to relieve himself against the wall. He waited for ten minutes to make sure that no one had missed him from the crowded room, then walked along the riverbank and up the track to Lynton. The moon came and went through the broken clouds and in its light, before he reached the church, he saw two shadowy figures standing under a tree. After some murmured instructions to de Blanchefort, they went boldly to the covered lych-gate and found both guards sound asleep. Gwyn poked one with his foot and the man leaped guiltily to his feet.

'Shall I report to you to the constable and sheriff?'

said de Wolfe with mock severity. 'They may have you hanged for failing in your duty.'

The man was both abashed and relieved that the coroner was not going to make trouble 'All quiet here, sir. They've been cutting their hair and beards earlier – and losing more blood than on a battlefield!'

Leaving the guards at the gate, they entered the church. This was the most sensitive part of the stratagem for de Wolfe, but he put the options baldly to the men. 'You can co-operate with me or not – but if not, I promise that you will hang, for I'll withdraw your sanctuary. The sheriff would be only too willing to string you all up, I assure you.'

They all muttered their assent and the coroner went on, 'I suspect that all of you will come back again from Wales before long. I am well aware that abjuration is but a temporary state for many people. Once the sheriff and his men have left, they are unlikely to return for years. Your reeve and your bailiff are your own problem but, again, I suspect they are not unaware of your activities and keep a tight mouth if they are bribed well enough.' De Wolfe saw a few sheepish grins in the dim, flickering light of the altar candles. 'As your exile is almost certainly temporary – and I want to know nothing of that – I wish to exchange my friend here for one of you, so that he may take passage on that vessel, disguised as an abjurer.'

There was another mutter, but of astonishment not objection.

'He is a large man, so I propose that you,' the coroner indicated the middle-aged villager, who was of a size with Bernardus, 'vanish into the woods for a day or two until the coast is clear and let this man take your place.' He held up his hand to stifle queries. 'The reasons for this are none of your business, but I say that one of you can go free now – and, no doubt, the rest of you will find a way to slide back home before long. The alternative is a rope around your neck tomorrow!' he added harshly.

There was no argument and the older man, beaming with relief, got out of his clothes and changed with de Blanchefort, who seemed not desperately pleased with the arrangement, but forced by necessity to go along with the coroner's plan. Though he had only stubble and no beard or moustache, the crude removal of his head hair with a dagger blade did not increase his enthusiasm for de Wolfe's machinations but, again, he submitted with ill grace.

As soon as this had been done, the fisherman muffled himself in Bernardus's dark cloak and hat and walked out between Gwyn and the coroner. With the moon hidden behind a cloud, the sleepy sentinels at the lych-gate took little notice of the three men who emerged, except to heed the coroner's terse warning to try to keep awake for the rest of the night.

Once out of sight at the head of the glen, the local man vanished into the undergrowth, gratefully taking a good cloak and hat with him as a bonus on top of his freedom.

At dawn, the coroner and his two assistants were back at the church. After creeping back into the alehouse John had hardly slept for the remainder of the night. He was anxious that his ruse should be successful, and concerned at how keen an interest the Templars and Cosimo would take in the departure of the abjurers.

The five were there, dressed in their ragged sackcloth, tied around the waist with lengths of creeper from the churchyard. They looked terrible, with hacked clumps of hair and bare, bleeding patches of scalp, their faces cut and scratched from their crude attempts at shaving. De Blanchefort looked as bad as the rest – in fact, little Eddida was less ravaged as he had had no facial hair to start with.

Before they started from the church, de Blanchefort took John aside at the back of the nave. The coroner stared at his ravaged face in the dim dawn light. As well as the effects of the dagger on his head and stubble, a few days' poor eating and sleeping and the constant stress of being a fugitive had taken a dreadful toll on the man, who looked haggard and drawn. Though not old, he had loose pouches of skin under his eyes and deep lines at the angles of his mouth, which had put twenty years on his appearance. His eyes were sunken in their sockets, but the the actual orbs had a strange glint that made de Wolfe wonder for his sanity. 'The others have given you their oath of abjuration,' he said. 'I wish to do the same.'

De Wolfe stared at him. 'What the devil for? This is all a sham for your benefit.'

The other man shook his head emphatically. 'I would feel better – and appear more convincing – if I had done what should be done to become an abjurer.'

To humour him, de Wolfe quickly administered the oath and the Templar solemnly repeated it.

'Satisfied?' snapped the coroner, anxious to get them down to the ship.

'Partly – but now I also wish to confess, as did the others.'

'Confess? Since when have you been a pirate?' Exasperated with the man's nonsense, de Wolfe watched the daylight strengthening through a window slit and was anxious to be gone.

'I know that you are no priest, but I would feel better if I confessed.'

'For God's sake, de Blanchefort, stop this idiocy. We must leave now.'

The renegade Templar seized his arm, and his face, suffused with a strange obsession, came close to his. 'I must confess to someone!' he hissed. 'For it was I who killed Gilbert de Ridefort.'

De Wolfe froze into the immobility of disbelief. '*You* killed him?'

De Blanchefort leaned on his crude cross. 'I had to – he deserved to die for his lack of faith. He had decided to retract his promise to me to reveal the secret. After all we had been through – losing our membership of the Order, putting our lives at risk – after all the months of heartrending discussion and decisions, he decided that he could not, would not, do it. So I killed him, for being a craven coward and a traitor to the new truth.'

His voice became fanatical. 'It is now left to me to reveal it! That is why I must survive to get to a place of safety, to preach and write the reality of Christendom.'

De Wolfe's shock was passing into anger, but he needed to know how it had been done. 'How did you find him?'

'I suspected that his determination was weakening, even before we left France, so I came to Devon some days earlier than I told you in order to observe him. I also followed you, Crowner, and saw you meet with him. I saw you leave the city with him and, by questioning people, easily guessed that you would have taken him to your family home at Stoke. So I went there to meet with de Ridefort.'

'Intending to kill him?'

De Blanchefort made an impatient gesture. 'Of course

not – I wanted to talk with him, to strengthen him. As I said, for some time I had sensed his wavering resolve, but not until we met in the woods near your manor did he tell me decisively that he had decided to give himself up to the Order and that he had abandoned our promise to reveal the truth.' His voice became so impassioned that de Wolfe now knew that his mind was unhinged.

Thomas had been standing by all the time, listening open-mouthed at these frightful revelations, but Gwyn was more concerned with getting the abjurers out of the church. 'We must go, Crowner, it is getting late!' he urged, but de Wolfe ignored him.

'So what happened?' he demanded.

'I was so incensed with him that we quarrelled violently, and I struck him on the head with a fallen branch. He fell dead, though I had not intended that. It was some freak blow – or maybe an act of God.'

'But those other injuries – in the side and the hands,' grated de Wolfe, holding his anger in check with difficulty.

'My rage made me inflict on him those marks that denoted his lack of faith in our resolve. They were tokens that reflected the nature of the awful secret wilfully concealed by the Templars for all these years.'

'The Awful Secret!' rasped de Wolfe scornfully. 'Was your secret worth the life of a brave man?'

'A brave man!' sneered de Blanchefort. 'De Ridefort was a spineless coward when it came to the one thing in his life that really mattered. He could wield a sword, yes, and cut down Saracens, but he could not keep a promise to defy the hypocrisy and deceit that we discovered in the Church that we had served all these years.' He waved his cross in de Wolfe's face, his own contorted with manic emotion. 'And as for the secret being worth one man's life, I tell you, John de Wolfe, that if I and others like me are silenced, there will be tens of thousands of lives forfeited soon, when Rome's scythe of repression slashes through the Languedoc. And in the centuries to come, the Inquisition that is blossoming now, like an evil flower, may annihilate millions who dare to question the autocracy of the Church.'

Gwyn tried again to get his master to move the men out of the building, but John silenced him with a wave of his hand as he glared at the flushed face and protuberant eyes of de Blanchefort.

'Listen, you mad rogue! I've no time to discuss your warped theology!' His anger was steadily rising. 'If this is true, you are a murderer and must be exposed! You cannot now go on that vessel. I must arrest you.'

The man's face was a mask of crazed cunning. 'I am a sanctuary seeker and an abjurer – I have taken the oath and you have heard my confession. I am entitled to abjure.'

'Nonsense, you arrogant fool! They were meaningless, obtained on your part by trickery and not sworn on the Holy Book!'

'Then how are you to explain why I am here, deviously planted amongst your abjurers? And where is the man I replaced, the one you have wilfully let escape? You are guilty of deceit, perverting the course of justice and God knows what other crimes. You are trapped, de Wolfe, so let things take their course.'

After rapid reflection on his position, de Wolfe had to resign himself to the inevitable. If the sheriff discovered his plotting, he would never let him forget it. In fact, he would probably pursue every legal avenue to have him condemned, to take revenge for the recent humiliation that the coroner had visited on him over the Prince

John affair. In addition, the Templars and the Church would be after his blood for deliberately engineering the escape of such a notorious heretic.

Fuming with anger, but powerless, he capitulated and signalled to Gwyn to lead the abjurers out of the church.

The other men were lined up inside the door but just as de Blanchefort began moving to join them, the coroner grabbed him roughly by the shoulder and swung him round so that they were face to face again.

'Listen, you evil bastard, before you go, I want to know what this damned secret was that has caused me so much trouble. Understand?'

The former Templar shook his head slyly. 'That will be revealed to the world at large soon, not dribbled out in whispers behind the hand.'

De Wolfe put a hand behind him and whipped out the dagger from his belt. In a second it was at de Blanchefort's neck, already drawing a drop of blood where the needle-sharp point pricked the skin. 'Tell me or, by God, I'll kill you now and be damned to the consequences!' His tone left the other man in no doubt that he meant exactly what he threatened.

'All right, let me go. I'll tell you.' John backed the knife off a few inches, but kept it hovering before Bernardus' face.

'We couldn't discover the whole story, we had to piece together overheard fragments of talk between the Master and other more senior officers. Then we accidentally came across some documents no one was supposed to see, which sent us covertly searching amongst the secret archives in Paris. It took a year to make sense of it all.'

'Come on, get on with it! My sister told me that de Ridefort hinted it was something to do with the mass.'

Thomas, who stood listening open-mouthed alongside them, groaned and convulsively crossed himself, but de Blanchefort smirked. 'The mass? You could say that, though it's a detail. The early Templars found inscriptions on tablets in the catacombs beneath the Temple in Jeruslaem that recorded that Christ, though crucified, did not die on the Cross. The resurrection was a revival of the near-dead body, all prearranged by some influential friends. He lived for another thirty years, a great man, teacher and prophet, but he was mortal, so the concept of the Trinity is fiction, knowingly perpetuated by Rome.'

There was a second's silence then, with a strangled cry of desperate fury, little Thomas de Peyne launched himself at de Blanchefort and futilely tried to batter him with his small fists. The other pushed him away impatiently and the clerk subsided on to the floor, his face in his hands, weeping and keening.

De Wolfe pulled him gently to his feet, as Gwyn and the other abjurers watched in astonishment from across the church. 'Don't fret yourself, Thomas. This madman's pack of lies isn't worth a clipped penny.'

He turned back to de Blanchefort. 'And is that all your precious secret amounts to? A fairy-tale, some legend peddled by Templars as deluded as yourself?'

A supercilious expression came over the man's face. 'There's more. The Templars have always had a special regard for Mary Magdalene and we discovered that not only was she Jesus's wife but she bore him several children. She went with many other Jews to live in southern France, though we could not discover whether Christ himself went there or remained in Palestine.'

This all sounded so outrageous to de Wolfe that he never for a moment contemplated that there was the slightest truth in de Blanchefort's babblings. 'I'm not sure whether you are to be condemned for your blasphemy and sacrilege or pitied for the unhinged state of your mind,' he said scornfully. 'Where is the proof of these preposterous ideas?'

'Buried in a hillside in the foothills of the Pyrenees,' replied de Blanchefort sharply, now incensed at being ridiculed. 'The early Knights of Christ were ordered by Rome to place the evidence where it could never be rediscovered, so they brought it back to France when they returned in about 1127 and, with the aid of German miners, buried it within Mount Cardou, concealed for ever by an immense rockfall.' He paused, as if momentarily overcome by his own revelations. 'It was even suggested by some documents – though I can hardly credit it myself – that the bones of Christ himself were also found and buried with the tablets.'

There was another groan from Thomas, who was rocking back and forth, his face still covered by his hands.

'My own family comes from this area and the Chateau de Blanchefort, a former Templar possession, sits opposite Mount Cardou and guarded it in the early part of this century. You see now why I have such a personal interest in this momentous discovery!'

De Wolfe was still convinced that the man was a dangerous lunatic, but any further revelations were cut short by Gwyn, who bellowed from across the church. 'We have to go, Crowner! It's broad daylight and the tide will soon be ebbing.'

De Wolfe gave the former Templar a rough push and sent him stumbling on his way. With a shaken Thomas trailing behind, mumbling in Latin under his breath, they filed out of the church and into the final and most dangerous part of the escapade.

* * *

The tide was full and the *Brendan* well afloat when the procession came down the track alongside the stream. A soldier walked in front, then came the five abjurers, each barefoot, each holding their cross two-handed before their faces. They looked like a line of scarecrows, shuffling along in their shapeless hessian robes, with their scratched, tufted scalps. The dwarf Eddida was the leader, and after the last man, another soldier was followed at a distance by the coroner, his officer and clerk. The older, tallest man came in the centre, the hands holding his cross tight against his face.

De Wolfe was tense with anger at Bernardus and apprehension in case his elaborate plot was discovered at the last moment. As he walked, he cursed himself for allowing his sense of duty to Gilbert de Ridefort to have landed him in this situation. Far from wanting to help this man escape, he would now have cheerfully cut his evil, demented head from his shoulders – but it was too late and he was caught in a trap of his own making.

The sad cavalcade reached the bottom of the track where it became pebbled. This was the most dangerous spot for the venture: it was nearest the alehouse where, in the doorway, Abbot Cosimo and the three Templar knights stood to see the departure of the abjurers. The sheriff was not there: he was too incensed at their easy escape to want to witness it and was at the back of the tavern with Ralph Morin as they supervised the impending departure of most of the men-at-arms, the rest being left to secure the village for a few days.

As he came level with the alehouse door, de Wolfe saw that Cosimo's gaze was again directed at Eddida and he wondered what strange emotions so attracted the abbot to the dwarf. He suspected that unnatural desires were the most likely reason for his fascination, though these little men were always objects of curiosity and cruel derision. The Templars watched the procession clamber across the pebbles, then turned back into the room behind to collect their arms and saddle-pouches ready for the journey home.

De Wolfe sighed with relief, especially when the Italian priest also vanished into the tavern to join them. He strode across the stones to where the forced emigrants were wading through the knee-high wavelets to reach the side of the knarr. As the crew hoisted up little Eddida with coarse comments about his size, John splashed into the shallows and caught up with de Blanchefort. For a moment, he even considered sticking his dagger under the killer's ribs, but good sense prevailed. 'You evil bastard, I hope you rot in Hell!' he offered as a farewell.

As he grabbed the ship's side, de Blanchefort gave him an enigmatic smile. 'If there is a hell, brother – though I've come to doubt it – then I'll see you there!'

He swung himself aboard and de Wolfe backed away in frustration.

The small vessel was pulled astern by a pair of long oars until it had enough sea-room to raise the clumsy sail and turn out into the bay.

In sullen anger, the coroner walked back to where Gwyn and Thomas waited for him at the edge of the beach. The little clerk was still pale and shaking with the insult his faith had received from de Blanchefort's blasphemy.

'Shall we saddle up with the rest of them?' asked Gwyn, pointing to the preparations behind them where the men-at-arms were checking their horses' harness. The sheriff and constable were already mounted and the Templars were helping Cosimo's surviving guard to saddle the abbot's mare.

'Let's wait a while. I've no stomach for listening to de Revelle complaining half-way to Exeter.' John turned to watch the *Brendan* moving away from the shore, her sail now filled with the breeze. 'Maybe a bolt of lightning will strike that black-hearted swine out there.'

A few minutes later, the horsemen moved off and Ralph Morin shouted across to de Wolfe that they would see the Templars and abbot on their way for a few miles, then return to Exeter through South Molton, a more direct route than via Barnstaple. 'We'll catch you up in an hour or two, or when you stop to eat,' promised the coroner. He watched the procession plodding up the track through the glen, lined by silent widows, fatherless children and old men.

'Why didn't we go with them?' asked Gwyn.

'I want to see that damned ship well out of sight,' answered the coroner bitterly.

They saddled their own horses and climbed up to Lynton, then to a nearby headland on the seaward side of the valley of rocks. Here they had a panoramic view of the coastline in either direction, from the great prominence of the Foreland Point on their right across to a headland near Martinhoe on the left. Sitting in their saddles, they watched in silence as the little ship clawed its way across the westerly breeze, making slowly northwards towards the Welsh coast, clearly visible over twenty miles away.

Then, suddenly, from around the Foreland, they saw two long lean ships racing side by side, each propelled against the wind by a dozen oars on either side. High curved posts rose at stem and stern and their whole appearance was blatantly foreign. Like two greyhounds after a badger, the predatory galleys sped after the clumsy knarr, the gap closing rapidly as the three men watched.

Thomas de Peyne crossed himself for the tenth time that morning and murmured quietly to himself in Latin, 'Requiescat in pace!' while Sir John de Wolfe's feeble belief in a jealous God was suddenly strengthened.

POCKET
B O O K S

**This book and other Simon and Schuster titles are available from
your book shop or can be ordered direct from the publisher.**

Ramses:

0 671 01020 4	The Son of the Light	Christian Jacq	£5.99
0 671 01021 2	The Temple of a Million Years	Christian Jacq	£5.99
0 671 01022 0	The Battle of Kadesh	Christian Jacq	£5.99
0 671 01023 9	The Lady of Abu Simbel	Christian Jacq	£5.99
0 671 01024 7	Under the Western Acacia	Christian Jacq	£5.99
0 671 01805 1	The Black Pharaoh	Christian Jacq	£5.99
0 684 86628 5	The Stone of Light: Nefer the Silent	Christian Jacq	£10

0 671 51673 6	The Sanctuary Seeker	Bernard Knight	£5.99
0 671 51674 4	The Poisoned Chalice	Bernard Knight	£5.99
0 671 51675 2	Crowner's Quest	Bernard Knight	£5.99

Guenevere:

| 0 671 01812 4 | The Queen of the Summer Country | Rosalind Miles | £6.99 |
| 0 671 01813 2 | The Knight of the Sacred Lake | Rosalind Miles | £6.99 |

Please send cheque or postal order for the value of the book, free postage
and packing within the UK, OVERSEAS including Republic of Ireland
£1 per book.

OR: Please debit this amount from my
VISA/ACCESS/MASTERCARD _____
CARD NO: _____
EXPIRY DATE _____
AMOUNT £ _____
NAME _____
ADDRESS _____
SIGNATURE _____

Send orders to: SIMON & SCHUSTER CASH SALES
PO Box 29, Douglas, Isle of Man, IM99 1BQ
Tel: 01624 675137. Fax: 01624 670923
www.bookpost.co.uk
Please allow 14 days for delivery.
Prices and availability subject to change.

POCKET
B O O K S

GUENEVERE 2
The Knight of the Sacred Lake
ROSALIND MILES

Camelot, and Arthur and Guenevere are holding a glittering
feast to celebrate their knights of the Round Table. But
amidst the joy of the ceremony, one key figure is absent. Sir
Lancelot of the Lake has left court, sent away by Guenevere,
who is tormented by a love for him she may neither honour
nor deny.

As Guenevere struggles to reconcile duty and destiny
Lancelot, too, is torn by conflicting loyalties to his Queen
and King. Guenevere holds staunchly to her faith in her
knight. But can she endure his absence, and the shattering
news that she has a rival for his love?

(published in November 2000)

£6.99

ISBN: 0 671 01813 2

POCKET
BOOKS

GUENEVERE I
The Queen of the Summer Country
ROSALIND MILES

Across the many kingdoms and islands of ancient Britain,
Arthur begins his quest to become High King. But even
as he battles to reclaim his birthright, an impassioned and
beautiful woman is waiting to claim her destiny.

With a rare and intuitive magic, acclaimed novelist and
historian Rosalind Miles vividly brings to life a legendary
woman's greatest and most glorious time, revealing
Guenevere's bravery, passion and inner torment as she ruled
a truly ancient kingdom.

Price: £6.99

ISBN: 0 671 01812 4

POCKET
B O O K S

CROWNER'S QUEST
BERNARD KNIGHT

Christmas Eve, 1194. Sir John de Wolfe gratefully escapes
a party given by his wife Matilda, to examine the body of
a canon who has been found hanged. Suicide is suspected,
but it is soon apparent that there is more to this case than
meets the eye.

As usual, John's investigations are hampered by his brother-
in-law, Sheriff Richard de Revelle. But when a local lord is
killed, John begins to suspect that the cases are linked and
Sir Richard's reasons for delaying the investigation may be
more sinister than the usual petty vengeance.

PRICE £5.99

ISBN 0 671 51675 2

POCKET
BOOKS

THE POISONED CHALICE
BERNARD KNIGHT

The well-born ladies of Exeter are not having a good week.
First, Christina Rifford, the daughter of a rich merchant, is
raped. Then Lady Adele de Courcy is found dead in one of
the poorest areas of Exeter.

John's suspicions fall on a local merchant who had dealings
with both girls, but before he has been able to establish
proof, the girls' vengeful families are taking the law into
their own hands.
John slowly begins to put the pieces together. But a
final, brutal act of violence brings a new twist to John's
investigation before he arrives at the truth.

Price £5.99

ISBN 0 671 51674 4

POCKET
B O O K S

THE SANCTUARY SEEKER
BERNARD KNIGHT

November, 1194 AD. Appointed by Richard the Lionheart as
the first coroner for the county of Devon, Sir John de Wolfe,
an ex-crusader rides out to the lonely moorland village of
Widecombe to hold an inquest on an unidentified body.
But on his return to Exeter the coroner is incensed to find
that his own brother-in-law, Sheriff Richard de Revelle, is
intent on thwarting the murder investigation, particularly
when it emerges that the dead man is a Crusader, and a
member of one of Devon's finest and most honourable
families . . .

PRICE £5.99

ISBN 0 671 51673 6

Further Reading

Those readers who wish to learn more about the nature of the Awful Secret, are recommended to read the following paperbacks:

Andrews, R., and O. Schellenberger, *The Tomb of God*, (Warner, London, 1996; ISBN 0 7515 1961 8)

Baigent, M., R. Leigh and H. Lincoln, *The Holy Blood & the Holy Grail*, (Arrow, London, 1996; ISBN 0 09 968241 9)

Gardner, L., *Bloodline of the Holy Grail*, (Element, Shaftesbury, 1996; ISBN 1 86204 152 0)

Theiring, Barbara, *Jesus the Man*, (Corgi, London, 1993; ISBN 0 552 13950 5)

Also many Internet sites reached through *Rennes-le-Chateau* etc.